Brokedown
cowboy

MAISEY YATES

Brokedown cowboy

HQN™

Recycling programs
for this product may
not exist in your area.

ISBN-13: 978-0-373-78842-2

Brokedown Cowboy

Copyright © 2015 by Maisey Yates

All rights reserved. Except for use in any review, the reproduction or
utilization of this work in whole or in part in any form by any electronic,
mechanical or other means, now known or hereinafter invented, including
xerography, photocopying and recording, or in any information storage
or retrieval system, is forbidden without the written permission of the
publisher, HQN Books, 225 Duncan Mill Road, Don Mills, Ontario
M3B 3K9, Canada.

This is a work of fiction. Names, characters, places and incidents are
either the product of the author's imagination or are used fictitiously,
and any resemblance to actual persons, living or dead, business
establishments, events or locales is entirely coincidental.

This edition published by arrangement with Harlequin Books S.A.

For questions and comments about the quality of this book,
please contact us at CustomerService@Harlequin.com.

® and TM are trademarks of Harlequin Enterprises Limited or its
corporate affiliates. Trademarks indicated with ® are registered in the
United States Patent and Trademark Office, the Canadian Intellectual
Property Office and in other countries.

www.HQNBooks.com

Printed in U.S.A.

Brokedown
cowboy

Dear Reader,

I have a soft spot for a strong, wounded hero. I always have. I think in part because I always want to fix their pain. I write romance because I believe in the power that love has to heal, because I believe that no one has ever missed their chance at happily ever after. Even if they need a second chance at it.

Connor Garrett is desperately in need of a second chance.

If you've met Connor in *Part Time Cowboy* then you know what a grumpy, surly, heartbroken man he is. From the moment I "met" him, I knew I needed to write his story.

I like a broken hero, and I love a story about friends discovering there's more between them. *Brokedown Cowboy* gave me a chance to play with two of my favorite themes.

Liss and Connor have so much history together, and no one knows Connor's pain like she does. But she's also fully aware that what he's been through means loving again will be a challenge for him. Luckily, Liss is up to the task.

I hope you enjoy Connor's road to happiness as much as I enjoyed writing it (if you're still in the store, you might want to buy a box of tissues...you've been warned).

Happy Reading!

Maisey

CHAPTER ONE

CONNOR GARRETT WAS a grown-ass man. He knew there was nothing to fear in sleep. He knew the darkness of his room didn't hide anything more sinister than a pair of carelessly discarded cowboy boots, waiting for him to stub his toe on them in the dead of night during a sleepy trip to the bathroom.

He knew these things, just like he knew the sun would rise over the mountains just before six this time of year, whether he wanted it to or not. He knew these things as surely as he knew that an early-morning breeze tinged with salt meant a storm would blow in from the coast later. That unintentional run-ins with barbed-wire fences burned like a son of a bitch. That wooden barns burned and people you loved left.

Yeah, he knew all that.

But it didn't stop him from waking up most nights in a cold sweat, his heart pounding harder than a spooked horse's hooves on arena dirt.

Because the simple truth was that Connor Garrett knew all these things, but his subconscious had yet to catch up.

He sat bolt upright in bed, sweat beading on his bare chest and his forehead. If this weren't standard procedure for his body, he might've been concerned he was having a heart attack. Unfortunately, though, he knew at this point that the racing heart, accompanied by chest pain, was just stress. Anxiety.

Damn lingering grief that refused to lessen even as the years passed.

He wasn't surprised when he woke up alone in bed, not anymore. It had been three years, after all. He wasn't surprised, but he *noticed*. Every time. Was acutely aware of how cold the sheets were on her side of the bed. It wasn't even the same bed he'd slept in with Jessie. He'd bought a new one about a year ago because continuing to sleep in the bed they'd shared had seemed too depressing. But it hadn't accomplished what he had hoped it might.

Because no matter how hard he tried, whether he lay down in the middle of the bed at the start of the night, or even on the side nearest to the window, he always ended up on *his* side.

The side by the door. In case of intruders or any other danger. The side that allowed him to protect the person sleeping next to him. The side he had taken every night during his eight years of marriage. It was as if his late wife's ghost was rolling him over in his sleep.

And then waking him up.

Unfortunately, Jessie didn't even have the decency to haunt him. She was just gone. And in her place was emptiness. Emptiness in his bed. In his house. In his chest.

And when his chest wasn't empty, it was filled with pain and a kind of dread that took over his whole body and made it impossible to breathe. Like now.

He swung his legs over the side of the mattress, the

wood floor cold beneath his bare feet. He stood and walked over to the window, looked out into the darkness. The black shadows of pine trees filled his vision, and beyond that, the darker silhouette of the mountains, backlit by a slightly grayer sky. And down to the left he could barely make out the front porch. And the golden glow of the porch light that he'd somehow managed to leave on before he'd gone to sleep.

His chest tightened. That was probably why he'd woken up.

Abruptly, the dream he'd been having flooded back through his mind. It hadn't been a full dream so much as images.

Opening the door late at night to see Eli standing there, his brother's face grim, bleaker than Connor had ever seen it. And a ring of gold light from the porch had shone around him. Made him look like an angel of some kind. An angel of death, it had turned out.

As stupid as it was, he was half convinced that leaving that same light on downstairs brought the dreams back stronger.

It didn't make sense. But if there was one thing he'd learned over the years, it was that grief didn't make a lick of sense.

He jerked the bedroom door open and walked downstairs, heading toward the entryway. He stood there in front of the door, looking at the porch light shining through the windows. For a second he had the thought that if he opened it, he would find Eli standing there. Would find himself transported back in time three years. Listening to the kind of news that no one should have to hear.

There was a reason his darkest nightmares consisted of nothing more than his younger brother standing on his front porch.

Because in that moment his life had transformed into a nightmare. There was nothing scarier than that. He was confident he could take the bogeyman if need be. But he couldn't fight death.

And in the end he hadn't been able to save Jessie.

And he was not opening the damn door.

He flipped the light off and found himself walking into the kitchen and opening the fridge, rather than going back upstairs. He looked at the beer, which was currently the only thing on the shelves besides a bottle of ketchup and a bag that had an onion in it that had probably been there since the beginning of summer.

He let out a heavy sigh and shut the fridge. He should not drink beer at three in the morning.

Three in the morning was clearly Jack Daniel's o'clock.

He walked over to the cabinet where he kept the harder stuff and pulled out his bottle of Jack. It was almost gone. And no one was here. No one was here, because his fucking house was empty. Because he was alone.

Considering those things, he decided to hell with the glass. He picked up the bottle and tipped it back, barely even feeling the burn anymore as the alcohol slid down his throat.

Maybe now he would be able to get some sleep. Maybe for a few hours he could forget.

He'd given up on getting rest years ago. These days he just settled for oblivion.

And this was the fastest way he knew to get it.

"YOU SHOULD JUST INSTALL a drain in the house so you can hose it down and let all the dirt wash out. Just like you do out in the barn."

"What the hell are you doing here, Liss?"

Felicity Foster refused to be cowed by the overwhelmingly unfriendly greeting her best friend had just issued. It was just Connor, after all. She was used to his less than sparkly demeanor. She was also used to finding him passed out on the couch in the morning.

It would be nice if that occurred less frequently, but if anything, he seemed to be getting worse.

Not that she could blame *him*. She blamed his barn burning down. As far as the loss of Jessie was concerned, things might have continued to get better had he not lost that, too. It was just a building, bricks and wood, but it was his livelihood. It was just another piece of Connor's dream burned down to the ground. He'd had enough of that. Too much of it.

She was officially pissed at life on his behalf. How much was one man supposed to endure?

"And to answer your rather charming question, Connor," she said, stepping nearer to the couch, "I brought you groceries."

He sat up, his face contorting, making him look a bit like he'd swallowed a porcupine. "Groceries? Why did you do that?"

"I know it's been a while since you've gone out and socialized with actual people, rather than simply sharing your space with cows, so I feel compelled to remind you that the normal human response to this would be *thank you*."

He swung his legs over the side of the couch and

rubbed his hand over his face. She wanted to do something. To put her hand on his back and offer comfort. She was used to those kinds of impulses around Connor. She'd been fighting them for the better part of her adult life. But her conclusion was always that touching him would be a bad idea. So she stood there, her hands held awkwardly at her sides, leaving him uncomforted. Leaving the appropriate amount of space between them.

That was part of being a good friend. At least, it was part of maintaining a healthy friendship as far as she and Connor were concerned.

"Thank you," he said, his voice gruff. "But why the hell did you bring me groceries? And why did you bring them by before work?"

"I brought you groceries because man cannot live on booze alone. I'm bringing them this morning because I was too tired to lug them over last night, when I actually bought them. So I thought, in the spirit of goodwill and breakfast cereals, I would bring them by now."

"I do like breakfast cereals. I'm ambivalent about goodwill." He stood up, wobbling slightly. "Feeling a little bit ambivalent about gravity, too."

"I'm surprised you feel like eating. How much did you drink?"

He looked away from her and shrugged in a classically Connor manner. Playing things off was an art form with this man. "I don't know. I woke up in the middle of the night. I couldn't get back to sleep so I had a little bit to drink and ended up staying down here. Anyway, I don't really notice the hangovers anymore."

"I don't think building up a resistance to hangovers is a crowning achievement."

"For my lifestyle, it certainly is."

She rolled her eyes. "Come on, cowboy. I'll pour you some cereal."

She shouldn't offer to do things like that for him. She knew it. But she did it anyway. Just like she brought his groceries when she knew his fridge contained nothing but beer. Just like she still came to his house every day to make sure he was taken care of.

"Whoa, wait a second, Liss. We do not know each other well enough for that shit."

"I've known you since I was fifteen."

"The preparation of cereal is a highly contentious thing. You don't know how much milk I might want. Hell, I don't know how much milk I might want until I assess the density and quality of the cereal."

"Are you still drunk?"

"Probably a little bit."

"Kitchen. Now."

Connor offered her a smart-ass smile, one side of his mouth curving upward. She couldn't help but watch him as he walked from the living room into the kitchen. His dark hair was longer than he used to keep it, a beard now covering his once clean-shaven jaw. She didn't mind the look. Actually, *didn't mind* was an understatement; she thought he looked dead sexy. Though, in her opinion, there was no look Connor had ever sported that she'd found less than sexy. Even that terrible haircut, gelled and spiked up, that he'd had for about a year in high school, his one and only attempt at trendiness. No, on that score, the beard and hair were fine. The real issue was that his mountain-man look wasn't a fashion statement, but an outward sign of the fact that he just didn't take care of himself anymore.

They walked into the kitchen, and with the sun shining through the window like it was now, she could clearly see the coat of neglect that everything wore. The stove had a grease film over the top of it, a shocking amount of splatters on the white surface considering that she knew Connor never cooked anything here beyond frozen pizza. The pine cabinets looked dingy, the front window dotted with a white film of hard-water stains.

The house didn't wear its neglect with quite the same devilish flare its owner did.

Connor reached up and opened one of the cabinets, taking out one of the brightly colored boxes of cereal she had just placed there. It struck her, in that moment, how funny it was she had known exactly where to put the cereal, and that he had known she would.

He grabbed a bowl and placed it on the counter, turning to face her, and she realized then that Connor wasn't wearing his neglect quite as well as he would like everyone to believe. Sure, he was still sexy as hell, the tight lines by his eyes, the deep grooves in his forehead not doing anything to diminish that. But they were new. A map of the stress and grief of the past few years, deepened by his recent losses.

She ached for him. But beyond buying the man's food, there was very little she could do.

She had been about to unload on him about all the crap that was happening with her rental. But it wasn't a good time. Though she doubted with Connor there was ever a good time. Not because he wouldn't care, but because she didn't want to pile on.

Connor poured milk on his cereal, milk she had brought, and set it back on the counter. He picked up his bowl and started eating, crunching loudly on his first bite. "Are you going to have some, Liss?"

"I never say no to cereal. I have important accounting stuff to attend to. I find an early-morning carb rush is the best way to handle that."

"Coffee?" he asked, talking around the food in his mouth.

"I had a carafe before I came over. I don't play around with caffeine consumption."

"Well, I need some." He set the bowl back down on the counter and made his way over to the coffeemaker.

"So you had coffee. Beer, and coffee."

"I'm not an animal."

Liss snickered while she got her own bowl and set about preparing her cereal. There was a strange domesticity to the scene. Mundane conversation, easy morning sounds. Water running in the sink, clattering dishes. The soft filter of early sunlight through the thick wall of evergreens that surrounded Connor's front yard.

There was something poignant about sharing this with him. This moment that seemed to have slipped right out of time. Like something she'd stolen, something she shouldn't have.

Seriously, you would think she was the one who had been drinking. She was maudlin.

Connor started the coffee then returned to the island where he'd prepared his cereal. They stood across from each other, eating in silence, except for the crunching. And the sounds of the coffeemaker.

More morning sounds she was not entitled to.

Because this was the kind of thing a guy shared with his lover or wife. Not with his oddly codependent best friend.

"Have you heard back from the insurance company about the settlement?" The barn had burned down in July thanks to a few kids carelessly playing with fireworks, and while Liss knew that insurance companies could drag their feet to a pretty insane degree, this was going somewhere beyond that.

It was mid-September, and as far as she knew, Connor's bank account remained void of settlements.

"Nope."

"Well, that's a little bit ridiculous, don't you think?"

He shrugged one shoulder then took another bite of cereal. "Probably. Just haven't had the energy to go chasing it down."

"Don't you think you should find the energy? All that equipment…"

"I'm very aware of what I lost in the fire. I don't need you to summarize. Anyway, I've been making use of Bud's old tractor. Plus, Jack had some extra tools."

"That's very nice. But don't you want your own things?"

"Yes, Liss," he said, his tone getting hard. "I would very much like to have my own shit. Actually, what I would really like is for my barn not to have burned down."

Connor Garrett was six feet four inches of solid muscle. When he crossed his arms over his chest, showing off the strength in his powerful forearms and the full-sleeve tattoo he'd gotten a couple of years ago, he made a very intimidating picture. To other people. But not to her. "Too bad it's not a perfect world, isn't it?"

Connor snorted. "Yeah, Liss, I have noticed that the world isn't perfect."

"Noticing it isn't enough. You have to do something about it."

"I was not aware that my cereal came with a lecture."

"It wasn't supposed to. I have to go to work." She set her bowl down on the counter then turned away from him, shoving her hands in her jacket pockets.

"Wait." She heard footsteps, and no small amount of rustling behind her.

She turned back toward Connor, who was pouring coffee into a travel mug. "I'm waiting."

She watched as he put two spoonfuls of sugar and a splash of cream in the cup. Exactly the way she took her coffee. And of course he knew. "Coffee. You're allowed to leave mad, but you're not allowed to leave without caffeine."

She took the cup from his hand, holding her breath as her fingers brushed his, tightening her stomach muscles before they could do so involuntarily. "Thus ensuring that I don't leave mad." She lifted the cup. "Evil genius, Garrett."

"I am that, Foster. As you should well know by now."

"I'm familiar. Poker tonight?"

"As far as I know. Eli has campaign stuff he's working on, so I'm not sure if he'll stop by, but I'm pretty sure Sadie is coming. And unless Jack is getting laid with some random stranger…"

"Oh, Jack. It's a real concern with that one." Jack Monaghan was Connor's other best friend. Between

Eli and Connor in age, he'd been terrorizing Copper Ridge with the Garretts since the three of them were adolescent boys. And he had grown up to be a bigger terror than he'd been at twelve.

Unlike Eli, who was staid and responsible, running for sheriff of Logan County and in a serious, committed relationship with onetime bad girl Sadie Miller. And unlike Connor, who had gotten married in his early twenties and settled into ranch work. Jack had never settled into much of anything. Except sleeping his way through the female population, and steadfastly refusing to grow up by opting for a career as a rodeo cowboy.

Jack was hell on cowboy boots, but he was a lot of fun to have around. So long as you weren't counting on him for much.

"Yeah, well, one of us should go out there and get some."

Liss resisted the urge to ask for any details regarding Connor and his getting-some status. She was willing to bet he wasn't, but then, it wasn't like he told her everything. And Connor's sex life was absolutely none of her business. In fact, she had spent the better part of the past seventeen years ignoring the fact that he had a sex life. Or at least trying to.

"I'm happy for Jack to be the getting-some ambassador. Down with relationships!"

Connor chuckled. "I don't think Jack orders his sex with a side of relationship."

"He's a better man than I am," Liss said.

"Yeah, me, too."

Well, that might answer her question. The one she

wasn't going to ask. The one she certainly wasn't going to dwell on. Though she was dwelling a little bit.

"Okay, Connor, I really have to go now. Thank you for the coffee."

"Thank you for the cereal. And the other things."

"My unending friendship, my support, my willingness to give you the hard truths?"

"I meant the milk and the half-and-half. But sure."

She shot Connor a mock dirty glare and gave him a good look at her middle finger before turning and walking out the door. The crisp air touched her skin, bathing her in a feeling of freshness. The weather had already cooled quite a bit, and mornings were starting to take on that tinge of salted frost that signaled the fact they were leaving summer further and further behind.

She walked down the stairs and toward her little Toyota. Good thing she had this car free and clear. And hopefully it stayed running. Since, thanks to Marshall, her credit was on life support. That asshole, driving off one day in the brand-new truck that had both their names on it. And then proceeding to not make payments. And then also continuing to use credit cards that were in both their names without her knowledge.

She'd been able to get a certain amount of dings on the report taken care of, but some of it the bureaus had been unwilling to reverse. Right about now she couldn't get a car loan, or a new rental house, to save her life.

Which, because of the general stability of her lifestyle, wasn't the biggest problem. Until a couple of days ago when she'd found out that her landlord needed her out of the house in thirty days because she was selling it.

Yes, that had thrown a wrench in the works.

But she would figure it out. She always did.

She could always move in with her mother, though the very idea of it made her shudder. She wouldn't be living on the streets, anyway, ideal situation or not.

But she would worry about that later. First work, then poker. She could panic tomorrow.

CHAPTER TWO

"GET OUT OF my house, Miller."

His brother's girlfriend looked up at him, the expression on her face comically innocent. "I came bearing gifts, Connor. Is that any way to greet a guest with presents?"

"You brought Beavers paraphernalia into my house. OSU fans can stay out on the lawn. We worship at the temple of green and gold here."

Jack, who was already sitting at the table, thumped the side of the green ice bucket, proudly displaying the large University of Oregon O. "This is Duck country, sweetheart."

Sadie batted her eyes. "I had no idea. I just found this bright orange bowl and thought it would be a great bowl to bring black and orange M&Ms in."

"She's a witch! Burn the witch!" Jack chanted from his position at the table.

"Light anything else on my property on fire and I will roast you over the flames, Monaghan," Connor growled.

"Sorry, Con," he said. "Bad joke, all things considered."

Connor supposed it was. But then, if you couldn't laugh at life's shit, you might as well lie down in it and die. Which…he was closer to doing some days than he'd like to admit.

Sadie ignored him and walked into the house, putting her giant orange bowl on the table, an ugly blot near his hallowed Ducks ice bucket. "Eli should be by later. I invited Kate, too."

This elicited a groan from Jack, and, he realized after the fact, from him, too.

"What?" Sadie asked. "Kate is my friend, and I want her here."

"She's my little sister," Connor said.

"And I have to watch my mouth when she's around," Jack said.

"But you *don't*," Sadie said, arching her brow. "Anyway, your boys club gets stale. The testosterone is so thick a girl can hardly breathe."

"Hey," Connor said. "What about Liss?"

"She is an excellent source of estrogen, but firmly on your team," Sadie said, reaching into her godforsaken bowl and taking out a handful of candy.

He supposed he couldn't argue that point. Liss was his friend. And had been for years. She'd stuck by him almost as long as Jack. And she wasn't obligated by blood the way Eli was. Considering that, he definitely owed her an apology for being such a jackass this morning. But hangovers were not his friend.

Considering *that*, he spent way more time with them than he should.

"She's coming, right?" Sadie asked.

"Yeah, I'm surprised she's not here yet."

As if on cue, the door burst open and Liss all but tumbled into the room, dropping her purse on the wooden floor and letting out a frustrated growl. "My damn car wouldn't start." She straightened and pushed her dark, coppery hair from her forehead, her hazel eyes telegraphing her evil mood with supreme effect. "I tried for twenty minutes in the parking lot at work, and then when I was getting ready to call a tow truck, it started for no apparent reason. That's not a good sign."

Sadie closed the distance between herself and Liss and picked Liss's purse up from the floor, not because Sadie was big into neatness, but because she seemed to like picking up after people. A therapist before she'd come back to Copper Ridge to open her bed-and-breakfast, Sadie liked fixing other people's problems more than she liked just about anything else.

Except antagonizing them with sports rivalries, apparently.

"That sucks, Liss," Jack said, leaning back in his chair, his eyes on the forbidden bowl of candy.

"Eat the candy, Jack," Connor said, keeping his eyes on Liss.

She was wearing the same clothes she'd had on this morning, a pair of black dress pants and a blue button-up shirt, her hair hanging loose around her shoulders. She looked flustered, which was unusual for Liss.

"Just one more thing I don't need," she grumbled. "Something smells good."

"Frozen pizza, à la me," Connor said.

"Yum!" Liss said, her crabby expression lightening. "Anything else?"

"I brought pizza rolls," Jack said.

"Anything else?" Sadie asked.

"There's cheesy garlic bread in the oven. And marinara sauce to dip in," Connor said.

"So," Sadie said, "pizza, pizza that's folded in on itself and deconstructed pizza."

"Pretty much," Connor said.

"Any vegetables?" Sadie asked.

"It's like you don't know us at all," Jack said.

"I'm on board with your choice of menu for the evening," Liss said, sitting down at the table across from Jack and immediately snagging a beer from the Ducks bucket. "I require carbs, cheese and grease to deal with my mood."

"I'm sure Jake will take a look at your car," Connor said, referencing Copper Ridge's new mechanic. Jake was still building a client base, and he was counting on word of mouth to help do that.

"Probably. But I don't really want to go begging for free work. Anyway, as long as it's a minor issue I can afford to deal with it. But I am not in a position to buy a new car."

Jack snorted. "Who is?"

"Probably you," Liss said.

Jack just shrugged. Jack might be in the position but Connor certainly wasn't. Not with his barn reduced to ash and charred ranch equipment. Though, truly, he supposed that was a fixable problem. But somehow, every time he went to fix the paperwork the insurance place had sent over, he got distracted and ended up doing something else. So the changes never got made. And the paperwork never got fixed. And his bank account stayed empty. And his barn stayed ash.

Damn, he needed a beer.

He took one out of the bucket and rested the bottle against the corner of the table, pulling it down as he slammed his hand on the top of it.

"Show-off," Sadie said.

He shrugged. "Yeah, I just figured I'd put all my skills out there tonight. Putting frozen food in the oven, popping beer tops without a bottle opener. I'm a badass."

"A superepic one," Liss said, taking a drink of her beer. "And after I've had this entire bottle, and possibly another, I might even upgrade you."

"To what?" he asked.

"Superepic rock-star badass."

"I like that. But I think cowboy should be in there somewhere."

Jack winked. "You're not a real cowboy, though, Connor. When was the last time you rode a bucking bronco?"

"No, asshole, you're confused. *You're* not a real cowboy. You just play one in the ring," Connor said.

Sadie started humming "Rhinestone Cowboy," and Connor decided he liked her a little more than he had a few moments ago.

The oven timer went off and Connor crossed the living room and went to the kitchen, getting some hot pads and taking the bread and pizza out of the oven. The pizza rolls were sitting in a ball on the counter, and he stacked the pan laden with the real pizza on top of the bowl and carried the tray of bread in his other hand, taking it all into the dining area.

He set the food down in front of Liss and Jack, and Sadie gleefully reached for a plate, hovering near the bowl of pizza rolls.

"Next time, I promise to bake something," Sadie said. "Quiche. That might elevate this a little bit." Although her expression said she didn't really mind slumming it with their subpar pizzas.

"Sure, Sadie, you could do that," Connor said.

The door opened again, and Kate burst through it, followed by Eli, who was still in his uniform. Everything a stranger might want to know about his two younger siblings was conveyed by the way they walked into his house. Kate was exuberant, her footsteps loud, her grin irrepressible. Eli's steps were measured, cautious. And when he saw Sadie, the slow, subtle smile that spread across his features expressed a depth of happiness that made Connor's bones hurt.

That had been him once. At least, that was how he remembered it.

When he'd walked into a room, there had been only one place his eyes had gone. Jessie. She had been his focal point, his North Star, from the time he was eighteen years old. And then suddenly, she was just gone.

And so was his star.

He cleared his throat and took another drink of beer. There was no point in following that train of thought. No point in thinking about her at all. Except it was hard on nights like this. On the one hand, he depended on these get-togethers. They were his one opportunity to smile. To laugh. But when everyone was together like this, it was impossible to ignore the fact that it wasn't everyone. And it never would be again. Jessie had always sat next to him when they played poker. And sometimes she cheated, and he pretended he didn't notice.

He hadn't played a hand since without wishing she was there to look at his cards.

Still, it was better than drinking alone.

Liss sat next to him now. And he figured if he couldn't be with his wife, he should be right near his best friend.

Eli winced and reached into his jacket pocket, producing a vibrating cell phone. He let out a long-suffering sigh. "I've got to take this. Campaign stuff."

"It's fine," Sadie said, answering for all of them.

"I'll turn it off for the game."

"It's fine," Connor reiterated.

Eli waved a hand and walked back outside, the phone pressed to his ear. Sadie was smiling dreamily after him.

"He's so sexy when he's doing political stuff," she said.

Connor and Kate groaned. Then Kate moved farther into the room, offering her greetings.

"Hey, Jack. Hey, Sadie, Liss," she said, walking over to the table and taking a big piece of pizza off the pan, not bothering to use a plate. No greeting for him, but whatever. That was what younger sisters were for. "Did you sort out the rental situation?"

It took him a moment to realize that Kate had directed the question at Liss. "What rental situation?" he asked.

"Sorry. I didn't realize you hadn't told everyone," Kate said, her expression sheepish.

Liss looked slightly embarrassed. "Oh, no, it's not a big deal. Anyway, no, not yet. But I will."

"Wait a second, what rental thing? Is something happening with your house, Liss?" Connor asked, feeling annoyed now, because his little sister knew something about his best friend that he didn't.

Liss let out an exasperated breath. "I'm dealing, Connor. Put away your duct tape and superglue. You don't need to fix this."

He almost opened his mouth to say he hadn't offered to fix a damn thing. Because it was true; he hadn't. He hadn't offered to fix a damn thing in years.

There was no one around to complain if he didn't. So sinks stayed leaky, windows stayed drafty and...well, he got drunk while his friend was having a problem, and *motherfucker*, he didn't like that at all.

"Well, maybe I want to fix it if I can," he said.

"That's nice of you, Connor, but I don't think you can. Unfortunately, I'm uncovering a lot of damage Marshall did to my credit when he took off a couple of years ago. Some of it was obvious and came to my attention pretty quickly. Some of it has been less so. There were other credit cards, an additional car loan, plus what I already knew about. Basically, even with the credit bureaus correcting some of it, I can't get a new rental easily. And now that my landlord is selling..."

"That's not fair!" Kate said around a mouthful of pizza. "Most everybody here knows you, Liss. And a lot of us knew Marshall. So we kind of know he was an ass."

"If you had always known that, Kate, you might have let me in on it," Liss said, smiling ruefully.

"I think I *did* tell you that," Connor said through clenched teeth. "Repeatedly."

Liss tightened her lips into a bud, and Connor could tell she was holding back a deadly reply. He didn't really care. She'd been warned. She didn't listen. And while he didn't hold it against her, he had pretty much told her so the minute she'd shacked up with that idiot who was, well, an idiot.

Of course, Connor'd had to acknowledge, just to himself, that he might've been being unfair, because no man seemed good enough for Liss. Kind of like how no man would ever seem good enough for Kate.

But in the end, his instincts had been right on. Marshall had been a loser. Marshall had run off with Liss's money and the truck they had just bought. And now this.

"That's beside the point," Connor continued. "How long do you have to move out?"

"Legally, I have thirty days. But it's a private sale, and everything is moving really quickly. I figure I'm going to be out on my rear one way or the other. I mean, if it's that or going to live with my mother, then I will stay until the very last second, but…"

"You should stay here," Kate said.

Liss's eyes widened, and he felt his own mouth fall open. "Here? As in…*here* here?"

"Well, Sadie has the B and B."

Sadie winced. "I'm booked solid through Christmas. People coming to visit family, combined with the off-season discount, created a deluge of reservations."

"Your bed-and-breakfast is your livelihood, Sadie," Liss said. "I'm not going to take advantage of that. No one would expect *me* to do accounting for free."

"I wouldn't do accounting for money," Jack said.

"You probably *couldn't* do accounting for money, either," Liss returned.

"I'm wounded, Liss," Jack said. "However, speaking of all that, maybe somebody has a room and could use your services?"

Connor thought about all the paperwork he had left to do for the insurance. No, it wasn't accounting, but he *had* accounting to do. Though Liss already did it for him. And he even paid her. It was one of the few administrative things that still got done on time and well, because he paid for the service, rather than pretending he would do it himself one day. And Liss had brought him groceries this morning. In exchange for nothing but a bowl of cereal. He used her services already, many of them, and gave back very little in return these days.

"You can stay with me, Liss," he said, before he had time to fully process the implications of what he was offering.

"Really?" She looked shocked, and that made him feel even worse. Because why should she be shocked that her best friend was offering basic hospitality to her in her time of need? She shouldn't be.

He was clearly an asshole.

"Yes, really. This house is huge. And I'm here all by myself. I've got three completely empty bedrooms, plus office space I never use." Jessie had used the office to manage ranch staff, but he never had. It felt weird offering her space up. But she was gone, and Liss was here. Liss needed him, and he was going to help. "Anyway, it would just be until you can figure out a way to get a place of your own. Until you can find somebody who's willing to go outside the box for you. Or until your credit improves, or whatever. And you can save up for your deposit and first and last month's rent and all that."

"Connor, I can't stay here for free."

"No, you'll be staying here in exchange for groceries." She already bought them for him, anyway. "Plus, I might need a little bit of help with my organization."

Jack snorted. "You think?"

"We don't all have obsessive-compulsive tendencies like Eli," Connor said drily.

Eli, of course, chose that exact moment to walk back in, looking as if he was willing and able to lay down a little law and order. Sure, Eli was younger, but the two of them had banded together at a very young age to take care of the ranch and raise Kate. He'd had to start seeing Eli in a new light very quickly. There were only two years between them, anyway, but Connor had begun viewing him as an equal from the moment Eli had taken on household responsibilities.

And now that Connor lived alone in the big house, barely able to clean up after himself, he really appreciated all that Eli had done to make their lives better when they'd been kids.

Since then, Eli had gone from protecting the family to protecting the entire town. And while Connor didn't go around gushing about it, he couldn't be prouder. Even when Eli looked at him like he was a lost cause. Much like he was doing now.

"What did I miss?" Eli asked.

"Connor is defending his lack of housekeeping skills," Jack said.

Sadie crossed the room to Eli and wrapped her arms around his neck, kissing him deeply as though they hadn't just greeted each other a few moments ago. "Hey, Sheriff," she said.

"Not yet," he said. "Don't jinx it."

"I'm not a jinx! I'm the human incarnation of a lucky rabbit's foot!"

"Are you?" he asked, cocking his head to the side, the whole interaction way too cute for his formerly stoic sibling.

They separated slowly, Eli's hand sliding over her hip before resting there. Connor's stomach twisted.

"Connor isn't just defending his housekeeping," Sadie said. "He's offering Liss a place to stay until she can find a new rental."

"What happened with your old rental?" Eli said, frowning deeply.

Liss sighed. "I should have known that once the Garrett family got involved this whole thing would get epic. Long story abridged, my credit sucks because of Marshall, and my landlord is selling."

Eli's breath hissed through his teeth. "That's a bad combination."

"But it's going to be fine," Connor said, his tone insistent. "Because she can stay with me until she figures something out. I have plenty of room here. Anyway, she's here every night as it is. And she already brings me groceries."

"You're a little too attached to the grocery thing," Liss said.

He shrugged. "Hey, it's your rent. A small price to pay for a bedroom at Chez Garrett."

Liss fidgeted, looking around the room at all the expectant gazes. The Garretts were her surrogate family, so it was no surprise they had all rushed to her aid. But she hadn't told Connor for a specific reason. She'd found herself talking to Kate today during her lunch break, when they'd run into each other at the Crab Shanty during lunch hour. She should have known that the youngest Garrett wouldn't employ discretion.

Anyway, this was a solution, and she *did* need a solution. It was just the idea of living with Connor was sort of a loaded one. For a variety of reasons.

Though resisting would be…well, stupid. Because it was this or living with her mother, and she could genuinely imagine nothing worse than living with her mother. Except, maybe, living under a bridge. Actually, though, the bridge might be preferable.

But Connor had a point. This was a huge house. She spent a lot of time here, anyway.

Though, under normal circumstances, she would've wanted a little bit of time to think it over. Just because it was a change. Just because any commitment to move was kind of a big deal. But with the Garrett clan, Sadie and Jack all staring at her as if she had to issue a formal statement now, she felt as though she could hardly leave them waiting.

So she just ran through a quick laundry list of excuses and drawbacks, to be on the safe side:

Connor's house was farther from work.

She had never been that into the rustic look. Which his place had in spades.

She would have to put some of her furniture in storage.

Being in close proximity to Connor might make her loins burst into flame, starting another fire, leaving him homeless as well as barnless.

Yes, that. *That* was a problem. But then, she had done a lot of work in the loin department where Connor was concerned. She should be able to handle it. Honestly, she had been friends with the man for more than fifteen years, so her coping skills where he was concerned should be more refined. They were possibly even more refined than she realized. High exposure to Connor might actually help. If so, things like this morning, and that intimacy she had felt in the moment, would seem more commonplace.

So, there was a theory. And it was helping with her attempt at a snap decision.

"Thank you, Connor. I… Thank you. I really appreciate the offer. But we're going to have to talk about logistics, because I'm not just going to stay here and sponge off you."

"I'm not worried about that. Honestly," he said.

"Well, I am. I don't want to take advantage of you or our friendship."

"You won't," he said, his tone carrying a note of finality. "If anyone has been taking advantage over the past few years, it's been me. I didn't even realize you were going through something. You didn't tell me. That says a lot."

"Connor," she said, her voice quiet, "I just didn't want to pile on."

"That's the thing. You sure as hell should not be thinking of sharing things with me as piling on. I'm your friend. Yeah, I've had my share of bullshit going on for the past couple of years, but that doesn't mean you need to keep all this to yourself. I should've made that clearer."

Liss's chest tightened. She didn't like putting her crap on other people. Especially not someone who was already going through so much. Regardless of what he said, it did matter. She didn't like to be a burden to people. Least of all people she cared about. Why would anyone keep her around if she was taking more than she was giving?

"You should definitely stay here, Liss." It was Eli's turn to give his two cents. Apparently.

"I'm going to. Thank you."

Jack took another piece of pizza off the tray and leaned back in his chair. "Are we going to play cards, or are we going to stand around debating living situations? Not that you asked, Connor, but I might like to come and stay here, too."

"Why would you do that? Your house is nicer than mine."

"Yes, but Liss is going to be in your house, buying groceries. I'm assuming she might even cook some of those groceries."

"I never said anything about cooking," Liss said. "And even if I were going to cook, I would not be cooking for *you*. I will, however, kick your ass at poker."

Jack spread his arms wide. "Bring it on."

Everyone jostled and started taking their spots at the table, Eli reaching out to the center of it and grabbing a deck of cards. "It's about to be brought, Monaghan," Liss said.

And for a moment things felt normal. Things felt sane.

Pretty soon all of that would change, but for now they were just going to play some cards.

CHAPTER THREE

"Hey, Liss," Connor said, following her out the door to his house and down the steps of the porch. The poker game was done, and Jack had already gone home, while Kate was in the dining room lingering over the bowl of pizza rolls, and Eli and Sadie were just sort of happily sitting in the same chair.

Liss was ready to go, blaming an early work schedule, but they still had some things to figure out as far as Connor was concerned.

It was dark outside, cold enough that Connor could see his breath as he exhaled, the sharp bite of air in his lungs a signal that fall was fleeting and winter was biting at its ankles.

"We need to talk just a little bit before you go," he said.

Liss paused and turned on her heel, the gravel crunching beneath her feet. "Do we need to talk tonight?" She sounded tired, and he couldn't blame her. Had she sounded tired this morning? Had she sounded tired for longer than that? What else hadn't he noticed?

"It's not going to be long and involved, I promise. I just want to get a few things straight. You're not paying me rent."

"I'm going to have to compensate you somehow."

"Sure you are. You will bring me food, like you already do, and I will actually give you something in return."

"Connor, don't be difficult about this. At least let me go over some of the paperwork for the ranch. Get things organized. And maybe the house, too. If I'm going to be living in it, then I need things at a slightly higher level of cleanliness."

"Fine. Done." He ignored the tightening in his stomach. All of these offers of payment sounded very... domestic. Which was fair, he supposed, since they would be sharing the same house.

"Good," she said, nodding. "I'm glad we could come to an agreement."

Something about the situation struck him as funny then, loosening the knot in his gut. "I feel like we should shake hands or something."

"It does feel a little formal, doesn't it?"

"Yeah. Better idea." He reached out and pulled Liss into a hug, not really thinking about it until she was pressed up against him, warm, soft and *very* feminine. He didn't hug people often. He didn't hug people ever, really. *Sometimes* he hugged Kate, an awkward half hug. And he was more likely to punch Eli in the face than pull him into an embrace.

Very likely for those reasons the contact hit him with the force of a two-by-four. And while he was still reeling from the hit, time seemed to slow, and he became acutely aware of small things he would never normally notice. Of how soft she was, how tiny she was, folded into his arms, and—of course—the press of her breasts against his chest, because he was only human.

Connor breathed in deep, inhaling a hint of wood smoke coming from his own chimney, a bit of sea salt mixed with pine and a floral note he knew was coming from Liss's hair. The kind of girlie shampoo that had once cluttered up his shower, but had been absent from his house and his senses.

And for some reason, in this strange slow-motion moment it seemed perfectly acceptable for him to run his palm up Liss's back.

"Connor, you're kind of squishing my face."

Liss's muffled voice broke the moment, time suddenly returning to its normal speed. He laughed, a short, harsh sound that wasn't really intentional. But apparently, the release was necessary.

He let go of her and took a step backward. "Sorry about your face."

"Hang on to that, Connor. That could be a really useful insult later."

"I meant it sincerely. The squishing of your face, not the features of your face. The features of your face are fine." He had a feeling he wasn't making any of this better, or less weird.

"Thank you," she said, her tone letting him know that he definitely seemed weird to her. "I'm going to go home now. If I don't get my sleep, the numbers will not be effectively crunched tomorrow."

"That would be a shame."

"Not really. But I need the paycheck."

"So when do you want to move, then?"

She kicked her foot across the top of the gravel, the rocks clacking against each other. "I don't know. I mean, I have time…"

"Well, whatever you want. I'll even help you move."

Liss pulled a face. "What exactly has come over you? You're being all helpful and things."

"I guess it's the realization that I haven't been very helpful at all recently." They both knew exactly since when.

"I understand. I'm not going to tell you how you should handle all this. It's not my place."

"You're about the only one who thinks that. Eli thinks I need to get over it. Jack thinks I need to get laid."

Liss cleared her throat loudly. "With that in mind, I will be the one who thinks you just need to do what you can."

"I can do this," Connor said. "I can give this to you. So let me."

She scuffed her toe over the gravel, the rocks clicking together. "I am. We'll work out the logistics later. Thank you."

He gave her a halfhearted wave and turned away from her, walking back up the steps before pausing and watching her get into her car. Waiting until it started to go back inside. At least the thing would get her home tonight.

He shut the front door behind him and walked into the dining area, coming face-to-face with three very rapt sets of eyes. "What?" he asked.

"So, Liss is going to move in?" Eli asked.

"Were you not here for the entirety of this?" Connor returned.

"Just confirming."

"She needs me. She's a friend."

"I know," Eli said.

"Well, you look too interested. There's nothing to be interested about."

Sadie's expression turned placating, which only irritated him more. "Of course not." She reached into her offensive orange bowl and started digging around for candy. "It is very nice that you're doing this for her."

"You all have the wrong end of the stick," he said, pointing at the group. "You would not be reacting like this if I offered Jack a place to stay. And if Jack needed me, I would have him stay here, too. And he's a way bigger pain in the ass than Liss."

"True," Kate said. "On all counts."

"See? Katie agrees with me."

"Not," Kate said, her tone filled with warning, "if you keep calling me Katie."

A smile tugged at his lips. "Whatever you say, Katie."

It was Kate's turn to reach into the bowl. She pulled out a couple of M&Ms and hurled a couple at his head. "Serves you right," she said when one clocked him in the temple.

"Oh, no," he said, in mock terror. "You threw candy at me."

"*Beaver* candy," Sadie said.

"Okay, ladies, let's get out of Connor's hair," Eli said, showing an uncharacteristic amount of sensitivity. Eli usually thought nothing of running roughshod over him. Mainly because Eli always seemed to think he knew how other people should live their lives, and Connor was no exception to that.

Eli lifted Sadie from his lap and stood, raising his arms behind his head and stretching. "I need to sleep," he said. "With the election so close now, I'm not doing very much of that."

"But you're going to win," Sadie said, her tone confident.

"You are," Kate agreed.

Both women looked at Connor. "You are," he said, and he wasn't just saying that to stroke his brother's ego. He was the best choice for the county; there was no question about that.

Eli was a professional at sacrifice. He had sacrificed for Kate when he'd been a teenager. Had sacrificed his safety when he'd agreed to wear the uniform. And Connor knew, and never took for granted, the fact that Eli had sacrificed by being the one to come and tell him about Jessie's accident. Connor knew that no one in the department would have ever asked it of him. But Connor also knew that Eli would have never given the responsibility to anyone else.

For those reasons, and for so many more, Connor knew his brother was the man Logan County needed as its sheriff.

"Well, I appreciate the votes of confidence. Just make sure they're also physical votes on election day."

"Are you kidding? I'm going to go stand by the ballot drop boxes with my shirt off and my chest painted," Connor said. "A big painting of your face."

"I will arrest you. And I'm not joking," Eli said, lacing his fingers through Sadie's and heading toward the door.

Kate stood up and followed after them, offering him a goodbye wave.

"Goodbye, Connor," Sadie said as they headed out, shutting the door behind them.

And he was left alone again, by himself and in his big empty house.

But that was about to change.

Disquiet lodged itself in his gut. He'd had quite enough change over the past few years, and this was more of it.

But he wouldn't be alone. He was really fucking tired of being alone.

But he was alone now so he took another beer out of the ice bucket. A couple more drinks would help drown out the silence. Would help him fall asleep.

And there was no one here to tell him no.

"I THINK I SOLVED my rental problem," Liss said, sliding a paper clip onto a stack of papers and looking up at Jeanette, her coworker, who sat at the desk opposite her.

"You found someone to rent to you?" Jeanette asked, licking an envelope and smoothing it closed.

"Not exactly. But Connor has a lot of empty rooms, and he's agreed to let me stay with him until I can find a place."

Jeanette arched a dark brow and looked to the left to make sure no one else was lingering nearby. Maria and Sandra were the only others in the office today, but the older women didn't necessarily enjoy listening to her and Jeanette gossip. "Is this fine-ass Connor? The one with the bulging forearms and very delicious tattoo? Your friend? The one who's been by to pick you up from work a few times?"

Jeanette had been in town for only a couple of years, so she didn't know everyone's life or life story in as much detail as most of the locals did.

Liss cleared her throat. "Yes, that Connor."

"Get it, girl."

Liss's face burned, and she knew full well that she was blushing. "There will be no getting of it. He's just helping me out. And he really is *just* a friend."

Jeanette frowned. "Sorry. I did not imagine for one second that you were really only *just friends* with a man who looked like that. I just thought you were slow on the rebound after that jerk left." Jeanette never remembered Marshall's name, or at least, she pretended she didn't remember his name. Because Jeanette was a goddess like that.

"It's not like that with us. I was really good friends with his wife. Him, too. But Jessie and I were friends for…years and…well, that would be weird. And you know. Too much baggage."

It was a refrain she had repeated to herself often.

"Yeah, that makes sense. That's a lot of history."

"A book full of it. That's the problem with small towns," Liss said, sighing heavily. "There's history everywhere. That is perhaps why I've been single for so long." Except she knew it wasn't just that.

"Thankfully, I came with a man in tow." Jeanette and her husband, Tom, had been married for five years, and Tom had come to Copper Ridge to work as a fisherman.

"It was a better plan than mine. Which was to grow up here, never leave and ensure every man in my age group knew me far too well to see me as anything other than a friend. I'm thinking Copper Ridge could almost single-handedly cause a boom in the mail-order-husband market. Maybe I could get myself a nice biddable Russian groom. One who would chop wood and open jars for me."

"Let me know how that works out. I might sign up." Jeanette winked and pushed a stack of papers beneath a hole punch, pressing it down firmly. "Not that I need another husband. It would just be nice to have someone around the house to do hard labor when Tom is out on the boat."

"I could really start something here. A nice little

secondary career." Liss stuck the papers she was holding into a file. "Of course, I think living with Connor is going to be my secondary career."

"If it's rent-free…"

"It is."

"And comes with a very handsome roommate," Jeanette said, smiling.

"Yes. A cranky, high-maintenance, handsome roommate."

"That's what they call a fixer-upper."

"I think when I put out my ad for my mail-order husband, I'm going to request a man who's turnkey."

Jeanette laughed. "Good luck with that. They all come with baggage. Even the good ones." She pushed a couple buttons on her computer then paused. "Actually, especially the good ones. It's the ones who have been through a lot and come out the other side that are really worth it in the end."

Liss let Jeanette's words hang there for a moment, willing them to just roll off, hoping they wouldn't sink in. Because she didn't need to harbor any more false hope where Connor was concerned.

Finally, she responded. "Great. I'll let you know when he comes out the other side. Although, it *still* won't be like that."

"Whatever you say, Liss. Whatever you say."

Liss's cell phone vibrated against the surface of her desk. Her landlord's number flashed over the screen and she frowned, answering the phone as quickly as possible. "Sorry," she said to Jeanette, grabbing the phone and picking it up, answering quickly. "Hello?"

"Hi, Liss?" Marjorie asked, before plowing into the rest of her sentence. "Our buyer is very motivated to move. In fact, they really need a place to stay, so if we can't clear out the house fast enough for them, they might look somewhere else. They're able to pay cash, so they're very mobile, and this is moving very quickly. I'm sorry to inconvenience you, but if you are able to move out as quickly as possible, I would really appreciate it. I know what your rights are legally, but I thought I would just talk to you personally."

Of course, because this was Copper Ridge, and your landlord was never *just* your landlord; they became your friend, too. So when they overasked of you, it was impossible to say no. That was the economy of a small town. Everyone knew they could borrow help if need be, and interest was paid in small favors and homemade pies.

But then, her landlord had not become a good enough friend to refuse to ask something like this of Liss. Of course, she also knew Marjorie would never push or throw her out on the street or anything.

"It just so happens that I lined up a place to stay last night. And I can move in whenever." She thought of Connor and his house, and her stomach did something weird. Kind of a twist and turn at the same time.

Marjorie breathed out an audible sigh of relief right into Liss's ear. "If you could start moving out this weekend, it would be really helpful. I just don't want the sale to fall through. Norm and I are much better off in Arizona, and the sooner we can cut ties with everything here, the better. It isn't that I don't love the town, but my joints don't love the damp."

"I understand." Even though she didn't, really.

"Thank you, Liss. You've been a great tenant." Most especially since Marshall had moved out, but Liss didn't say it. "Most especially since that boyfriend of yours moved out." Oh, so Marjorie was going to go ahead and say it. "I hate to lose you, but I'm just too old to be managing properties and going back and forth between places. And if we have to hire a company…"

Liss let her mind wander. She'd heard Marjorie's hand-wringing on the subject already. She was agreeing to move out; she didn't know why she needed to subject herself to her landlord's woes. Which was potentially a little bit unsympathetic, but she was the one who was being massively inconvenienced, so maybe not.

"Okay, sweetie, I've got to go," Marjorie said.

"Okay, talk to you later." Liss hung up and set her phone on the table. She looked up at Jeanette. "Is it okay if I make one more personal call?"

Jeanette waved a hand. "I'm not the warden. Do your business."

Liss picked her phone up and dialed Connor's cell phone number. He still had a flip phone, and half the time it didn't ring, but it was still worth a try, because she knew he was out in the field right now, rather than at home.

Much to her very pleasant surprise, Connor answered on the second ring. "Liss?"

"Hi, Connor. I just wanted to say…I guess I'm moving in this weekend."

"I guess I'll be at your house early Saturday with a truck." He sounded a little bit dazed, and she couldn't blame him. She *felt* a little bit dazed.

"I'll be waiting. With groceries. As per the agreement."

"All right, then, Saturday."

"Saturday," she repeated, before hanging the phone up.

It wasn't that big of a deal. It wasn't a deal at all.

Maybe if she repeated that to herself a few more times she would start to believe it.

CHAPTER FOUR

IT WAS MOVING DAY. Connor had to be at Liss's house by nine. Which meant he'd been out on his horse by six. The morning air had a mean bite, but he didn't mind. The needle pokes of wind against his skin, combined with the pounding of his horse's hooves on the soft ground, went a long way in wiping his mind clean.

Connor rode through the empty field, clumps of mud and grass flying up behind him, hitting the back of his shirt. The clearing was flanked by a grove of trees on the left, and a steep, evergreen-covered pitch of rock on the right. The sky above was filled with gray, misty clouds that seemed to be rolling down toward earth, swallowing the tops of the mountains that surrounded the ranch.

This was morning here in Copper Ridge. All shades of deep green, blue and gray. Until the sun came out and burned the cloud cover away, flooding the ranch with golden light, drawing the scent of dirt, moss, pine out, then washing it all with an ocean breeze. For Connor this was as close to spiritual as it got. Being in this place, this town, where vast stretches of water met vast open land. Where all the essential sources of life were ready and available. This place was in his blood, in his soul.

This land had been here before him, before his family had fenced it, cultivating it, but never taming it. To the best of his ability he would see it was here long after he was gone. In his mind, progress could never mean man-made development on land like this. Progress would be when people realized that everything they needed was already here.

He ignored the hollow ache in his stomach that was trying to remind him even here, even now, he felt a little bit empty.

That even now, with the golden sunlight poured over the evergreen trees, he felt cold down to his soul. That no matter how bright the light shone, it never seemed to touch him.

He ignored that, because there was nothing he could do with it.

He pulled back on the reins, bringing his horse to a stop, taking a moment to survey his surroundings. It was still here. It was early enough in the morning that even the wind was still. It was the kind of vast silence that would swallow up the sound of a man's voice, consuming it as if he had never spoken.

One man wasn't powerful enough to disturb beauty like this. It made him feel small, and consequently it made some of his problems feel a lot smaller.

He dismounted from his horse, dropping the reins and leaving her standing there. He walked forward, toward the middle of the clearing, and looked up. For the first time he saw a small patch of blue sky, a ray of sun bursting through.

He closed his eyes, keeping his face angled upward, letting the warmth seep through his skin, praying it would reach his bones.

It didn't. But it hit him just then that this was the

first morning he had woken up without a hangover in quite a while. He hadn't had a drink last night. He'd been too focused on what it would mean to bring Liss into the house.

He opened his eyes and looked at the sun, and his head didn't hurt.

All things considered, he figured it would be a pretty good moving day.

THEY'D ATTACKED THE PROJECT of moving Liss much like a barn raising. All hands on deck, finished by the end of the day. Ultimately, nothing was left undone except for a few empty boxes still in need of disposal, and paper plates with the remnants of pizza, along with a few empty beer bottles, stationed throughout Connor's house. Of course, there hadn't been much to move into the house itself.

A bedroom's worth of furniture, and all her clothes, books and a few kitchen gadgets she hadn't been willing to part with.

Everything else had gone into a vacant outbuilding on the Garrett property. Which was going to save her a lot in storage fees. Between letting her borrow space on the ranch, space in Connor's house and the use of their muscles—including Jack's—Liss was starting to feel as if she was taking an awful lot.

And that feeling, that feeling of being in debt to somebody else, always made her feel uncomfortable. She felt as though it forced her to keep a running tally on what she had contributed versus what someone else had contributed. Because she never wanted to be on the wrong side of that balance.

She took a deep breath and tried to banish the tightness in her chest. The moving crew, comprised of Eli, Sadie, Kate, Jeanette and Jack, had all gone home, leaving her there in her new space, with her new roommate.

She took a deep breath and walked over to the kitchen sink, looking out at the wall of trees that stood between the house and the mountains. It didn't feel weird to be here. Of course, she didn't know why she had thought it might. Well, she supposed it was because she was living here now, instead of visiting. But then, she was much more than a casual visitor. Always had been. Even more so in recent years. Because she was bringing him food, having dinner with him, trying to prevent him from drinking himself into a stupor every night, which she had managed with mixed success.

It didn't feel weird at all to be standing here. No, it felt comfortable. This would be comfortable. Yes, comfortable. Like a broken-in pair of boots. Like a late-July afternoon on the hiking trails that wound through the mountains and beneath a canopy of trees.

That kind of comfy.

She heard footsteps behind her, and she turned.

Connor shoved his hands into the pockets of his jeans and rocked back on his heels. "You need anything?" he asked.

"No. Still full from the pizza."

"I know there's no bathroom right off your bedroom. But I figure you can have that one that's nearby in the hall. I only use the one off my bedroom."

She'd kept all of her toiletries in her travel case. She just hadn't felt comfortable unloading makeup and hair-care products all over a common area. There was moving in, and then there was invading. "Only if you're sure. I don't mind keeping that stuff in my room."

"No way. That's not practical at all. Just unload it all in there. As far as I'm concerned this is your place, too. I mean, it's mainly my place, but we're sharing. Seventy-thirty."

She laughed. "Generous."

"Yeah, I think so. Come on, though. This place is huge. I basically have a trail worn between my bedroom and the kitchen, and I hardly go anywhere else. I spend most of my day outside working. Of course, that means I barely clean any room in the house, so I'm sorry about that."

"Well, I kept my house clean. I have no problem transferring that to here. Honestly, you have no idea how much I've been wanting to wipe down your cabinets."

A lopsided smile curved his mouth. "That kind of sounds dirty."

"Wiping down your cabinets?" she asked, barely suppressing a grin. "I don't even want to know what that could be."

"Do you know what I want?"

She narrowed her eyes. "What?"

"Pie."

"That had better not be euphemistic pie." The line of conversation was making her feel strange. A little bit light-headed.

"No, this is literal pie." He walked to the fridge and opened the door, pulling out a white bakery box and setting it on the island in the center of the kitchen. "Remember Alison? She made those pies for the Fourth of July thing. You know, then my barn burned down and Eli ran her husband off the property."

"Oh, yes, I vaguely remember that night," she said drily.

"Anyway, she's selling pies independently, not just baking for the diner. Because she left her husband right after the thing."

"Did she?"

"Yep. So I hear from Sadie. It's not the kind of gossip I would keep up on on my own." He opened the box and shrugged a shoulder. "Still, I figure it's nice to help support someone starting a new life."

Connor being Connor, he was downplaying anything even remotely nice about what he had done. "That's very thoughtful of you," she said, moving closer to examine the dessert that was in the box.

"I got pie in exchange for my good deed. I think that nullifies the good deed. My reward is pie."

"And what variety of pie are we talking?"

"Marionberry."

"Excellent reward. Do you have ice cream?"

Connor looked up at her, handsome face contorted into an expression of horror. "And whipped cream. I know I might seem uncivilized, but even I have some boundaries."

"You're a god among men, Connor Garrett. You have saved me from homelessness—or at least living with my mother—and you've given me pie."

"You can begin paying me back by getting out some plates," he said.

"Will do."

She made herself busy getting out plates, ice cream and the whipped cream, which was in the fridge as promised. Apparently, Connor could grocery shop when dessert was involved. Well, dessert or alcohol.

She brought the plates over, and Connor put one

piece on each, a very generous-sized piece, because Connor knew she didn't mess around with desserts.

He didn't even ask if she wanted the pie warm, because he knew better than that. He put each piece in the microwave for about thirty seconds, and when they were done, she was waiting with a scoop of vanilla ice cream for each.

They both dove right into their pie, eating wordlessly, exchanging looks during bites. "This is good," Liss said when she was halfway through with her piece.

"Understatement," Connor said around a mouthful.

"I don't even know why we bothered to put pieces on the plates. We should've just eaten straight out of the box."

"Because it takes longer to heat up a whole pie?"

"Yeah, good point." Liss's thoughts turned to Alison. "So, is Alison still working at the diner?"

"Search me," Connor said. "I just know she's trying to make a business out of the baking. It's hard to start over."

"You would know."

"It's not really the same."

"Sure it is," she said, taking another bite as if she could stuff her statement right back into her mouth. She should not be pushing him on this topic, and she knew that.

"No, it's not the same. She was married to an asshole. She very rightly chose to end that marriage, and because of that finds herself with increased options in life. I didn't make any choices about changing my life. It just changed."

But you could make some now. She did not say that out loud. "Fine. But you are still in a new chapter of your life."

"I should have put that book down a few chapters ago, then. Called it good."

Liss's stomach pitched. "I really hope that wasn't supposed to mean what I think it did." Right now she was ready to hit him in the face with her pie plate.

"What do you think it meant?"

"I hope you don't think you should've stopped living. Because I don't want to think about that. Connor, Jessie was one of my best friends. I know it isn't the same as being married to somebody. I do. But I can't think about losing you, too. I just can't. I can't lose both of you."

"That's not what I meant, Liss. I didn't really mean anything by it."

"Don't say things you don't mean."

"Sorry, honey. I guess you missed the memo about me being a gigantic bastard."

Liss sighed. "You are not a bastard. You do a very good impression of one, but I know you aren't one. Case in point, I am standing in your kitchen with you eating dessert. Your kitchen, that is now my kitchen, too. Because you gave me a place to stay when I needed one. Because you are actually kind of a kick-ass friend. And a good man who buys charitable pies. So enough with the bastard talk."

"I think you're the only one who still thinks I'm decent, but I'll take it."

Her eyes met his, dark, enticing, with a hint of bitterness, like a coffee bean. Her heart squeezed tight, and she looked down. She didn't know why this happened sometimes. Why she could stand there and talk to him and feel perfectly appropriate, neutral friendship feelings that she would have while speaking to someone like Jeanette. And then suddenly she would look at him, and things would change. Her breath would catch in her throat, her heart doing tricks. And in those moments he was the furthest thing from just a friend. In those moments he wasn't *just* anything. He was everything.

"You are more than decent. And don't argue with me. Anyway, maybe we should talk about what I can help you with around here?"

"You're very effectively helping me demolish this pie. That's appreciated."

"I will be sure to add pie demolition to my résumé. But beyond helping you reduce the snack foods in your house, I'd like to help. Cleaning for sure, because that benefits me, too. I already do your accounting. But if there's any other paperwork that you have, I'd be happy to help. I know that Jessie used to handle a lot of the admin." She had already invoked Jessie's name once in the past few minutes so she might as well do it again.

"Yeah, I'm pretty behind on some things, I can't lie about that." Connor braced his hands on the island, and her gaze was drawn to them. He had nice hands. Strong, square, masculine. He had never worn a wedding ring all that often. The kind of work that he did made the little gold band a hazard. More than one rancher had lost a finger by getting a wedding ring caught on an animal or a tractor. But she was still surprised that he'd taken it off and never put it back on again. In so many other ways she could see he was holding on tightly to the past, but not in that way. Of course, that wasn't something you asked about. He sighed heavily. "I would like to lie about that. I pretty much *do* lie about it to Eli."

"But what's the point of lying to him? He would just want to help."

"Yeah, that's the thing. He wouldn't be able to help

himself. He would jump right in. And then he would resent me for it. And it's not the resentment I'd mind so much, it's the fact that he should have his own life. And I shouldn't be interfering in it with all of my shit."

"He's your brother, though. Your shit is his shit."

"It's been that way for too long, Liss. I'm not going to do that to him anymore. He has Sadie now, and I just know he's going to marry her. He's got to make a family with her. And he should be free to do that. He's been dealing with other people's messes for way too long. I don't need him to do it with mine."

"That's what family does. We clean up each other's messes, because it's better to do that than to not have family at all." At least that was what she often told herself, because Madeleine Foster was a mess and a half. And Liss had spent a very good portion of her life cleaning up those messes. She was all in trying to keep her mother happy. Trying to prove her worth. But over the past few years it had started to wear on her. It was an insatiable well she could continue to pour into forever and never satisfy. Never get the one thing she was actually after.

"That's why you're good family to have."

She wondered for a second if he was going to hug her again, like he'd done the other day. Stupid, but that hug was burned into her consciousness. There had been something about it, something that differentiated it from the hugs they'd shared before. It had left her warm and a little bit breathless. Or, more to the point, it had left her a little bit turned on. She'd had a very restless night that night.

All things considered, she really shouldn't want another hug from him. But she did. Base creature that she was.

It was sort of the story of her life. Stealing a few cheap thrills now and again from innocuous Connor contact. Oh, she didn't mean to. She didn't mean to let sparks fly through her veins when his fingers brushed against hers, didn't mean to go weak-kneed when he smiled and caught her eyes. It was involuntary. And unnecessary. But it happened all the same.

"Well, I'm happy to be your family." She took a step backward, just in case he did intend to hug her. She needed to curb that before it happened. Because sanity. Because even though her reactions to him were involuntary, and in some ways not entirely unpleasant, it did not mean she had to encourage them. Because, as he just said, he felt all familial toward her. And it was what he needed from her. He did not need her getting gooey over hugs. "If you could leave me a list of things you want to look at tomorrow, I'll go over it when I get up in the morning and get started."

"I don't want you to spend your Sunday doing chores for me."

"And I want to start as I mean to go on. These are chores. I want to help you. I think I've made that perfectly clear by showing up once every couple of weeks with groceries. And by bringing you food so you don't starve and die."

"You were sharing that responsibility with Eli."

"Sure. But I called and reminded him most of the time. Anyway, just leave me a list, and tomorrow I'll get started."

"Okay, but I'm afraid you're going to regret this a little bit."

She laughed. "Maybe. But that's future Liss's problem. Present Liss is going to skip off to bed with a full stomach and not worry about it."

He shook his head. "Fine, but when future Liss becomes present Liss she's going to be cursing past Liss."

"Maybe. But I'll worry about that tomorrow."

Yes, this was going to be comfortable. Comfortable, indeed. And as Liss settled into her new bedroom, she knew that she had made the right decision. She was going to be just fine.

CHAPTER FIVE

BY THE TIME Connor got back to the house Sunday night he was tired, dirty and grumpier than a bear with his ass stuck in a beehive. All he wanted to do was grab a beer, sit in front of the TV and pass out.

The damn cows had collapsed the fence on the far end of the property and had ended up scattering into BLM land. It had taken multiple four-wheelers and men to get the craven beasts back where they belonged.

Steak. He wanted steak. That was the other thing he wanted.

He had a feeling it wasn't a coincidence, considering how obnoxious the damn cows were.

He remembered the list he had left on the counter for Liss that morning, and he perked up slightly. With any luck, the kitchen would be cleaner, and his paperwork would be done. And probably, just because she was Liss, she would've made dinner, too. After all, she had to eat, and she had worked all day.

By the time he walked through the entryway and into the kitchen he was almost smiling.

But there was no warm, inviting smell of a home-cooked dinner. Neither was Liss in the kitchen, prancing around in an apron and high heels. He had no idea why he was picturing her wearing that, since he had never seen her wear any such thing; he only knew he had pictured it.

What he had not imagined was Liss storming into the kitchen, barefoot, and wearing jeans and a T-shirt, scowling at him like he'd just voiced his desire to have found her cooking in high heels out loud. "We need to talk."

"Do we?" he asked, walking to the fridge, opening it, hunting for a beer. He was in trouble, and he wasn't sure why. He was rarely in trouble with Liss, and Lord knew he had probably earned some that she had never doled out. But as far as he knew he hadn't done anything wrong today. In fact, all he had done today was work hard and come home to a frowning woman. That was one thing about marriage he had not missed.

"Yes, we do. I was doing that paperwork that you asked me to take care of."

He arched a brow. "You got a paper cut?"

"I wish, Connor, *I wish.*"

"I told you it was going to be a pain. You said you wanted to do it."

"The thing is, Connor, it was not a pain." She was saying his name a lot. The amount of times she used his name in a sentence seemed directly related to how pissed she was. "Connor, it took me about five minutes to deal with. There were just a few things that needed to be clarified and refilled out. In order for you to get your insurance money. You got the paperwork more than a month ago. I saw the date that was stamped on it. Why didn't you send it?"

Well, that explained why he was in trouble. He hadn't realized a whole month had passed since he'd last spoken with the claims office. But in his defense, he hadn't really thought it was a simple fix. In fact, every time he thought about doing it, a hard knot of stress started to form in his stomach, and he broke out into a cold sweat. So he went and did something else. Anything else. And okay, it might have been easier than he'd imagined it would be, but there was no way it had taken her only a few minutes to do the task.

"I don't know," he said, because right then he honestly didn't.

"That's not a very good answer. In fact, it isn't the answer."

"It's an answer. It's the only one I have. I don't know why I didn't finish it. It just… Every time I thought about doing it, I didn't."

"Connor, this is the only way you're going to get your barn built. You led me to believe, me and everyone else, that the insurance company was dragging their feet. But they didn't have all the paperwork because you didn't do it."

"I didn't ask you to get in my face about what you found in the house. I just asked you to take care of it. That too difficult?"

Liss crossed her arms beneath her breasts. "Yes, it is too difficult. I want to understand what's going on."

"There isn't anything going on. I just didn't get it done."

"That's bullshit, Connor. You even had it signed. You just needed to finish the body of the paperwork. All I had to do was fax it over today, and it's being processed. It was that simple."

"It wasn't simple." He slammed the refrigerator door shut and dragged his fingers through his hair. "Obviously, if it was simple I would've done it."

"But you didn't. Somehow, I managed."

"Yeah, well," he said, throwing his arms out, "I guess I just wonder what the point is. Everything I build, every single thing, just ends up getting destroyed. If I get the money it would just burn, too. Or maybe I would rebuild the barn, and then what? Is it going to be safe?"

His heart was thundering hard, his hands feeling a little bit shaky. He hadn't realized the outburst was coming until it was over. But he realized, as soon as he had said the words, that they were true.

This ranch had been in his family for generations. And if there was one thing every generation of Garretts had in common, it was loss. When they loved someone, that someone left. When they loved something, it got destroyed. Connor had loved a lot of things. He had added one major bit of himself to this operation, the barn, and it had burned to the ground.

How many more signs from God did he need before he just stopped trying? A guy would have to be a damn hardheaded fool to not realize when things just weren't going to grow where he planted them.

"You don't really think that's going to happen, do you?" Liss asked, her eyes full of concern. She'd looked at him like that twice in the past couple of days. Like he was crazy, like she wanted to hug him and slap him at the same time.

"There are no guarantees." And she couldn't argue with him about that. Because he knew it was true. He knew it was true more than anyone. "That barn was something that Jessie and I both wanted for this ranch. I dreamed about something like that. I hated that I had to get it through tragedy. With the money from my old man dying. Hell, who would want that? But I had it. Eli,

Kate, they gave their share so that I could have that. So that we can take this ranch and make it better. And then Jessie died, and all of my plans went to shit. Because it doesn't matter anymore."

It was hard to describe the kind of desolation he had felt when he lost Jessie. The way the future felt as if it had been erased. But then, there was more to all that than he could tell Liss. More to all of it than he could ever tell anyone.

Because everyone had grieved with him over Jessie's death. He didn't want to add to it.

"Connor, I know you've been through hell. I remember what a big deal it was to you to have that barn built in the first place. How bittersweet it was, because of your dad. I was there. I remember how excited you were, how excited Jessie was. I remember all of your plans. I know all of those dreams that you had are still somewhere inside of you."

Pain washed over him, through him. Because he wished what she was saying was true. The simple fact was that those dreams were gone. Dead and buried. He was just doing his best to get through the day. To work the ranch.

The fact that he got up every morning and did his work was about the only thing that separated him from his dad.

The thought was like spikes of barbed wire pushed under his fingernails. He wasn't like his dad. Michael Garrett had checked out of his children's lives completely when his wife had left. Leaving the ranch to rot, leaving his kids to take care of themselves, while he drank himself into a stupor on the couch.

Connor took care of the ranch. Connor didn't have children to neglect.

He rubbed his hand over his heart, trying to ease the intense pain that was spreading from there and moving outward.

"I don't really have dreams anymore," he said, feeling stupid talking about this. He wasn't the kind of guy to drag his feelings out into the open and examine them. He didn't even like to examine them by himself, under the cover of darkness.

"That's not what I want for you," she said, her tone all sad and desperate.

"I can't… I can't." She looked down, blinking rapidly. Great, he had made Liss cry. "Don't cry for me, Liss. I don't even cry for myself."

"Then somebody should cry for you," she said, looking back up at him, her eyes shining.

"No way. Cry over something that's worth it. Cry over puppies that are left in the pound, and ice cream scoops that fall off ice cream cones. But don't cry over me."

"I can't make any promises. Connor, the money is going to come soon now. Promise me that you'll get the barn rebuilt. Or go to Hawaii." She closed her eyes and shook her head. "No, get the barn rebuilt."

"Why, because Jessie wanted it?"

"No, because *you* wanted it."

He had wanted it, though he could barely remember wanting much of anything. Could barely remember being the man he'd been three years ago, ready to start a new phase of his life, everything stretching ahead of him all bright and sunny and new. Instead of a wasteland of routine, of loneliness and grief that never seemed to ease no matter how much time passed, no matter how much he drank.

"It's hard to remember back that far. Or at least it's difficult to remember why I cared."

"You cared because this ranch is in your blood. It still is, Connor. I know it is."

"Right now the ranch is just under my skin. I spent hours trying to get damn cows back into their pens. Not coincidentally I want to eat a hamburger."

Liss clapped her hands together. "Right. So let's make the hamburger happen. The question is, do we want to go to Ace's? Or the diner?"

"I sort of feel like throwing sharp things at a corkboard. So I vote for Ace's."

This was good. If they went out, there would be no more chance for talking. Because there would be too much laughing, and drinking and interacting with people who weren't him. So Liss wouldn't be able to hold him under the microscope to the same degree she just had. Their conversation had gone to way too much of a navel-gazing place.

Liss pulled a bright pink rubber band from around her wrist and quickly swept her hair up into a ponytail. "I should just go put some makeup on."

"What do you need makeup for?"

"If the barn needs painting, you have to paint it, right?"

He stood and stared at Liss, standing there fresh-faced, and damn pretty in his opinion, and puzzled over why she would need painting. "Natural wood is good, too," he said, somewhat lamely. He was bad at complimenting people. He was out of practice. Not that he'd been all that good at it even when he was in practice.

"Thank you," she said, her cheeks coloring a little bit. "I think I will at least add a little bit of stain, though. I don't know. This metaphor has gotten weird."

"Okay, you go paint. I'm going to hop in the shower because I smell. I'll only be about five minutes."

THE BAR WAS CROWDED, as per usual on a Sunday night. It was very likely most of the town had gone from church straight to drinking. But likely it was needed to get them through the workweek that lay ahead.

But in spite of the impending doom of Monday, the atmosphere was exuberant. Country music was playing over the jukebox, almost every table filled, a small crowd gathered by the dartboards. Some people were still in coveralls, wearing the evidence of the day's labor, while some were still in suits and ties, evidence of labor of a different sort.

All the bits and pieces of Copper Ridge collided here, and it was easy to see why.

The whole bar had a rustic feel to it, knotted wood on the floor and on the walls, exposed beams on the ceiling. There was half a red rowboat mounted to the ceiling, old fishing nets spilling out of it. It was everything a coastal hole-in-the-wall needed. And, in defiance of its hole-in-the-wall appearance, it had darn fine food.

"You know what you want?" Connor asked.

"Fish-and-chips. Tartar sauce and malt vinegar."

He nodded once. "Snag a table, will you?"

"Sure. Just a Diet Coke to drink."

He nodded again, walking over to the bar. She couldn't help but watch him go. He had put on a plaid button-up shirt, pushed the sleeves past his elbows, revealing that tattoo that fascinated her so much, and the muscles that fascinated her equally.

Only Connor knew what the tattoo meant. He'd come back home one Saturday with the start of it and finished it over the next few weeks. But he'd never said anything about it. And she had never asked. Because the omission was so glaring, it had to be purposeful.

So she let him have it. But after today, she was starting to think she let him have a few too many omissions.

She'd been livid when she'd discovered the paperwork. But then he'd said all those things, and her heart squeezed tight, and all the anger had sort of leaked out and drained away.

And it was impossible to be mad at him now, as he was ordering her food and standing there with his broad back filling her vision, slim waist tapering down to slim hips and… Well, there was no use denying the fact that it was a damn fine ass.

Her cheeks got hot, and she looked down at her hands. She was not going to keep staring at him. Not like that.

She looked up again when he pulled his chair out and sat across from her. He set her Diet Coke down in front of her, his own hand wrapped around a dark brown beer bottle. "Food will be up in a minute."

"Good," she said, "I'm starving."

She looked up, behind Connor, and saw a group of three women, all bleached blonde, all much more made up than she was, staring Connor down. Blonde number one leaned over and whispered something to blonde number two, who then turned her focus to Liss, her frosted-pink lip curling upward into a sneer.

Well, Liss had clearly been measured and found wanting.

Blonde number three tossed her hair over her shoulder and stuck her chest out, as if she was gearing up to go on a mission. And her mission seemed to pertain to Connor.

Oh, dammit. They were headed this way. All of them were headed this way. They made their way up to the table, one moving to Connor's left, the other two standing on his right. "Hi." The one Liss had arbitrarily dubbed number three spoke first. "My friends and I had a question."

Connor looked up, a crease between his brows, his lips pulled down into a frown. "Yes?"

He looked so confused, it was almost cute.

"We were just wondering if your table mate here is your girlfriend or your sister?"

Liss sputtered.

Connor's frown deepened. "You came all the way over here to ask me that?"

Number three, whom Liss clearly should've named number one, reached out and touched Connor's forearm. Ran her manicured fingertips over the vines of his tattoo. Rage burned in Liss's chest. *She'd* never done that. She had never touched his tattoo, and some random woman was trailing her fingertips over the ink on his skin.

"It seemed important," she said, winking at him. Her eyelashes were fake. Liss was certain.

"She lives with me," he said, turning his attention back to his beer.

"Doesn't really answer my question," Blondie said.

"I don't see why I should," he said, his tone uncompromising.

The woman rolled her eyes and gestured to her friends

to move on. "Sorry you aren't in the mood to play, honey," she said, her parting shot as she wiggled back over to the other side of the bar.

Liss snorted. "Can you believe that?"

"What?"

"Obviously, they did not think I was pretty enough to be your girlfriend."

"I don't see why they cared."

She arched a brow. "Do you *really* not see?"

He shook his head. "Not really."

Liss looked closely at his face to see if he was being serious. "Because she was hitting on you. Now, I don't think my being your girlfriend would've deterred her, but I think she wanted to insult me first."

He waved his hand. "I doubt she was hitting on me."

"Yes, she was. Women must hit on you all the time."

"Maybe." He shrugged, the gesture more uncomfortable than casual. "I don't really care."

She should not be happy to hear that. She should be concerned. "You don't care at all?"

"I'm not in the market for anything."

"That woman was not in the market for a relationship, Connor. She just wanted…you know, naked stuff."

"I'm not really in the market for that right now."

She should not be happy about that, and she should *not* be interested in exploring the topic further. "Not at all?"

"No. And don't try to change my mind. You said that you were going to support me being where I wanted to be. Eli has already pushed me about it. Jack won't shut up about it."

"I just… I figured…"

One of the new waitresses, someone Liss didn't

know, set their food down in front of them. Both in red baskets, piled high with french fries. "What did you figure?" Connor asked, eating a fry.

"Well, I figured at this point you would be in the market for that. If you had not…gone to market already, so to speak."

"I don't have enough energy to fill out my insurance paperwork. Why would you think I had the energy to screw somebody?" He took the top bun off his hamburger and started squirting ketchup on the patty.

Her stomach twisted, and she did her best not to examine it. "Because, typically, it's something people make time for." She should talk, since she'd been single for two years, and there had been no screwing.

Connor shrugged and took a bite of his hamburger. "I didn't come here to get a psychological evaluation. I came here to take out my rage on the cows by eating their brethren. So we can drop the subject now." He set the hamburger down and looked at his thumb, which had a spot of ketchup on it.

He raised his thumb to his lips and licked the red sauce from his skin. The sight of his tongue moving over bare flesh, even his own flesh, sent an arrow of longing straight down between Liss's thighs.

"Okay, fair enough." Yes, she was more than happy to abandon this line of conversation.

"Hey, guys."

Liss looked up, and Connor looked behind him, to see Jack standing there. "Mind if I pull up a chair?"

"Please," she said. Anything to break the weirdness of this moment. Why were things weird? Was it because she had moved in?

"Glad you're here, Jack," Connor said. "As soon as I finish eating, I'd love to kick your ass at darts."

"You're welcome to try."

Jack joining the group added an air of familiarity, of normalcy. A much-needed injection of it, after the roiling jealousy she'd experienced watching Connor get hit on, and the flash of heat that had assaulted her only moments later.

She had to get a grip. Because, like Connor said, he was in no place to hook up. And even if he were, it wouldn't be with her.

She wouldn't want it to be her, anyway. Some things in life are too important to screw up with sex. Her friendship with Connor was one of them. She had decided that years ago, and other than one brief lapse, a few months where she had thought things might be changing between them, she had always thought that.

It was true then; it was true now.

Connor was the best friend she'd ever had, and she would do anything to protect that friendship. Anything.

CHAPTER SIX

CONNOR WAS GETTING a late start to the day. Fortunately, his team was good, and he knew that the animals would be taken care of. Still, he hated oversleeping. But he, Jack and Liss had stayed way too late at Ace's last night, flinging darts at the board, laughing about stupid stuff and in general ignoring the reality of life.

Reality that had slapped him in the face pretty hard this morning when his alarm had gone off. It wasn't just the fact that they had stayed at the bar late. Once they'd made it home, Connor had had a hell of a time sleeping. It had been as if something was sitting on his chest, making it impossible to breathe, impossible to do anything but lie there, sweat beading on his brow, panic rising in his throat.

Not for the first time, he wished he had accepted medication for his anxiety.

But when the doctor had offered it a couple of years back, Connor had just laughed it off and said he didn't need a pill when a beer would do the job. But he was getting tired of the hangovers. He was tired of the anxiety, too. Hell, he was tired of all this shit. He would never have thought he'd be the kind of guy to become a head case over a little grief. Or a lot of grief.

It seemed as if he might be, though.

I don't have enough energy to fill out my insurance

paperwork. Why would you think I had the energy to screw somebody?

A flash of last night's conversation popped into his mind. Had he really said that to Liss? Yeah, he had. He didn't suppose it was normal to still be this tired. To still be this overwhelmed by what was left. But then, there was nothing normal about losing your entire future. All of your plans. Everything you were.

The finality was the worst part. It just happened. Unexpected, fast. Jessie had gone out to visit with her friends. A normal night, nothing unusual at all.

And she hadn't come home.

Just like that, every plan for the future gone.

And he was sort of stubbornly sitting here in the present, afraid to plan for a future he'd never wanted in the first place. One where he was alone, single. But here he was, and now… He couldn't readjust, not again.

He let out a heavy breath and walked to his dresser, jerking open the bottom drawer and digging for some underwear. And there were none. Because he didn't keep up on his laundry, because he sucked. He sucked at taking care of himself, and he had sucked at taking care of his wife.

Of course it was too late to fix a marriage that had been put asunder by death. But it wasn't too late to fix the situation with his underwear.

He walked downstairs—wearing nothing but yesterday's underwear—and headed toward the laundry room. Hopefully there was something in the dryer. He was not the best at keeping up on laundry. Because laundry was terrible. But sometimes he ended up with one or two baskets full of clean clothes, just sitting in there, because he hated to put things away.

Liss had accused him of being a man-child on more than one occasion. He was starting to think she might be right.

It was a pretty sad-sack thing, now that he thought about it. A grown man not being able to see to his own household. But Eli had always done that when they were growing up, after their mother had left. And then Connor had married Jessie, and she had handled all of it. It wasn't a great excuse. He had always expected for it to be taken care of, and it had been. While he had spent his days working himself blind on the ranch.

He'd intended to change. Because Jessie had asked him to. And because she deserved for him to.

Only then it had been too late.

So he'd gone right back to how he'd always been. Because there was no one to be different for. No one to be better for.

And because of that, he had no clean underwear.

He opened up the laundry room door and saw two baskets filled with clothes on the floor. He opened up the dryer door, and there was a full load in there, too. Okay, he was bound to come up successful in this pursuit.

He started to dig through the dryer and realized pretty quickly he wasn't looking at his own clothes. He grabbed a basket and stuck it underneath the opening to the dryer, pulling the clothes that were inside out and into said basket.

His hand got caught around something lacy and flimsy, and he looked down and froze. Well, he had found clean underwear. They just weren't his.

For a full ten seconds he sat there and looked at the mint-green panties that were in his hand. They were delicate, feminine. And very, very tiny. He had never imagined that Liss wore underwear like this beneath her rather sensible outfits. Well, in fairness, he had never thought about Liss's underwear before.

But he was thinking about them now. He couldn't stop himself from running his thumb over the soft, flat waistband. He swallowed hard, lifting them up so that he could see the shape.

It was a thong, which was very unexpected. Even more unexpected was the quick image that flashed through his mind of what Liss must look like wearing them. A shadow of copper curls beneath the flimsy lace, and the round, shapely ass that would be displayed to perfection.

He dropped the panties back into the basket and stood up, taking a step back as if there was a rattlesnake in there amid the clothes. Since when did he imagine Liss in her underwear? More important, since when had he noticed that her ass was shapely?

He never had, not consciously. It must be something his subconscious had absorbed. Some kind of male instinct he had thought long destroyed busily cataloging desirable feminine attributes even while his conscious mind was shutting it out.

He reached into the basket next to the one containing Liss's clothes, stripped off his old underwear and quickly pulled on a new pair, before jerking the laundry room door open and walking out into the kitchen.

Unfortunately, just as he walked in, so did Liss.

Her eyes flew wide, and she took two steps backward, her cheeks turning bright pink. "Sorry." She turned and walked out of the room as quickly as she had just walked in.

"Dammit," he growled, stalking back to the staircase and heading back to his room as quickly as possible.

He put on a pair of tan Carhartt pants and a black T-shirt, before going back downstairs to do some damage control. Although, really, there should be no damage to control. It wasn't as if she hadn't seen him in various states of undress over the years. It just felt more inappropriate, because he had just been handling her panties.

"Liss?"

"In here," she said, her voice sounding muffled.

He walked toward the living room and into the room, just in time to see Liss scrambling up from the couch, throwing one of the decorative pillows back onto the cushion. She looked at him, her lower lip sucked between her teeth.

They just sort of stood there, frozen, staring at each other.

Then a gust of air tried to escape Liss's mouth, turning into a sound that was somewhere between a growl and a snort.

He frowned. "Are you laughing at me?"

Her shoulders shook, her face turning redder. She shook her head, still biting her lower lip.

"I'm serious, Liss. You just saw me in my underwear, and you're laughing? I have to figure out if I'm insulted by this or not."

She shook her head again, sitting down on the couch, her face getting redder, the shaking in her shoulders getting increasingly violent.

"Either you're having a stroke, or you are laughing at the sight of me in my undies."

She released her lower lip and heaved in a deep breath, a guffaw escaping a second later. "No! No."

"You're *not* laughing."

"No," she hooted, "I'm not laughing."

"Yes, you are."

"Not at the sight of you in your underwear. I mean, not like you think," she said, breathless. "It was just so absurd. You were looking at me. I was just looking at you. I happened to walk in and you were in the kitchen, and you were pretty much naked." She was rambling now, but it was a whole lot better than the alternative.

Because things were kind of jumbled up in his head. And for some reason, he was still picturing her in *her* underwear, even though he was the one who had been caught in his.

"I thought you were at work."

"I forgot my cell phone, so I came back because I didn't have any important appointments this morning. I guess this is a part of negotiating the living situation."

"I guess."

She cleared her throat. "Really, though, it's nothing I've never seen before."

He tried not to be offended by that comment. As though any man in his underwear was exactly the same as him. Really, he had no place to be offended by that comment. Because the sight of him mostly naked should not be remarkable to his best friend. And yet, his masculine ego—which along with his nice-ass radar, was not as dormant as he had believed—was slightly dented.

"True. But then, I've seen plenty of women in their underwear—" only one, now two, in person and others in pictures, but Liss didn't need to know that "—and that does not mean that you're going to be prancing around in here in a state of undress." He regretted saying that the moment he did, because it brought to mind those images he was working so hard to banish. "Are you?"

"No. Would you rather I act completely scandalized? Should I have had you fetch the smelling salts?"

"I don't have smelling salts. All I have is barbecue steak rub. I don't think it's the same."

She rolled her eyes. "Yeah, I don't think so."

"Okay, so here's the deal. I won't assume that you're not in the house anymore. And I won't come walking downstairs in my underwear."

"Deal."

"Okay," he said, taking a step away from her, rubbing the back of his neck. "I suppose you need to get back to work. I know I do."

"Yeah, I should."

He nodded, a thread of tension stretching between them, and he wanted to banish it. Wanted to do something to get rid of it, because this wasn't normal. "Great, I'll see you for dinner."

"I might go out with Jeanette," she said quickly.

"Okay. I'll see you later, then."

"Yeah, later."

Connor turned and walked out of the room. It was probably a good thing Liss was going out tonight. After only a couple of days of cohabitation, he felt as though they could maybe use a little space.

But this was normal, this adjustment period. Connor hadn't lived with anyone in a few years, and he'd lived with Jessie for a long time. Even then, they had a lot of miscommunications and a lot of ups and downs. There was no reason to believe it would be any different with a roommate.

He opened the door and took a deep breath, banishing all the weirdness that lingered inside him. There was no time to worry about any of that. He had a ranch to work on.

SHE'D HAD FANTASIES about Connor before. Here, in the darkness of her room, she was woman enough to admit that. And yes, she had seen him without his shirt on. They spent a lot of time on the lake, down by the river and on the beach. Copper Ridge was surrounded by water and they, like most of the other residents, made the most of it.

But somehow, seeing him in his underwear was different. Because it wasn't just his perfectly muscular chest, with a very perfect amount of chest hair sprinkled over it. Or his washboard flat abs and the tattoo that was starting to drive her crazy. No, it was combined with the full scope of his very muscular thighs, compliments of years in the saddle, and, it just…well, and… the very prominent bulge at the apex of said muscular thighs. There. She'd admitted it.

It was burned into her brain now. The image of him standing in his kitchen nearly naked, looking as if he'd just been slapped upside the head with a two-by-four.

She rolled over onto her stomach and buried her head beneath her pillow. She had to be adult about this.

She snorted and rolled back over, uncovering her face. That was the problem. She *was* being adult about this. *Very* adult. With lots of adult thoughts and desires and needs.

What were you supposed to do when your adult needs were for your best friend and roommate? Where was her handbook?

"Ignore it," she said out loud, "like always."

It was the only thing to do. They would have to go on as though undiegate had never happened. She was just having a little Connor relapse due to the close proximity. Probably not aided at all by the recent amount of time she'd been spending taking care of him. And definitely not helped by her extremely long bout of celibacy and singledom. When things settled down she would have to focus on getting a date. Yes, that would help. A little bit of normalcy, a man who wasn't Connor filling her time.

Yes, that would help. And if in the meantime, she spent just a little bit of time thinking about how Connor had looked in his underwear, well, she was only human. It didn't mean anything. Just a little healthy female-to-male appreciation.

That was her story, and she was sticking to it.

CHAPTER SEVEN

THE MORNING THE INSURANCE settlement money went into Connor's bank account he felt as if there was a timer ticking down. And there was a part of him—a much larger part of him than he might have imagined—that wanted to take the money and go down to Cancun. Just disappear from all this for a while, from Copper Ridge, from responsibility.

But he couldn't do that. Because of the ranch, because of his family, because Eli's election was coming up, and he had to be there for that.

Damn responsibilities. He would rather have a margarita.

But his family needed him here, and if there was one thing he wouldn't do, it was abandon them. Their mother had walked out when things had gotten tough, and Connor wasn't going to do the same.

No, he wasn't his mother in this little play. He was the one who was left behind.

He was a lot closer to being his father.

He gritted his teeth. *No*, he wasn't. He saw to his responsibilities.

Like getting the barn built?

Yeah, he had to get the barn built. He had enough money to hire a crew to come out and get it done, which meant he needed to get started as soon as possible.

There was no excuse. Maybe that was something else Liss could help him with.

Liss. That was also feeling slightly difficult at the moment.

And it was his fault. Because she had seemed fine after their little mostly naked run-in a few days ago. But his brain had latched on to the vivid image of what she might look like in the mint-colored thong and hadn't let go. It was starting to drive him crazy.

On the long list of things he never wanted to talk to anyone about was the effect grief had on his sex drive. It just wasn't something anyone needed to know about. Yes, they all had a fair idea he wasn't getting any, if only because it was a small town, and they all lived in each other's pockets.

Okay, the town at large didn't know, but Eli knew that he didn't see women coming back to the property, and Jack knew that when he left the bar with a woman, Connor always left alone.

They wouldn't have to ponder his actions too hard to figure that out. Plus, he had admitted as much to Eli during the world's most horrific conversation a few months back. But what he hadn't admitted was that it was more than not feeling like engaging in a flirtation or a hookup.

It was that his give-a-damn was busted on such a bone-deep level that he didn't even *fantasize* about hooking up. It was pretty easy to abstain when you didn't even feel like jacking off to deal with a morning erection.

A morning erection that had become a lot more insistent since Liss's thong had come into his life.

Connor groaned and scooped up a pitchfork full of

manure from his horse's stall and chucked it into the back of the truck. He was going to deal with this the way he had dealt with it back in high school. Hard work. That was, in his experience, the world's most effective boner killer. Except for the obvious. And he wasn't going to do *either* obvious thing. For equally obvious reasons.

"Hey, Connor, did that pitchfork do something terrible to you?"

Connor turned and saw Eli standing at the entrance to the stalls. "I'm shoveling shit, Eli. How excited am I supposed to look?"

"All right, fair enough. You just don't normally look actively angry while doing it."

Connor stuck the pitchfork into the shavings and leaned against it. "I got my insurance money today."

"Well, damn," Eli said, monotone. "Those bastards. Finally settling the score with you. I have half a mind to go and slap handcuffs on them."

"I didn't ask for your sarcasm."

"I don't know why you're standing there looking so upset about finally getting what you've been working toward for the past few months."

Connor winced internally. But he was not about to have the same argument with Eli that he had already had with Liss. "I guess it's just time to rebuild. And I have a hard time feeling very enthusiastic about rebuilding. I don't have a great track record, Eli. I don't know if you've noticed."

"What do you mean by that?"

"I tried to do the best I could by this ranch. By the family. But every time I try to make something better, nature finds a way to burn it to the ground, for lack of a less obvious metaphor."

Eli frowned. "I know things have been hard, but everything that's happened…do you really think that's all about you?"

"Sure, or I have a lightning rod above my head. It's either that or it's random, Eli. Tell me which one is supposed to make me feel better."

Eli rubbed his hand over his forehead. "I doubt anything I could say would make you feel better. Except that no matter the answer, you have to keep doing things."

"Sometimes I'd rather not."

"That was what Dad did," Eli said. The total lack of judgment in Eli's voice made the statement even worse. As though he couldn't blame their dad, and wouldn't blame Connor, either. But Connor would. Connor *did*.

"Yeah, well, it's not what I'm going to do. I work, don't I? I work the ranch every day. Not leaving it to my kids to do, not that I have any, but you get the point." Connor let out a long, slow breath. "It hasn't escaped my notice that anything new I bring onto this ranch seems to die." He met his younger brother's gaze. "Tell me that's not true."

"I can't," Eli said, his voice strained. "Connor, you're probably the only person on this earth more connected to Jessie's death than I am. I was there. I was the one who had to tell you. I feel it. The brutality of it, the suddenness of it. I feel it down to my bones. Please know that I don't take what you've been through lightly. And when I tell you I think you need to move on, when I tell you that I want to see you happy, it's not because

I don't realize what you went through. Because I was there, Connor."

Connor knew Eli was talking about his reaction to his wife's death. Eli was the only witness to that moment, and he was probably the only one who remembered it with any real clarity. Connor could hardly piece together the memory, and it was probably all for the best. The moments after the words had left Eli's mouth had been a blur.

IT WAS LATE, and the only person he'd been expecting was Jessie, so the knock at the door was a surprise. Connor opened the door, and his brother turned to face him, something in his expression strange. Wrong. The porch light was on, a ring of gold surrounding Eli's frame.

Eli stepped inside, not saying a word. Another thing that seemed wrong.

"Connor, go on and sit down."

He complied, because he'd never seen his brother look quite so desolate. Not even when their mother had left. Not even after their father had died.

"There was an accident tonight," he said, his voice breaking.

And he didn't even have to finish the sentence, because right then Connor knew. His whole body went cold, and something in his gut turned, and he knew. He knew it wasn't Eli, his brother, just paying a visit, but a sheriff's deputy doing his duty. A brother doing his duty.

"Jessie died tonight, Connor."

THERE HAD BEEN nothing after that. Just a kind of strange buzzing in his head that wouldn't go away. And he was aware of saying things, but not of what he'd said. He couldn't remember anything that had happened after Eli spoke those words. He couldn't remember the rest of the night or the whole next day. A full twenty-four hours that were gone forever.

A gift, he imagined.

"Even knowing that," Eli continued, "I want you to have more."

But Eli didn't know *everything*. And Connor knew, in spite of his brother's good intentions, he thought he understood and empathized a bit better than he did.

"I want you to have what I have," Eli said. "I didn't think I wanted to find love, but then I met Sadie. And everything changed."

Everything changed.

For some reason that part of the sentence stuck out in Connor's mind. But he didn't want to overthink it. "Yeah, and after what we'd been through as kids, deciding to go ahead and get married wasn't the easiest decision for me. But that's what happens when you fall in love," Connor said. "I know Sadie is this new chapter of your life, and I think because of the timing, you don't quite equate it with me losing Jessie. But that's what it is. What if you lost her, Eli? Would you want someone else?"

Eli looked away. "No," he said, his voice rough. "But I only mean it… I was afraid, too. Remember, we had this discussion. That love came here to die. But I found love again, and there was no room for me to stay scared when I found it. Just stay open. And…maybe start small. Like with building a barn."

Connor cleared his throat. "I can do that."

"If Jack were here, he would suggest adding sex to that list."

Heat burst through Connor's veins, because that word had become inextricably linked to the mint-colored thong. "I don't want to have this discussion with you. We tried it once. Let's never repeat it."

Eli shifted, obviously uncomfortable. "Well, I don't *want* to have the discussion. I just worry about you, dammit."

"Stop it. I don't need you to worry about me. I need you to focus on your woman and your campaign."

"Speaking of my campaign, and speaking of your barn..."

Connor crossed his arms over his chest. "What about it?"

"If you can get the barn built in time, I'd love to have a party out here on election night. We'll set up a TV and watch the results and we'll have a party. A big barbecue."

"Sadie has bewitched you. Because only six months ago you would've gagged and died thinking about having a party here." Connor rubbed his chin. "Come to think of it, last time we had a party here, planned by Sadie, you burned my fucking barn down."

"And I'm willing to take the risk again. Because a barn is meant to be used."

Connor gritted his teeth and forced his brain not to apply that statement as a broader metaphor for life. Or for his dick.

"Fine. If it's on track to be structurally sound by election night, it's yours." And now the construction of the barn was for someone else, and that meant he had to get it done. "I'll make some calls today."

Eli took a step forward and slapped Connor on the back, which was about the closest they ever got to a touching moment. "Thanks, man. I appreciate it."

"This is your ranch, too. You live on the property. Name is on the deed. It's not a favor. It's your right."

"Stop trying to act like you're a 100-percent-mean son of a bitch," Eli said. "It's only about 85 percent."

Connor flipped him off and grabbed the pitchfork again. "You going to stand there all day, or are you going to help shovel?"

Eli smiled. "Guess I'll go get my own pitchfork."

"THE WEATHER SAYS this is going to be the last nice day in a while. I think we should head up the mountain and go to Horseshoe Falls." Liss finished her last bite of breakfast and looked up at Connor expectantly.

It was a little bit crisp outside, but the sun was already breaking through the clouds, and after a week spent behind her desk, all she wanted for her Saturday was to escape into the mountains. Solitude would've probably been the smarter choice, but once Connor had come downstairs, in flannel and worn jeans, she'd been unable to pass up the chance of spending the day with him.

Because he was her best friend, not because of his jeans. Or the way they fit. Or the way he looked wearing only the underwear that was undoubtedly beneath them.

It was not about that at all. It was about friendship and togetherness and not the fine muscular structure of his thighs.

"I shouldn't skip out on work," Connor said, gripping the edge of the counter and leaning back against it.

"Just a couple of hours, Connor. A quick hike to the top of the trail."

"Yeah, that long to the top, and then we have to hike down."

"If you lie down on the trail, I can give you a good shove and maybe you can roll back down to the ranch," she said, trying to look innocent.

He lifted his coffee mug to his lips. "Felicity Foster, if I fall I'm going to grab on to your ankles and bring you with me."

He was teasing her, a humorous light in his dark eyes, and yet for some reason his words made her stomach knot up tight. "Right. So, are we going to do this or not?"

"Okay, let's do this. But you have to pack peanut butter sandwiches."

"I think I can handle that," she said, smiling brightly.

"Then let's go."

THE TRAIL THAT led up to Horseshoe Falls was almost completely closed in by trees. Shades of green filled in every available space. Ferns grew over the ground like a lush, velvet carpeting. The sun could only peek through the few windows in the branches, moss thriving in the near constant shade, growing on all sides of the trees and over the gray, craggy rocks.

Liss's boot slipped on a patch of mud on the trail, and she pitched forward slightly, speeding up her steps to keep her balance. She reached out, grabbing a hold of Connor's shoulder to keep from doing a face-plant.

He stopped walking and looked at her. "Careful. I'm not chasing after you if you roll over the ledge."

"I am being careful. But some of this trail is a little bit sludgier than I anticipated."

"You were the one who said it was a good day to hike."

She released her hold on him, and they resumed walking. "It is. It's a fantastic day to hike." She breathed in deep, relishing the crisp air that smelled like pine and soil. "I don't think we've gone hiking up here since before summer."

"It's been a while."

"So," she said, knowing that she had just engaged in the clumsiest conversation transition of all time, "do you have plans for getting the construction of the barn started?"

"I'm working on it. I talked to Eli a couple of days ago, and he wants to have his election-night party in the new barn. Which means it needs to get going."

"Excellent. Because I have an idea."

He stopped in the middle of the trail and turned, his hands on his lean hips, one of his dark brows raised. "Oh, shit. You have an idea?"

"I'm really not sure how I feel about that reaction. Again, I feel compelled to remind you that normal people are thankful when their friends try to help them."

"You can sometimes be a little bit overexcited in your help. Forgive me for feeling cautious."

"You are forgiven," she said, waving her hand. The fact was, in Connor's estimation this would be considered overexcited help. And she knew it. But she also felt as if it was the best way to get things moving. "I think we should have a barn raising."

"I'm sorry, did you hit your head and start hallucinating that you lived in a 1950s musical?"

"No. I did not. But the fact is, most of the town was there when the barn burned down. I feel like they would love for this chance to give back to you and help you get back on your feet."

"I wasn't exactly down on my ass."

She crossed her arms beneath her breasts and stared him down. "Yes, you were."

"Not as much lately."

He was right; she had not discovered him passed out on the couch once since she'd moved in. So that was progress.

"Do we really need to make it a party?"

"I figured it would be great. I think it would be great for Eli, it would be wonderful for Sadie and it will get your barn off the ground a lot faster."

"We'll discuss it."

"We will. We're going to discuss it tomorrow, in fact. I already talked to Sadie, and she wants to have me come over tomorrow afternoon for tea and talk of logistics."

"Tea and logistics? You're going to do this whether I fucking want to or not, aren't you?"

"Yeah, I fucking am," she said, smiling. "And you should want me to do it because it's smart. And I'm smart. And Sadie is smart, and we're all smart. So get on and hold on, cowboy."

"Liss, you are lucky as hell that you buy my groceries. And that you're adorable."

Liss ignored the tightening in her stomach. "It's true, I am adorable. But I am fierce. And I will have my way."

"I am familiar with your fierceness. But look, I don't want this to get out of hand. And with the way the barn was originally, I'm going to have to have professionals do the finish work. But as far as getting the frame up, the more hands, the better. And I can definitely see your point where that is concerned."

"Excellent! I love when you can see my very valid, perfectly logical points. Even if it takes you a while."

He reached out, and her breath caught in her throat, resting there like a little ball. He reached behind her head and grabbed the end of her ponytail, tugging it gently. "Why do your logical points have to be wrapped up in my worst nightmares?"

He released his hold on her hair, but he was still very close to her. She was having a hard time breathing. Stupid fresh air. It had to be the fresh air. It was too pure or something.

"I don't mean to be…your worst nightmare," she said, hoping her voice didn't sound as thin and shaky to him as it did to her own ears.

"You aren't my worst nightmare. But your desire to see me socialize is."

She nodded, her head feeling a little bit fuzzy now. If she wanted to, she could reach right out and touch his bottom lip. Could trace the outline of it with her thumb. Not that she would. Why would she do that? Why would anyone do that? Why would anyone even think of that?

Never mind the fact that it was a very nice bottom lip. Even framed by his beard. Or maybe especially framed by his beard. Really, it was hard to find fault.

Better than tracing the outline of it would be tasting it.

That thought found her stumbling backward, away from him.

"Whoa!" Connor reached out and grabbed her forearm, tugging her back toward him, obviously afraid she had tripped, rather than rightly guessing that she was scurrying away from him because she had just had a fantasy about licking his face. And suddenly, she was on the exact opposite trajectory from the one she had intended to be on. She was not only closer to Connor than she had been only a moment ago, but her breasts were pressed against his chest.

Holy crap. She was dizzy.

She should say something. She should break his hold. She should step on his foot and run screaming down the trail back toward civilization. Really, she should do anything but what she was doing. Which was just staying in his hold, resting up against his solidly muscled chest, allowing the heat from his body to wash over her.

"Are you…okay?" he asked, still holding on to her.

"Yes," she said, swallowing hard.

She realized with no small amount of uncertainty that had Jack stumbled back on the trail, Connor would not be holding him to his chest at this moment. She realized that the only reason he was still holding on to her was that she was a woman. Even if she was his friend.

She wasn't sure what to do with that information.

Obviously, they didn't view each other as *genderless*. They never had. It wasn't as though they changed in the same locker rooms. But still, this was interesting. And he was still holding her.

What would happen if she leaned in? The idea entered her head and stuck. But she didn't do it. She simply froze, waiting. Waiting to see what he would do next. Waiting to see what *she* would do next.

"Well, we better keep going if we want to make it to the top."

"Yes," she said, extricating herself from his hold.

Suddenly, she was very conscious of the fact that she had just sort of melted into him, and had spent nearly a full minute lingering. She was also suddenly conscious of just how revealing that was.

Stupid. Stupid and dangerous and stupid.

"Yes, the top. Views, and waterfalls and shit," she said, her tone overly bright.

"Okay. To the top." Connor turned away from her and started to walk back up the trail, and Liss followed behind trying to get a grip on her sanity.

Though she feared, at this point, it might be beyond her reach.

CHAPTER EIGHT

CONNOR HAD SERIOUSLY fucked up. There was no doubt about it.

He walked into his bedroom and slammed the door behind him, kicking off his boots and leaving them where they landed, moving through to his bathroom.

Yeah, he was an idiot. When he had taken a hold of Liss back on the trail, he hadn't been thinking about the thong. Or more specifically about the fact that his best friend was a woman.

Which was the crux of the issue. He imagined that her underwear could've been cotton with full coverage on the ass and little white bunnies printed on the fabric, and it would have had the same effect. Okay, maybe not the exact same effect, but an effect nonetheless. Because it reminded him that she was very much female. With female undergarments.

He hadn't touched female undergarments in way too long. He was thinking of them as *female undergarments*, and if that didn't say it all, he didn't know what would.

But now he had held her up against his body, in combination with feeling her underwear. And somehow he was having a barn raising.

Yes, somewhere in all of this he had gone wrong. Very, very wrong.

He stripped his shirt off and turned the water on in the shower, working at his belt before taking his jeans and underwear off. He was a mess. But then, that was nothing new. It was just suddenly some of his mess was tangled up in Liss, and seeing as she was usually his well-ordered sanity, that was a problem.

He took a deep breath and thought of that moment on the trail again. How her skin had felt beneath his hands as he caught her, how her breasts had felt pressed up against his chest as he held her tight.

And his dick was getting hard. Perfect.

His dick had basically been asleep for the past three years. And now he was getting wood over his best friend. Because he had touched her panties, because she lived in his house, because he knew how soft her skin was and because he hadn't gotten laid in three years.

He gritted his teeth and stepped into the shower, not caring if the water was hot or cold. Actually, cold might be good.

It wasn't cold, and he couldn't bring himself to add to his torture by freezing his balls off.

He rested his forearm against the shower wall and leaned his forehead against the tile. What was happening? He had very little in the way of stability in his life, and Liss was a cornerstone of the crumbling foundation he did have.

You did not mess that shit up for the sake of a hard-on.

He turned around and took the bar of soap off the wire rack that still hung around the showerhead, in spite of the fact that he never put anything in it but a bar of Irish Spring, and it had space for all kinds of shampoos and conditioners.

He gritted his teeth as he rubbed the soap over his

skin, trying to keep himself detached from any of the sensations he was feeling thanks to the slickness of the suds combined with the hot water.

It felt good. And it made him want *more*. Made him want to reach down and take a hold of himself, because damn that would feel nice.

But no. His penis didn't deserve nice things.

Especially not since it was getting overexcited about Liss.

Just thinking her name brought a picture of her into his mind again. Golden eyes looking at him, all wide and surprised, and those breasts... Yeah, they were nice breasts. He was acutely aware of that fact now that he had been in such close contact with them.

His cock jerked and he lowered his hand, wrapping his fingers around himself and squeezing tight.

Heat tore through him, and he braced himself on the wall, a harsh sound ripping from his lips. How long had it been since he'd come? A long time. Pretty much not since the last time he'd had sex. And he knew how long that had been.

But he'd wanted to fantasize about his dead wife. In his mind, that just hadn't seemed right. And he'd never been in a space where he felt as if he could fantasize about anyone else, either. Well, *want* hadn't really come into it. His body had violently rejected both options for sexual satisfaction, and so he had remained unsatisfied. But for some reason, this was working for him.

He was so tempted.

No one will know. Just do it. Just do it and get back to normal.

He did not argue with his internal voice of reason for too long.

Mainly because getting off was on the horizon, and he desperately wanted to get off. Just a few minutes of oblivion. A couple of seconds of blank white light were all he felt was good. He hadn't realized until this moment just how badly he missed it. How badly he needed it.

So he squeezed himself tighter, running his palm along his hard length, his breath hissing through his teeth. Yeah, this would be fine.

He closed his eyes as he continued to touch himself, visions of Liss, Liss as she had been today, how soft her hair had felt, how she had looked at him. And then he went deeper, into those forbidden fantasies he had been fighting since that day in the laundry room.

Images of Liss wearing nothing but that thong, the color vibrant against her skin, her coppery hair spilling over her shoulders. She was so pale. Her nipples would be pale, too.

His heart was thundering hard, his blood running through his veins. He lowered his head, quickening the strokes of his hand, bracing himself against the shower wall with the other as his release tore through him, raging around inside him like an animal. And for a glorious moment, there was nothing. There was no pain, there was no barn, no responsibilities at all.

There was nothing but complete, pure pleasure. And seductive, golden eyes that could only belong to one woman.

And he grabbed that moment and held on to it for as long as he could.

But as always, damn reality started to crowd in far too soon.

And then he was just standing there, bare-ass naked

with the realization that he had just gotten his rocks off fantasizing about his best friend.

Shame crawled over his skin like an army of ants.

He turned and shut the water off, grabbing a towel and drying himself off as roughly as possible. He deserved for the towel to scrape off his skin. He certainly didn't deserve to hang out basking in good feelings.

He was an asshole.

An asshole who was suddenly exhausted. Who still had a barn raising looming in the future, and would have to face his friend at some point in the near future.

He sat down on the edge of his bed. He considered going down to the kitchen to get a drink. But there were two problems with that. The first being that Liss might still be up. The second being that if he got even a little bit drunk he couldn't be responsible for what else might happen. For the past three years getting drunk meant one thing, seeking oblivion. But now that his libido seemed to be back in action, getting drunk might mean lower inhibitions and poor decision making, much like it had back in his early twenties. And with Liss in the house, with him this close to the edge...

No, no alcohol for him.

Fortunately, he was actually feeling tired. Nothing like an orgasm to knock you out. He had forgotten how effective it could be.

He had forgotten how good it was.

And he was going to forget again. Well, maybe not the orgasm part. But what had gotten him there. That was off-limits. Never again.

He closed his eyes and let his exhaustion wash over him. He was sleeping now. Everything else could wait until tomorrow.

When Connor came back to the house for lunch, he hoped very much to avoid Liss. Because unfortunately, last night's little slipup had not been forgotten about in the cold light of day. On the contrary, it seemed more vivid.

His first thought when his eyes had opened that morning had been of Liss in her thong. And then, because it was morning, he had an erection. And his immediate thought had been to take himself in hand, using the image that he now knew was tried and true, while he worked his way toward the kind of oblivion that couldn't be found in the bottom of a bottle.

He had not. Because, dammit, he had a moral compass even if it was wonky.

So he had gotten into a cold shower, got dressed as quickly as possible and stomped out of the house without eating any breakfast.

He was back now, and thanks to the past four hours of hard labor with no breakfast to fuel him up, he was now starving and willing to take a chance of running into Liss.

And of course, thirty seconds after walking through the door, he did.

She was wearing a loose, low-cut gray sweater, with a pink tank top underneath that was peeking out the top, looking a little bit too much like a bra for his liking. Paired with that was a tight-fitting black skirt, a pair of textured tights and some knee-high boots. It was as if she was trying to kill him. Felicity Foster, in his kitchen, with her Grade A cleavage.

"Hi," she said brightly. Too brightly in his opinion. It was almost as though nothing had changed between them.

And then he realized that as far as she was concerned, nothing had. She had been acting completely normal, even since the underwear incident. He was the one with the issues.

The one dealing with hormones that rivaled those of a fourteen-year-old boy.

"Hi," he said, probably also too brightly, since he usually lacked brightness altogether.

"I am actually headed over to Sadie's to discuss you. You should come."

"Is this the tea and logistics thing? Because I don't think I should be involved in that." He started to move away from Liss and edged closer to the kitchen.

"Yes, it is the tea and logistics. And it is about you and your barn. Also, I have been assured that there will be cupcakes. Not only will there be cupcakes, there will possibly be quiche."

He grunted. "That is a whole lot of very girlie food."

"And you want it. Don't bother to deny it. You know, it's probably quiche with bacon in it."

His stomach chose that very moment to growl. Traitor. "Okay, I could use some food."

"Great. So why don't you walk me over?"

He gritted his teeth. "Sure."

He pulled the front door open again and held it for her, waiting for her to get out onto the porch before he followed her, slamming it shut behind them.

She tromped down the stairs, obviously oblivious of just how her skirt tightened around her ass. He was not oblivious, dammit. It was as though a veil had been ripped from in front of his eyes. And suddenly, Liss was a woman. With breasts, and a perfect ass and interesting underwear.

It was a disaster.

"It's about time for the oaks to start dropping their leaves," Liss said, kicking at a dried brown leaf on the ground.

"Yeah, about the time the madrones stop dropping them."

"If Oregon has one thing, it's trees."

He grunted. He was not in the space to be making small talk. Really, he was not in the space to be walking through the property with her. He needed to be in avoidance mode.

They crossed the little grove of trees that ran between his driveway and the driveway that led back to the Catalogue House. No oak trees here, just thick evergreens.

When they reached the end of the road, Connor was shocked again by all that Sadie had done with the place. He didn't come by very often. Usually, when Eli and Sadie were feeling social they came to the main house, and occasionally Connor went to Eli's. But he didn't often have occasion to stop by the bed-and-breakfast.

The front yard was perfectly manicured, with little patches of green lawn surrounded by rhododendron, pansies and a whole bunch of other flowers he didn't know the names for.

Flowers had been Jessie's thing, not his. Even now, something about the sight of little flower beds like this made him want to go get her, so he could show her. Or made him think she must have just been around. And if he went back to the house he would find her on the front porch, wiping the sweat off her forehead and taking off dirty gardening gloves, having just finished planting.

It was such a strange feeling, and so persistent once it took hold, that it was hard to shake.

Frankly, he preferred the post-masturbation shame. Though if he had a choice, he would take neither.

He turned his attention away from the flowers and focused on Liss again. On the way she looked when she walked up the stairs.

He was officially a bastard. Oh, well. Everyone already thought he was. Might as well embrace it.

Liss knocked on the door, and it took only a few moments for Sadie to answer. When she saw him, Sadie's blue eyes widened. "Oh, Connor, I didn't know you were coming."

"Is it a problem?"

"No! I'm glad you came."

"I'm not!" a voice called from inside the house.

"And Kate's here," he said.

"Yes, she wanted to come and help. And she was already acting as assistant baker. I have a full house. Though everyone is out on a whale-watching tour right now."

"How fun," Liss said, walking inside. "It's funny, when you live here you never do half as much as people visiting seem to."

Connor listened to them make small talk as they walked through the entryway and into the dining area. There was indeed a decent selection of food on the table, though he maintained that the food on offer was girlie.

His sister was sitting at the head of the table, a slice of quiche on a plate in front of her, a dainty little mug with something hot inside sitting next to it. He didn't think he had ever seen Kate with something so feminine that close to her.

In spite of her floral cup she was in her usual uniform of plaid shirt and shapeless work jeans, her dark hair in one long braid. His sister was definitely a contrast next to Liss with her skirt, and Sadie with her armful of bangles, long dress and blond hair loose around her shoulders.

Part of him worried that being raised by a couple of half-civilized men had done Kate a disservice. Another part of him was just glad he didn't have to beat the boys off her with a stick.

"Go ahead. Grab a plate and a chair, Connor," Sadie said.

He complied, sitting in the chair next to Kate. He declined the generous offer of tea, because he was not going to drink out of one of those pansy-ass cups. He did not, however, decline the quiche, which did indeed have bacon in it.

"Thank you so much for agreeing to the barn raising," Sadie said. And it took him a moment to realize she was talking to him.

"I didn't really agree to anything," he said. "I got steamrolled by Liss."

Liss snorted. "You did not. I don't do that. I don't steamroll."

Kate laughed, slapping her hand on the table. "Sorry, Liss, but you kind of do. I mean that in a good way. You get stuff done."

"Well, it's a good idea," Liss said, her tone insistent. "And I knew you would need pushing. It's…aggressive assistance, is a nice name for it."

"Steamrolling," he said.

"Well, however we arrived at this point, with you at my table eating quiche and agreeing, I'm thankful," Sadie said. "My guests are thrilled at the prospect of being a part of this. So you know this helps me in ways I hadn't even considered."

And he really was glad about that. Because Sadie was a good person, and he certainly appreciated all that she had done in Eli's life.

"Great. I just don't want things to get out of hand."

"What's out of hand to you?" Sadie asked.

"Anything more than two people and a cooler full of beer," Kate said.

His sister was mocking him, but she was pretty close to the truth.

"I don't know, maybe no sponsors," he said.

"I already called Ace," Sadie said, speaking as though he hadn't, "and he agreed to donate some beer. On tap."

"He's too giving," Connor said. Plus, his gesture would attract a hell of a lot of people.

"Lydia wants to help spread the word," Sadie said, talking about Copper Ridge's president of the Chamber of Commerce. "We were thinking of touting it as an old-fashioned barbecue and barn raising, to help a family who has given so much to the community."

"Eli has given so much to the community. All I do is play darts and ranch cattle."

"Look," Kate said, picking at her quiche with her fingers, "people love you. Don't ask me why, because I think you're a rather unpleasant cuss. But they do. They want to help. So many people saw the barn burn, and they feel connected to this."

"Did you take an informal poll?" he asked.

"Well, seeing as I work at one of the town's main hubs, yeah, I kind of did. Or rather, I didn't have to," Kate said, looking defiant. "Because people ask about you. They ask about the barn, they ask about the ranch. They want to know how you're doing."

Connor shifted in his seat. It wasn't really as if the town's concern surprised him. Everybody had been very concerned about him when Jessie had died. He'd had more casseroles than one man could humanly consume. Yeah, he knew they cared. But he didn't know what to do with all that caring. Because it kind of made his chest tight, and then that made him angry and he just wanted to be left alone. Or drunk. And it was a really bad combination in the end.

Being ignored was better than receiving sympathy. Or it had gotten twisted into that in his mind. Dealing with sympathy was hard. It felt as though you needed to be strong and reassuring for the people who showed up at your doorstep with sad eyes and layers of tuna and cheese in a pan.

They wanted to know that you were okay, so you had to look okay. They asked if things were getting better. But they wanted only one answer. You couldn't tell them that things were getting worse, because your wife was still buried six feet under the ground, and that wasn't likely to change anytime soon.

Yeah, Connor sucked with sympathy.

"Talking to people is hard," Connor said.

"You're talking to us right now," Sadie said.

"Do I look like I'm enjoying myself?" he asked, taking another bite of his quiche.

"If you're not enjoying yourself, you had better spit my quiche out and walk on home," Sadie said. "Oh, yeah, cranky man, I have your number. And I'm not going to put up with your crap."

He grumbled and took another bite of the quiche. "I will eat as much quiche as I damn well please."

It was Liss who looked at him, sympathy in her golden eyes. Sympathy he did not deserve, considering what he had just done over her image the night before. "Connor, I actually do understand that this is hard. Because I know how people used to look at you, and how they look at you now."

His throat tightened. "What the hell does that mean?"

"It means that before you lost her everybody knew you were strong. They treated you like a man. And now they treat you like something that might break. They look at you like you're a widower. And nothing else. And I know that's a serious pain in the ass, especially because you don't want to feel that way."

He gritted his teeth, trying to ignore the way Liss cut right through with the truth, like a precision blade sliding right up under his skin.

"It really is only because they care, though. So let them care. And show them that you're okay," she said.

He nodded slowly. "Fine, do what you want."

"We're going to have caramel apples," Kate said, smiling widely.

"Sounds festive."

"You couldn't sound less thrilled," Liss said.

"I have fillings. Caramel apples are more of an obstacle course than a treat," he said drily.

"We got a band," Sadie said, almost exploding with her joyousness. Joyousness he did not share.

"I'm getting the feeling that you were going to do this even if I said no."

Kate had the decency to look somewhat sheepish. "Eli and I were going to outvote you."

"Damn part owners. You don't even do anything." He was joking. Mostly.

"Yes, I know family can be a real pain in the ass," Kate said, her tone cheery.

"I'm not going to fight you anymore. I surrender." He held his hands up and earned smiles from all three women. It was a rare thing in his world, to have a woman smile at him. Having three of them do it at once was sort of amazing.

"As soon as we can get all of the materials we need for the frame, we can have the barn raising. So I'm thinking we'll schedule it for two weeks from now. How does that sound?" Sadie asked.

"Does it really matter what I think, Sadie?"

"No," Liss said.

"When I die, I'm half convinced my gravestone will read *here lies Connor Garrett, good intentions were the death of him*."

"Better than wolverines," Kate said. "Death by wolverine would suck."

"That depends," Sadie said. "Are we talking Hugh Jackman Wolverine, or flea-infested, forest-dweller wolverine with the hinky little claws?"

"I was thinking the flea-infested, hinky version, but Hugh Jackman would be a pretty decent way to go," Kate said.

"This has been great," he said, standing up from the table. "But I think I'm going to go back to work now."

Kate stood up and wrapped her arms around him in an uncharacteristic hug. He threw one arm around her shoulders and squeezed. "Don't be mad, Connor. I love you. I just wanted to do this because I love you."

He took a deep breath, and for some reason it was

difficult. Like Kate was squeezing him too tight. But that wasn't it. It was something on the inside. "I know, Katie. I love you, too."

"Okay, let's stop with all this now," she said, pulling away from him and smiling. "I can only take so much mushiness."

"I think my tolerance is even lower than yours."

"I'll walk you back," Liss said.

"You trust these two with the rest of the details?" he asked.

"Trust me, Connor, I'm a professional," Sadie said.

"You aren't a professional party planner," he said.

She shrugged. "Yeah, but I'm a professional something."

"Ha-ha. That's very comforting," he said.

"Bye, Connor. Bye, Liss," Sadie said, clearly eager to get rid of him so she could start figuring out how to hire party clowns, balloon-animal artists and other things that were sure to horrify him down to his bones.

"Behave yourself," he said as he and Liss walked back out onto the porch.

"She is not going to behave herself," Liss said sagely. "She doesn't know how."

"You," he said, holding his finger out toward her. "You started this."

She snapped her teeth near the end of his finger, and he lowered it. "Do that again and I'll bite it off," she said. "Anyway, you deserve this."

"Why does that sound like an insult and not something positive?"

Liss smiled. "Because it's a little bit of both."

"I ought to send you out to the shed to live. You can

nest in all of your stored belongings instead of sleeping in my nice warm house."

"You wouldn't do that to me," she said, walking past him and starting down the stairs, putting him in direct line of sight with her butt again. "Because I am adorable. We went through this already."

"You keep forgetting that I am not very nice."

"No, you keep forgetting that you are all bark and no bite. I, on the other hand, have a little bite, as I believe I just proved."

"That was not a bite. That was a snap. Threats don't count." He walked down the stairs after her, quickly catching up to her on the path. "And you were right. I don't know what to do with people. There, I admitted it."

"You didn't need to admit it to me. I already knew."

"It's just that I don't really know what to do with casseroles and sympathy. Honestly, I don't know what to do with casseroles. What the hell is that? Why do people bring you food that seems designed to make you sadder? It isn't like people actually make that shit for themselves. It's the designated bereavement food, and it's terrible. I lost my wife, not my taste buds. People should bring cake and Jack Daniel's."

Liss laughed, and he appreciated that. Not very many people would have laughed, because his brand of dark humor tended to make normal people uncomfortable. *He* made people uncomfortable. "I think it's just because they're easy to transport. I don't think it's because they're actively trying to sadden you with their one-pot meals."

"Sure. Nobody is ever trying to actively hurt you."

"They do a pretty good job, though, don't they?"

Connor reached up and grabbed a twig off a low-hanging branch and snapped it off. "Mainly because people make everything about themselves. How your pain feels to them. And what they think you should do with it. I don't think they mean to. It's just that we're all really selfish when it comes down to it. And I've been selfish, God knows. But I feel a little justified."

"You are."

He threw the twig off to the side. "I guess I have to try sometime, though, right?"

"To not be a big surly beast? Yeah, probably."

He closed his eyes and stopped walking. "I just never want to…" He opened his eyes. "You never want to make other people hurt like you do. So you keep a lot of stuff to yourself. I'm not sure it's the best."

Liss stopped, turning to face him. "Connor, you never have to keep things from me. You don't have to protect me."

The words were hovering on his lips, words that he had never spoken out loud. But he held them back. "Good to know."

There was no point in talking about any of it now. No point in telling Liss the secret he had kept for three long years. It was better to just keep it inside. At least there, it would hurt only him.

"So," he said, changing the subject, "if I wanted a dunk tank, could we use you as the victim?"

"I am not going to get in a dunk tank. Not even for you."

"Come on, Liss, you're ruining the carnival atmosphere."

"You get in the dunk tank."

"It's my barn raising. I should not have to get in the dunk tank."

Liss laughed and turned away from him, and he followed after her. This felt normal.

This did not feel like an interaction he would have with the Liss of his late-night fantasies. This was Liss, his best friend. This was just how it should be.

CHAPTER NINE

Liss looked around at the collection of people who had turned out for the barn raising. She wanted to go around and give each and every person a hug and a kiss, except she wouldn't, because that was gross. And because she really wasn't that much of a toucher. But in spirit, she felt like doing it.

While the turnout was not as grand as it had been for the great Fourth of July barbecue a couple of months back, it was still very impressive.

A few guys from town had brought out their barbecues and were grilling Garrett beef, hot dogs and veggie burgers. Alison had brought several pies and cakes, while Ace was a one-man refreshment machine.

Everyone was about to fuel up before the volunteers took to raising the frame. The pad had been cleared, and the pieces assembled and laid out the previous week by the crew Connor had hired to do most of the fine detail work.

And today the bulk of the structure would get installed, speeding up the construction.

Eli was making his way through the crowd of people, making sure to greet everyone. Out of uniform today, he looked handsome in his black T-shirt, jeans and cowboy hat. But, in Liss's opinion, he couldn't compete with Connor.

Connor, who was not making the rounds, but was standing near the building materials nursing a beer. He was still rocking his beard, though he had trimmed it a little bit for the event. He was wearing a battered baseball cap, a tight white T-shirt that exposed the hard muscles beneath and faded jeans with holes in the knees.

Just looking at him made her mouth dry. Made her stomach tight. Made her want things that she absolutely shouldn't want. Living with him was definitely the special kind of torture she had anticipated. In the three weeks since she had come to his house, she had seen him in his underwear only once, but she was coming to realize that Connor in constant doses was dangerous whether he was fully clothed or not. She had thought that maybe being immersed in daily domestic tasks with him would make it all feel commonplace. That was not the case. If anything, the web of intimacy that she had felt caught in that morning she brought him cereal had tightened around them both.

Of course, he probably didn't feel it. Because men didn't worry about things like the intimacy of eating cereal.

Of course, whether or not *men* worried about it was moot. Connor just didn't see her that way. He never had.

She looked at him again and her heart started to beat faster. How on earth could you be friends with a man for as long as she had been friends with him, and still not be immune to him?

Her…attraction, feelings…whatever, had lessened over the years, of course, but they seemed to be intensifying again.

She tried not to think about the year when Jessie had gone off to college. She and Connor had both stayed in town, and their bond had intensified during that time. And sometimes she'd imagined… But then, when Jessie had come back, Connor had proposed.

And she'd just felt stupid. And small. And mean. For wishing that her two best friends would break up. For wishing that she could have Connor to herself. For hoping that, while Jessie had been away, the bond between herself and Connor had become strong enough that it would become something more.

She was a terrible friend. Fortunately, nobody knew.

Just like nobody knew that the night of Jessie and Connor's wedding, Liss had snuck onto Garrett property and gone down to the river they had spent so much time at when they were teenagers. She'd sat on the swing, the one Connor had talked her into jumping from on a hot summer day years before, and she'd rocked back and forth, inhaling the familiar breeze. Getting used to being alone. Getting used to being without him. She'd gotten drunk on champagne from their wedding reception, still wearing her maid of honor dress, while she cried until her throat hurt.

But the next morning, with only her hangover as a companion, she'd been certain she'd purged her feelings for him from her system. Connor and Jessie were married; the fairy tale was over. She wasn't the princess. That was life.

She'd done a damn fine job of believing that. But then Connor's happily-ever-after had gone terribly wrong. The story had changed again.

It was all her body, her heart, needed to rekindle the flame. Apparently.

And that just made her feel like the biggest dick of all time. As if there was an opportunity open to her because of Connor's grief. Because of the loss of Jessie. Yeah, a huge dick.

She looked away from Connor, and over at the "dance floor"—which was really just some boards that had been anchored to the ground temporarily—where people had already coupled off and were holding each other close as the band played a slow country song.

"Did you get a drink?"

Liss looked over and saw Ace standing beside her, holding out a red plastic cup with beer filled to the top. "I didn't," she said, taking his offering. "Thanks."

"I'm taking a break," he said, rocking back on his heels. "Do you want to take one, too?"

"Are you hitting on me?" she asked. She had known Ace in passing for years, and while he was definitely sexy, she had never really thought of him that way. Mainly because she had either been in a relationship or pining after Connor. Which didn't leave a whole lot of time to look at the perfectly nice eligible men who littered the town.

That should change.

He smiled, his blue eyes glittering. "Maybe. Unless you don't want me to. In which case, maybe let's just start with a dance."

She set her beer down on the table next to her. "I can't remember the last time I danced. Sure."

His smile broadened, and he held his hand out. She took it. It was warm and strong. It was nice. But it didn't turn her on. Nothing like when Connor had taken hold of her arm when he caught her on the trail.

Of course, she hadn't even begun to think of Ace in a sexual way, and Connor had the benefit of more than fifteen years of fantasy built around him. So maybe that was the reason.

They moved to the edge of the dance floor, and he pulled her up against his chest, one hand around her waist, the other holding hers. "How come we've never danced before?" he asked, a hint of double entendre lacing his tone.

"No good reason I can think of," she said.

Liss saw movement out of the corner of her eye and saw Connor walking toward the dance floor. For one heart-stopping second, she thought he was coming for her. And if he did, she would go with him. There was no question. Yes, Ace was hot. And being held up close against his body felt nice, but that was all it was. Nice. Kind of comfortable like a pair of socks. And she barely knew the guy. She'd known Connor for the better part of her life, and try as she might, she couldn't make touching him comfortable.

Touching Connor was like standing in a field during a lightning storm. Exhilarating, beautiful, terrifying. Probably dangerous. It had been, from the time she'd been a fifteen-year-old girl until now as a thirty-three-year-old woman.

But Connor wasn't walking toward them. He wasn't even looking at them.

Instead, Connor walked straight past all of the dancing and went right for the stage.

The band stopped playing, and Connor went to stand in front of the lead singer's microphone. "Nobody panic. I'm not going to sing."

Everyone laughed, and Liss suddenly became aware that she was still standing, holding on to Ace. Which, when she thought about it, was a little bit weird when there was no music.

"I just wanted to thank everyone for coming out today," Connor said, clearing his throat nervously. Other than when he'd spoken his vows in front of the guests at his wedding, Liss didn't think Connor had ever spoken in front of a group of people before. She felt nervous on his behalf. "Everyone here has been a lot better to me than I've ever been to them. And that's the truth. Eli is the best of us Garretts. Kate comes in a close second. I think I'm somewhere way down the list, even though most of the spaces on the list are blank."

Liss extricated herself from Ace's hold, offering him a smile and tucking a strand of hair behind her ear, trying to minimize the little bit of awkwardness that always followed when you'd just squirmed out of a guy's arms.

"All that to say," Connor continued, "let's raise a barn."

There was a smattering of applause after his announcement, but Connor was already moving away from the stage and toward the building site.

"I guess that's my cue," Ace said, offering her a smile and walking toward Connor.

But Liss's brain ceased to process anything when Connor gripped the hem of his white T-shirt and tugged it over his head, sending his baseball cap flying to the ground, exposing his broad, muscular back and his lean waist.

Those jeans were riding dangerously low on his hips, and she absolutely stared as he bent down to retrieve the cap he'd lost during his unintentional strip show.

Connor wasn't the only worker who decided to ditch

his shirt. It was a veritable all-male revue. Of course, none of them flipped her switch quite the way Connor did.

"Not bad." Kate Garrett was standing at Liss's side, obviously enjoying the show. Though Liss imagined for very different reasons.

"No, indeed," Sadie said, coming to stand on the other side of Liss. "Of course, the object of my affection has left his shirt on. He's far too appropriate sometimes. Well, not in all venues." She winked, and Kate groaned.

Liss couldn't help but feel as if there was something slightly pointed in the way Sadie had worded the previous sentence. And she didn't like it at all.

"Ace left his shirt on," Liss said, talking directly to Sadie.

"Shame," Kate said.

Sadie offered her a look that spoke volumes. "A real tragedy for you."

Kate made a noise in the back of her throat. "Oh, look, Jack took this opportunity to take his shirt off, too. I don't think he likes to keep his clothes on if he can help it."

"Not if the rumors about him are true," Liss said, more than happy to take the focus off her.

"Do you think they are?" Kate asked.

For some reason Liss didn't really want to confirm for Kate that she was 99 percent sure the rumors about Jack were understated if anything.

"I feel like we should help," Kate said.

"I organized most of this, so I do not feel the need to pick up a tool of any kind," Sadie said.

Kate rolled her eyes. "A little sweat isn't going to hurt you," she said, rolling up the sleeves on her plaid shirt.

"I can only think of a couple good reasons to sweat," Sadie said. "Scratch that, I can think of one good reason to sweat. And it has nothing to do with raising a barn."

"I get it, Sadie. You have sex with my brother. We don't ever need to speak of it." Kate flipped her braid over her shoulder. "Now, if you'll excuse me, I'm going to go make myself useful."

Kate turned and walked toward the action, and Liss and Sadie watched her go. Then Sadie turned her far too keen blue eyes onto Liss. "So, how are things going?"

"Well, my car is starting almost every time, so that's nice."

"I meant with Connor. With the arrangement."

Liss narrowed her eyes. "I don't know what you're getting at."

"Yes, you do. You were dancing with Ace, who, may I say, is a pretty hot specimen, and you were holding on to him like he was a toad."

Liss gasped. "I was not. I was dancing with him like he was an attractive man."

"And you kept looking at Connor."

Liss sputtered, her protest stumbling on her lips. And in the end she decided against voicing it at all. "Okay, so I'm not attracted to Ace. I'm not going to pretend. But nothing is happening with me and Connor. Nothing ever will. There is history wrapped in issues between us, not to mention the fact that we're basically siblings."

Sadie held her hands up in mock surrender. "All right, all right. No need to get touchy."

Liss sneaked a peek at Sadie. "You believe me, right?"

She shook her head. "No. I don't believe you. I think you want to jump his bones. But I won't push you."

"Even if I wanted to, I can't." Just saying the words made her feel desolate. She hated that.

"Why not?"

"Friendship. Nearly two decades of it. Plus, the baggage. The fact that his late wife was one of my best friends." Liss looked down, her heart beating heavily. "I know you didn't really know Jessie, but she was wonderful."

"She's also not here anymore," Sadie said. "And he is. And you are."

"I… It's not that simple."

"I didn't say it would be simple. I just said you wanted it."

She should deny it. She really should. But she felt as though any denial would be feeble, and epically transparent. "I really want simple. Mainly, I would like to not lose the good things I have."

"What if you added better things?"

"I think this is when I ask when Eli is going to propose to you," Liss said.

Sadie arched a brow. "Nice. He's probably waiting until he's sure I won't skitter off. I'm a proven flight risk."

"Somehow, I don't think you are anymore."

Sadie smiled, a happiness in her eyes that Liss craved with an intensity that shocked her. "No, not anymore. He's got me for good. And he didn't even have to handcuff me to anything."

"True love."

"Yeah, it is. And in my experience, it was worth facing down a little bit of fear."

Liss cleared her throat. "Well, I will keep that in mind should it ever become relevant."

"Someday we'll talk about your denial," Sadie said.

"You didn't get your therapist license renewed, did you?"

Sadie just smiled and walked over to the table with all of the pie. Liss stayed in her spot, watching as the walls of the barn went up.

By the end of the evening, everyone was exhausted, but the frame and the roof were intact. Looking at it now, as all of the people in town started to dissipate, as the laughter faded, Liss felt her throat tighten. It was such an amazing thing, their town. The community that was here. The way they all supported each other. The way they were here for Connor, the way Connor had been here for her. Given her a place to stay when she needed him.

It was something that ran so much deeper than attraction. Something she prized more than anything else.

It was loyalty—unbreakable, unconditional and deep. It was something she'd never had with the father she didn't know. Something she hadn't had with her mother, who was content to take until Liss had nothing more to give.

It was real. And, Liss decided, standing there in the fading light, looking at the barn, not worth risking for anything.

IT HAD TO be close to midnight. Everyone had gone home hours ago. But not Connor.

He couldn't sleep. And he didn't want to drink. Not after he'd gone so many nights without doing it. But he was pissed, and his brain was going double time. Energy was pouring through his veins, making it impossible for him to sit still.

So he was in the barn, hammering siding up himself, in the light of the big yellow work lamp he always used for this kind of project. Sweat was rolling down his chest, in spite of the fact that the dark air was cold.

He put another board in place and started to hammer the nail. He should be using a nail gun. But he wanted to pound on something. He wasn't sure if he wanted to get the barn up, or if he was trying to knock it down. Wasn't sure if he was happy about it, or if he hated it.

When the original barn had been built, it had been with a view to the future. It had been his dream, and Jessie's dream. This was something different. Something he wasn't sure he was ready to have.

This restlessness had been eating at him since they first started preparing the site for the raising today. And it had only gotten worse over the course of the day.

Then Ace Thompson had put his fucking hands on Liss. Sure, it was just dancing. She probably hadn't even gone home with him. Probably. He didn't know, because he hadn't gone back to the house. He didn't want to know.

He didn't want to be upset about it, either. But he was.

Seeing as he had recently decided that he wanted to put his hands on Liss. No, *decided* was a terrible word for it. *He* hadn't decided anything. His dick had made that decision. And it was a terrible decision. He knew it. But it didn't stop him from hating the man who had perfect freedom to touch her.

Because Connor couldn't. For so many reasons. So many damn reasons.

All perfectly valid.

Because she was his best friend. Because he hadn't

felt this way until she'd moved in. Because he was pretty sure he felt this way only because of the close proximity. And because of the fact that he hadn't had sex in three years.

And those were all terrible reasons to screw up the best relationship you had.

So he was out here hammering nails. Because he couldn't get hammered, and he couldn't nail Liss.

If he hadn't been in such a crappy mood, he would've laughed at his own joke.

He kept on hammering the nail long past when it had been driven into the wood. But he wasn't even thinking now, wasn't even trying to be productive. He was just trying to burn off the feelings that were crawling around inside him, like living things that needed to be choked out with movement.

"Connor?" A feminine voice rose up above the hammer strikes.

He turned and saw Liss standing there, her eyes wide, her face washed in light. "Are you just getting home?" he asked, instantly enraged.

"What?"

"You. Are you just getting home?"

"Where would I have been?"

"I don't know. With Ace. Getting laid."

"For your information, asshole, I was in your kitchen getting warm milk. Not that it's your business either way. If I want to have more milk, I will have more milk. And if I want to have sex, I will have that, so just… Yeah."

"Not at my house." He knew he was being unreasonable, and he didn't care. Because the moment she had walked in, he had pictured her with Ace, his hands on her skin, and he had seen red.

"What are you, my dad? You know what, you can't be my dad, because he was never around, so he didn't care who I brought home. So I don't even know what you are."

LISS HAD NO IDEA what had gotten under Connor's skin. She had been out looking for him, because when she had realized that he hadn't come in, she'd been afraid he was off somewhere drinking himself into a stupor. Frankly, she didn't trust him. Not when emotions were this close to the surface; and where the barn was concerned, clearly, there were emotions.

The fact that they were standing here yelling at each other about something as stupid as him thinking she hooked up with Ace was evidence of that. The fact that he was in here at midnight putting up siding with a hammer, pounding on the board as if he wanted to put a hole in it, was yet more definitive evidence.

"Just your friend, who opened up his house to you, and worries about you. And who, frankly, does not want you to sleep with a skanky bartender."

"Since when is it your business who I sleep with?" she asked.

"When I said it was."

"What is your problem?"

"What isn't my problem?" he asked, throwing his hands wide, the hammer still gripped tightly in one of his fists. His chest was bare, a golden beam from the work light throwing the muscles on his torso into sharp relief, highlighting the beads of sweat on his skin that were trailing down through the ridges of his abs.

It was difficult to have a fight with somebody when you were light-headed from looking at them.

"Things are moving. They're moving faster than I want. Moving on, and I'm not ready," he said, dropping his arms to his sides. "This barn is getting built, whether I'm ready for it to be built or not. I'm starting to want sex again, even though I don't *really* want it."

Liss blinked, her heart stuttering as she absorbed his words. "Wait, what?"

"And you," he said, taking a few steps toward her, "you are not helping."

"What again?" she asked, blinking rapidly, her heart pounding so hard she was afraid she might pass out. Just think that away, onto the floor of the partially built barn.

"You," he said, his voice rough, "and your lacy panties. I saw them in the laundry. And now I can't stop picturing you in them."

Her stomach twisted into a knot, her heart thundering against her breastbone. "You thought about me in my panties?"

"I can't *stop* thinking about you in them."

"Well, I saw you in…your underwear. You didn't see me in mine."

"You seem fine. I am not fine." He dropped the hammer with a dull thud and took another step toward her, wrapping his arm around her waist and drawing her up against his chest. "I'm not fine." He raised his hand, brushing her cheekbone with his thumb. "I'm just not."

She could hear the pain in his voice, the confusion, the plea. He wanted her to fix this, wanted her to make it better, to take away the anguish that was tearing at him from the inside out. But she couldn't.

She didn't want him to stop picturing her that way.

Because she didn't want him to let her go. As far as this was concerned, she didn't want it to be okay. She wanted to be different. She wanted to be everything.

He needed her help, and she wanted something else entirely.

She hated herself for that weakness, but she couldn't fight it. And she didn't move away from him.

"I'm not fine, either," she said, her voice small.

For a moment he just looked at her, his chest rising and falling with each breath, his eyes glittering. Then he moved.

"Fuck," he said, just before his mouth covered hers.

Liss was glad that he was holding on to her, because if he hadn't been, she would've crumpled straight to the ground. Years of fantasies could not have prepared her for the reality of Connor's lips on hers. It was new, and it was familiar in the most beautiful way. Like Christmas. Different all the time and somehow the same. With surprises and tradition all wrapped into one. That was kissing Connor. His scent surrounding her, so familiar, but mingling together now with his flavor. She had never tasted him before, and it was the most wonderful thing. The most perfect thing.

He angled his head, sliding his tongue across the seam of her mouth as she opened to him, sighing as his tongue moved against hers. She wrapped her arms around his neck, pressed herself hard up against him and kissed him back with all of the repressed enthusiasm that had been building inside her since she'd first imagined what it might be like to taste his lips.

He was everything. The sunset on the ocean, the salt breeze through the pine trees, a burst of the season's first ripe blackberry on her tongue. He tasted like heartbreak and hope, and it made her ache down so deep it was physical pain.

He shifted their positions and cupped her face, the kiss intensifying. His mouth was firm, his beard rasping against her skin, his tongue slick against hers. The depth to the kiss, the intensity of it...it couldn't be anyone but him.

She'd spent years studying his lips, and now she finally knew what it felt like to have them beneath hers. She'd talked to him, but she'd never heard him groan like he did as she swept her tongue across his bottom lip. She knew him, as well as a friend could ever know another friend, and yet, she hadn't known what he sounded like when he was aroused. But she did now. And it was better than anything. Better than ice cream.

When he pulled away from her, she was shaking, a strange, sick feeling in the pit of her stomach. Terror mingling with desire, excitement, adrenaline.

She didn't know what to say; she didn't know what to do. She wanted to lean in and kiss him again, and she wanted to run away. She couldn't really do both at the same time. Unless she kissed him really quickly and then ran for the hills.

There was no question that she had just revealed a hell of a lot. Because you didn't kiss a guy like that if you hadn't thought about it before. If you hadn't thought about it for years and years, over and over again.

But he had kissed her back. And even though he was looking at her now as if she had sprouted a second head, the fact remained he had instigated this.

And he had thought about her in her panties.

She didn't want to speak, because that would mean the moment was over. And it was a moment she had spent so many years waiting for, she didn't think she could face the end of it.

But she did have to deal with the fact that this could very well be the end of the moment. Because he wasn't moving toward her again. Didn't look like he was leaning in for another kiss. Didn't look like he would extend his hands to her and lead her to his bedroom.

A shiver ran through her body. She wanted to go to his bedroom. She just let the thought sit there, fully formed, acknowledged. She wanted to go to Connor's bedroom. She wanted more of what had just happened. She wanted him naked, wanted to touch him everywhere, taste him everywhere. Once would never be enough. One touch of his mouth against hers was nothing more than a glimpse at paradise.

How could she go back now that she'd experienced this? Connor was fantasy made flesh. And now that she knew desire like this was real and living, how could she ever go back to what she'd accepted before?

This was heat and fire, the kind that left scorched earth and devastation in its wake. The kind that reshaped everything it touched.

Too soon it was over.

"Sorry," he said, taking a step away from her.

It was over. That step backward made it official. She hated it. Hated that she was only going to kiss Connor once. She had spent a very long time accepting the fact that she was never going to kiss him at all. But this was worse.

"Don't apologize," she said. "It sucks."

That was probably too honest. She should stop talking. She should go back into the house and not say anything. She should just say it was okay and nod along when he said it shouldn't happen again, that their friendship was too important. Because it shouldn't, and their friendship was too important. But she didn't want to have that conversation. And she didn't want to nod along. Seeing as she didn't agree.

"I just grabbed you and kissed you. We don't kiss. If that doesn't merit an apology, I'm not really sure what does."

"Just don't say you're sorry you kissed me. Because I'm not sorry."

"Why aren't you sorry?" he asked.

"I liked it."

The words hung there between them, like dust in the air, highlighted by the work light, swirling around them. "You liked it?"

"Yeah," she said, shrugging a shoulder. "I haven't been kissed in a while."

"And you didn't kiss Ace."

"No, I did not kiss Ace. I didn't even want to. In spite of the fact that it has been a long time since I've been kissed."

"But you wanted to kiss me?" He looked so confused, and if she didn't feel so conflicted, so tied up in knots, it might've been funny.

"Well, I wasn't opposed to the idea."

He lifted his hands then lowered them, slapping them on his thighs. "What does... Well, what the hell does that mean?"

"I don't know." She started picking at the remnants of pink polish on her thumbnail. "Does it have to mean anything?"

"Does a kiss ever mean...nothing?"

"I think sometimes it just means that people like to kiss." That sounded lame.

"Well, but usually it means people have certain feelings. Things they want to do that are kissing. That are more than kissing."

"This is the most awkward conversation I've ever had," she said.

"Well, how is it supposed to be not awkward? We've spent a lot of years not kissing. And then I kissed you. It would've been a lot easier if you would've just let me sweep it under the rug with an apology."

"I know. But I didn't feel like it."

"Liss, you are a pain in the ass."

"Well, thank you, Connor. You kissed me and then you called me a name. The state of our friendship is a little bit weird at the moment."

Connor put his hands on his head. "I know. I think there's something weird happening to me." He let out a long breath and relaxed his arms again. "There has been for a long time. And I think something is happening, with you living with me, and it having been… a while. Three years."

"So it's proximity, then." That hurt.

"Probably. What else could it be?" Ouch again.

"Nothing," she said, leaving it at that. Anything else would be admitting that her attraction was long-standing, and his, apparently wasn't. If he was even really attracted to her. He hadn't really said. He was talking about sex deprivation and proximity, which wasn't the same thing.

"We should forget this. Apparently, I'm kind of dangerous when I don't drink."

He also had some spark back. A little bit of wildness,

like the Connor he used to be. She liked it. She liked it a whole lot better.

"No, don't do that. If it's a choice between drinking or making out, I think you should just make out with me."

Her aim had been to make him laugh. But he wasn't laughing. Instead, his eyes caught hers, a serious light in them. A predatory light. Connor had never looked at her that way before. It made her feel light-headed, made her feel like maybe that step back hadn't meant the end, after all. "Medicinal making out?"

Liss swallowed hard, feeling dizzy. "Sure."

"What scares me is the hangover," he said, his tone grave.

Yeah, that was the thing that scared her, too. Because the kissing was fine, and she was sure sex would be better. The aftermath was the concern. It made her feel panicky, made her feel like a wild beast was clawing at her insides. Possibly Kate's wolverine.

"Yeah. Those can be a bitch."

"I'm well acquainted." He extended his hand, fingertips drifting over her cheek. "We should go inside," he said, breaking contact with her.

Suddenly, she was freezing. Her teeth chattered, and she wrapped her arms around her midsection. "Good idea," she said.

It was very inconvenient that she and Connor had to go back to the same place tonight. She needed distance. She needed it badly. Because depending, she had a feeling she could be easily convinced to run away screaming into the night, or fall right into his arms and spend the night screaming with him, in his bed.

Oh, boy.

They were both still standing there, neither of them making a move to go in.

"We should go," he said again.

"Good idea," she repeated.

"I don't know why it's hard," he said.

Liss tried to hold back the laugh that built in her chest, but she was unsuccessful. It burst out, somewhere between a snort and a sputter. "That's what she said."

"Really, Liss?"

"I'm sorry. I'm so inappropriate. This is really uncomfortable. And I guess when things get uncomfortable, I figure you might as well add a penis joke." Connor turned away from her and started out of the barn. "What? At least this is more normal." She trailed after him, pleased that somehow she had managed to break the tension, even if it was accidental.

"It is that," he said, not turning back to look at her.

They walked on for a while, not saying anything. If you didn't have anything non-penis-related to say, you shouldn't say anything at all. Or something.

The house came into view, the porch light off, the only light provided by the moon. Connor walked up the steps, his hands shoved in his pockets. Liss hung back. He looked at her, his expression serious. "You can come in. I'm not going to jump you."

"Good to know," she said, walking up the stairs and joining him on the porch. "I didn't really think you were going to." She had a feeling there was a much higher chance of her jumping him.

"Well, good, I'm glad you realize that."

"I trust you, Connor."

"I'm not sure you should," he said.

"Connor, let me tell you something. I don't even

know my dad. I think he sent a card once, but I don't know for sure, because my mom took it and burned it. She never could separate what happened between them from my relationship with him. It would have been one thing if she had been angry at him because of the way he ignored me, but that was never it. She was just never over the fact that he didn't stay with her. That he didn't take care of her. Unlike my dad, she's always been there. But she's never hesitated to tell me how difficult I've made her life. Being a single mom is hard, and she made sure I knew. But I did learn very quickly that there were ways I could make things easier. When I kept the house clean, when I got myself to school, things were easier. And…" Liss swallowed hard; she was embarrassed to tell him the next part, not because the story was embarrassing, but the level of emotion she still felt about it was. "This is going to sound really stupid. But remember how I didn't go to senior prom?"

"Vaguely. I was kind of over prom, since I'd already been to mine and as a graduate it all felt like kid stuff to me, but it was important to Jessie, so I went."

"Well, I wanted to go. I was waiting tables at The Crow's Nest to save up to buy this dress that I saw at the bridal store. With hindsight, and some maturity, I think it was a very ugly dress." She didn't. She still thought it was beautiful. Cotton-candy pink with spaghetti straps, clear beads on the bodice and heavy satin skirt. And if she ever saw it, she would buy it. Just because she could. "Anyway, I saved up for a few months for that prom dress. And I bought it. I put it in my room, still in the little plastic garment bag, hanging on the outside of my closet so I could look at it whenever. Then, like, three days before prom, my mom saw the dress and got really upset. She started telling me about all these problems. The car wasn't working well, and our power bill was really big. And I shouldn't spend my money on something like that. She said I needed to help around the house more, because she did so much for me. I was so angry at her, and at myself. I knew she was manipulating me. And I knew there was nothing I could do about how it made me feel."

Connor grimaced. "Liss…"

"I returned it. And I gave my mom the money I had saved. The night of the prom, we went out. We had hamburgers and milk shakes. She was happy with me. And that is what I have to do to have a relationship with her. But you don't do that to me. And that's why I trust you. So don't tell me that I shouldn't." She paused, her heart up in her throat. "You're the best I have."

"Oh, Liss," he said, taking a step toward her, wrapping his arm around her waist, drawing her in for a hug.

"It was just a dress."

He moved his hand over her back slowly, the motion so unintentionally erotic she was besieged by both guilt and arousal. "It's not, though."

He was right. It wasn't just a dress. It was yards of pink satin as a metaphor for her mother-daughter relationship. Or maybe for her life. She certainly hadn't been any better off living with Marshall than she had been with her mother. He always needed something, always wanted something. Always something she needed to sacrifice to make his life easier, so that she was fulfilling her position as girlfriend to the best of her ability.

And still, no matter how much she had given, it never seemed as if it was enough. Marshall had taken off with the truck she had bought with him for heaven's sake.

She cleared her throat. "Yeah, well, it's easier if it's just a dress."

"Yeah, I get that."

Suddenly, she became very aware of his heart beating hard against her chest, of the heat of his body, the strength in his hold. She should move away from him, but she didn't want to. So instead, she leaned into him, resting her head on his shoulder.

Liss shifted in Connor's hold, pressed her cheek against his chest, could feel his heart rate start to speed up. And along with that, she could feel...

She wiggled a little bit, trying to see if she could force her hip into more definitive contact with what she was almost certain was a very inappropriate erection.

She felt his muscles go rigid, felt him freeze. And now she was completely certain. "Connor?"

"What?" He sounded strained, like he was in pain.

"Do you... I mean..."

He moved away from her, his hands up as he backed away. "Sorry."

She stood there for a second, feeling stunned. As if she'd been slapped upside the head with a piece of barn siding. And then, before her brain could catch up with her body, a decision was made.

She started to close the distance between them, and he took another step away. But she reached out, looped her arm around the back of his neck, her momentum propelling him back against the side of the house, her chest flush against his. Then she stretched up on her tiptoes and closed the distance between them.

Connor growled, lacing his fingers through her hair and pulling her more tightly against him. This was different than the kiss in the barn; this wasn't a test. This was rough, intense. Angry. Both of them realized that a horse had been let out of the gate, and they couldn't figure out how to put it back.

He reversed their positions, pushing her back against the wall, pressing the erection that had started it all hard against her stomach. She moaned, biting his lower lip, because she wasn't quite able to help herself. She'd never done anything like that before. And under normal circumstances, she might have felt a little bit embarrassed about it, or at least a little bit afraid that the guy hadn't liked it. But she wasn't, not with him. Because there was no doubt based on the sound he made, based on the way he tightened his hold on her hair, that he had enjoyed it. And this was Connor, and she knew how to read him better than any other person on the planet.

She slid her hands down the front of his chest, relishing the feel of his bare skin, his muscles. He was so hot, and hard and perfect. He was so everything a man should be, and nothing she had ever had before. Marshall had been a backseat driver, in life and in bed. He had no trouble asking her to do things differently, but he never took control.

Connor suffered no such problem. Connor led by example. And it was a very good example.

Liss let her fingers drift over the ridges of muscle on his abs then reached to the side, feeling around for the doorknob. She managed to get the door open, and let them both inside, still kissing him. She was dizzy now, but really, who needed air? She was kissing Connor Garrett. She didn't need anything else.

They half stumbled to the couch, Liss landing on his lap, her thighs on either side of his. Connor put his hands on her waist, sliding them upward, beneath the hem of her top. She wrenched her mouth from his, a gasp escaping her lips. He released his hold on her and gripped the front of her T-shirt, tugging the neckline downward, revealing a healthy amount of cleavage, and the tops of her lacy bra cups.

"Damn," he said, the word like a prayer.

He leaned in, pressing his lips to her breasts, before tracing the line where fabric met skin with the tip of his tongue. This was getting a lot further a lot faster than she had imagined it might. Well, the truth was, she hadn't really thought ahead the moment she had decided to kiss him out on the porch. And in her imagination, in her fantasies past, things had always been hazy. Sensual, but hazy. There was a limit to how deep and detailed she could go with her fantasies about him and still look him in the eye the next day.

This, while sensual, was not at all hazy. It was sharp, to the point of pain, pleasure so acute it twisted into something decidedly different, wholly unique, like she had never felt before.

She slid forward on his lap, her knees hitting the back of the couch, bringing her into very decisive contact with his arousal. Need pierced her, and she rocked her hips against him, need rolling through her like a wave.

She reached between them, fumbling with his belt buckle. When did she get so clumsy? When did basic things like undoing belts become a near impossibility? Maybe around the time getting a belt open had started to feel like a life-and-death situation. "Connor," she said, panting, and not even caring that she was, "Connor, I need… I need…"

Before she could get the words out, he had pulled her shirt up over her head in one efficient movement while working at the clasp of her bra with his other hand. He seemed to be having as much trouble as she was.

"New plan, you get the belt, I'll get the bra," she said.

His hands immediately went down to his belt buckle. "Works for me," he said.

She unhooked her bra and tossed it to the side, and Connor froze. "You, belt. I held up my end of the deal."

"I can't... I... Just a second." He cupped her breasts, sliding his hands beneath them, pushing them together before releasing his hold, watching her intently. "Fuck." He leaned in, tracing the outline of her nipple with the tip of his tongue before sucking it in deep, his tongue slick, his whiskers burning her sensitive skin in the very best way. She arched her back, rocking her hips forward, chasing the climax that was building, strong and low inside her.

Then she looked down, and the sight almost sent her over the edge.

Connor. This was *Connor*. Finally.

He lifted his head, his dark eyes meeting hers. "Sorry about that. It's been three years since I've seen actual breasts in person. And breasts are, like, my favorite thing. Your breasts specifically are my favorite thing right now."

Heat assaulted her cheeks. "Could you stop apologizing to me every time you do something that feels amazing? Otherwise you're going to be groaning an apology about the time I make you come."

"You have to stop talking right now, or it won't be long until the apology happens." He reached down and undid his belt buckle, sliding his pants down his hips, leaving his underwear in place.

She reached down, sliding her hand over the black

fabric, feeling the hard ridge of his cock. She nearly whimpered. She had hit the jackpot. She would have wanted Connor either way; she had for enough years that she could honestly say size didn't matter. But it turned out he was extremely impressive, and she found she was very happy about that.

She moved her palm over his length, squeezing him gently. He let his head fall back, air hissing through his teeth. She lifted the waistband of his underwear and slipped her fingers beneath, making contact with his skin. She wanted to freeze this moment. This moment, where she was touching him for the very first time.

Arousal and emotion curled around her stomach, twisting it tight. She had her hand wrapped around Connor's cock. And the thought alone was enough to send her straight to the edge.

She pushed his underwear down, pulling him out so she could see him. "Oh, Connor."

She slid off his lap, getting on her knees in front of him, her hands planted on his thighs. His gaze was intent on hers, his jaw clenched tight. If all she had was tonight, and she feared very much it was all she would have, then she was going to fulfill her every fantasy.

Yes, she would love to believe this would be the start of something lasting. Would love to believe this was only the first of a thousand times. But she wasn't quite that naive. Tomorrow the sun would rise. The light would clear up the fog that had settled between them, and they would be left with trying to figure out what to do with their friendship. With trying desperately to get things back to the way they were.

She didn't mind that she still had a light grasp on reality. It made her more determined to take this moment and make it everything. Everything she had always wanted. She curled her fingers around his shaft and leaned in; keeping her eyes on his, she flicked her tongue over the head of his cock.

He gripped her hair and tugged her head up. "Liss, I don't…"

"What?" He couldn't stop it now. He could *not* stop her now.

"I've never… I don't…"

She froze. "Well, you aren't a virgin, that I know."

He didn't say anything for a moment, his expression pained, the tendons in his neck standing out. "I've never had anyone do that before."

A shock wave rolled through her body, immobilizing her. Then she shook it off, fantasy taking hold and blunting reality just enough. "Okay. Well, you're about to. We're going to talk about this later. Right now I'm not interested in talking."

LISS LEANED IN, picking up where she had left off, sliding her tongue over the head of his cock before tilting her head and taking him in deep, moving her hand in time with her mouth. Connor kept his hand buried in her hair, his fingers clenched into a fist.

His best friend in the entire world had his cock in her mouth. And all he could do was sit there, his fingers tangled in her hair, and think one word over and over again.

Fuck fuck fuck fuck.

He only wished he had let her get *this* far before he had gone and confessed that he was a blow job virgin. Hell, he wished he hadn't confessed at all. It was a stupid thing. A stupid thing he'd never worried all that much about. Until, of course, a woman unexpectedly got on her knees in front of him. Then it seemed like a big freaking deal. A huge deal.

She made a satisfied, throaty sound as she took him in deeper, the slick friction of her tongue over his skin almost too much to handle. But then, this was the first time anyone had put their hands on him in three years. The first time anyone had put their mouth on him in ever.

His stomach muscles tightened, fire roaring through his veins. He was dangerously close to coming, and he didn't want to. Not yet.

"Liss…"

She shifted position, gripping the base of his shaft with her hand, tilting her head and sliding her tongue along the length of him. He released his hold on her hair, sifting it through his fingers, watching as the copper strands caught the light. Gold, red and deep brown all highlighted by the lamp near the couch. And her skin, so pale and pretty and very, very bare.

He looked down at the elegant line of her back, at the hint of her ass, visible thanks to her position, and her very low-cut jeans. She straightened slightly, still teasing him with her tongue, her breasts visible now, her pink nipples tight, so perfect.

Desire built in him, the heat in his blood intensifying, drawing close to a boil. And he knew he couldn't fight it any longer.

"Liss," he said, her name a plea now. Because he needed her to stop or else he was going to lose all control.

She looked at him, those golden eyes lit with a matching fire to the one that burned through him. She knew. Knew he was close to losing it. But she didn't stop. He closed his eyes, tightening his hold on her hair, embracing the release that was roaring through him as she continued to slide her hand over his length, drawing his release out of him in long, slow waves of pleasure.

When his blood cooled, his vision coming back into focus, he looked at her. Fuck. He'd come all over her tits like some kind of animal.

"Oh, shit," he said, unable to catch his breath.

Liss blinked. "Don't apologize."

Dammit, he *had* been about to apologize. Because who the hell did that? Who lost their control like that? Who just did that to a woman without even talking about it first? He certainly didn't. His first reaction was to apologize, because he couldn't imagine her feeling anything but disgust.

"This wasn't a good idea," he said.

Liss recoiled, getting to her feet, scrambling for her T-shirt. She picked it up and held it over her breasts, her expression fierce. "Okay, so that's nice. This is a bad idea after you get your orgasm?"

"No, it was a bad idea from the beginning."

He expected a fight; he expected her to get mad. Instead, her shoulders sagged, a sadness that made him ache filling her eyes. "You know what? Obviously, it was a bad idea. We weren't thinking. Like we discussed in the barn, it's been a long time for both of us." She gestured toward him. "Apparently, it's been forever for you, for that. And…and…I need a shower."

Of course she did. And it was his fault. Because she had to wash him off her.

She turned and walked out of the room, and Connor stood, doing his pants back up, pacing the length of the room. He was such an asshole. He'd let all of his sick fantasies get out of hand, and then it had ended up like that. With him completely disrespecting his best friend. With him taking advantage of her.

His brain rebelled against his revision of the events, trying to remind him that out on the porch Liss had been the one to kiss him. But it butted up against his desire to cast himself as the bad guy. So he dismissed it. Because he was comfortable as the bad guy. This was what he did. He let people down. He fucked stuff up.

And Liss was no exception, apparently.

He pushed his hand through his hair and walked into the kitchen, on a hunt for alcohol. It had been a few days. But hammering apparently didn't fix anything.

Jack Daniel's didn't, either. Not permanently. But it made for a nice temporary haze. And he needed that. More than anything. Needed something to keep him from going into Liss's room and finishing what they'd started.

He took a glass down from the cabinet, and for the first night in weeks, Connor Garrett poured himself a drink.

CHAPTER TEN

IN LISS'S OPINION, the morning after should come with a whole lot more buzz than this. But then, in her opinion, the night before should have concluded in an entirely different manner.

Instead, the entire day had been filled with the sound of clattering dishes, awkward no-eye-contact greetings and a whole lot of scampering around each other like frightened cats when they had accidental encounters.

And yay, hooray, tonight was the poker game. Which meant they were going to have to take this awkward little show on the road, in front of all their friends and family.

She felt as though she had a stamp on her forehead that said "I totally sucked my friend's dick."

The strangest thing was, she still didn't regret it. Or maybe, it wasn't that strange. How could she regret the culmination of half a lifetime's worth of fantasies? Well, *culmination* was a strong word. There was still unfinished business. Namely the fact that he had gotten off and she hadn't. Watching him come had certainly been an aphrodisiac, but she would have really liked a little bit of that action herself.

She should be more regretful. She really should be. But it was hard, with the memory of Connor's lips, and Connor's…other things, still fresh in her mind.

Well, when she was by herself she wasn't regretful. But the idea of seeing him again in a few minutes, with a room full of other people, made her slightly regretful.

She wasn't entirely sure what insanity had exploded between them. Wasn't sure what had dropped the invisible barrier that had always been there, stripping them of their inhibitions and their clothes.

She closed her eyes and imagined him as he'd been last night. What it had been like to be on her knees in front of him.

And he had never had… No one had ever… She didn't even understand how that was possible. How could any woman resist that? She and Jessie had never talked about her and Connor's sex life because Liss was not a masochist. So she'd had no idea her friend had hang-ups about oral sex.

Dear Lord, why was she going there now? It was just that she didn't understand. And she was obsessing about it now. Obsessing about the fact that she was the first to ever go down on him.

"Is the oven preheated?"

She jumped as Connor came into the room, knocking over the stack of red plastic cups that she was next to. "Yeah," she said.

"Good. I want to have everything ready when people get here."

"Yes, because this is the classiest of dinner parties. We don't want people's beer to get warm while they await their frozen pizza."

"There's chips and salsa. Everyone will live."

"Good," she said.

Their eyes met and held. It was the first time all day. She regretted it instantly.

Now she really wished everybody would just hurry up and get here.

She heard the front door open, and she almost groaned with relief. "In here!" she said.

Heavy footsteps crossed the wood floor, and then Jack appeared in the doorway of the kitchen. "I'm here to take your money," he said. "Now give me a beer."

"Get your own," Connor said, and Liss was nothing but grateful to have a buffer between her and her best friend. She could honestly say it was the first time she had ever been pleased about that.

"Is the ice bucket out?"

"Yes," Connor said, "but there isn't any beer in it yet. You can make yourself useful, Jack. How about that for a change of pace?"

"Well, I don't have much experience with that," Jack said, shrugging, "but I can try."

Jack walked over to the fridge and opened it, bending down and pulling out a few bottles of beer. "So I spent my day dealing with sperm. How was your workday?"

Liss's head whipped to the side, and her gaze collided with Connor's. Then looked away. "What?"

"We artificially inseminated one of my horses today," Jack said, straightening, two beer bottles in each hand. "And that was way closer to that sort of thing than I've ever wanted to be. It feels mean, really, making it all such a sterile process. But it's cheaper to ship frozen horse semen than it is to ship the horse."

Connor winced. "Could you stop saying that word? And words related to it?"

"You run a ranch, Garrett. I would've thought you had a little more fortitude than that."

Yeah, normally he did, and Liss knew it. Though

it was a little bit trickier to be discussing these topics considering what happened last night.

"Man, I just let a bull loose in the field and he can have at it," Connor said, holding his hands up. "I don't order containers of champion baby gravy."

"Because you raise these guys for meat. I'm breeding champions."

"Just don't use that as a pickup line," Liss said, side-stepping through the room, hoping to escape. Hoping to put a little bit of distance between herself and Connor.

"I do okay with the pickup lines I have," Jack said, a half smile curling his lips.

Liss went into the dining room and set about doing busywork. Fanning out paper napkins, helping Jack put the beer in the ice and arranging the paper plates in various positions.

Connor stuck to the kitchen, his excuse that he was babysitting the frozen pizza that was baking in the oven. She was not going to call him on the fact that a frozen pizza did not need to be babysat. If Jack thought it was weird, he didn't say anything. So he probably didn't think it was weird, because Jack almost always said something.

As soon as the pizza came out of the oven, Sadie, Eli and Kate came in as if the kitchen timer had called them.

After much jostling, everyone took their seats around the table, except for Connor, who was back in the kitchen taking care of something that probably didn't really need to be taken care of. But when everything settled, the only vacant chair that remained was the one to the right of Liss. Because of course, it would be assumed that she and Connor would want to sit next to each other. Or, if not want to, that they wouldn't have a problem with it. In truth, very likely no one had thought of it at all. But she had.

She had a problem with it right now. Mainly because she was caught in this weird place where she wanted to run away and hide from Connor and also put her hand in his lap.

Connor walked in then stopped as he saw the vacant chair next to her. Clearly, he was caught in a similar place. So maybe he just wanted to run away. He was the one who had stopped things between them last night, after all.

After he'd had an orgasm. Typical.

"I guess I'll sit next to Liss," he said, his announcement making things extra weird.

"You sound kind of bummed out about that, Connor," Kate said. "Do you think she has cooties?"

"No," he said, shooting a glare at Kate before he moved to the table and came to sit beside her.

Their eyes met again, and she felt as if they had an actual collision. The impact of his gaze was like getting hit in the face with a brick.

And much like getting hit in the face with a brick, it was impossible for her to hide her reaction.

He leaned back in his chair, and his shoulder brushed hers. She swallowed hard, certain that everybody must be able to feel the tension that was wound so tight between them. Because it was obvious. It all came back to that stamp. The one that was on her forehead, advertising last night's activities.

"What's the game?" Eli asked, putting his hand on the deck of cards that was at the center of the table.

"Five-card draw," Kate said.

"No preference," Sadie said. "Because I still pretty much don't know what any of the games are."

"Yes, you do," Jack said. "And it's that kind of acting that gets us fleeced every week."

"I guess you should have learned by now," Sadie said, smiling sweetly.

"I'm a slow learner when it comes to pretty faces," Jack said. Kate contorted her mouth into a sneer, sticking her tongue out. "Faces like that," Jack said, winking.

"Don't even try it," Connor said, giving Jack a warning glare.

"Oh, please," Kate said, rolling her eyes.

Jack just smiled.

"Are we going to play cards, or what?" Connor asked, taking the deck of cards from beneath Eli's hand and starting to deal.

He went around the table, flinging out cards quickly, then placed the remaining cards back at the center of the table. "Okay, let's do this."

They went a few rounds, raising the pot by five and ten cents apiece each time. They played for loose change around here. But a big pot wasn't the point. It never had been.

"Anyone else?" Jack asked.

"I call," Kate said.

"Me, too," Sadie said.

"Call," Eli said.

"Call," she and Connor said at the same time, their unison annoying her.

"Cards down," Jack said. "Royal flush. Suck it."

Jack always talked like that, especially during cards. But for some reason, his little comments and double entendres had become very, very apparent today. Okay, not for *some reason*. She knew exactly the reason. Because last night, she had been sucking it. And so tonight, when Jack said things like that, all she could do was imagine sucking it again.

She felt her face getting hot, and she knew that her cheeks were red.

"It's just a card game, Liss," Jack said. "Relax. Don't look so much like you want to tear my throat out with your teeth."

She realized that she was still clutching her cards, and that everyone was staring at her. She put them down. "I don't have anything," she said, her words tumbling out quickly.

"I knew I would end up with all your money," Jack said, pulling the pot toward him.

"Just one more game," Connor said, "then I need to get some sleep."

"Rough night?" Eli asked.

Liss knew that Eli was not implying anything, and she knew that Eli didn't know anything. But it did not stop the heat in her face from intensifying.

"No, it was fine. Why would you ask that?" Connor asked.

"You're kind of twitchy," Eli said. "And grumpy."

"I'm always grumpy," Connor said.

If Connor was grumpy, Liss hadn't noticed, because she had been too busy being wrapped up in her own blanket of awkwardness.

"True," Kate said. "He is always grumpy."

"See? I'm a professional asshole."

"But you do make great pizza," Jack said, taking a slice from the pan at the center of the table.

"Yeah, I'm very proficient at opening cardboard boxes."

"How is it you're still single?" Jack asked.

Connor tensed, a muscle in his jaw ticking. "Because my wife is dead."

Silence settled over the room. Eli shifted uncomfortably while Sadie looked to him as if pleading for him to solve the mess that had just landed in front of them. Kate looked straight ahead, her gaze fixed, her eyes glittering. Like she might cry.

Jack cleared his throat. "Shit, dude. I was just teasing. I wasn't thinking."

"No, I know you weren't thinking. Why would you? It's been three years. Should be over it."

"No, you shouldn't," Jack said. "I'm an ass."

Right then, Liss felt the hole at the table. The empty space where Jessie had been. Her pretty friend, whose laugh could fill up a whole room. Jessie, who had been so lovely that Liss could never hate her, even when she'd married the man of Liss's dreams.

And thinking of her now…it made her want to curl into a ball and cry. She was gone, and that hurt. It was also a reminder of everything that stood between her and Connor. Not just a friendship, but a grief that was still bigger than both of them.

"You know what? I'm really tired. I'm going to bed." She stood up and walked out of the room, feeling shaky, feeling weak. What was her problem? She was acting like a child. And everybody was going to think she was crazy. Especially since she'd been nuts through half of the game. And now Connor had gotten his feelings hurt, and she was acting like it was about her.

She just needed a shower. And to sleep. One night hadn't dealt with their mistakes. Maybe another night would.

CONNOR STARED DOWN at the center of the table, not quite sure what had just happened. "I think the party is over tonight," he said, pushing himself up. "I probably need to go talk to her."

"I'm sorry, Connor." Jack looked genuinely remorseful, which was so unusual for him that Connor didn't have it in him to be mad at all. Just annoyed that everything made him think of the past. That even when well-meaning townspeople weren't taking him back there with their sympathetic comments, he brought himself back there. That he couldn't let go, because he didn't want to. Even though he did.

Basically, he had too many damn feelings for a man who didn't like dealing with feelings.

"Don't be."

"No, do be," Eli said. "I don't know what's going on," he said, turning his attention to Connor, "but go fix it."

"Yeah," Connor said, nodding at his brother. He wasn't going to pretend that nothing was happening between him and Liss, because even if they wouldn't guess they'd crossed the line last night, things were obviously tense. Hell, if they weren't tense, she wouldn't have stormed out like that. "Kate, feel free to take the pizza."

"Thanks," she said, picking up the pan that still had a quarter of a pie on it.

"Is that my punishment?" Jack asked. "I don't get the pizza?"

"Yes, now go home and think about what you did," Kate said, grinning unrepentantly.

"Or I'll follow you home and eat your pizza," Jack said.

"Better not," Kate said, "or I'll mess up your pretty-boy face something good."

"She probably will," Sadie said. "She's very serious about pizza."

Eli jerked his head in the direction of the door. "Come on, let's go." He wasn't wearing his uniform today, but his tone certainly was, and Jack and Kate rushed to obey.

Sadie lingered, a line deepening between her brows, her lips turned down into a frown. It was that look he often got. Worry wrapped in sympathy. But coming from Sadie it didn't gall as much as it did from others. She reached out and put her hand on his shoulder. "Are you okay?"

He looked at her. "As okay as I ever am."

"That's what worries me. You're never all that okay, are you?"

He thought back to last night, to the moments of pure, heady sexual desire that hadn't been tied to anything heavy or sad.

"That's not true," he said. "Sometimes I'm drunk."

"Connor," she said, pure censure lacing her tone. "Don't joke like that."

"You really are like having another sister. That's not a compliment," he said, but it was.

"Yeah, I try. I also worry. What's up with Liss?"

"I don't know." Which was partly true. "But I'm going to find out."

"She was really good friends with your wife, wasn't she?"

"She was."

"I wish I could've known her. Because with as much as you all loved her, I know I would have, too."

"You would have," he said. "She was very organized. She took great care of me. Probably a little bit too great. Probably why I'm such a big baby now."

"You aren't a baby. But you are in pain. If you ever need anything, you can talk to me. I was a professional at this in another life. Also, I care about you."

Emotion tightened his chest, and he cleared his throat, trying to get rid of it. "Thanks, Sadie. I probably won't take you up on that. But it means something that you offered."

Sadie forced a laugh. "At least you're honest."

He lifted a shoulder. "Sometimes."

"Good night, Connor. Good luck." Sadie turned and left, closing the door behind her.

Connor let out a long breath and looked around at the mess on the table. He would have to deal with it later. For now he had to deal with the mess that was between him and his best friend.

He walked out of the dining room and up the stairs, then down the hall to Liss's room. He thought about knocking then just opened the door.

Liss was sitting on the end of her bed, her forearms resting on her thighs. She looked up at him, a bleak expression on her face. "Did everyone leave?"

"Yeah," he said, crossing the room and sitting down next to her on the bed. "What's up?"

"I don't know. Today was weird."

He laughed, not really because it was funny, but because he was relieved that she was admitting it. Relieved that they weren't going to ignore what had happened anymore. "It was so freaking weird."

"Because last night was weird. And then Jack made that comment. And I realized that you aren't over what happened. Of course you aren't. Why would you be? But I wanted… I want to fix it. And I can't."

Connor rubbed his hands over his face then rested them on his thighs. "I want to apologize about last night, but you got mad at me for apologizing already."

"I will accept an apology about last night as a whole."

He let out a heavy sigh. "I'm sorry. I'm screwing this up. I'm screwing everything up. I don't know if I'm more sorry that I crossed that line with you, or more sorry about the way I finished it. But I basically sucked."

"No, that was me, remember?"

He laughed again. "Do you have to go making inappropriate jokes right now?"

"Is there a better time to make inappropriate jokes? I'm already mortally embarrassed. How much worse could it get?"

"I'm embarrassed. I can't believe that I…" He leaned forward, resting his forearms on his thighs, matching Liss's position. "Okay, I have to tell you something. And I've never told anyone this before, mainly because… Well, you've never asked and I wouldn't tell Jack under penalty of death. Also, Eli is my brother and we don't talk about this shit. But I've only been with one woman."

He wasn't embarrassed by the fact that his wife was the only woman he'd slept with. It just wasn't something he'd ever had to share before. But he wanted to explain to Liss why all of this felt like a huge deal.

"Only… You've only ever slept with Jessie," Liss said.

"Right. I liked her from the beginning. And I waited until she was ready. And I was never with anyone else. I never wanted to be." He looked down at his hands. "Going out and hooking up has never been me. It's not who I am. It's not what I do. But dammit, I am so sick of being celibate. Obviously, I have a little bit of sexual frustration that I'm dealing with."

Liss looked down and picked at the edge of her fingernail. "So I'm the result of your sexual frustration boiling over?"

"Hell, Liss, I don't know. That's part of why I freaked out when I kissed you in the barn. Because I can't tell you why this is happening. And if you like, that's a terrible thing to say to your friend right after you kiss her. I feel like it's a terrible thing to kiss your friend just because you're sexually frustrated. And it's an even worse thing to let your friend do what you did just because it's been three years since a woman has touched you." He rubbed his hands over his face. "And I just don't know. I just know that things are different. And I know I'm not ready for them to be different. I know I'm not ready to want someone else. But I do."

"Is it the worst thing to want me?" Her voice was small, timid, and he hated the note of insecurity that wound through it, because he was afraid he had put it there.

"In some ways, kind of. Because I don't want anything but sex and friendship. Not touching and in completely separate corrals. And I'm not sure that's possible."

"Why not?"

"Because I've never done it before."

"Neither have I. I've had two semiserious relationships, so it isn't like my list of experience is a lot longer than yours. Though I have given a blow job before."

"Did you have to bring that up?"

"I'm fascinated."

"It feels wrong to talk about it."

"Okay, regardless of where we go from here, we just have to deal with the fact that I have gone down on you. No take backs. And, as the first bestower of oral sex upon you, I sort of want to know why you've never had it before."

He straightened, letting his head fall back. "Liss, you are killing me."

"Am I making you blush?"

"Or something," he said, battling with the extreme embarrassment that was swirling around with arousal, making his gut feel unsettled.

"There's no room for you to be embarrassed about this topic. Once you've done it with someone, you have to be able to talk about it."

He gritted his teeth and clasped his hands together. Especially now that she was gone, he didn't like to say anything bad about Jessie. And while this wasn't technically bad, it felt slightly like a complaint. And that felt wrong. But Liss was right. She had given him his first blow job and was therefore entitled to details of some kind.

And blow job or not, she was his best friend. He didn't talk to very many people. Hell, he didn't really talk to anyone. Didn't he owe her this? Honesty?

"She just didn't ever want to," he said. "She very early on told me she thought that was gross. Granted, we were in high school, and I was trying to talk her into doing things that weren't going all the way. But that was her stance. And that was the stance she kept through all of our years of dating, and eight years of marriage."

Silence settled over them like an itchy blanket. But then, what did you say after something like that? There wasn't anyplace good to go.

Finally, Liss cleared her throat. "Okay, I think my curiosity is satisfied. But for the record, it's not gross."

He shifted, feeling like an absolute ass, because his cock was getting hard while they were discussing this. "Good to know."

"I'm saying that because I feel like that's part of why you freaked out afterward. Because you were worried I would be disgusted. But I wasn't. I did that because I wanted to. Because I think…I think you're sexy. You must realize that. I wouldn't have done any of that if I didn't."

"You think I'm sexy?"

"Connor, I'm not going to make out with a guy I don't think is hot."

"Or…other things."

"Oh, definitely not other things."

"So," he said, shifting position on the bed, "what do we do? Do we just try to let things go back to how they were? Do we try to forget that this happened?"

"Well, we tried that after we kissed in the barn. Then ten minutes later we made out on the porch and went further on the couch. Then we spent the entire day avoiding each other. So I'm not sure that's going to work."

"So the alternative is what?"

Liss shrugged. "Having sex, I guess."

Connor nearly choked on his tongue. "You can't just say things like that."

"I just did. Look, we are in close proximity, and it's obviously bringing things up. Some things literally," she said, looking pointedly at his lap. "And…like you said, you want to have sex, but you're not ready to go out and hook up with somebody random, because for you sex has always been intimate. Well, it's always been that way for me, too. But I think between us, even though our connection is friendship, we have intimacy that's already built-in. And maybe the thing with you is just psychological. You've only been with one woman, so the second one feels like a big deal. Plus, the first woman after your wife is always going to feel like a big deal. So…this might make it easier. And then you'll be able to kind of move forward."

He was pretty sure his dick was doing all of his thinking, because what she said made a strange kind of sense. Just a few months ago he'd told Eli he never wanted to have sex again. And a few months ago he had believed that. But now he knew that wasn't true. He was going to have to deal with a whole heap of personal crap before he did. Maybe this was a way to have his cake and eat it, too.

"I don't want to ruin our friendship," he said. What she said made sense, but he still wasn't convinced.

"I don't, either," she said. "But we already crossed the line. We already started this. We can't go back and forget it happened. Wouldn't it be better to just try to make it work for you?"

Her words sent a spark of discomfort along his veins. The kind he felt when townspeople showed up at his door with food and sad eyes. And he didn't like it one bit. "You want to make this work for me? What about you?"

"What do you mean what about me?"

"I am not going to be a pity fuck, Liss." He felt like an ass the minute he said the words, because Liss's face turned bright red, and she looked away from him as if he'd just flashed her on Main Street. "I'm tired of pity. I've had too much of it. I don't want casserole sex."

"I'm genuinely insulted that you would compare my sexual skill to casserole, which I know you hate."

"That isn't what I meant. What I meant is it's one of those things that people only give you when you're sad. Kind of like when your best friend gives you a blow job on your couch."

"A couch blow job is totally not the same thing as a casserole."

"I just don't get what's in it for you."

"You just don't get that I think you're sexy as hell and that I want to sleep with you?"

Just when he thought Liss couldn't shock him anymore, she managed to lay the verbal equivalent of wrapping his hand around hot wire on him. "Since when do you want to sleep with me?" he asked.

"It's one of those things. It comes and goes," she said.

"No way, baby, that doesn't fly."

"*Baby?* You're calling me *baby* now just because I felt you up?" she asked.

"You did a lot more than that, and you know it. And I'll *baby* you if I feel like it. Give me an answer."

"You're so demanding," she said.

"You don't mind," he said, shifting his position slightly on the bed.

"No, I don't." She took a deep breath. "I don't want

you to doubt our friendship because of this. So don't freak out. But I've been attracted to you off and on for a long time. Like, long time. But we were friends, and you were dating Jessie. So you know, you starred in some rather formative fantasies of mine, but that was it. I never wanted to compromise what we had. Or what I had with Jessie. But if it's on the table now? Then yeah, I want it. And trust me when I say it's not because I feel sorry for you."

"I don't know how to have this conversation."

"It's a terrible conversation for a lot of reasons," Liss said. "But either we have the conversation or we continue unsuccessfully ignoring it. And eventually one of us is just going to blurt out what happened in the middle of a poker game. Kate would die of embarrassment. Jack would never let us hear the end of it. In fact, Jack would probably ask why I've never done the same for him. Eli would be too nice to say anything."

"Eli would be too nice to say anything to *you*."

"Whatever, I'll take it."

"Can you imagine how asinine everyone would be if they knew?"

"Oh, I need one thing to be very clear," she said. "They must never know."

That suited him just fine. He wanted for himself and Liss to be able to go back to being best friends when all of this madness was over. And that meant the fewer people who knew, the better. That meant only the two of them could ever know.

"You cannot tell Jack," she said. "He would be the biggest, most obnoxious frat bro about it—"

Connor cut her words off with a kiss, deciding this was as good a moment as any. His heart was raging fast, his hands shaking, his whole body shaking from the inside out. Liss grabbed the front of his shirt, pulling him closer to her, and he pushed forward, letting them go down backward onto the mattress, settling over her body.

This was Liss, his friend. He'd touched her a thousand times, his hands brushing against hers, fingertips meeting as they'd passed things between them, but he had never touched her like this.

"Connor." She sighed, arching against him, parting her thighs and letting him settle between them.

This was Liss. He'd heard her say his name more times than he could count, with a giggle in her voice, in anger, and happiness. But he had never heard her say it like this, thick with pleasure, with need. She wanted something that only he could give her right now, and that feeling, that realization, sent a shock of desire through him so sharp, so intense, it nearly buckled his knees, even though he was already lying down.

This was Liss, and he was damn glad it was.

LISS FRAMED CONNOR'S FACE with her hands, kissing him back, deeply, passionately. Frantically. She couldn't believe this was happening. Could not believe that he wanted this, too. Finally. After so long. After so many years of fantasy, he wanted her, too.

He groaned and shifted, pressing a kiss to her jaw, and her eyes started to sting. She was going to cry. She didn't want to cry. She squeezed her eyes shut tight, fought against the wave of emotion that was swelling inside her.

He pushed his hands beneath her shirt before taking it up over her head. She lifted her arms, helping it go smoothly. Because she really was anxious to get naked with him. They hadn't been naked together yet. The very realization that they were about to sent a shiver through her.

Yes, she had taken him into her mouth, but this was a new level of intimacy. A skin to skin they hadn't shared before.

She pulled his shirt over his head, sliding her hands over his bare back, relishing the feel of his muscle definition beneath her fingertips. "Connor Garrett, I should have gotten you naked a long time ago," she said, moving her hands down his back and cupping his ass.

"I guess we've just been waiting for the right time."

"Timing is a bitch."

"Not right at this second. She's being pretty sweet."

A half smile curved Liss's lips, and she brought her hands around to the front of his belt, undoing the buckle as quickly as possible before shoving his jeans down his lean hips. Now she had him completely naked. Just like she wanted him. And now she needed to be naked, too.

As if he were some kind of mind reader, his hands went to the snap on her jeans, opening it, the brush of his fingers against her stomach so erotic it almost pushed her over the edge then and there.

Then he gripped the tab on the zipper, drawing it down slowly, and she trembled. She had never trembled during sex before. But then, she had never had sex with Connor before.

He hooked his thumbs in the waistband of her jeans, his rough skin abrading her thighs as he drew them down, taking her panties with them.

He leaned back, his eyes intent on her. "Fuck," he said.

"Your vocabulary has become very limited recently," she said, her voice breathless.

"I blame you." He leaned in, pressing a kiss to the inside of her knee, moving up to the sensitive skin of her thigh. "Hey, Liss?" he asked.

"What?" she asked, anticipation knotting unbearably in her stomach.

"Remember when we made that rope swing at the creek?" He moved his hand down her thigh, parting her legs a little bit more, leaning in, pressing a kiss a little bit higher.

She did not get why he was stopping to engage in story time. Not now. Not when she was liking so very much where this was going.

"And you were scared, but I told you it would be fun," he continued. "And you said you had never done it before, but I said you just had to take a chance. And you did, and you screamed and screamed. But in the end, you told me you loved it."

Oh, yes, she knew that swing. That summer. And the summer years later when she'd wept her heart out over losing him. She knew that swing well.

"That's a really great story, and it's a nice memory. I do recall. But I'm not sure why you're telling me now."

He kissed her again, higher on her thigh, and she trembled. "For a couple of reasons." He moved his fingertips along her sensitive skin, perilously close to where she was aching for his touch. "I've never done this, but I know I'm going to have fun. And I'm pretty sure, just like when you rode that swing, you're gonna scream."

Liss was pretty sure she was going to spontaneously combust then and there. She may have already done it.

She might be nothing more than a little Liss-shaped pile of ashes. She was trying to process too many things at once. He had never done this before, either; he was going to do it now; he wanted to make her scream…

And then he lowered his head, sliding his tongue over her clit, a low sound rumbling in his chest. And she lost all ability to think entirely. She looked down, the sight of his dark head in between her thighs the most erotic thing she'd ever seen in her life. She was so very aware that it was Connor, that it was her best friend, the man she had always wanted. And what he lacked in experience, he certainly made up for in enthusiasm.

He tasted her with deep, long strokes, holding tightly to her hips, drawing her toward his mouth as he did. He lapped at her like she was ice cream on a hot day, trying desperately to get every last drop before it melted entirely. And she was definitely close to melting.

He teased the entrance to her body with a fingertip before sliding in deep, continuing to lavish pleasure on her with his mouth as he did. Forget enthusiasm, he was just good at this.

He added a second finger, increasing the rhythm of the strokes of his tongue, and everything went bright, like the sun through the trees on a hot summer day. And she was flying. Just like she had on the rope swing. And hell, yes, she screamed. And when she came back to herself, Connor was right there with her, kissing her lips now, his cock hard against her hip. Not only had he been enthusiastic, and very, very good, he had enjoyed it. She could feel the very irrefutable evidence of that.

"Condoms. We need those," he said.

"Yes," she said, barely able to force words to her throat. "Those."

"I… My bathroom?"

"I have no idea," she said, feeling helpless and just plain irritated. If they'd come this far only to be stopped by a lack of contraception, she would have to go ahead and give the universe a serious talking-to.

"They expire, don't they?" he asked, his tone dire.

She groaned. "Yeah, they do."

"Great. I'll just go check that. You don't have any…"

She shook her head, holding back a weird, inappropriate giggle. She didn't know why, as turned on as she was, as concerned as she was about the condoms, as slightly awkward as she felt, she wanted to laugh. "I don't have any. I haven't been with anyone since Marshall. And along with the truck, he took the condoms."

"He took your four-wheel drive and your safe sex? What a bastard."

"In his defense, condoms are pretty cheap. I just haven't needed them."

"Shortsighted." He kissed her, getting up from the bed. "I'll be right back."

Liss lay flat on her back, her arms up above her head, her breathing irregular, her heart thundering fast. She couldn't believe that had happened. She could not believe this was happening.

More than that, she couldn't believe how right it felt. Sure, there was going to be awkwardness later, she knew that. There had been awkwardness every step of the way as they'd started down this road. The aftermath of the kiss had been awkward; the aftermath of the first bit of serious intimacy had been awkward, and this was going to sting in the morning. But all things considered, it was easy to be naked with him. Easier than it had ever been with anyone else.

He returned a moment later, holding a box. He was still naked, and she couldn't stop staring. Could not believe that he was walking across the room as bare as the day he was born right in front of her. After so many years of waiting to see him like this, she felt as if there should be fanfare.

In the absence of fanfare, though, she would just stare.

"They're still good. Not for much longer, but they are still good," he said.

"I'm very encouraged by this."

"Because my only other option was going to ask Eli, or driving to town."

"You would not have gone to ask Eli."

"I would've had to send you. It would've been less shocking, and you could've pretended you had someone else here," he said.

"You cannot send the girl to get condoms. I'm pretty sure that's some kind of Round Table, King Arthur's knights, courtly love shit."

"If it had been a serious emergency, I would've had to send you." He pulled a plastic packet out of the box. "Fortunately, we are covered."

"Well, you aren't. Yet." She sat up, scooting to the edge of the bed and holding out her hand.

"You want the honors?" he asked, one eyebrow raised in a very Connor sort of expression.

"Any excuse to get my hands on you." He closed his eyes and let his head fall back, and she snatched the condom from his hand. "I haven't even touched you yet tonight," she said, looking at the pained expression on his face.

"It just feels so good that you want to," he said.

Her heart crumpled a little bit. "You know how much I want peanut butter and chocolate. Like all the time."

"Yes," he said, his eyes locked with hers.

"I want this more. I want you more." She tore open the packet and positioned the protection over the head of him, rolling it down his hard length, her breath hissing through her teeth as arousal tore through her. "Seriously, I would give up Reese's peanut butter cups forever to have this."

He growled, and suddenly she found herself flat on her back, and Connor was kissing her as though it was more important than his next breath. She laced her fingers through his hair, and he grabbed a hold of her wrists with one hand, holding them together and lifting them above her head as he deepened the kiss.

She gasped as he settled between her thighs, the blunt head of his erection probing the soft entrance to her body. And suddenly she just wanted to stop everything, to stop time so that she could be here for a moment longer. About to experience the one thing she had fantasized about more than anything else. Being with Connor. Actually being with him. Having him inside her.

She was going to know what it was like in just a few seconds. Have every question answered about him. What it was like to feel him inside her. And she just didn't feel prepared. She almost felt terrified.

But she wasn't going to stop him, wasn't going to stop this.

She arched her back, her breasts pressing against his chest as he pushed deeper inside her. Buried himself to the hilt. She kept her eyes locked with his, kept the connection between them. He flexed his hips, retreating slightly before thrusting hard into her, closing his eyes. And she got lost in the rhythm, in the moment, in him. She watched his face as he moved inside her then looked over and saw his forearm, his muscles straining as he held her wrists above her head still, his tattoo rippling and flexing with each movement.

The tattoo. The tattoo she had been dying to touch. And he was holding her hands so she still couldn't.

She angled her head, parted her lips and traced one of the vines etched there in dark ink with the tip of her tongue. He shivered, a harsh sound escaping his lips.

"Liss," he said, "you have to be careful."

"I don't want to be careful. I want it all."

Still holding her wrists tight with one hand, he put his other hand beneath her ass and lifted her up, increasing the momentum behind his movements. She arched against him, meeting his every thrust. Pleasure bloomed low, intense, in her stomach. She was not a multiorgasmic girl, at least not usually. But she had a feeling she was going to be tonight.

The back of her hands hit the headboard, the intensity of Connor's movements pushing them both back against the hard wooden surface, the brass detailing biting into her knuckles, her hair catching beneath one of the edges and tugging a bit. But she didn't care. She didn't care about anything but the driving need to find her release.

He thrust deep, rolling his hips, and she braced her hand on his chest, felt his heart hammering beneath her touch. She opened her eyes and looked at him, at his expression, his eyes squeezed shut, his jaw clenched tight. Connor. Her Connor. Lost in her.

She looked away, shutting her eyes. Unable to deal with the intensity of looking at him. And he pushed into her one last time. Pleasure exploded behind her eyelids, and she felt as if she was lying down outside on a sunny day again, flashes of light popping through the trees, leaving bright-colored spots in her vision.

He lowered his head, his forehead pressed against hers, his lips just a whisper away. And then his big, muscular frame shook, a deep, low sound reverberating in his chest as he froze, his cock pulsing inside her as he found his own release.

He rolled away from her, lying on his back. She felt cold, freezing, with the warmth of his body removed from hers. But she didn't know what she should do next. Didn't know if it was okay for her to hold on to him like he was a lover. If she should talk to him like he was a friend. Because they had agreed on sex, sex to help them get over his hang-ups, and she didn't think cuddling was included in that kind of therapy. Of course, it wasn't like there was a handbook.

There should be a handbook. Maybe after this she would write one. *How To Have Sex With Your Best Friend Without Losing Your Mind.* At least, she hoped that after this she would be qualified to write that book. If not, it would mean she had lost her mind, and possibly her friend.

But no, she wouldn't think that.

"I'll be right back," he said, getting off the bed and walking out of her room, leaving her there by herself.

She debated the wisdom of scrambling to get her clothes on and going after him. But he had said he would be back. The last thing he wanted was her getting all clingy on him. The last thing *she* wanted was her getting all clingy on him.

But she felt clingy.

She gritted her teeth and rolled onto her stomach, burying her face in her pillow, fighting back the tears that were starting to build behind her eyelids. This was supposed to be about dealing with Connor lust; this was not supposed to be about feelings.

She didn't want to have feelings for him. She had done her best to let go of those over the years. He had married one of her best friends. He remained one of her best friends. And those things are far too valuable to mess up.

They still were.

Just when she was starting to think that he was not coming back, he walked back through the door and crossed the room quickly, getting back into bed. She almost sighed with relief when he climbed in beside her.

"I just realized I didn't ask if I could sleep with you," he said.

"You can," she said, her throat tightening, her chest aching.

"I might just stay for a while," he said.

She nodded wordlessly, knowing that he probably couldn't see the gesture. He didn't speak, and neither did she, not for a long time. They didn't hold each other; they simply lay next to each other, naked, in bed together, an intimacy that they had never shared before.

Finally, she turned over onto her side so that she was facing him. She stared through the thin darkness, broken up by the full moon outside, at his profile, at his arm, which was raised up over his head. At his tattoo. She'd touched it now. A very specific fantasy now fulfilled. She hadn't just touched it; she'd licked it. Because hellfire and brimstone, that man made her want things that went way past logical. Way past civilized.

But it hadn't satisfied everything. No, she still wanted more. Needed more.

She imagined that would always be the case.

She lay there for a moment, her heart still thundering hard. And then she decided to go ahead and push. She had never asked him about the tattoo. Because it felt like a bridge too far. But here and now, with all of their skin out in the open, it seemed like maybe some other things could come out in the open, too. "What does your tattoo mean?"

There was nothing but silence for a moment. "It's a pretty shitty story," he said, his tone strained.

"Yeah, I had a feeling."

"And that's what you want to talk about right now?"

"It's either that or the weather. Or we talk about how amazing the sex was."

"I'm okay with talking about how amazing the sex was," he said.

Her face got hot, and she felt silly. Stupid. Like some inexperienced girl instead of a woman in her thirties. What was it about Connor that made her feel that way? How did a man she knew better than anyone else on earth make things feel so new and scary? It didn't make sense.

"Was it amazing?" She cleared her throat. "I mean, for you. Obviously, for me it was amazing."

"Do you really have to ask?"

"I'm asking. So obviously I had to."

"Yes, it was amazing. But that kind of feels like a stupid thing to say. Like it's not enough. I don't know what to say about it."

"That's not stupid. It makes me feel good."

"I think I can do better, though. It's like…like you woke part of me up again. Like I'm waking up."

"I'm glad."

Silence settled between them.

"Jessie really liked her flowers. She always did," he said, his voice rough.

She swallowed hard, her stomach clamping down tight. It was strange to hear him talk about his wife when they were in bed together. To hear him talk about the friend she never would have betrayed this way, if she'd lived.

"I know she did." It was all Liss could think to say.

"A few weeks before the accident she went out of town for a few days to visit her parents. She told me to make sure that I watered her roses. I said I would, but then I didn't think about it again, because it didn't have anything to do with the ranch, and they weren't necessary, at least not to my mind. So I went about my business, and when she came back, they were dead. She was furious. She said I never listened when things were important to her. That I didn't take her seriously. That I didn't care about her. And none of that was true, but…I was so wrapped up in the ranch. I just didn't think. It wasn't just the roses. They were just one thing. One in a long line of mistakes I made that showed I thought a lot more about this place than I thought about her."

"That's not true, Connor," she said. "You loved her."

"I did. I do. But sometimes I didn't show it." He paused. "I was going to change. I was going to do better. For her. For us. And she died." He lowered his arm, held it in front of him, tracing the intricate lines in blossoms etched into his skin. "These are Jessie's roses," he said, his voice strangled. "I got this because this way, I haven't let her roses die."

CHAPTER ELEVEN

CONNOR HAD NO IDEA how he had gone from the throes of the most intense sexual release of his life to confiding his most intense regret and shame. And all with the same person.

On the bright side, the general confusion was working to defuse the horror, fear and realization that now he had seen his best friend's tits, he would never be able to unsee them, that he had no doubt would rear their ugly heads soon enough. Like a giant Hydra made of awful and awkward. There was no fighting that thing. Every time he cut off one of the heads, the fact that he had seen Liss naked would grow back ever larger.

You have to get a grip. Because if you don't, you're going to fuck up the most meaningful relationship you have.

Which was really par for the course with him. His tattoo was a reminder of that. And now Liss knew it.

So at least she wouldn't be surprised when he handled all of this less than gracefully. Not that she would've been, anyway. They had known each other for too long for her to expect him to start spouting poetry right now.

"I don't know what to say," Liss said, her voice muffled.

"I have a knack for killing conversation. Earlier tonight was kind of exhibit A."

"That was Jack's fault."

"No, it wasn't. I don't expect everybody to think of my tragic backstory every time they open their mouths around me. Actually, I would prefer if they didn't, so pulling crap like I did earlier runs counter to my objective."

"We all have a tendency to be our own worst enemies."

"Oh, I'm well aware of that." He had a feeling he had become his own nemesis tonight. And yet he was having a difficult time regretting it.

He sucked in a sharp breath, his ab muscles tightening as Liss placed her fingertips on his forearm, slowly tracing the outline of one of the roses that was inked into his skin. "She knew. She knew how much you loved her."

"I don't think she did," he said. "No, I know she didn't. Because I didn't know. Marriage is… It's long. I didn't fully appreciate that before I actually got married. But I don't know that anyone does. And at first it feels hard. The newness wears off, and then you're just living with this person who's around all the time. Eventually it gets easier. You settle into a routine. But at some point you settle in so deep you can go for days living in the same house, sleeping in the same bed, hardly saying a word to each other. It gets comfortable. That's one of the beautiful things about marriage. But it's one of the dangerous things, too." He took a deep breath, trying to ease the tension in his chest. He never talked about this stuff. He didn't really like thinking about it at all. But they were already talking about his tattoo, so they might as well just have the talk and get it over with.

There wasn't really anything about tonight that could

carry over into tomorrow morning. That made it a safe space. And he was going to take advantage of that.

"It's weird. I swear to God, Liss, I could go a whole day without thinking very much about her when she lived here. I didn't feel her presence. I was so damned used to it. But I felt it when she was gone. I had no idea emptiness was so fucking heavy. How can it be when it's nothing? But it is."

"That's life, though, Connor. We take things for granted. Because we can't always have perspective."

"Yeah, well, why the hell not? It doesn't absolve me, just because other people do it, too. Doesn't fix anything."

"Neither does guilt."

"Oh, thanks. I guess I'll just be done with that, then."

"Stop it," she said, her voice faintly chastising, her fingers still moving over his skin. This new intimacy was a strange thing. They had never been into casual touching. And now they were lying next to each other, completely naked. But more notable was the fact that she was just touching his forearm because she could. Because a line that had been drawn between them for years had been suddenly erased. "I'm trying to help."

"I know."

"So don't be such a grumpy bastard."

He rolled onto his side, and the motion shook her hand from his forearm. He could see her skin clearly thanks to the pale moonlight filtering through the window. Could make out the outline of her nipples, see the dark shadow at the apex of her thighs. And it occurred to him then that he was in bed with his best friend, only the second woman to ever touch his body, only the second woman he'd ever been inside, and he was talking about his wife.

That feeling of being out of time, of being in a safe zone, vanished as a wave of reality washed over him.

With that revelation came the feeling of being something more than naked. As though he hadn't just removed his clothes, but peeled back his skin, as well, exposing the contents of his chest. As though everything had been dragged out into the open. His guts, and not a whole lot of glory.

He pushed himself into a sitting position and swung his legs over the side of the bed.

"Connor?"

"I need to go to bed," he said, standing.

"You can stay in here."

No, he couldn't. That was nonnegotiable. But he didn't say that; he didn't say anything. He didn't even stop to collect his clothes. He just walked toward the bedroom door and wrenched it open, stumbling out into the hall. He paused for a second, hoping that Liss wouldn't come after him. She didn't.

Which, he supposed, was the benefit of conducting your ill-advised sexual encounter with someone who knew you so well.

Something in his chest twisted hard and tugged down, just about dropping him to his knees.

This had gone beyond what he felt ready to deal with. At least it had gone past what he felt ready to deal with while sober.

He went down the hall and down the stairs, not caring that he still wasn't dressed. The only person who was here to see it had already seen it. Because he had gone and made one of the worst decisions he could've possibly made.

This was the wrong time to have that revelation. After he'd already done it.

Now that his dick had gone to sleep, his brain was back in action. And his brain knew that he was a dumb ass.

He walked through the living room and into the kitchen, opening up the cupboard and taking out his bottle of Jack Daniel's. Then he opened up the cupboard next to it and took out a glass.

He bent down, bracing himself on the counter, one hand in front of the glass, the other in front of the bottle, as he stared at both. His heart was hammering hard, his stomach so tight he could barely breathe.

He didn't feel as though he'd betrayed Jessie. Because she was dead, and he wasn't stupid. That was when your marriage vows ended, after all. But he did feel as if he betrayed Liss.

More than that, he felt as if he'd jumped into the river with both feet without bothering to learn to swim first.

His chest was crowded with emotions. Worry slithering around in his brain like a pissed-off rattlesnake. And much like dealing with a rattlesnake, reaching in to try to manage that mess would probably be fatal.

He straightened and took the cap off the bottle.

He knew this wouldn't solve his problems. It never did. It gave him oblivion, and the next day gave him a headache, but it didn't solve his problems. Not permanently. All it did was provide a nice little window of time where he could forget he had any.

He wrapped his fingers around the bottle, squeezed it tight. Then he picked it up and poured a generous amount into the glass, putting it back down and screwing the lid back on, shoving it back against the wall.

If he didn't drink, then everything would just keep growing. The feelings in his chest would just keep expanding until he exploded, his thoughts turning around until they drove him nuts.

And who was he going to talk to about it? Eli? Certainly not Liss. Not now. Not now that she was a part of the torrential wave of crap he was dealing with.

It isn't like you ever talk to her about it, anyway.

He ignored his voice of reason and picked up the glass, raising it to his lips. He tipped it back, the amber liquid touching his lips, the promise of sleep and peace so close he could taste it. And it tasted like damn good whiskey.

Completely without his permission, an image of Liss's face swam in front of his vision. And in that image she was looking at him with wide, sad eyes.

"Well, this is your fault, anyway," he said, knowing she couldn't hear him.

Unsurprisingly, she didn't answer him. But he could still see her in his mind. Those big golden eyes begging him not to drink anymore...for her.

And then with a growl, he slammed the glass back down on the counter. He braced his palms flat on the granite, leaning forward, lowering his head. Yeah, the last thing he needed was Liss finding him hungover in the morning and blaming herself. Because she would. Because she was like that.

But the alternative was spending the night sober.

Considering he had just screwed his best friend and abandoned her, naked and in bed, he imagined he deserved whatever penance there was to be paid.

He swore and tipped the contents of the glass over into the sink. Immediately regretting that piece of dumb-assery. He could've at least saved it for later. But apparently, he wasn't thinking clearly tonight.

If he ever was. If he ever had.

He tightened his fingers over the rim of the glass, lifting it from the counter. He turned toward the cabinet then suddenly decided against putting it away. Because everything was stupid. And his entire life was a mess. So why even bother to keep the kitchen clean?

Instead, he released his hold on it and let it crash to the hardwood floor, sending a spray of glass across the pine surface.

He would deal with that in the morning. Right now he couldn't give a rat's ass.

He walked across the kitchen, stepping on remnants of the glass, knowing he would regret that in the morning, too. Right now, though, he didn't care. Mainly because he knew he would have a whole host of regrets in the morning, and all of them bigger than a few pieces of glass in his feet.

He walked up the stairs, taking a quick look at Liss's room, and noticed that the door was firmly shut now. For the best. He continued on into his bedroom and slammed the door behind him, lying facedown on the bed, not bothering to get dressed.

His head was already starting to pound, which just seemed like adding insult to injury, since he had skipped the alcohol.

He closed his eyes tight and spent the rest of the night in that uncomfortable space between gritty-eyed exhaustion and unconsciousness. Peppered with images of his brother standing on the front porch, a ring of light

YOUR PARTICIPATION IS REQUESTED!

Dear Reader,

Since you are a lover of our books – we would like to get to know you!

Inside you will find a short Reader's Survey. Sharing your answers with us will help our editorial staff understand who you are and what activities you enjoy.

To thank you for your participation, we would like to send you 2 books and 2 gifts – **ABSOLUTELY FREE!**

Enjoy your gifts with our appreciation,

Pam Powers

SEE INSIDE FOR READER'S SURVEY

For Your Reading Pleasure...

#1 NEW YORK TIMES BESTSELLING AUTHOR

DEBBIE MACOMBER

"Macomber can be depended on for an excellent story."
—RT BOOK REVIEWS

The Reluctant

#1 NEW YORK TIMES BESTSELLING AUTHOR

SHERRYL WOODS

DOGWOOD HILL

A CHESAPEAKE SHORES NOVEL

FREE!

We'll send you 2 books and 2 gifts
ABSOLUTELY FREE
just for completing our Reader's Survey!

YOUR READER'S SURVEY
"THANK YOU" FREE GIFTS INCLUDE:
- ▶ 2 FREE books
- ▶ 2 lovely surprise gifts

PLEASE FILL IN THE CIRCLES COMPLETELY TO RESPOND

1) What type of fiction books do you enjoy reading? (Check all that apply)
- ○ Suspense/Thrillers
- ○ Action/Adventure
- ○ Modern-day Romances
- ○ Historical Romance
- ○ Humour
- ○ Paranormal Romance

2) What attracted you most to the last fiction book you purchased on impulse?
- ○ The Title
- ○ The Cover
- ○ The Author
- ○ The Story

3) What is usually the greatest influencer when you <u>plan</u> to buy a book?
- ○ Advertising
- ○ Referral
- ○ Book Review

4) How often do you access the internet?
- ○ Daily
- ○ Weekly
- ○ Monthly
- ○ Rarely or never.

5) How many NEW paperback fiction novels have you purchased in the past 3 months?
- ○ 0 - 2
- ○ 3 - 6
- ○ 7 or more

YES! I have completed the Reader's Survey. Please send me the 2 FREE books and 2 FREE gifts (gifts are worth about \$10) for which I qualify. I understand that I am under no obligation to purchase any books, as explained on the back of this card.

194/394 MDL GH6X

FIRST NAME	LAST NAME

ADDRESS

APT.#	CITY

STATE/PROV.	ZIP/POSTAL CODE

◄ If offer card is missing write to: Harlequin Reader Service, P.O. Box 1867, Buffalo, NY 14240-1867 or visit www.ReaderService.com ◄

BUSINESS REPLY MAIL

FIRST-CLASS MAIL   PERMIT NO. 717   BUFFALO, NY

POSTAGE WILL BE PAID BY ADDRESSEE

HARLEQUIN READER SERVICE

PO BOX 1867

BUFFALO NY 14240-9952

NO POSTAGE
NECESSARY
IF MAILED
IN THE
UNITED STATES

all around him, his expression grim. And interspersed with that was the image of Liss, her breasts bare, her name on his lips like a prayer.

LISS SAT AT the kitchen table, her eyes feeling like they'd been rubbed with sandpaper, her hands wrapped around a hot cup of coffee. She was simultaneously terrified and praying with intensity that Connor would show up and they would be forced to interact.

She took a deep breath, her chest aching as she did. She drummed her fingers on the mug, fighting back a feeling of misery and some tears.

Huh. She hadn't really imagined that the culmination of a decade and a half of fantasies would end in her having the sensation of being dipped into a vat of feelings and wrung out to dry. No, when she had imagined all this going down, she had focused decidedly on the physical aspect of it.

Right now she wished that she could recapture the simple buzz that had come with the physical side of what had happened. Because right now? Right now it was all feelings. Damn, miserable feelings.

She wanted to see him, to try to gauge whether or not they were okay, or if things were terminally weird. She also wanted to avoid him for the rest of her life. Possibly move to Bulgaria, change her name and work in an apple orchard.

Those two very strong desires warred with equal force inside her. But since she didn't have a passport she figured hanging out and trying to face this thing head-on was probably her best bet. Anyway, Felicity Foster was many things, but a coward wasn't one of them.

She heard the front door open behind her then footsteps on the threshold, and she jerked her arms backward, sloshing coffee over the edge of her mug.

She rolled her eyes at herself and got up from her seat, making her way over to the paper towels, which had been refreshed since she had moved in. She pulled one off the roll, getting ready to turn around and face both the coffee spill and Connor.

But when she turned she came face-to-face with the only person it could possibly be more horrifying to see right now than the man whose brains she had thoroughly screwed out the night before. His little sister.

"Good morning," Kate said, walking into the kitchen.

"Good morning," Liss responded, moving back to the table and awkwardly dabbing at the spill. "What brings you by?"

"I have the day off at the Farm and Garden, so I figured I would come grab a coffee and maybe see if Connor needed any help today."

"Oh, well, I haven't seen him this morning," Liss said, her face heating. She had the distinct feeling that she was telegraphing all of her memories from last night straight into Kate's brain. All of her X-rated memories. The horror of that did not even bear pondering.

"That's okay. He was doing something with the fencing today, right?"

"I'm not sure," she said, feeling really uncomfortable and a little bit as if she was getting the third degree. It made her feel like a kid with her hand caught in the cookie jar. Or a teenager caught with condoms in her purse.

"Just wondering. Jack usually comes by to help with things like that."

And suddenly Liss felt relieved, because she realized

that the line of questioning had nothing to do with her and Connor. "Were you hoping to see him?"

Kate's expression went through several different incarnations. Shock, embarrassment and finally disgust. "No, not especially. I was just curious."

Liss had a feeling Kate was a little more than curious, and she could think of nothing worse besides her own current situation than dear sweet Kate having a crush on the much older, much more experienced Jack. "Right. Idle curiosity about the whereabouts of Connor's dear friend." She was pushing, mainly because it was better than focusing on her own issues.

And as diversionary tactics went, it wasn't a bad one.

"Idle curiosity about the amount of help Connor was receiving on a project," Kate said, her tone measured.

Kate certainly didn't look as though she was out trying to impress a guy. She was dressed in her typical daily wear of extremely untrendy work jeans, a shapeless T-shirt tucked into the waistband and a belt with a silver buckle. Her dark hair was restrained in a braid, a cowgirl hat firmly in place on her head. As far as Liss knew, Kate did not own makeup of any kind, and she had never seen evidence to the contrary.

Still, she wondered.

"Well, I'm very sorry that I can't answer the question. Because I haven't seen Connor, Eli or Jack today. I have seen coffee, and that's about it."

"I would like to see some coffee," Kate said, obviously letting her subtle Jack accusations go.

"Feel free," she said, smiling back.

Kate was like a little sister to her, which meant she felt at liberty to give her some grief.

Up until recently, she would have lied and said that

Connor was like a brother to her. She would've been very aware of the fact that it was a lie, but she would have tried it all the same. But *now* she wouldn't even be able to pretend. Because now it would be creepy.

She heard the front door open again, and this time it was Connor who came walking into the kitchen, freezing when he saw both her and Kate standing there.

Great, the only thing that could be more awkward than Connor walking in earlier was Connor encountering her for the first time in the broad light of day with Kate there.

"Good morning," he mumbled, crossing the kitchen and heading toward the coffeemaker.

"Morning," she and Kate said in unison.

"Are you doing the fence today?" Kate asked.

"Yep," Connor said, bypassing Kate and grabbing a mug, taking the carafe from the coffeemaker before Kate could and pouring himself a cup.

"Do you need help?"

"I could always use an extra pair of hands," he said.

"Great," Kate said. "I'm happy to do it in exchange for coffee."

"After I have some." He finished pouring his cup and walked back to the table, his expression contorting when he put weight on one of his feet.

"Are you okay?" Liss asked.

Connor gave her a measured look. "I'm fine."

"Why are you limping?" Kate asked.

Connor shot her a deadly glare. "I stepped on a nail. Luckily, my tetanus is up-to-date."

Liss frowned. "Are you okay?"

"I already said I was," he answered, clearly in a vile temper.

"Great." Fine for him to be in a mood. He was the one who had stormed out last night after they'd had sex. He was the reason she felt so teary this morning. He had no right to be grumpy. She was grumpy.

The stupid thing was, it wasn't even surprising that he had done that. It was a classic Connor move. He was not the kind of guy who talked about his feelings, and yet last night he had started talking about them. Logically, she knew he was hardly going to cuddle with her after doing something that made him feel so exposed, so uncomfortable.

But dammit, whether she understood or not, it still hurt.

"Yeah, Connor," Kate said, "you seem totally fine. Like always. By which I mean you seem like a jackass."

Connor gave Kate a look that could only be categorized as deadly, but Kate didn't seem to notice. She was busy getting her coffee, and probably thinking she was just dealing with normal everyday grumpy Connor. Liss knew differently. Liss knew that Kate was treading on dangerous ground. However, jumping in to save Kate might put her in the line of fire, and she wasn't sure if she wanted to do that or not.

Mercenary, perhaps. But she wasn't all that concerned about it at the moment.

"Watch it," Connor said.

Kate crossed her arms, her expression fierce. "Or maybe you lighten up and stop acting so much like a guy who just peed into a live electric fence."

"Stay out of this, Katie."

"Don't. Call me that." Kate's eyes were glittering fiercely now.

"Stop being such a baby and get out there and fix my fence."

"First of all, I own one-third of that fence, you raging asshole. Second of all, I don't have to be here helping you. It's my day off," Kate said, her cheeks flushed red. "And third of all." She held up her middle finger and said nothing else.

"Go home, then," he said.

Kate scrunched up her face, took a sip of coffee and set it down on the table with a mighty thump. "No. See you out at the fence line." She turned on her heel and stormed out of the kitchen.

All things considered, Liss was not surprised that she had still opted in to fence work. And if she was right about Kate's Jack feelings, all she could do was feel sorry for her. Because she knew all about harboring feelings for someone who would never return them.

Though in Kate's case, it was for the best if Jack never looked twice at her. Because as bad bets went, he was like going all in on a pair of twos.

Of course, Connor was a close second. So she supposed she should probably work on her own issues, rather than focusing on someone else's. But it was a lot more fun, and less crazy making, to focus on someone else's.

"What was her problem?" he asked.

"You. You were her problem," Liss said.

Connor grunted. "She shouldn't be this annoying this early."

"And maybe you shouldn't treat her like she's fifteen. But that's a different conversation."

"Is it a different conversation? We could have it now."

"You mean instead of the one we should have?"

Connor looked up from his coffee, his expression baleful. "Pretty much."

"How long do you think we can avoid it?"

"I'd give it another ten minutes. For the caffeine to hit my system."

"What happened to your foot?"

"I told you I stepped on a rusty nail."

"And for some reason I don't believe you." She didn't know why; she only knew she didn't.

"Fine. I broke a glass. And I stepped on the broken glass."

Liss frowned, a growing feeling of unease rolling over her like fog. "How did you manage that?"

"Not pouring myself a drink last night. Okay, well, I did pour myself one. But then I dumped it out. I didn't drink it."

Suddenly, Liss's eyes felt prickly. "Well, that's good."

"Right. Glad you think so."

"You don't?"

"I don't know. Progress, I guess. But you know, I slept like hell. Alcohol probably would've helped."

"Staying with me might have helped, too." She shouldn't have said that. It sounded needy, which was fair, because she felt needy, but she should have played it a little bit more cool.

"Couldn't," he said, lifting his mug to his lips and taking a sip.

Really, she should not expect more out of Connor than one-word answers. But unfortunately, she wanted more out of him than that. Because it was one thing to accept being shut out of his emotional storage locker as a friend. But as a lover?

Yeah, but are you really his lover?

Good question. Maybe one night of sex didn't make her a lover. Really, it wasn't fair for her to want things to change in some ways, when she desperately wanted to believe that one night of sex wouldn't change other things. She imagined it wasn't something you could cherry-pick. Which just sucked. She wanted to cherry-pick, dammit.

She wanted a customizable menu of options with boxes she could check. Access to his finer feelings? Check. Awkward self-consciousness? No. A solid, unshakable friendship? Check. Crippling loneliness and despair? No.

Consequence-free orgasms on tap? She would double check that.

She had a feeling, however, she would not be getting any of those things. Except the things she didn't want. Those she would probably get. Because life was a superhelpful bitch like that.

"Right," she said. "Probably should've just grabbed your penis again instead of trying to talk about feelings."

Connor sputtered, coffee sloshing over the edge of his mug. "What the hell, Liss? You can't just say stuff like that."

"Now is not really the time to get precious. The horse has left the barn, run across the pasture and trampled the daisies. If you go after him now, he'll just get spooked and kick you in the head."

"Come to think of it, I do feel a little bit like I've been kicked in the head by a horse. Which just reinforces my theory that I probably should have just gotten drunk last night."

"Instead of having sex with me?" She was just digging herself in deeper and deeper.

"I meant…after the sex. Probably, though, your idea is better, and I should have just gotten drunk before we had sex instead of having sex, because then we wouldn't be having this discussion now."

"Wow. You're really good for my self-esteem."

"Come on, Liss." He sighed, a heavy, defeated sound. "I needed last night. I'm not going to lie to you. But I have no idea what it gave to you. And there's really nothing…beyond what happened that I can offer to make it more for you."

"Who said I needed more? I think it's pretty obvious what I got out of it. The same thing you did."

"I don't…"

"I did not have sex with you under sufferance, Connor. I wanted to. I liked it. I got orgasms, and really good oral sex and skin-to-skin contact out of it. And you're not sure why I enjoyed it?"

"Well, it's just that you're a woman…"

"Whoa. Put that truck in reverse, cowboy."

"I'm worried about your emotions."

She let out a sharp, one-note laugh. "Oh, my emotions! I forgot about those somewhere around the time I was screaming your name."

"Not just your emotions. I'm worried about our friendship. But I feel like a massive jerk seeing as I'm basically using you for therapy."

"I thought I agreed to that."

He dragged his hand over his face and let out another long, drawn-out sigh. "You did. But that doesn't make me feel any better about it."

"After the fact. Which is very convenient."

"Nothing about this is convenient," he said, shouting now.

Well, this was going worse than she had imagined it might. Which was really saying something, because her imagination was not overly optimistic. "Good. I don't want to be convenient sex."

"Congratulations. You aren't. You're the most inconvenient sex I have ever had."

"What, you are... You are just...the most postorgasmically grumpy human being on the face of the planet. Being this unpleasant after getting some that was *that* good is a real commitment to being an asshat."

"I'm good with commitments. Long commitments. Marriage. Being a jackass. It's kind of my wheelhouse."

"Oh, go build your barn."

"I'm working on the fence today. The crew is coming by later to deal with the barn."

"Whatever. Just get out of here. I'm trying to drink my coffee, and you are ruining it."

"This is my kitchen."

"For the time being it is our kitchen. I live here, too."

"If you want equal share, you need to pay at least half of the mortgage," he said.

"Well, no, thank you."

"Somehow, I thought that would be a deterrent. I think I'll stay in my kitchen for a while, all things considered."

She picked up her coffee mug and raised it in salute. "You do that."

"I did a lot of thinking last night. Sometime after I stepped on the glass and before I got up this morning. And then a little bit more thinking when I walked on cut feet out to the barn."

"And?"

He took a deep breath, his dark eyes meeting hers. "We can't do that again."

Her stomach withered and sank into her toes like a dried-out leaf falling from a tree. "Oh?"

"I've lost too much. And you know, the reasons we did it still stand. You were right. I was building it up to be something huge in my head. It was like a mental block. And now I've pushed past it."

"So…you pushed past your mental block…with the help of my vagina?"

"Dammit, Liss. I'm trying to be sincere."

"I'm just trying to figure out what exactly is happening between us."

"Nothing. Nothing new."

"So you can just forget? You can just pretend that you never saw me naked? You can just pretend that you never…you know, all those things you did? Everything we did?"

"I'm not going to forget. I won't forget. But I still think we need to draw a line under it and call it done," he said, his tone firm, authoritative.

She wasn't used to him being like this. Decisive, commanding. It was hot. Which was completely inconvenient, since he was currently telling her that they were not going to do the sex thing anymore. Which meant his being more of a turn-on was not okay.

"I…" And she realized she was standing in the man's kitchen, barefoot and wearing pj's, about to beg him for more sex. She had never felt sorrier for herself. And that included when she had returned her prom dress. And also the moment she had found out that the man she had lived with, supported, made lackluster love to for years, had stolen her identity then gotten the hell out of Dodge.

Yes, realizing that you were on the cusp of begging your best friend for more sex while wearing sheep-festooned flannel pants was a new low.

"What, Liss?"

"I think you're right." Even though she didn't.

"About?"

"If this is the end result of what happened last night, we're not doing it again. Whatever has been happening the past couple of days...I just think it accomplished what we needed it to. I was...well, not back in the game after Marshall. And obviously you weren't. And now we kind of broke the wall down, like you said, before I got all gross." She took a deep breath, trying to keep her voice from shaking, trying to keep from crying. Weird that she felt like crying. Weird that this felt like the end of something. But it wasn't really anything. Their friendship, all eighteen years of it, that was something to protect. One night of sex should hardly show up on the radar.

They were getting back on track. They were putting things back the way they should be.

It wasn't really a change. And it shouldn't be sad.

"I'm glad we're on the same page." He looked slightly shocked, as though he had not expected her to agree quite so quickly.

"The same side of the bed, so to speak." She didn't know why she was trying to make the conversation more awkward. Apparently, it was her natural instinct. No wonder she'd been single for two years.

"Or in agreement, in different bedrooms. Since that is what we are agreeing on."

She took a deep breath. "Connor, I'm sorry if I added confusion to what I know has been a seriously effed up few months."

"Months? Try years."

"Sure. But I want to help you. And you can't keep going the way you have been."

"I know. And now I've changed some things. Had sex. Started building a barn."

"Nice to know I'm on par with barn building." She winced. "Sorry, I should probably stop mentioning the thing that we did that we aren't going to do again."

"Like I said, I'm not going to forget that it happened. I don't think there's any point in pretending it didn't happen. Unless we're in front of the others."

A shiver of horror wound through her. "They must never know."

"Never."

That, she could agree to with no reservation at all.

"I had better go get to work."

"Yeah, probably. I imagine Kate is out there ordering Eli and Jack around like she's the foreman."

Connor rolled his eyes. "Likely."

She waved a hand. "Intervene."

He looked at her hard, too hard for her liking, because she had a feeling he was seeing a layer or two deeper than skin. Down to all of her vulnerabilities and bare, fragile emotions. "Are you going to be okay?"

She forced a smile, fully aware that it stopped well short of her eyes. "I'll be fine. I need to reorient is all."

"Yeah, well…last night was…intense."

"And we don't usually do intense," Liss said, rocking back on her heels.

"No. And I haven't done intense at all in a while. I

think I maxed myself out and…shut down. Kind of…
hibernation or something. But yeah, less of that now."
He offered her a smile in exchange for hers. Just as
manufactured and superficial as the one she'd given
him.

She tried to feel happy for him. That last night had
been some sort of transcendent experience as far as he
was concerned. Therapy by orgasm. But it was hard
when she was feeling so damn sad for herself.

Last night was less transcendent for her and more a
weird, very final confirmation of the fact that she was
destined to forever feel more and different for Connor
than he did for her.

She wasn't sure what she felt for him, but it was
somewhere past simple friendship. Not like either of
the romantic relationships she'd had in the past, either,
but then, that wasn't too surprising.

Over the past three years she'd been helping him glue
his life back together, making sure he was functional,
getting his groceries, that she'd stepped into a different
role in his life than the one she'd grown up in.

She'd become more like a wife without the benefits.

And without the love.

That thought had a sharp point on it, and it stabbed
straight through her skull and down into her chest, hitting her heart.

She did her best to ignore it. To make eye contact
with Connor and to try not to look as though she was
having some sort of emotional meltdown.

"Great," she said. She could feel the inadequacy of
the word as it hit the air and went flat. But she couldn't
find it in her to add to it. To try to dig deeper and say
something encouraging when she frankly felt like shit

and wanted to crawl beneath a fuzzy blanket for the rest of the day and hide.

As it was her day off, she could if she wanted to. And she just might. She needed to watch *Sense and Sensibility*. And maybe find out if Alan Rickman wanted to come and marry her to rescue her from her wayward feelings.

"All right, then. I'll catch you later."

He turned and walked out of the kitchen, and Liss sagged against the wall, unable to prevent an epic whining sound from escaping her lips.

She'd been so caught up in what it would be like to make love with Connor that she hadn't spent nearly enough time imagining what it would be like after she made love with Connor.

Though, even if she had spent time thinking about it, she doubted she could have possibly guessed how horrifying it would really be.

But she was living it now. So she would just have to deal.

But for a while she would be dealing with it from beneath a fuzzy blanket. So for a few hours at least, it might not seem so bad.

CHAPTER TWELVE

CONNOR FELT...RESOLUTE, if not better.

He had made his decision, and he stood by it. By it, behind it, in front of it. Basically, he had a whole fence around the decision so that it couldn't escape and flee off into the wilderness, leaving him with no decisiveness and a hard-on that wouldn't quit.

Because, even though he knew it was the right decision, it wasn't the one he'd wanted to make.

No, the one his body wanted to make was the one that would see him back in bed with Liss, her legs wrapped around his hips as he sank deep inside her.

But that was the wrong choice. So his body didn't get a vote.

He straightened, pushing his hat back and looking around. Eli was leaning against a post, drinking a cup of coffee. Kate was down the fence line with Jack, holding a wire straight while he worked something with a pair of pliers.

It was an overcast day, gray clouds rolling over the caps of the mountains, lowering the sky so that everything felt a little bit more closed in. This kind of weather suited Connor just fine when he was doing heavy labor. The cool, damp air refreshing rather than freezing, since they were out there working their asses off.

Normally, a project like this helped him exhaust his

body until it was numb. Which he usually only needed to help with the loneliness, the sadness and the general soberness he went about his day in until he was able to reach for a little alcohol at the end of the day to help him out.

But he was trying not to drink. And really, sadness and loneliness weren't his issues right now.

It was the fact that his libido was suddenly wide-awake. And hungry.

There was a whole hibernating-bear analogy in there, he was sure of it.

Actually, that applied across the board. Something about dealing with the barn, breaking through the barrier of lust and sex, putting down the bottle and just dealing with things was making him feel a lot more awake in general.

Too bad doing things had consequences. That was one point in favor for lying around being a drunk. The only consequence you had to deal with was the hangover. And what he was dealing with now was a lot more complex. Complex, emotion-type things. And he didn't like that.

But the alternative was essentially sinking into the same kind of pattern his dad had been in. Hell, he'd pretty much been there. And now, with the benefit of it being in hindsight, he could see that. He had been excusing it, since he had been getting the ranch work done. But he hadn't gotten anything else done, and he imagined a sad drunk was a sad drunk as far as family and friends were concerned, whether he did his ranch work or not.

"Everything going okay down there?" Eli asked.

"Fine," Connor said, realizing his answer had come

out somewhere between a grunt and a growl. He was going to have to work on that, too. Since he was working on things. Making decisions, and having normal human interaction and shit. "Almost done." There, the last part of that sounded a little bit friendlier.

"What's on the schedule for the rest of the day?" Eli asked.

"I'll probably see what's going down with the barn. The crew should be by later today. A lot of it is finish work that I can't contribute much to. But I should at least go check it out."

"Do you think it will be done by election night?"

Connor laughed. "Just asking out of idle interest?"

"No, I'm asking out of selfish interest," Eli said, crossing his arms over his chest.

"At least you're honest."

"Hey, it feels like a lot is riding on the election. I mean, if I don't win I still have a job I love, and I still have a position in the community. But I would never have started running if it didn't mean something to me. If I didn't feel like I was the best man for the job."

"You are the best man for the job," Connor said. He had always thought that, but he had never said it. Because sincerity was hard for him; because tapping into any kind of real emotion was hard for him. But Eli deserved to hear it.

Eli offered him a half smile. "Thanks."

"And my offer to paint your face on my chest and direct voters to check the appropriate box stands."

"One too far."

Connor grinned, actually feeling it a little bit. "I have limited skills. But I could do that."

"If we were going to strip anyone down and use sex to sell my campaign, it would be Jack," Eli said.

"I heard my name and sex," Jack said, walking up to where they were standing. "Not too unusual, but I am curious."

"Should I leave?" Kate was standing a little bit behind Jack, barely visible, peering around his shoulder.

"No, we aren't actually going to pimp Jack out for Eli's campaign," Connor said.

"Why not? I would probably do it," Jack said.

"That is probably not the best way for me to start my political career. You have to wait a couple of years to get involved in sex scandals," Eli said.

"If you ever do get involved in a sex scandal, it will probably be somehow related to your association with Jack," Kate said. "And Sadie will have to stand behind you at a press conference looking grave. Maybe it's time to defriend Jack."

"You aren't getting rid of me that easily, Katie," Jack said, turning to face Kate. "I'm what you call a fixture. It would be harder to get me off Garrett land than it would be to uproot a stump."

"I'm pretty handy with a winch and a tractor, Monaghan," Kate said, her expression fierce. "If anyone could uproot your ass, I could."

"But why would you want to?" Jack asked, turning on that charm of his that seemed to get him anywhere and everywhere he wanted to go in life.

"Let me count the ways," Kate said.

"Stop trying to scare my friends off," Connor said. "I have two." Of course, he had done a fairly good job of alienating the other one. But he was trying to fix that. By not undressing her again.

"Maybe choose better friends," she said, her words cut off when Jack put his hand over her face. "Jack!" Her shout was muffled.

"Katie is no longer available for comment," Jack said, smiling broadly.

"If only it were that easy," Connor said.

For the second time that day he earned a one-finger salute from his younger sister. At least this one seemed a little bit more good-natured than the one in the kitchen. So it was possible all was forgiven. Now, if only things with Liss could be smoothed over quite so easily.

Jack hissed and pulled his hand away from Kate's face.

"Dammit, Katie! You bit me."

"You face-palmed me."

"Son of a bitch. You left teeth marks." Jack looked at Connor, and Connor shrugged. In his estimation, any guy who was dumb enough to try to pull shit with Kate had swift retribution coming.

He was protective of Kate, but truth be told, she mainly protected herself.

"Okay," she said brightly, ignoring Jack's evil eye. "We have one more section to finish shoring up. So maybe we should get back to work."

"Who died and made you foreman, Kate?" Eli asked.

"In the absence of adequate leadership, someone has to rise to the occasion," she said, crossing her arms and giving them a smart-ass smile.

"Or, in the absence of leadership, we can skip work and go get a hamburger," Jack said.

"Hamburger after work," Kate said resolutely, turning around and heading back toward the section of the fence she and Jack had been working on earlier.

"I should go help her, or she'll put a rattlesnake in my boots. Or bite my ankle herself," Jack said, turning and following after Kate.

"Do you want to go check out the barn while we let them finish the less desirable work?" Connor asked Eli.

"Absolutely," he said.

A DAY OF HIDING beneath a blanket had not done much to defuse the feelings that were rioting through Liss. She had done nothing but sit in bed wearing woolen socks, drinking warm beverages and watching saccharine movies, and, unsurprisingly, she did not feel better. She felt cozy, but slightly stale, and as twilight settled over the scenery outside, more than a little bit maudlin.

Because her greatest fantasy had come to screaming, sweaty life, and it had been everything she had ever wanted and more from a physical standpoint. But it had left her feeling hollowed out emotionally. Now it was over, never to be repeated. And it just didn't feel like enough.

Actually, that was the world's biggest damn understatement.

It was like the incredible crash that came after Christmas morning. If Christmas only came once in eighteen years and then promised to never come again.

She let out a heavy sigh and flopped backward, one of her throw pillows just under the center of her spine. She contorted her expression, reached underneath herself, grabbed the edge of the pillow and yanked it out, throwing it across the room. Everything was against her and her comfort. She let out a long, drawn-out groan and then rolled over onto her stomach.

She lifted her head slightly, pitifully, and looked

over at her nightstand. There were four mugs on it. Representing the progression of the day. One that had contained coffee, one that had contained tea, one that had contained cocoa and then another coffee mug from when she had gone into the kitchen, forgotten the first mug and been too lazy to correct the error.

"You are a pathetic creature, Felicity Foster," she said to the emptiness of her room.

But what could she do? And how could she be anything but pathetic? She had peaked. Fantasy-wise, anyway. And she was currently living with the man who had peaked her fantasies. And then crashed her fantasies.

She rolled off the bed and stood up, scrubbing her hands over her face. Then she walked over to the window and looked outside. She could see the line of pine trees that stood sentinel along the yard, separating Connor's home from Eli's, Kate's and the rest of the ranch. And she could see the porch, the light on, casting the lawn in a yellow glow.

She was as familiar with this house, with this property, as she had been with her own former house. Very few things had changed over the years, and ironically, in this house that seemed so unchanged, her relationship with Connor had changed past the point of no return. And they were trying to return. Because it was what Connor wanted.

She frowned.

She didn't want that. And she hadn't fought for anything else, for anything more. Because she was so used to being accommodating that it had just never even occurred to her. What Connor wanted was what she had agreed to. Just the idea of asking for something more had seemed like begging to her. Had seemed sad and pitiful rather than a reasonable thing.

Why did she do that? Why did she think what she wanted shouldn't matter? That it was wrong somehow?

Stupid question; she knew why she did that. She did that because every single person in her life whom she cared about always made her feel as if she had to earn her spot.

Except for Connor. Connor had never done that.

She moved closer to the window, pressing her forehead against the glass and letting out a long breath, fogging up her view.

She was so tired. Her relationship with her mother made her tired; the fact that she had spent years in a relationship with Marshall made her tired. The fact that she had been acting the part of Connor's wife, while getting nothing of the good part in return, for the past three years, made her tired.

And the worst part was, she had no one to blame but herself. She'd established these behaviors; she'd continued in these behaviors.

Connor hadn't asked her to take over his grocery shopping, to bring him dinner. She hadn't been married to Marshall; she could have walked out the door at any moment, or rather shown him the door at any moment. She could have told her mother that guilt trips weren't going to work.

But she hadn't. Because she had not wanted to risk it.

And where had that gotten her?

Here. Here in this exact moment. This exact, unhappy moment, staring down a future where sex with Connor was done, and never happening again.

"Well, forget that." She pushed back away from the

window and took a couple of steps toward the center of the room, breathing hard.

She wanted more. She wasn't done.

She walked over to the door and opened it, making her way down the hall, down the stairs and into the living room. Connor's boots were by the door, which meant he was home. Or out running barefoot in the field. But she would put her money on him being home.

At that exact moment, he came walking in from the kitchen. "Hey," he said, stuffing his hands into his pockets, his expression both adorable and sheepish.

The muscles on his forearms flexed, her eyes drawn, yet again, to his tattoo. Seeing it now felt kind of poignant. Also, still sexy. That was the power of her attraction to Connor.

"Hi, how was work?"

"Good. The barn is looking good," he finished lamely. "How was your day?"

"Oh, you know. I sort of spent the day lying around in my room. Dealing with things of the emotional variety."

He winced and pulled one of his hands out of his pockets, rubbing the back of his neck. "Right. You okay?"

"Yeah," she said. "Just...processing."

"I did a little bit of that today myself. But you know, it works best for me when I'm outdoors."

"Your method is probably healthier. Mine involves pastries and a lot of warm drinks."

"I'm not sure I do anything more emotionally healthy than you do. Maybe if I drink more hot chocolate I would be in a better space?"

"All things are possible with cocoa. Provided you have marshmallows."

"Obviously."

Liss took a deep breath, gearing up to say what she was thinking, then decided against it. Probably this wasn't the best moment to tell him that she would really like to keep going with the physical side of their relationship. Not when he was dirty from working on the ranch all day, exhausted. Not when there was still this much awkwardness between them.

Yeah, but that isn't going to just go away. And he's an idiot to think it will.

Thinking of Connor as an idiot cheered her slightly. Anyway, it was true.

"Do you have any serious Sunday plans?" she asked.

"Not really. Eli and Kate will probably come for dinner, and I'll do the regular ranch stuff in the morning."

"But your afternoon is free?"

"I feel like you're leading me somewhere, Liss."

"I am. I was wondering if you wanted to go on a hike down to the swimming hole."

"It's too cold to swim. I'm not in the mood to freeze my ba—" Much to Liss's surprise, color darkened Connor's cheeks, and he cleared his throat and redirected. "I'm not in the mood to swim in an ice bath."

His sudden discomfort with saying the word *balls* in front of her was exhibit A for the case she was mounting. Things were not back to normal. Not having sex would not put them back to normal.

"I don't want to swim. I want to hike. I want to eat and look at scenery." She rocked back on her heels, her hands clasped behind her back, a bit of guilt tightening her chest. She was scheming. And she was being dishonest.

But it was for the greater good. Or something.

"Well, that sounds fine. Do you want me to see if anyone else wants to come?"

"No!" Her answer came out a little bit too quick and a little bit too emphatic. "I mean, I think it would be nice for us to do something."

His eyes narrowed. "Okay."

"What? Don't look at me like that."

"Like what?"

"Like you're afraid I'm going to jump on you and violate your person." She wasn't going to jump on him; she was going to talk to him and use rational points to lay out why they should in fact continue on with the physical relationship. Completely different.

Now, if that failed, she might jump on him.

He cleared his throat. "I did not look at you like that."

"You did!" She held her hands up and curled her fingers in, making little claws. "I'm not that scary."

He reached out and grabbed one of her fingers, squeezing it tight and shaking it gently. "Scary."

The contact sent a rush of heat through her body, and she jerked her hand away, taking a step back, hoping he couldn't tell that she was blushing. Good grief. You would think she was a teenage girl dealing with her first crush, and not a woman in her thirties who had seen love's first bloom wither and die a couple of times at this point.

"I promise not to scare you." Except, she was sort of lying. Because she might very well scare him.

"But do you promise to bring hot chocolate and marshmallows? Because now that you've mentioned it, I want some."

"That can be arranged."

"Okay, then. Sounds like a good plan." They both

stood there, lingering awkwardly, silence filling the space between them and forcing the awkwardness to expand. "I need a shower."

"Right." She fought against the mental images of Connor, naked and wet, for a full thirty seconds before she just went ahead and let her imagination have a field day. "Enjoy that."

"I will."

He walked past her and back up the stairs. And she let out a breath she wasn't aware she had been holding.

Her plan might be a little bit evil, but it had to be better than this. Because if everything went according to her plan, she could have Connor again, and it might even fix some of what seemed to be broken between them now.

Anything was better than this.

CHAPTER THIRTEEN

CONNOR HAD SOME reservations about disappearing into the woods with Liss. Especially considering that his resolutions were on a shaky foundation at present.

When he'd tried to go to sleep at night his dreams had been plagued, not by images of his brother standing on his porch, but by images of Liss, lying next to him in bed, her body bare, pale, highlighted by the moonlight filtering in through the window.

And when he woke up, he was alone.

Still, he couldn't cancel on her. Because that would require honesty. And he didn't want to give honesty on that score. Not even a little bit.

Well, it didn't *require* honesty. But he would feel kind of like a dick if he didn't give it to her. Especially since she had gone out of her way to be honest with him. Yesterday she hadn't put on a brave face and pretended everything had gone back to normal. She had admitted that it was a rough day, and it was more than he would have been inclined to do.

He ran his hand over his hair and put a baseball cap on, walking out of his bedroom and shutting the door hard behind him before heading down the stairs.

His heart hit the back of his breastbone hard when he saw Liss, standing in the entryway holding a picnic basket, wearing a fluttery, floral dress that went down just past her knees and a pair of brown, lace-up boots. Her rich, coppery hair was pulled back, a few strands escaping the confines, framing her face.

As far as he could tell, she wasn't wearing makeup, but there was something sexier about that just now. Maybe because it left her skin bare, exposed to him.

Get a grip, Garrett. You go three years without sex and suddenly everything gets you hard because a chick actually touched you?

It was a hell of a lot more than that, but minimizing it seemed like it might help. It didn't, but he had thought for a brief shining moment that it might.

"You're ready," he said, because if all you could think about was your friend's bare skin, you were better off saying something inane.

"Yes, I am. Positively laden with foodstuffs."

"Good," he said, continuing down the line of inane comments, "because I'm hungry."

A spark of tension crackled between them, the dual meaning in his words impossible to miss. Dammit. Would conversation ever not be loaded between them? Or would he be doomed to think of the sexual every time he said something innocuous?

Liss didn't seem to notice. And if she did, she didn't care.

"Good," she said, a smile curving her lips.

She turned and opened the front door, walking out onto the porch. And his eyes were glued to the way her skirt hem swished with each step, revealing a little bonus leg each time.

Liss had always been in possession of a great set of legs. But now those legs had been wrapped around his waist. As a result his admiration had a slightly different context.

He wrenched his damn dirty eyes away while she took the stairs. And he knew her skirt rode up even more as she did. It was costing him to play the part of gentleman right now. Costing him dearly.

Connor decided to focus on the scenery rather than Liss's legs. It was certainly safer. If not more satisfying.

They walked through the line of trees that separated his portion of the property from Eli's, and they made their way along the dirt driveway that ran past where the barn was being constructed, and past one of the vast, fenced-off fields that contained the livestock.

It was a gray afternoon, mist hanging in the air, thick with salt from the sea, casting a dull shade over the green around them. The clouds hanging over the pine trees made them look as though they'd been wrapped in cotton. Like department store Christmas decorations stuck down into the landscape.

The old barn, the one that had been in use back when Connor was a kid, came into view, and Liss took a right past the dilapidated structure. The path that ran through the field here was still well-worn and familiar. They had taken it down to the river all the time when they were kids. Hot summer days always made more bearable by a quick dip in the water. Days made more bearable by escaping the house, his father's drunken slurs and the empty liquor bottles that littered the floor for most of the day. Until Eli was able to get Kate to bed, so he had a chance to clean up.

A whole host of memories hit him as they wandered down this path. They had spent a lot of time down here during their high school years. When a lot of their peers had opted for bonfires and beach parties, their small, close-knit group had chosen instead to do their underage drinking on Garrett land.

Not Eli, obviously, ever the upstanding citizen. Though he had always come, looking over his shoulder nervously as Jack passed beer around. And Liss had been there, of course. Jessie, too.

It hit him then that he hadn't been back here since before Jessie died. He didn't know why he hadn't realized it last night. It was one of the many places, including the stretch of road she'd died on, that he'd eliminated from his geographical vocabulary.

This wasn't one of the particularly weighty ones, just a place with happy memories he'd preferred never to confront.

His stomach tightened as they entered into the grove of trees that grew along the riverbank, stepping around creeping blackberry vines as they made their way closer to the water. He half expected to see a ghost down at the river's edge, but when they came to the sandy bank there were no apparitions.

It was just him and Liss.

And it was just now, not the past.

The water moved slow here, the surface of it nearly still, smooth like a green glass bottle. The rope swing they'd used back in the day was still there, tied to a tree limb that stretched out over the river.

They'd spent a lot of lazy days here. Days when he'd allowed himself to relax and be a kid, a luxury for him and Eli, since they'd been working men raising a child for most of their teenage years. Picking up the slack their father couldn't, because he was lost in his pain.

It made him ache to be here. Not the bad kind. In a

wistful, bittersweet way. He avoided certain places and memories of the past for this very reason.

But right now…right now he felt pretty happy to be here.

"It's been too long since we've been down here," Liss said.

Yeah, it had been. And now that he was here, he knew avoiding it hadn't been necessary. Or at least it wasn't anymore.

"I'm starving," he said.

"Was that a hint?" she asked, a smile tugging at her lips.

It was a hint that he was tired of thinking about the past. And ready to eat some of the feelings that were rioting around inside him. They weren't all bad feelings, but there was a lot of them. A damn lot.

Liss set the basket down on a moss-covered rock, bending at the waist, yet again giving him an unintentional and illicit showing of her legs. This time he didn't look away. He was having a weak moment. Year. Lifetime.

She opened the basket and took a patterned blanket off the top, unfolding it and spreading it out on the sand. Then she took out a few colored bowls with lids that she must have brought from her house when she moved in, because he certainly didn't have anything like that intact. A few scattered lids that went with nothing. Which had not concerned him for a while, since he didn't really keep actual food in the house, either.

She set the bowls down on the blanket and gestured at the spread. "Have a seat."

"Don't mind if I do," he said, settling down on the blanket, dampness from the sand seeping through and

into his jeans. He didn't really mind that, either, because it was so nice to have someone do something like
this for him because they wanted to, and not because
he was sad or hungover. At least, he was going to pretend that was why.

This wasn't casserole. This was a picnic. And this
was different.

Liss sat down beside him, pulling one of the largest
bowls onto her lap and taking the lid off. There was a
small knife inside, berries and peaches.

"Did you bring me out here to kill me?"

She grinned at him, holding the paring knife up. "I
would need something a lot bigger to take you down,
Garrett. Though it would be effective on parts of you."

"Too far," he said.

"Is it?" she asked, her smile widening. "I don't feel
like I've gone too far yet."

"Yeah, because none of your body parts have been
threatened. You better be slicing peaches."

She arched a brow. "That could be taken two ways."

"Stop," he said, feeling uncomfortable, like he had
yesterday when he'd just about said *balls* in front of her.

Which was dumb, because he had said a whole lot
crasser things to her over the years. But now that they
had actually been naked together, every comment
seemed a lot more pointed. And seemed to hit him in
the gut, low and hard, making heat spread through his
veins.

"Okay," she said, looking all innocence and light
as she wrapped her hand around a peach and pulled it
out of the bowl, sliding the edge of the blade through
the skin, a bead of juice breaking through and running
down her arm. She switched hands and lifted her arm

to her mouth, running her tongue along the wet line left behind by the juice.

He felt the impact of the movement as though she had run her tongue along his skin. It was such a sensual thing to see. And he could hardly be bothered beating himself up for feeling that way. Because he was only human. Only a man. With a newly reinvigorated sex drive.

And she had run her tongue over his skin. Intimately. The only woman to ever do that...

And he really needed to redirect his thinking now.

She went back to the task of dividing the peach into equal sections, throwing the pit into the water and disturbing the surface, creating ripples that expanded slowly and blurred the reflection of the trees. She took another peach out of the bowl, and she lingered over slicing that one, too. It took him a moment to realize that they were just sitting there in silence, and that he was watching her every movement with the kind of attention he gave to very few things. His cows, football and Liss slicing peaches.

She mixed the cut peaches in with the blackberries then scooped a bit onto his plate, doing the same for her. Then she opened the other bowls, revealing some pasta salad, and in the other one a couple of sandwiches with what looked like turkey on them.

"You do a little too well taking care of me," he said, taking a bite of the sandwich.

Liss's cheeks turned pink, and for some reason it made his own face feel hot. "Is that even possible?" She looked down and picked up her own sandwich. "I mean, what are friends for?"

"A friendship that's a two-way street?"

"Our friendship *is* a two-way street."

"It's okay, Liss. I realize that none of my relationships have been for the past few years." He let out a long, slow breath. "A few months ago, when Sadie left, Eli told me off. For being a drunk. For leaving all the responsibility to him. He wasn't wrong. I needed to hear it. And I obviously didn't correct everything right when he called me out, but I have been working on it."

"I know." She picked up a slice of peach and took a bite. "You haven't been hungover once since I've moved in."

"Baby steps and all that shit," he said.

"Big man steps. The way I see it, Connor, it's pretty easy to judge you from the outside looking in. But nobody else is in your boots."

"Sure. But even though there is no handbook for stuff like this, common sense says that if you don't keep moving, you're just going to die where you're at. And I haven't been moving."

Admitting that felt like a step forward. And steps forward were, after all, what he was aiming for.

"You have been lately," she said. She took a deep breath and looked away from him, staring out across the water. Connor examined her profile, the elegant line of her nose, the faint sprinkling of freckles across her skin. They weren't very prominent, only visible if you were up close.

His breath caught on the sudden thought that he was not up close to her often enough. He missed things, keeping his distance. Little details that he was soaking in now. Little details that suddenly seemed essential.

As if sensing his careful study of her profile, Liss shifted, setting her plate down on the blanket beside them, moving away from him. Then she stood slowly. Then her hands went to the buttons on her dress, undoing the first four, letting the top fall down past her shoulders, then letting the garment fall down to her feet.

"Liss?" A whole riot of questions went through his brain, so many that they got bottlenecked at his mouth, and he couldn't say another word.

She bent at the waist and untied her boots, slipping them off and throwing them into the sand. Then she made quick work of her bra, pushing her panties down her hips, her legs, and leaving them on the ground with her dress. Then she reached up and took a couple of pins out of her hair, letting it fall loose down her back.

And he still couldn't say anything. All he could do was sit there transfixed. Looking at the way her copper curls contrasted with her creamy skin. Admiring the easy slope of her waist that dipped first, then flared out to form the rounded curve of her hip, the dimples, low on her back, just above her perfect ass.

She turned her head, her hair rippling with the motion, and looked at him, her eyes meeting his, her expression both fierce and timid at the same time. Then she looked back at the river, her eyes fixed straight ahead as she walked down to the bank and stepped into the water.

She lifted one foot up fast, a reflexive response to the cold, he imagined. Then she put it back down, straightening her shoulders and wading in deeper, the water closing over her body. A slight shiver racked her frame, but she kept going. And he just watched.

He didn't know what the hell was going on, but he didn't want to break the silence. For some reason, the idea of it seemed tantamount to swearing in church. And even he knew better than that.

She raised her hands up over her head then slipped entirely beneath the surface, leaving nothing but a ripple where she'd been standing. Connor stood, his eyes glued to the water. His heart pounding fast.

Only a couple of seconds later she resurfaced on a shriek, shattering the air around them, just like she'd shattered the surface of the water a moment before. She pushed her hair and droplets of water off her face. She was facing him now, smiling. "I think you should join me," she called.

"You are insane."

"Maybe," she shouted.

"I told you I do not want to freeze my balls off today."

She lifted a shoulder. "Suit yourself."

She went under the water again, and when she resurfaced she was farther away from shore, treading water.

He hadn't paid all that much attention in school, but she brought to mind that story about sirens who lured men to their deaths.

It hit him then that she was the most beautiful thing he had ever seen. And he was standing on the shore, *watching* her, when he could be out there with her. He was holding himself back, as an observer, when he could touch all that beauty, taste it. Get out in that water and sink down deep in it.

Along with that realization came the crushing weight of time. That it was passing. That he wasn't guaranteed a set amount.

He was guaranteed this moment. If he wasn't too afraid to take it.

And who knew exactly what shape it would take.

Maybe it would just be a moment to recapture something he hadn't done since he was a teenager. Swimming naked, not caring if anyone saw. A last grasp at the kind of freedom age, grief and too much hard work had stolen from him.

Maybe it would become something more.

But he would never find out if he stood there on the bank, not moving.

One thing he was sure of now more than ever: if he didn't move forward, he would die where he sat.

He gripped the hem of his shirt and wrenched it over his head, his hands going to his belt buckle, working it through the loop as quickly as possible, then undoing his jeans.

He shrugged them and his underwear down, kicking them to the side.

Liss was watching him from out in the middle of the river. It wasn't anything she hadn't already seen. Still, he felt a little bit self-conscious. Bare-ass naked out in the broad daylight.

He stepped into the water and bit back a curse. "This is cold," he called.

"Yes, it is. But I don't think you have to worry about freezing your balls off, Connor Garrett."

"You don't?" He crossed his arms over his chest, going in a little bit deeper.

"No, because I'm not convinced you have any."

He snorted and picked up the pace, sliding into swimming when he reached chest-high water, gritting his teeth against the bone-aching chill. He closed the distance between himself and Liss quickly.

"What are you, twelve?"

She looked at him, her expression impish. "Do I look twelve?"

No. No, she did not. "Okay, I'm out here. Now what?"

"Do I have to make all your decisions for you?" she asked, a note of teasing in her voice, but a thread of truth winding through it.

That wasn't fair, though. He had made a decision yesterday. A decision about not touching her again and getting their friendship back on neutral ground.

But then, he supposed changing your mind came with the territory of making decisions. And if not, that was just too damn bad. He would claim inexperience on that score, since he'd made so few in recent years.

He moved closer to her, and her smile faded. "No," he said, "you don't have to make my decisions for me."

He reached out and wrapped his arm around her waist, pulling her close to him, their legs tangling. She gasped, the shocked look on her face so satisfying it almost overrode the feel of her bare, slick body against his. Almost.

He kicked a few times, bringing them closer to the opposite shore to where their picnic was set, bringing them to a point where he could touch ground again.

He planted his feet as firmly as he could, avoiding any algae-covered rock, tightening his hold on her. Her breasts were pressed firmly against his chest, and he was pretty sure he could stay like this for the next hour, and in spite of the cold be completely happy.

"What are we doing here?" he asked. Because he felt like he needed to do the responsible thing and try to figure out just what she was expecting. If all she was expecting was for them to have some fun swimming naked together, he needed to know. Because his brain had shot straight past that and gone on to something else entirely. Damn open-ended. Damn the torpedoes and everything else.

He'd been open to a vague set of possibilities while standing there on the shore, but now that they were up close and personal, the options he was willing to consider had narrowed. A hell of a lot.

"Not nearly enough," she said, leaning forward and pressing a kiss to his neck, just beneath his jaw.

The brief contact of her lips against his skin sent a shock wave of needs through his body. And he wondered how he had ever thought he would just go back to seeing her as a friend. To forgetting what had passed between them.

To forgetting what it felt like to be naked with her, to be inside her.

His intentions had been valiant. Or maybe they hadn't been. Maybe they had just been more self-protection. Because this was... He didn't know what the hell this was. He knew what it couldn't be. He knew what it might mess up.

But he was still here. With her.

He moved his hands slowly up the line of her spine, the drag from the water keeping his movements slow, measured. They broke the surface of the water, and he moved his palms over her shoulders then up to cup her face, sliding his thumbs over her cheekbones, brushing away the droplets of water that clung to her skin, skimming over her freckles. He had never paid much attention to them before today, and now he found he wanted to count them, match the number of kisses to freckles.

He leaned in, kissing her lightly on one cheek then on the other.

"Connor," she said, her voice thin, shaky.

"Liss," he said, because he didn't want there to be any question that he knew whom he was with. When he looked at her, she was all he saw.

He tilted her face upward, leaned in and pressed a kiss to her lips. She wrapped her arms around him, holding on to him tightly, and she tilted her head backward, keeping her face just out of the water, watching her hair flow up around her like a copper halo. He could see her breasts just beneath the surface, pale, rosy-tipped. He bent down and licked a drop of water from her neck, mimicking what he had wanted to do earlier with the peach juice.

He turned his head and kissed her jaw, following the line until he came to her chin, then he moved to her mouth, deepening the kiss, tasting her. She parted her lips for him, sliding her tongue against his. And it didn't matter that the water was cold as freaking glacier melt; shrinkage was not a problem. He was so hard he thought he might explode the next time she flicked the tip of her tongue over his lips.

He abandoned her mouth and straightened slightly, taking in the view of her body. He covered her breast with his palm, moving his thumb over her tightened nipple. She shivered beneath his touch. Or maybe it wasn't his touch so much as the water.

"Cold, baby?" he asked.

"No," she said, her teeth chattering.

"Liar," he said.

He slipped his hand behind her knees and lifted her, holding her close to his chest and walking until he couldn't touch bottom anymore. He swam across the short distance where the waterline went over his head,

Liss kicking along with him. When his feet connected with solid ground again, he picked her up again, walking them both out of the river and onto dry land. He didn't set her down again until they got to the blanket. Then he knelt down next to her, watching the water drops roll over her skin.

"I want…" He bent his head down and captured a drop with his tongue, following the trail over her breast, to one tightened peak. He drew it deep into his mouth, sucking hard. Liss arched against him, a hoarse cry escaping her lips.

"Are you going to finish your sentence?" she asked, gasping for breath.

"I thought I would just lead by example," he said, his lips brushing against her skin as he spoke. He sipped more water from her body, moving to her other breast, tracing the outline of the tightened bud with the tip of his tongue. "You're beautiful, do you know that?"

"It's never mattered to me that much. But I'm happy to know that you think I'm beautiful," she said, her voice trembling.

He moved away from her slightly, giving himself a better view of her body. "I do. I'm not good with… poetry and shit. I never have been. I can show you." He leaned in and kissed her inner thigh, moving closer to where he really wanted to be, to the part of her he really wanted to taste.

He liked this. He really liked it, and he had a lot of catching up to do.

She said his name again, like a prayer, half a sob. Oh, yes, he liked this a lot.

He put his hand between her thighs, her flesh hot beneath the cool water that clung to the curls that covered her sex. He slipped his fingers through her slick heat, pressing one deep inside her body. Then he leaned in, moving his tongue over her clit in time with the movement of his finger.

She tasted like heaven. And he'd been stuck in hell for far too long.

He reached down and wrapped his hand around his cock, squeezing tight. He didn't have any protection with him, which meant this was not going to end quite the way he wanted it to.

He tasted her deeper, urged on by the sounds of pleasure she was making.

"Connor... Connor, I need you. I need you inside me."

He raised his head, breathing hard. "No. Can't." It took every ounce of self-control he possessed to refuse. He didn't want to refuse. But he wouldn't put them at risk for pregnancy.

That was something he just couldn't deal with.

"Can," she said. "I brought condoms."

That brought him up short. "Later. Later I will question you about that."

"That doesn't sound good," she said.

He moved up her body and kissed her deeply on the lips. "It might not be. But right now it doesn't matter. Right now? I just need to be inside you."

"They're in the picnic basket," she said.

"The picnic basket?"

"It was dessert."

He snorted, surprised that he could find anything amusing when he was this close to spontaneously combusting. He reached out and put his hand in the picnic basket, coming up victoriously with a handful of protection. "Ambitious," he said.

"I have a healthy fantasy life," she said, her tone innocent.

He tore open one of the packets and positioned the latex sheath at the head of his cock, drawing it down slowly over his length.

"I will never get tired of watching you do that," Liss said, her eyes on him with rapt attention.

"This? Really?"

"So hot," she said.

He watched her face, watched the way she looked at him, appraised him. No one had ever looked at him like that. Like he just might be the beautiful one.

It made his chest feel strange. Tight.

He positioned himself at the entrance of her body, leaning in and kissing her lips, testing her before thrusting deep inside her.

"Not as hot as this," he said, sliding his hand beneath her ass and drawing her hard against him.

"No," she said, holding tightly on to his shoulders, her fingernails digging into his skin. But he didn't mind. If anything, he welcomed it. Welcomed the little bit of pain to help defuse the intense pleasure that was threatening to overtake him. He wanted to make this good for her. He didn't want to make this a forgettable five minutes.

He wanted it to be a lot more minutes than that. And he wanted them to be memorable.

It would be for him. He knew it without a doubt.

He flexed his hips, beginning to move inside her, establishing a steady rhythm that kept him on edge, without putting him over. She arched against him, meeting him thrust for thrust. The feeling of her, tight and hot around him, was too good. Too much.

He looked down at her, their eyes clashing, a sharp shock of pleasure traveling down his spine and settling heart of the base of it. Looking at her like this, while buried deep inside her, in the light of day, made him feel more present than he had in years. Everything felt sharper, brighter, pleasure cutting into him like a knife. Liss arched up beneath him, her hold on him tightening, her name on his lips as she gave herself up to her own release. Her internal muscles tightened around him, and he couldn't hold back anymore.

He buried his face in her neck and let go. Of everything around him, of everything in the past, of any worry in the future.

And when he came back to himself, the only thing he was still holding on to was Liss.

CHAPTER FOURTEEN

WELL, SHE HAD done it. And she hadn't even said a word. She'd been planning an entire speech in her head. She'd intended to list all of the reasons why she wanted to continue sleeping with him. She'd planned to tell him that she deserved to have what she wanted.

In the end, staying silent and taking her clothes off had been a lot easier. And a hell of a lot more effective, she imagined.

Go figure.

She closed her eyes, relishing the warm weight of Connor's body on hers. She was soaking wet from her time in the river, and they had managed to crumple the blanket so that she was half in the sand now, some of the grains sticking to her arms, but she didn't care.

Because she felt too good everywhere else to worry about a little bit of sand. Sand was the least of her concerns. Sand was worth it.

She was starting to think just about anything was worth it for sex with Connor. It was unaccountably satisfying just how well he lived up to the hype that her brain had built up around him.

She felt…justified. Vindicated. Something. She felt like giving the part of herself that had been devoted to a secret Connor obsession for years a cookie and a pat on the back.

You did well, little obsessive part of me. Obviously, you knew just how good it could be.

The discovery that years of fantasy had been useless because he couldn't live up to her fictional imaginings would have been a hard one to swallow. Fortunately, that was not the case.

Connor moved away from her, the sudden loss of his body heat leaving her shivering.

He didn't look at her while he moved around the riverbank, collecting clothes. He dumped hers in a heap in front of her while hurrying to put on his own.

"Where's the fire, Garrett?"

"Hopefully not in my new barn," he said, his tone dry.

"You know what I mean."

"I'm not too fond of the idea of getting caught out here bare-ass naked," he said.

"Yeah, I guess that wouldn't be the best," she said, pushing herself into a sitting position and digging through the clothes pile for her bra. "Does anyone come out here?"

"I don't think so. But then, it's not like I keep real close tabs on Eli and Kate." He pulled his jeans on, and Liss's stomach sank. It was disappointing to watch him cover his body back up. Like watching someone box up a beautiful gift, only moments after she'd opened it.

"Well—" she set to work hooking her bra "—I thought maybe you knew something I didn't. Like, maybe the city council plays lawn darts here on Sunday afternoons."

"If they do, it's secret lawn darts, and they're illegally trespassing."

"You're no fun," she said, finding her panties and pulling them on before straightening out her dress, shaking the sand out of it. "I think if the city council was having a secret, illegal lawn dart game on your property, you would have to throw your support behind it."

"I would not."

She shrugged her dress on and started doing the buttons up. "Then you'll be forever known as that cranky Connor Garrett who wouldn't let politicians engage in a friendly game of lawn darts down by the river."

"Honey," he said, pulling his T-shirt over his head, pulling the hem down over his abs, a slow, reverse strip show that ended in disappointment instead of confetti and glitter, "I am already known as that cranky Connor Garrett."

"No, you aren't."

He raised his brows. "Yes, I am. Sad, cranky, widower Connor Garrett. I'll probably never be known as anything else."

"Unless you grow your beard longer and start weaving flowers into it like those weird hipster kids do. Then they'll probably call you Connor Garrett, sad, cranky, widower, flower beard."

She did the last button on her dress and stood, brushing the last remnants of sand from the flimsy fabric. And then they were both dressed, and it was almost as if they hadn't just had sex on the blanket. Anyone just joining them might believe all they had done was eat turkey sandwiches and gone for an innocent swim.

Except...

"What did you do with the condom?"

For the second time in as many days, she seemed to have made Connor Garrett blush. "Picnic basket," he said quickly, his words running together.

"You put a used condom in my picnic basket?"

"If I had buried it in the sand, like, a fox would have come and dug it up and dragged it somewhere. Probably deposited it at my feet while I'm trying to work or something. Then I'm going to have to explain why there's a used condom on my property."

"First of all, I don't think a fox is going to bring the used condom to your feet. Second of all, there are a lot of explanations for why a used condom might be on your property. Reason one—post city council lawn dart orgy."

"A duck might choke on it." His face was so comically serious that Liss could not hold back the laughter that was building in her chest.

"Okay, fair enough. Please tell me you did not put it in one of my bowls."

He looked away.

"Connor," she said, shaking her head. "Gross."

"It was that or endangering wildlife. Or foxes digging in the sand."

"Okay, I'm going to let that go. You know, if I ever told anyone about this, there would definitely be some new adjectives assigned to you."

"No," he said, his expression still serious.

"I won't," she said, putting her hands up.

This was weird, because they were giving each other a hard time, like usual. Talking about the absurd. Like the friends they had always been. Only, they were talking about the sex they had just had. Or rather, the aftermath.

Connor had drawn a pretty clear line in the metaphorical sand yesterday. And today she felt as though it had been blurred irreparably. Down there in the actual sand.

"I suppose we better head back. Everyone is coming up for dinner."

She cringed inwardly. "Great."

"About as great as sticking your dick in a beehive."

"I'll take your word for it."

At least he hadn't stumbled over that word. So he seemed to feel less awkward this time, as opposed to last time. Which meant more sex was making things better. She was going to ponder that.

DINNER HAD BEEN a lot less awkward than Connor had imagined it would be. He'd managed to, more or less, make eye contact with Liss when they spoke, rather than looking down at her breasts, and he had managed to make it through the meal without thinking too much about their encounter down by the river. Which was good, because the last thing he wanted to do was imagine what it had been like to lick water off Liss's bare skin while sitting across from his younger sister.

Things had not devolved into awkward double entendre that felt specific to what he and Liss had been involved in, either, which was a nice change. Though the fact that Jack hadn't been there had probably helped with that.

Now everyone was gone, leaving him with a stack of dirty dishes and the prospect of dealing with Liss one-on-one. Lucky, lucky him.

He went straight to the sink and for the dishes. Which was unusual for him, but honestly, it seemed a lot less scary than trying to figure out what the hell was going on between him and his best friend. Because he had made a decision yesterday, and today he had violated that decision. And he couldn't even bring himself to feel that sorry about it.

He felt a lot sorrier about the fact that he now had to deal with the fallout. Again. This felt a whole lot like history repeating itself.

Again, he recalled something from school. Something about those who don't learn from history being doomed to repeat it.

Apparently, his penis was a slow learner.

And apparently also, something about Liss reminded him of school. Maybe because they had been friends since they were in school.

This was so fucked up.

And he felt as if he was due for something un-fucked but he couldn't seem to manage that.

Really, he should've just burned off his newfound sexual desire with some buckle bunny down at the bar. But no, he'd opted to do it with his best friend.

That wasn't strictly true. The decision had been taken out of his hands. Or rather, he had taken things into hand in the shower, and then they had gotten out of hand, and then he had kissed Liss, and everything had felt a little beyond his control. Or a lot.

Right, like you weren't totally complicit in the decision-making down by the river today.

He scowled and turned the tap on, waiting for the water to warm up before dumping the dishes into the empty sink. Yes, he was complicit and shit. But that didn't make it a good decision.

"You're doing dishes?" Liss's surprised voice came from behind him, jerking him out of his self-pitying thoughts.

He didn't turn around. "They aren't going to do themselves."

"No, I know that. It's just that usually they are more likely to do themselves than they are to have you do them." She cleared her throat. "Incidentally, a lot like my orgasms. Except for lately."

He whirled around. "That's how you're going to open up the conversation?"

"There is no smooth, nonawkward way to do it."

She had a point. "Fine. Speak your piece."

"I disagreed with your unilateral no-sex decree yesterday."

"I sort of figured that. Seeing as you stripped naked in front of me this afternoon."

"Yes, well, I was going to just talk to you about my feelings. What I was thinking. And then, all things considered, I decided I would just show you. But now I imagine we can't avoid the talking anymore." Whiskey-colored eyes met his. "We need to talk about this."

"You know, that's the perk of being with the same person from the time you're too young to care about anything enough to want to talk about it."

"What does that mean?"

"When you're young, you don't ask a lot of questions. You don't worry about too much. You like being with someone, you want to get in their pants, that's pretty much love, and it's a done deal. But then you get to be in your thirties. And you have marriages, and jobs, and bad credit and enough carry-on baggage to ground a plane while they rebalance the load." He dragged a hand over his face and grimaced when he realized it was wet from the sink water. "Now I want to get in your pants, and I want to be your best friend. And I want things to stay the same. And I need things to change. And nothing is simple."

She cleared her throat. "I guess so. But then, when you're young, I'm not sure things are really simpler or if you're just missing the depth in everything. The possibilities. You see things big and simple. Like growing up here, I used to look around and see nothing but a lot of green and boring. And when it came to sex? You have friends, or you have lovers. They can't be the same. They don't even hang out in the same group. But I think the perk of being in your thirties is that you realize there's more than that. Now I don't look out there and see a simple blanket of green. There are so many shades of green in those trees, Connor. It can be deep or bright, cold or warm. Tinted with blue, covered in snow. I see so much more now. So it makes me wonder, why can't we be lovers right now and stay friends?"

"Anything that sounds that good is doomed to fail," he said, realizing as the bitter words fell from his lips just how deeply he believed them.

Liss bit her lip and closed the distance between them, wrapping her arms around his waist and resting her head on his chest. Connor's throat felt tight all of a sudden. He raised his hand and kept it at the back of her head, holding her against him.

"That isn't true. There are good things. There will be more good things." She moved her hands over his back, the movement soothing, but also sensual. Which only added to the confusion.

"I know. There have been…a lot of good things." He took a deep breath. "I mean, maybe there have been. I haven't been looking for them. I… Everyone leaves. One way or another. And…every time I think about changing something, or meeting someone, or building my barn…" He couldn't get the rest of the sentence out.

"I'm still here," she said, her voice muffled against his chest. "I'm not going anywhere."

He tightened his hold on her. "What if I mess it up?"

She pulled away from him slightly, meeting his eyes. "Connor, you are the best friend I have ever had. You're also the best sex I've ever had. How can that go wrong?"

"Don't ask that. It's me we're talking about here."

"Right. Cranky Connor Garrett. With the flower beard, the overactive fox-related imagination and a very nice-sized package."

He snorted. "I do not put flowers in my beard. I'll let you go ahead and keep the rest of it."

"See? This is working."

He gripped her chin between his thumb and forefinger. "And what about when it stops working?"

"We'll go back to the way things were before. But do you honestly think we can go back right now? Maybe later. Maybe after we…burn some of this off."

In truth, standing with her right now, touching her as if he had every right, he could not imagine going back to a world where touching her wouldn't be appropriate. Touch had been missing from his life for a long time. Now that it had been restored, in all its glory, he was reluctant to let it go.

Most especially when it came to Liss.

He was trying to take forward motion and he supposed, all things considered, that meant it wasn't a good time to take a step backward with Liss.

If it was even a step backward. Maybe sex would be a step backward. He couldn't tell anymore. But one of the options meant that he could keep having sex. And he was leaning heavily toward that option.

Since he had stopped filling the deep dark hole in himself with alcohol, it seemed as if his body was trying to compensate by filling it with sex. Or, less complex, perhaps he was just a man. And beginning to remember that fact.

Though he disliked reducing his attraction to Liss to something that basic. But then, the sex part could be basic, he supposed. His feelings weren't. But they were separate. And that was the beauty in it. That was a whole new shade of green.

If what Liss said was true, they could have this and then go right back to how things were before. He wasn't sure if he believed her.

But he hadn't been the same for a long time.

He hadn't wanted anything for a long time.

But he wanted her.

Whatever the hell that meant, wherever the hell it led.

"You're being very quiet, Connor."

"I'm not sure what to say."

"Something curmudgeonly?"

"I didn't really think this was the time."

"Then…just tell me that you want me. Because I want you, and it feels very exposing to admit that." She shivered beneath his touch, her eyes wide, so very vulnerable. And touched something deep in him that he hadn't even known was still there.

He tightened his hold on her. "I doubt a lot of things, Liss. But one thing I don't doubt, and one thing you don't need to doubt, is that I want you. Simple as that."

"As simple and complicated as that."

"It's like you said, there are a lot of shades of green. Maybe there are a lot of shades of friendship, too."

"That was almost...profound."

"I have spent a lot of time inside my head the past few years. Something profound should come out of my mouth once in a while."

"Profound, not profane."

He laughed. "Oh, right. Never mind, then. Profane is a whole lot more likely."

She extricated herself from his hold and took a step back. "So what do we do now?"

"Dishes?" She frowned at his suggestion. Of course, the first answer he had given her off the cuff, and it was the wrong one. That seemed about right. "Or something else," he added.

"Oh, you were about to do dishes. So that seems fair."

This strange, domestically tinged conversation pushed a line of tension up his spine, inch by inch, tightening his muscles.

It was too close to something he'd experienced before. Too close to the kind of thing he wasn't ready for again. Not now, probably not ever.

And he'd love to avoid it, but he and Liss lived together, so avoiding it wasn't possible.

Plus, she was Liss. He didn't hide from her.

"I guess that kind of leads into another conversation that is serious, and most definitely one I don't want to have."

"We don't have to have serious conversations," she said, turning toward the sink.

"Yes, we do. Because sex is serious. I mean, it is for me. I'm not Jack. I never will be. Even if I'm never ready for another serious relationship, I'm not going to go out and sleep with a bunch of strangers. Taking my clothes off with someone…being in someone…it means something to me."

"Well, it means a lot to me, too. I just meant…"

"I know. You're trying to spare me. But I think to avoid as much awkwardness as possible, and hopefully any hurt feelings, we do need some ground rules." He wasn't sure how he was the one spearheading this conversation. But he felt as if it had to be done. They were living in the same house, after all, and he desperately needed to establish boundaries.

For a lot of reasons, his sanity being chief among them.

"Okay, lay down your ground rules," she said, sweeping her hand across the room in a grand gesture.

He had a big one, and she probably wouldn't like it. But standing here, in his kitchen, with Liss in her bare feet, he knew he had to say it.

Sleeping together, holding each other all night, waking up tangled together…that was an intimacy he couldn't quite face.

And it definitely crossed the boundaries of friendship into…something else.

Lust was one thing, sex was another thing, but drooling onto your pillow right next to someone, waking up with morning wood and morning breath. Needing sex and also needing to pee…

Yeah, that was marriage shit.

That was the kind of thing he wanted to stay well away from.

He cleared his throat. "I think sleeping together is off the table."

Her facial features seemed to lower half an inch at that statement. "But you just said you wanted me."

"I do. But I'm making a distinction right now between sleeping together and having sex with each other," he said, shifting uncomfortably. Because this was uncomfortable. On a lot of levels.

"Okay. I understand that," she said, but her voice, along with her frame, had shrunk slightly, and he could see that she didn't really understand.

"Liss, I think it's important to make sure we keep things kind of…kept in their own corral."

Her brow crinkled, and the corners of her mouth turned down. "Mmm, cowboy sex wisdom."

"If you want cowboy sex, you have to put up with the wisdom."

"I get what you're saying. Boundaries."

"Exactly. Like, the property line of friendship extends to this point, and no further, and beyond that is the lover part."

"I think you have a breakdown in your metaphor."

"Probably."

"So when do we… How do we… There is no non-embarrassing way to ask you this."

"Is there anything to be embarrassed about between us anymore? You've seen me hungover. You've seen me naked. I had to admit to putting a condom in your picnic basket."

"Good point. But…it's not like when you're in a relationship, then. Because when you're sleeping with someone, you just do it when you get in bed."

"So you're wondering when we're supposed to…"

"Have the sex." She finished his sentence for him. Though he had not been planning on finishing it quite that way.

And, in spite of what he had just said, it was awkward. Damn awkward.

"When we...feel like it?" He cleared his throat. "I figure that's kind of a perk to being an adult, isn't it?"

"But how do we know if we both feel like it?"

"I'm a man who's been celibate for three years. I think it's safe to say I will always feel like it." After three years of not even wanting any, getting some was about all he thought about at the moment. When he wasn't thinking about trying to set boundaries, and trying to deal with the trauma associated with the fact that he only wanted to get some with the woman he considered his best friend.

He cleared his throat. "That does make things easier."

"Come to that, I don't really want to do dishes anymore."

She arched a brow. "Oh, yeah? What do you want to do?"

"You."

And that effectively ended the talking for the evening. And that was quite all right by him.

CHAPTER FIFTEEN

LISS DIDN'T USUALLY mind work. Work was a necessity, after all, and really, by and large she liked her job. But it was hard today. Because her head was full of Connor. Connor naked, Connor's hands on her skin, Connor's tongue on her...

Her face heated. Yeah, that was not the best thing to be thinking about while she was sitting at her desk.

"Did you have a nice weekend?" Jeanette asked from her position at her desk.

Liss felt unaccountably guilty, and completely transparent. "Yeah," she said, clearing her throat and trying to keep her blushing to a minimum. "It was fine."

Jeanette arched a brow. "Just fine?"

"Should it have been more than fine?"

Jeanette shrugged. "Me myself, I prefer to have weekends entirely comprised of awesomesauce. But how you spend your time is up to you."

"I just didn't do very much. Stuck close to home. A little hiking. A little swimming."

"You went swimming? It's cold."

"Yeah, but refreshing."

"You're also lying," Jeanette said, her eyes narrowed.

"I'm lying? No, I'm not lying. I went swimming."

"For what reason? Like, did you lose a valuable piece of jewelry in the bottom of the lake? Because that could be a good reason to go swimming right now. Otherwise I would just have to go ahead and say you're crazy. Except that you aren't crazy, so that means you had a reason to go swimming."

"Good Lord, Jeanette, what are you, a detective on the side?"

"Guilt. You reek of guilt, Foster." Jeanette narrowed her eyes further, tightening her lips. "Who did you hook up with?"

It was official; Jeanette had to be some kind of wizard. Liss didn't even have a hickey. She had double-checked this morning before she left the house. "Why would you think I hooked up with someone?"

"Because you question why I asked if you hooked up with someone, rather than just saying no."

"Fine. I was skinny-dipping in the river. That's why I swam."

"Not alone."

She bit her lip. She was caught. There was no getting out of it now. She looked down. "No, not alone."

"Good for you. You need to rebound from that asshole, and it's better late than never."

"Great. So this is me," Liss said, spreading her arms wide, "rebounding."

"I see that. Anyone I know?"

"I took a blood oath not to reveal it."

"So you broke and started sleeping with your friend after you moved in with him, didn't you?"

Heat poured into Liss's face. "No. It's just that… he's a prince. Of a small country. And he is engaged to marry someone else. So I'm, like, his last fling. And if the media finds out, the entire town will be overrun."

"Right. So how is Mr. Cowboy in bed?"

"You mean the prince. You want to know how the prince is in bed."

"Back in the early '90s I sort of wanted to know how Prince was in bed, but that's entirely different."

Liss cleared her throat, moving toward a subject change. "So that's settled. I had some sex. We don't need to make a federal case out of it."

"Oh, I have not even begun to make a case out of this. I want details. Is it weird? I've never slept with a guy I was friends with."

"How did you guess all that?" Liss was completely defeated now.

"You have no game face. You looked both satisfied and infinitely worried. And you have looked that way since you walked in this morning."

"Fine. I give. I slept with Connor. It's amazing. It's not as awkward as you would think. The fact that he has to wear clothes ever is a complete and total crime against humanity."

"I'm really glad to have that theory on him confirmed."

"I think I'm being an idiot," Liss said, covering her face and leaning forward, her elbows resting on the desk.

"Why, exactly? Because having sex that is both good and convenient seems nonidiotic to me."

"Because he's my best friend. And I feel… I feel a lot of things."

"Feelings are a bitch," Jeanette said. "But you never know how things will end up."

"I pretty much do. That's the thing. That is the primary problem with sleeping with your best friend while having feelings. When you're with a guy who's just like a boyfriend guy, there's mystery. You're not really sure what makes him tick. You aren't really sure what he wants. But I know Connor. I know what he's been through. I know what he isn't willing to go through again. And I even understand why."

"Yes, that does add another layer to it. But you're in deep already. Let's just face the facts. You were in deep before you ever touched him, am I right?"

"I'm transparent."

"A little bit, Liss. A little bit."

"I should put a stop to this, shouldn't I? I need to be strong."

"Oh, hell, no. Treat yourself."

"But he is not a treat. He is my friend."

Jeanette laughed. "Why can't he be both?"

"That's the question we both asked last night. And the conclusion was, we would try to be both. But we were weak. Weak and sex-addled."

"If a guy can make you sex-addled, stick with that for as long as you can."

"That's your official advice?"

She smiled. "I married it."

"Well, I will not be marrying him."

If there was one thing Liss was absolutely certain of, it was that there was no serious future with Connor. And even fantasizing about it wasn't worth the risk. If she let herself go there…she could almost imagine the look of horror on his face if she told him she wanted more.

So she wouldn't want more. Frankly, she was good at that.

She just needed this time. To deal with this desire. The desire she had been fighting off for the past too many years. It wasn't going to fade away. That, she already knew. So she was trying this method.

She ignored the slight ache in her chest.

"Then enjoy him while you have him."

Why not? Why shouldn't she? She was going to treat herself, because she had been too long without a man in general, and had been never with Connor. And she had wanted Connor for ages, so she might as well enjoy it while she had it. The horse had already left the barn and all that. So there was no use getting precious about it now.

Liss turned her chair sideways and stuck a stack of papers beneath the stapler, pressing it down hard. "I will, Jeanette. I will. And I will continue enjoying him tonight."

CONNOR COULDN'T AVOID going to town any longer. He did it as little as possible, unless he was going to the bar to hang out, but he needed to get some things for the ranch, so he'd gotten his ass into his truck and made the drive.

Fortunately, Kate was working at the Farm and Garden today, so that was one less person to deal with making sympathetic eyes at him. He had not been so lucky at the hardware store or the grocery store.

But he had managed to be cordial. He had almost managed to smile. Which was all thanks to Liss, really. He smiled again on his way out of the store, thinking about her scolding him for his inability to have normal human responses.

"I just had one," he said quietly as he jerked open the door to his truck and set the plastic bag with his soda, cupcakes and condoms in the front seat. He was trying his hand at not buying hard liquor, and instead had come up with artificial flavors and sugar, which seemed good to him. Also, more protection, since he and Liss had burned through the nearly expired box at record speed.

His phone buzzed in his pocket, and he took it out, flipping it open. He had the same cell phone for years and had never seen the point in upgrading. It still made calls, after all. "Hello?"

It was Eli. "Hey, you got some time? You're in town, right?"

"Yes, I am. Do you have time? I thought you were supposed to be protecting the citizens. Or at least stumping for votes."

"I'm on a break. Meet me at The Grind."

Eli hung up, and Connor stuffed his phone back into his pocket. Eli didn't ask much of him, so Connor figured he owed it to his brother to take a coffee break.

He got in his truck and started the engine, making the quick drive through the main drag of town to one of the newer coffee places that was quickly becoming a regular hangout, even among the old, crusty codgers, who were highly resistant to anything new.

Connor parked across the street, in front of one of the little tourist shops, just beneath the American and Oregon flags that were raised high and proud. He slammed the door shut and walked across the little two-lane road and into the coffee shop.

Eli was already sitting at a back table, his hand wrapped around a white cup with a lid. A latte, Connor assumed. He personally couldn't stomach coffee that had been diluted to that degree. There was a second cup on the table across from Eli, and Connor could only hope he had not ordered any froofy shit for him.

"It better be black," he said, pulling his chair out and taking a seat across from his brother, wrapping his hand around the cup on the table.

"It is. And strong enough to choke one of your bulls."

"You know me well." He took the lid off and watched steam rise up into the air.

"Okay. I have to show you something, and I have to ask you something."

"I'm a little nervous, Eli, I'm not going to lie."

Eli reached into his jacket pocket and pulled out a small black box, setting it in the center of the distressed-wood table, and opening the lid, revealing a very large diamond ring.

Connor looked up and stared at his brother then looked back down at the ring. Eli didn't say anything; he only looked at Connor with an overly fervent gaze.

"I'm real flattered, Eli, but I'm going to have to decline."

"You are such a dickhead."

"Did you just call me a dickhead, Sheriff?"

"Deputy Sheriff," Eli said through gritted teeth.

"Oh, that's right, the election hasn't happened yet. I would think you might be a little nicer to your constituents."

"If you don't vote for me, I'll kill you in your sleep. How's that?"

"Coercion. I think that's coercion. That's how it is."

"Be serious," Eli said.

"Okay. I'm ready to be serious."

"Obviously, I'm going to ask Sadie to marry me," Eli said. "Am I insane?"

"You would be insane not to."

Eli cleared his throat. "I don't mean am I insane to want to be with her. I want to spend the rest of my life with her, and I'm completely certain about that. I have been for a while now. But…she'll say yes, won't she?"

"Probably. Though I would ask her before the election, because if you lose she might move on to greener pastures."

"I really should have asked Jack."

"No, you should not have asked Jack. Jack would tell you to run from commitment."

Eli arched a dark brow. "And you won't?"

"No, Eli. I'm not going to tell you to run from commitment. Marriage is hard. I was married for eight years, and there were a lot of times when it just seemed like work. I loved my wife. But that didn't make every problem magically disappear. Life still happens, all of the problems you have interacting with a person on a daily basis still happen. But if you love them enough, it's worth it."

Eli picked up the ring box and turned it so that the diamond was facing him. "I know she's worth it. She's worth anything. Everything."

"Then it's the right thing." Connor reached out and patted his brother on the shoulder in a clumsy gesture of encouragement. He was out of practice at this older-brother stuff. But he was trying.

"Can I ask you something really personal?"

Connor shifted in his chair, lifting his coffee cup to his lips and taking a large gulp to give himself a little time to answer the question. "You're going to ask whether or not I give you the okay, right?"

"Probably."

"Then go right ahead."

"Would you get married again? I mean, if you could go back, knowing what you know now, how bad it hurts in the end when things go wrong. Would you do it again?"

He thought back. To the years he'd had with his wife, to full flower beds and nice smells in his kitchen. Someone in his bed at night, someone to share his life with. It was all kind of vague, impressions of a happy time. Feelings more than specific instances. And he didn't see her face. But the thoughts were…happy. Which was weird.

"Yes. I would."

Eli looked down. "That answer means a lot to me." He looked back up and met Connor's gaze. "You really don't want to have that again?"

"I don't know if I can," he said, because this wasn't the time to BS and cover up his dysfunction with a stupid joke. As much as he would like to. "When you talk about going back…that's a different man. I'm not the same as I was. The memories are… It was good. But I don't know if it's something I can do anymore."

"Still planning on dying alone and celibate?"

Connor just about choked on his coffee. "Alone, anyway," he said, clearing his throat.

Eli raised both brows in surprise. "Is that a confession?"

"You're not my priest. Hell, you're not even my sheriff yet. I don't have to confess anything to you."

"Fair enough. I'm going to ask her after the election party."

"Oh, thank God. Let's make this all about you again. I really don't like talking about me."

"Shut up, Connor. Is it a good time to propose? A bad time?"

"There is no bad time. Because that woman is head over heels in love with you. One thing I can tell you, Eli, with certainty, is that you love each other deep. When I'm around you, it almost makes me want to try it again. There, that was my allotted amount of sincerity and advice."

"You didn't answer my question, though," Eli said, rubbing his hand over his forehead.

"Ask her after the election party. Her answer will be yes either way."

Eli closed his hand around the ring box and slid it back toward him, putting it back in his jacket pocket. "Okay, I will." He stood, latte in hand.

"Eli," Connor said.

"What?"

"Congratulations."

He watched Eli walk back out of the coffee shop, and he stayed in his chair for a few minutes. He was happy for Eli. Genuinely so, which came as a little bit of a shock. Almost as shocking as the fact that he just had memories of the past that felt happy.

He picked up his coffee and took another sip before standing, waving at Cassie, the owner of the shop, and walking out the door.

There was a touch of bitterness to his happiness, though. Much like his coffee. Because what he'd said to Eli was true. He was too changed to simply go back to what he'd had.

And then there was what he had now. With Liss. Which was… Yeah, it was the best sex he'd ever had. He hadn't known sex could be this good. She just seemed to want everything he gave her, not just wanted, begged for it.

That was a damn powerful aphrodisiac.

Then, during the day, she was still his best friend.

A pretty damn good arrangement.

That might explain a good amount of the happiness he had felt today. Lately.

He pushed open the door to the coffee shop and walked out onto the street, making his way down the sidewalk past the collection of little shops that were popping up with alarming regularity lately. Tourism in Copper Ridge was booming. Thanks in large part to the renovated old town, events organized by the county, and city council and bed-and-breakfasts like Sadie's.

He turned to face the street, ready to jaywalk back to his truck, and paused. There was a secondhand clothing store just next to the knickknack tourist trap he was parked in front of. Rethread. If he was the type of guy who got any enjoyment out of puns, he might've laughed.

He crossed the street, drawing closer to the store windows, and stopped completely as a flash of pink caught his eye. Right there in the window, on a pale mannequin that was contorted into a very strange shape, was a pale pink, skinny-strapped prom dress.

The conversation he'd had with Liss on his porch a couple of weeks ago played back in his mind.

She'd said that in hindsight she thought the dress was ugly, but he'd seen the lie in her eyes even then. Because she was still hurt over it. She still loved it.

And this might look nothing like the dress she had

described to him, but it was how he'd pictured it. And he had no clue if it would fit her.

But he had to buy it.

CHAPTER SIXTEEN

CONNOR POUNDED THE LAST nail into the barn a full four days before the election and the election-night party.

And he felt satisfied.

Of course, given that the whole crew was in place, and most of the details had been finished by a specialty team, him putting in the last nail was more symbolic than it was necessary. But he was in a place where he was happy to take that.

He hadn't finished a whole lot of things in the past few years, but he had finished this. Fate had blazed through and burned yet one more thing in his life to the ground, but he had rebuilt. And it was better than the barn that had come before it.

There was a stone arch curving over the doorway and built partly up the first floor, adding detail to the red cedar planking that had been used to build the rest of the structure. The red metal roof shone bright in the sun, and the weather vane on top—shaped like a cow—was swaying back and forth lazily in the halfhearted afternoon breeze.

There was enough room for all of his equipment and a finished office on the top floor to help foster the idea that the running of the ranch was communal. Having it all centered in Connor's house kept the others too much on the peripheral. Which he had been happy about when he'd been letting everything slide. But he was ready for a little help, a little accountability.

He pushed open the door and walked inside. The space was empty, a blank canvas. It smelled like fresh wood and stain, the sweet smell of grass and hay blowing in the wide-open side doors and mixing in, almost christening it for use.

Only a few months ago, all that had been here was ash. He could hardly believe it now. Could hardly believe that so much destruction could be erased. That something as perfect as the old barn could be created again, stronger, better.

He heard footsteps behind him and he turned, half expecting to see Eli. But it wasn't Eli. It was Liss.

"This is... Connor, this is beautiful," she said, her eyes sparkling with unshed tears.

He cleared his throat, his chest suddenly tight. "Yeah. They did a good job. And it will be done in time for Eli's big election party. We'll be able to celebrate his new position in style."

"I dropped my ballot in the box yesterday," Liss said, smiling now. "He's got this."

"He better. Otherwise I'm going to think this place is pretty dumb. I mean, if Eli can take care of me, he can more than manage Logan County. Though it might justify me going deeper into my hermitage."

"No. No more hermitage," she said, closing the distance between them, standing close to him but not touching him.

He was tempted to close the small gap between them, to wrap his arms around her and pull her close against his body. But he had a feeling that violated the First Amendment of Connor and Liss's relationship Constitution. The separation of friendship and sex. Meaning there were normal friendship boundaries unless they were actually in the act.

Right now that separation seemed a little bit stupid.

"Then Eli had better win. Otherwise I'm building a cabin up in the mountains. Ordering all of my supplies out of a catalog."

"That sounds kind of lonely," she said.

"I'll get a sheep or something. Seems like the thing to do in a situation like that. Anyway, sure, there will be people, but there will also not be pants."

"You're planning on leaving civilization for a sheep and the chance to run around without pants? You know, Connor, if you really want to stop wearing pants at home, I'll let you," she said, the corners of her mouth turning up into a wicked smile.

This was sex talk, which made him wonder if they were in sex territory. Which meant that maybe, just maybe, he could put his arm around her.

So he did.

"You might be okay with that, but I imagine Kate would pitch a fit if she stopped by unannounced and saw that."

"It might keep her from stopping by unannounced," she said.

"That is a very good point."

She was smiling up at him, and she was just so pretty that he couldn't stand another moment of being this close to her without kissing her. So he did that, too.

She made a small noise in the back of her throat and he felt it burn all the way through him like a shot of whiskey hitting his blood. He cupped her face, deepening the kiss. It just felt so good. So good to be this close to someone. So good to be this close to her.

"So when is Sadie going to attack my barn with decorations and things?" he asked, his forehead still pressed against hers.

"We will probably start tonight so that it's finished in time."

"She roped you into helping?"

"Yes, she did. Me, Kate, Alison, Lydia and Jeanette. Oh, yeah, and Jack."

"How did she get Jack involved?"

"Did you not hear how many women are going to be there? She did not have to twist his arm."

Connor huffed out a laugh. "Well, when he gets in your way, just send him up my way and I'll give him a beer and sit him in front of the TV."

"Will do." He pulled away from her, suddenly conscious of the fact that really anyone could walk in on them. "Hey," she said. "This is beautiful. Really. And I'm so happy for you. And I'm proud of you."

"I could not have done it without your boot up my ass. And I mean that sincerely."

She smiled. "What are friends for?"

"A lot more things than I thought," he said, surprised at how easy it was to tease her. Surprised at how good it felt.

She pursed her lips, pulling a face. "Watch it, Garrett."

"Or what?"

"Or I might kiss you again."

"I wouldn't mind that."

He heard voices and footsteps coming from outside and was thankful that they weren't kissing again. Was thankful they were standing with a respectable distance between them now.

Eli and Sadie walked into the barn a moment later, talking loudly about how amazing everything looked.

"Really, they did an incredible job," Eli said, looking around.

Connor looked at Liss, who took a surreptitious step away from him, stuffing her hands into her pockets. "Yeah, they did," Connor said.

"I'm so excited!" Sadie said. "I can't wait to get my hands on this. I'm going to have Kate making flower arrangements," she finished, smiling broadly.

"You have a death wish, don't you?" Connor asked.

Sadie waved a hand. "It will be good for her. She was practically raised by wolves."

"Excuse me," Eli said. "She was raised by us." He gestured between Connor and himself.

Sadie made a sympathetic face at Eli. "Oh," she said, patting his face, "honey, I know."

He narrowed his eyes but didn't say anything.

"Do you have time to start decorating tonight, Liss?" Sadie asked.

"I am at your disposal," Liss said. And Connor felt a tug of something that reminded him a lot of jealousy. Because he had sort of wanted Liss at his disposal tonight.

"Great. I was thinking we could come out after dinner. It's going to be fun!"

"I can come and help," Eli said.

"No, you aren't allowed to. Because it's for you, for your election night, and it will make a really bad gift if you help. Plus, I don't want you to help because you're a control freak. And there's only room for one driver on this train. And that's me."

"I am not a control freak," Eli said. He paused for a moment. "Wait, yes, I am. Good point. I'll go to Connor's house and drink beer instead."

"Perfect," Sadie said. "And we'll stay in here and eat pie and drink hot cider."

"What if I want hot cider?" Eli asked, frowning.

"We might be able to make arrangements." Sadie wiggled her brows. "It'll be like prohibition. If you come to the back door of our barn speakeasy, you might be able to finagle some hot beverages."

"Or," Connor said, "I will come to the front door and get a cup if I ask. Because it is my damn barn."

"Poor Connor. I'll bring you cider." Liss patted him on the shoulder, and he jumped. It was totally appropriate contact, completely normal contact passing between the two of them, but it felt more intimate now, and something she probably shouldn't do in front of the others. He pulled away.

He could sense that he had done the wrong thing. But there wasn't much he could do about it here and now.

"All right, Connor will give you a few more minutes to admire your barn before we string lights and vomit cheer all over it. I know how resistant you are to cheer," Sadie said, smiling unrepentantly. "See you later tonight, Liss."

"I better go, too," Liss said, forcing a smile. "See you later, Connor."

And she left with Eli and Sadie, which left him alone. Knowing full well he had done something wrong, and not really sure what he could do to fix it.

Well, he still had the dress. And he suddenly had a very good idea for how to give it to her.

JACK HAD ONLY STAYED long enough to string the lights over the crossbeams on the barn's high ceiling, and in the tall branches of the trees outside. After that he had feigned a dramatic muscle injury and limped off, saying only a beer would cure it.

Sadie had her phone docked into some little speakers and was playing country music. Alison had brought pie, and Sadie had provided a slow cooker filled with apple cider, both of which were sitting on a rough-hewn wooden table placed in the back of the room.

Leave it to Sadie to throw an entire party that centered around preparing for a party.

Lights had also been strung outside, and tables set up with a few inside, as well. But there was enough space for dancing, and a temporary stage for both music and announcements.

And every single one of those tables that had been set up needed, per Sadie, three small flower arrangements, placed in Mason jars, and one larger one in a tall glass milk bottle.

Liss was sitting in a folding chair in front of a card table, arranging fatally dried flowers and burlap ribbons in jars. Kate was sitting on the floor, her expression a near comical scowl as she attempted to follow Sadie's example arrangement to the letter.

"It's really a shame she didn't need anyone to shoe a horse, catch a wandering calf or repair barbed wire to prepare for this party," Kate muttered. "That, I could have done."

"I would have fared better if she just needed her taxes prepared," Liss said.

Kate looked up at her. "I think you're doing better than I am. I should have left after the lights were done. Jack had the right idea."

"No, Jack is a lazy bum."

"Or he just knows his limitations. And his limitations are flower arrangements."

"True," Liss said.

"Less complaining, more arranging," Sadie chirped from across the room.

"You know, Sadie," Kate said, "I always wanted a sister. But it turns out it's overrated."

"I'm not your sister. Yet," Sadie said, smiling.

"She will be," Kate said, her tone hushed. "Not even Eli is stupid enough to let her get away."

For some reason that comment hit her close to the bone. Maybe because of the way Connor had pulled away from her in front of Sadie and Eli earlier. Because the fact remained Connor would be stupid enough to let her get away. Which was fine, wasn't it? Because this was all just physical. And when that burned away, their friendship would remain. So he would only let her get away in part. He would keep most of her. It's just that their interactions would always include clothes when this was over.

She swallowed hard.

"Do you think you'll get married in the barn?" Jeanette asked Sadie from where she was sitting.

Sadie's cheeks turned a delicate shade of pink. "We are not engaged. So that would be getting ahead of myself."

"But of course you are ahead of yourself," Lydia said.

"Of course I am," Sadie said. "I may or may not have a few secret files with inspiration pictures in them."

"I knew it," Lydia said. "And I'm glad. I'm glad he has you. Because he's most definitely the happiest I've ever seen him."

"True," Alison said, cutting a few more slices of pie. "He's happier with you than I am without my husband." The room got quiet. "It's okay to laugh at that," she added.

Jeanette did. "Let's hear it for good decisions," she said, raising her mug. "To choosing good husbands and getting rid of bad ones."

For some reason Liss looked down at Kate, who was looking back at her. "I would just like to get a first date," she said, quietly enough that only Liss could hear.

"Sometimes dating is overrated," Liss said.

Now she just felt weird and unsettled.

"To answer your question, though," Sadie said. "Yes, I would like a really country wedding. On the ranch, of course. I mean, why get married anywhere else when you have access to all of this?" She sighed. "Six months ago I could not have imagined being in a position where I might want to get married. It's amazing how love changes things."

The unsettled feeling grew, widened, into a sensation of gnawing envy.

Kate gave Liss another rueful smile. "We're going to have to arrange flowers for their wedding," she said, shaking her head sadly.

It suddenly occurred to Liss, as she sat there with dried flowers in her hands, just how much she wanted to arrange flowers for her own wedding someday. But not just a generic wedding, to a generic groom.

A wedding in this barn. A wedding to the man who owned it.

She was going to cry. She was going to cry right here and now, in front of everybody.

No, no, you aren't.

She bit the inside of her cheek and kept fiddling with the flowers.

There was nothing she could do about what she wanted, nothing she could do about the situation she and Connor found themselves in. The one where she wanted a whole lot more than he ever would.

Her mind kept going back to when he'd pulled away from her earlier today. That action had spoken a lot louder than any words ever could.

She was an idiot. How had she not realized it would end up like this?

Well, she knew why. Because she hadn't wanted to acknowledge just how much he meant to her. Just how much she wanted from him.

Frankly, she still didn't.

"Are you okay?" Kate asked. She looked concerned and also horrified that she had stepped into a forest of delicate emotions.

"I will be," she said, not sure if she was telling the truth or not.

"The idea of arranging flowers for their wedding is really that sad?"

Liss laughed. "Yes, if it's anything like this."

"I might fake my own death and change my name."

"But then you would miss the wedding," Liss said.

"I would make a dramatic return for the happy day."

Liss smiled. The entire Garrett family meant a lot to her. The entire Garrett family was like her family.

And on the heels of the realization of just how much she wanted from Connor, she also realized she couldn't risk it.

Because if something happened between her and Connor, something bad, she wouldn't just lose his friendship, she would lose the whole family.

"I might make you take me with you," she said.

"I'd be happy to," Kate said.

"Good. Then it's a plan. And I don't think it's an extreme reaction to flower arrangements at all."

Liss looked around the room at everyone here, people she was linked to, people the Garrett clan was strongly linked to. Yes, she wanted more, but the risk would outweigh the reward. Because there was no way Connor could give what she desired.

So yes, maybe she loved him. But this, the relationships in this room, they were love, too.

If she couldn't have everything, then she would just have this.

CHAPTER SEVENTEEN

LISS HAD SKIPPED sex with Connor the night of the barn decorating, claiming exhaustion as an excuse. She'd been feeling too raw after her realizations to risk getting naked with him. But she knew her resolve wouldn't last.

She didn't really want it to last, anyway. Because she had to make the most of whatever this was, for as long as she had it.

But she was exhausted after a day of taking abuse from a couple of very difficult clients at work. She hadn't gotten off until after six, trying to resolve various issues, and what she needed was some time to herself, and possibly a bath to build up some resolve before she actually came face-to-face with Connor.

She dumped her purse on her bed and went digging for her pajamas. So she wouldn't be looking all that sexy when she did come into contact with Connor. But he didn't seem to mind what she was wearing. He was more interested in what she wasn't wearing. That made her smile a little bit.

She found her flannel pajama bottoms in the bottom drawer of the dresser and straightened, turning around and facing the bed. Then she paused when she saw a white garment bag hanging over the back of her door.

There was a note taped to it.

She crossed the room and grabbed hold of the note.

It was attached to the garment bag with a rolled-up piece of duct tape. She laughed and unfolded it. It was short, and to the point, written in Connor's very square handwriting.

HOPEFULLY THE DRESS IN THE BAG FITS. IF IT DOES, AND YOU DON'T THINK I'M AN IDIOT, MEET ME IN THE BARN.

He hadn't signed it, but he hadn't needed to.

Unbearably curious now, she pulled the zipper tab on the bag, drawing it down slowly and revealing a wedge of pale pink. Her breath caught, and she undid the zipper faster, parting the two sides of the bag to reveal the dress inside. She slid her hands down the back of the skirt, pulling it more fully out of the bag.

It could have been the exact same dress she had purchased for the prom she had never attended. Satin, with vertical seams that ran from the bodice down the skirt. Spaghetti straps with clear beads sewn into them.

It was definitely dated. Not in the least bit fashionable.

She still thought it was beautiful.

"You shady bastard. How did you manage?"

She took it off the hanger and stripped her clothes off quickly. For a moment she was afraid to put it on. Just in case that was the end of the fantasy. And she couldn't get it zipped over her hips or something.

She took a deep breath and grabbed hold of the tiny little impractical zipper, pulling it down and stepping into the center of the pool of satin, pulling it up her body, working her arms through the straps.

She turned and looked at herself in the mirror that

hung on the opposite wall. She took a breath and zipped it up.

It fit.

Which meant she had a date in the barn.

LISS OPENED THE DOOR to the barn slowly, her breath catching as she saw the inside, the lights that were strung overhead casting a golden glow on everything. The tables were set with the flower arrangements they'd labored over, each chair placed around the table decorated with a burlap ribbon.

Everything in the barn looked and smelled new, sawdust and pine lingering in the air.

But the thing that made her heart stop was the sight of Connor, wearing a pair of black dress pants and a white shirt, tucked into the waistband of those pants. The shirt wasn't buttoned all the way, the collar left open, and he certainly wasn't wearing a tie. But for Connor, this was the ultimate in formal wear.

She stopped right in the doorway, laughing, and she wasn't really sure why. "What did you do?" she asked.

He stuffed his hands into his pockets. "I saw the dress in the window of a secondhand place, and I knew you had to have it." He cleared his throat. "But then I thought it was kind of stupid to have a prom dress and no prom." He shrugged. "So I thought since the barn was already decorated…"

Liss's throat was so tight she didn't think she could speak. She could barely breathe. So she didn't say anything. She just walked toward the man who meant more to her than any other person on earth.

"I didn't hang up any balloons or anything," he said. "But I did spike the punch."

She laughed, a kind of shaky, thin laugh. "You made punch?"

"No, actually I just brought wine coolers. Because I'm trying to cut back."

"Well, it's the thought that counts."

Except this went well beyond the thought. It was the most romantic thing anyone had ever done for her, and she knew he wasn't thinking of it as romance. The thought was like a knife cutting into her heart, as easily as she'd sliced through those peaches the other day.

"Since it's prom, I figure we should dance," he said, sounding grim.

"We don't have to dance," she said. But she wanted to.

"I know we don't." He moved away from her and crossed the room, going to where Sadie had left the speakers they'd been using last night. "Fortunately, Sadie left her thing in here. Because nothing I own could hook up to this."

He pressed Play, and a slow, instrumental song filled the room. Then he turned and held out his hand. "Since you're my prom date, Felicity Foster, I'd like to have this dance."

"Okay," she said, because it was all she could say.

She curled her fingers around his, and he pulled her close, wrapping his arm around her waist.

"I don't know how to dance," he said, moving slightly, out of time with the music.

"I don't care."

Because the rhythm didn't matter, the steps didn't matter, only her partner mattered. She slipped her hand out of his and wrapped both of her arms around his neck, and he put both of his hands on her hips. She rested her head against his chest, listening to the steady beat of his heart beneath her cheek.

Yes, she had wanted to go to prom back in high school. But he had been the date she'd dreamed of. Not the one she'd had. And Connor had gone with someone else.

She squeezed her eyes shut and tried not to think about what it would've been like if he had asked her back then.

And she realized there was no point in regretting it. Because she had been young then, and so had he. And as much as she had liked him back then, as much as her teenage hormones had panted after him, it was nothing compared to the way she felt about him now.

He was a man now. So different from the boy he had been. Shaped by the ensuing years and by the losses and triumphs that had marked each one.

Connor the boy had the top spot in her fantasies, but Connor the man held her heart.

And it didn't matter where they were fifteen years ago. All that mattered was where they were now.

She angled her head upward and kissed him. Deeper, longer, and with a lot more skill than she could have managed back on her real prom night, too.

He tightened his hold on her, returning the kiss, his hands moving from her hips down to cup her butt. He pulled her tightly against his body, against the hard ridge of his arousal.

"The song is over," she said, her lips still pressed against his.

"Yes, it is."

"Does that mean prom is over?"

"Prom, maybe. But not prom night."

"Oh, good. You know… You know what happens on prom night," she said, sliding her hand beneath the collar of his shirt.

"I don't know. I just dropped my date off before midnight, so if you're expecting something else…"

She pressed a kiss to his neck. "I am expecting to get lucky. I'm wearing a pink satin gown. How can I fail?"

"Oh, honey," he said, tucking a strand of hair behind her ear, "you're you. You couldn't fail no matter what you were wearing."

"How did you find a dress in my size?" she asked. "I have to know."

"It was actually too big. But I bought it then had a look in your laundry, and the woman at the store trimmed it down according to the size I gave her."

She blinked hard, trying not to cry. "That was… That was…" She took a deep breath to try to ease the pressure in her chest. "I don't… You gave this back to me and I…I can't give anything back to you. I can never make us even."

"Maybe there's nothing old for you to give me, but you've given me new things. And for a guy whose been spending all his time in the past, that's a hell of a thing."

"Connor, I don't… This is just too thoughtful. I can't repay it."

"There's no scoresheet with us, Liss. Not now, not ever."

"I'm not used to that," she said, sniffing.

"Liss," he said, bending down and brushing a kiss to her lips, "I hate that you gave that away for your mom. I hate that she made you feel like you owed her something just for being alive. You're not a burden."

She closed her eyes. "Connor…don't make me cry."

"I need you to know that. I need you to understand why I wanted to do this for you. I need you to understand that it wasn't a lot of trouble, that it isn't amazing that I thought of you. Who wouldn't think of you?"

"A lot of people," she said, her words thick.

"Stupid people." He kissed her again, and she just stopped thinking. She stopped doing anything but relishing the moment.

There was no point worrying about the future or the past when the present was so damn good.

She put her hands on the buttons of his shirt and started to undo them, pushing the fabric open and sliding her palms over his bare skin, relishing the feel of his heat and skin, of his muscles and the slight roughness of his chest hair.

She pushed the shirt off his shoulders and onto the floor and just looked at him for a moment. "You are… Connor, you have no idea."

His lips curved into a lopsided smile. "Show me."

She reached behind her back and undid her zipper, letting the dress fall to the floor. She took a deep breath and met his gaze. She didn't feel insecure or uncertain at all, another perk of being in her thirties instead of being a teenager.

She wasn't shy about showing him her body, and he wasn't shy about showing her how much he appreciated it.

"I'm pretty sure you didn't have any underwear that looked like that when we were in high school."

She looked down at the strapless, pink lace bra she was wearing, and at the matching thong. Then she looked back up at Connor. "No reason to. Since no one was seeing them."

"And right now I'm the only one who gets to see them," he said.

"Possessive."

He growled and closed the space between them, wrapping his arm around her waist and tugging her hard against his body. "Damn right I'm possessive."

"Why is that?" She needed affirmation, and she needed it now.

"Because I'm the only man who's going to touch you, Liss."

"Why do you care?"

"Because you're mine," he said, his tone firm, uncompromising.

"Why?" Maybe it was a stupid question, maybe there was no good answer to it. But she wanted to hear something that wasn't "because you're helpful," "because you make things convenient," "because you do my accounting." She needed something deeper, was starving for it.

Hungry for something she knew he wouldn't give her, but she would take whatever she could get. Whatever was closest.

"Because I can't stop," he said, tracing her lower lip with his thumb then following the same trail with his tongue. "I can't stop thinking about you, I can't stop wanting you, I can't stop having you." He shook his head. "Dammit, Liss, nothing has ever been like this."

His words rolled over her like warm oil, smooth and soothing and heating her blood at the same time. Liss shivered beneath his touch, her heart beating faster. It wasn't love, but it was enough. Right now it was enough.

He kissed her again, hungrier this time, deeper.

"Connor... I need... I need..."

"I know, baby." He turned around to one of the tables that was inside the barn. "We can never tell Sadie." His tone was grave as he took the flower arrangements off the table, and the tablecloth off the surface and spread it on the floor. "Obviously, I'm not as prepared as you were with your picnic. But problem solved."

"You could have had me on the floor, Connor."

"But then I would've spent the rest of the evening picking splinters out of your ass, and as nice as that sounds, that's not how I want to spend the rest of the evening."

"Yeah, not my idea of a good time, either."

He slid his hand down to her butt, palmed her cheek, squeezed it hard. "Yeah, I can think of much better things we could be doing."

He took her hand and led her to the makeshift blanket, drawing her down onto the floor with him. He made quick work of her clothes and his, retrieving his wallet before he discarded his pants, producing a condom just in time.

"You did think of some things," she said. "The important things."

"Thankfully." He bent his head to her breast, sucking her nipple deep into his mouth. "Yeah, thankfully. Because I have got to have you."

"Have me. I want you. Connor, I want you so much," she said.

She forgot about hiding any part of herself, forgot about concealing her feelings, from herself or from him. Because there was no room for that now.

He saw her already, anyway. So clearly that he had known, even when she'd told him that the prom dress she'd never gotten to wear was ugly, that what she really meant was the loss still hurt.

He'd known, and he had taken steps to fix it.

And she had nothing else to give him but her honesty. So she would. If she couldn't give it with her lips, she would give it with her body.

She shifted beneath him, arching her hips so that the blunt head of his cock met with her slick flesh, sliding over her clit, sending a shock of pleasure through her. "Nothing feels like this," she said, "like the way it feels to have you inside of me."

"Damn straight, baby. When I'm inside you it's like there's nothing else."

He ran his hand down her thigh, slid her leg up over his hip and pushed inside her slowly, stretching her, filling her. She squeezed her eyes shut, tears pressing against her lids, and she fought to hold them at bay.

"Don't hold back," she said, the words choked.

He shuddered, and it was as if her words snapped the thread that had been holding his control in check. He bucked hard against her, the motion bringing him into contact with her clit again. He slid his hands beneath her butt, raising her hips, bringing her up against him every time he thrust down deep.

"Liss," he said, his voice a growl. "Liss," he said again, broken this time, desperate.

He lowered his head, burying his face in her neck, and she felt him start to shake.

It was his surrender, his loss of control, that destroyed what was left of hers. He thrust into her one last time, coming on a growl just as her own release tore through her, leaving her breathless, spent and dizzy.

They were both breathing hard, and Connor lifted

his head, kissing her, deep, slowly. "Liss," he said, just her name. Nothing else.

But nothing else could have made her feel more special.

Nothing more than a pink prom dress and the most perfect moment with the man she loved. The man she had always loved.

And the man she always would love. No matter what.

A TABLECLOTH DIDN'T do much to shield a person from the hardness of a barn floor. But at the moment Connor couldn't say he cared. He didn't care about anything beyond the warm weight of Liss's naked body over his.

Doing this for her... It had felt essential. The need to do something for her, to *show* her he cared, a drive he hadn't quite understood.

Except maybe it was part of trying to move forward. Because he was trying to do that. And he wanted her to do it, too. If they could take on some of her old hurts, maybe he would have better luck tackling some of his own.

He wrapped his arms around her, holding on to her tight. Something about what had just happened had changed things between them, or at least it had changed something in him.

Something in this moment of laying the past to rest made him want to do the same.

"I..." The word died in his throat, blocking any more from coming out. He had never talked about this. Had never told another soul. But maybe this place, this new place that had been built over the ashes of a tragedy, was magic in some way.

Maybe it was the best place, the best moment, to say them.

He tried to breathe through the knot in his chest, sweat beading on his forehead, panic galloping through his chest like a herd of wild horses. He felt dizzy, his mouth dry, his stomach heaving.

The silence was costing him. And he couldn't hold it anymore.

"Her due date was September fifteenth," he said. They weren't exactly the words he had meant to say. But they were all he could manage.

"Whose?" Liss's voice sounded…horrified. Terrified. But then, he had never expected anything else.

It was just one of the reasons he had never talked about this.

But she had shared with him. And he needed to say this, needed to share it, because the secret, the pain, was like a living beast inside him, eating away at any ounce of happiness that tried to take hold of his soul.

And maybe telling her wouldn't help. But maybe it would.

"Jessie."

Liss didn't say anything; she just wrapped her arms around him, tightened her hold on him. She didn't speak, so he continued.

"We were having a hard time. The whole last year our marriage was really rough. She didn't like the amount of time I spent on the ranch. And I did a bunch of inconsiderate, boneheaded shit. I didn't think anything of finishing up work and going down to Ace's with the guys. I didn't remember to water her flowers. Hell, that year I forgot her birthday. Not that I forgot the date of her birthday, I just didn't realize what day it was and…

She was pretty fed up with me. And I can't say I blame her. Me? I was just pissed because I felt like I was the same. And she was angry that I hadn't changed. But… then she found out she was pregnant. And I was pretty damn grateful, let me tell you. Because I thought that was my lifeline. My second chance."

He released his hold on Liss, but she kept hers on him. He put a hand on his forehead, squeezing his temples tight. "I don't know, maybe she never would have left me, with or without the baby. But the baby… We had a baby coming. And I…I told her I was going to change. And I did. I was going to be a father, and I suddenly saw myself in a completely different way. Saw the man my father had been, the man whose wife had left him with his kids. And I…I knew I didn't want that. So I promised her that I would change. I promised I would be better. It was my wake-up call. I was going to fix things."

He took a deep breath. "I had barely started to try to get things back together. I never had the chance. I never even got to tell everyone about the baby. We never got to tell anyone. She was eleven and a half weeks pregnant. Just three more fucking days and we were going to tell everyone. But what's the point of doing a birth announcement when you're planning a funeral?"

He felt Liss's shoulders shake, and he realized she was crying.

He cleared his throat and continued. "What's the point of announcing something that's never going to happen? I didn't want… I didn't want to add to anyone else's pain. Because you all felt her loss like I did. I didn't want you being sad about the baby, too." He felt a drop of moisture on his chest. "See? I made you cry. I told you, sweetheart, you shouldn't waste your tears on me."

She took a deep, shaking breath. "Don't you know, Connor? It's not a waste. There's no one more worthy of my tears than you."

"Pointless tears. They don't fix anything," he said, his own eyes burning.

"But sometimes you have to cry, anyway," she said, burying her face deeper into his chest.

"I never did," he said, his throat so tight now he could barely breathe. "I just kind of screamed at the universe. At God. Whoever was responsible. I don't even remember that whole day after. I was a husband. I was going to be a father. And then, all of a sudden I was nothing. Just a dumb-ass guy with nothing to look forward to, and no one to come home to." The last word broke, something shifting in his chest. "I had all of these plans. And then it was all just blank. Wiped away in one second."

The ache in his throat was almost unbearable now, the tightness in his chest so intense he couldn't breathe. Something had to give. Something had to break. Or he was going to.

He tried to breathe but it caught, his shoulders shaking. "I lost my wife. I lost my baby." And for the first time a tear rolled down his cheek as he said words he'd barely ever let himself think. "I can't have them back. And I don't want to move on, because then I might forget. But I have to." Another tear rolled down his cheek, and he turned his face into Liss's neck and wrapped his arms around her again.

"Not right now," she said, her voice thick. "Right now all you have to do is lie here with me."

Another sob shook his body, but he held more tightly

to her. To Liss. And as the world around him fell away, and the dark pit threatened to swallow him whole, it was Liss who kept him anchored. Liss who kept them safe while he grieved.

There was no alcohol to numb the pain. It was pure, undiluted agony. It was everything he had been avoiding for the past three years.

He might have spent time in hell, but right now he was walking straight through the darkest part.

But he wasn't alone.

CHAPTER EIGHTEEN

LISS DIDN'T KNOW how long they lay together on the floor of the barn. Until Connor stopped crying. Until she stopped crying.

She felt as if her chest had been opened up, her heart scrubbed raw, before she was stitched back together.

At some point, Connor sat up then stood, extending his hand and helping her up, before erasing the evidence of their activities. Liss dressed slowly, and Connor did the same.

Then he turned to her. "Why don't we go to the house?"

"Okay," she said.

They walked back in silence, and Liss felt a growing sense of dread as they moved nearer to the porch. Because she felt as if this was leading up to something big. After this, there were pretty much only two things that could happen. Either he would push her away, because he felt too exposed, or he would pull her closer.

Her experience of Connor was that he tended to push people away. Everyone.

His revelation was a prime example of that. He hadn't shared. He had locked all of that pain inside himself, left screaming in his soul, a demon only he was fighting.

Until tonight. And it was you he shared it with.

She could only hope that he wasn't regretting it.

She kinda felt like a jerk making any of this about her. It was about him. But everything was all tangled up. Another problem with being a lover, and not just a friend. If she were just a friend, she would feel the stability of their relationship now. It wouldn't matter what he did after this. What he said. If he needed to be alone, she would understand.

But if that happened tonight, there was no way she wouldn't take it personally.

They walked up the front porch steps, and she felt a strange sense of déjà vu. Of that first night they'd kissed. A feeling like they were on the edge of a change, terrified of what the outcome might be.

Connor didn't seem to be suffering from the same sensation, since he just opened the door with no ceremony.

She followed him into the living room and stood there, not entirely sure what she should do.

"Are you tired?" he asked.

"Exhausted." And that was true.

"Why don't we go up to bed?"

His question hung in the air for a few moments, the significance of it slowly sinking in.

"We?"

"Yeah," he said, holding out his hand.

She didn't question him; she simply extended her hand and wrapped her fingers around his. He tugged slightly, and she followed his lead, up the stairs and down the hall toward his bedroom. "Connor…"

"I bought a different bed. Just…last year. I thought that might be relevant."

She wasn't sure if she would've thought of that. "Okay."

"I haven't ever had sex with anyone in this bed."

"Okay."

"You don't seem that concerned."

"I don't… I guess I wasn't."

"Well, that's good."

"You thought about it, though. So it matters to you."

He shrugged. "Just because it matters to me doesn't mean it matters. I make a whole lot of things bigger than they should be."

"Tell me."

"I just thought it might help. So I got a new bed. Because to me… You know, we bought it when she moved in. So I just wanted you to know, this isn't that bed. It's just my bed. And I want you in it."

"Thank you."

"I just told you I want you in my bed, woman. And the best you have is *thank you*?"

"It's better than apologizing. Which is kind of your thing," she said, her lips curving into a smile.

Her chest still hurt from their conversation, her eyes still burning, but smiling with him still felt right. Still felt natural.

"Sorry if I rocked your world back there," he said, his voice rough.

"You did. In a lot of ways." She cleared her throat. "Thank you for my dress."

He cupped the back of her head and pulled her close, kissing her deep. "Thank you for listening to me."

"Thank you for talking to me." She put her hand on his chest, her palm right over his heart. "You don't ever have to worry about protecting me. We're friends. Now and always. And that means we are here to help each other carry this stuff. You never have to carry double when I could share it with you."

He put his hand over hers, pressing hard. "Thank you. That's better than sorry, right?"

"Better," she said, a smile curving her lips.

"Let's go to bed, Liss."

CONNOR KNEW THERE was nothing to be afraid of in sleep. It wasn't as if the bogeyman could reach your dreams and get you. Still, when his front porch and a flash of light went through his mind, his heart rate sped up, panic invading his body.

But when he opened the door, it wasn't Eli standing there.

It was Liss. Looking at him. Wanting something from him. Something he didn't think he could dig deep enough to find…

He woke up breathing hard, a cold sweat covering his body.

There was a delicate hand resting on his chest, silky curls spread over his shoulder. Liss was there still. And he was holding her.

He wasn't alone. And his mattress wasn't cold.

He lifted his hand and brushed her cheek with his knuckles, relishing the feel of her softness beneath his touch. It was funny how he had expected to wake up alone. And funnier still just how much of a relief it was to wake up with someone.

And he hadn't been confused, even for a second, about who it was.

Because Liss was…Liss. She smelled like wild-flowers, courtesy of her perfume, and a little bit like sea salt thanks to the wind that tangled in her hair every time she walked outside.

Even in the dark, he would always know it was her.

He didn't want to close his eyes again. He just wanted to stay awake and look at Liss, highlighted by the pale moon that was shining through the window. He wanted to stay awake and live in this moment of not being alone.

Of being beside someone who knew the darkest, saddest part of it all.

What a failure he was. That he hadn't been the husband Jessie deserved. The giant crater of grief that was inside him, because he had lost not only the promise of a future with a new, better marriage, not only a wife, but a child.

That he had lost himself.

Because that was the bottom line of it all. The most important part of who he'd been was husband. But he had invested more in being a rancher. In being a cowboy.

Unfortunately, when you invested so much in a hunk of dirt and lost everything else, a hunk of dirt was all you had left.

That which a man sows is what he reaps. Or something.

Though he could see now that he had more than dirt. He had his barn, anyway. And it had been rebuilt. Which made a lot of other things seem possible.

The sky was turning a lighter shade of blue, and really, he could get up, take a shower and get ready to start his day. Go out and work on that hunk of dirt that had become his entire life.

But Liss was in here. And he was warm. And he wasn't alone.

So instead he decided to stay in bed.

"JUST A FEW hours now," Liss said, looking around at the barn, all decked out for the party tonight.

The sliding side doors were thrown open wide, white Christmas lights strung from the top of the frame, out to a tree outside, creating a twinkling canopy. Mason jars were strung from the tree branches, with flameless candles inside. Fire safety was important, for obvious reasons.

There were tables situated outside, and inside, everything set back up since the night she and Connor had spent on the floor.

Therefore, there was no ire from Sadie.

Though, while she wasn't filled with ire, she was wandering around the barn straightening things that were already straight and chattering like a ferret. Eli was hanging back, obviously well educated in what to do when Sadie was in full Sadie mode. Jack was outside, getting the barbecues fired up, directing those who had volunteered to come and help with food.

Jack was surprisingly organized and efficient when he needed to be. And it always came as a shock to Liss, because he seemed to work hard to keep his competence under wraps. He had the look of a man who ambled through life, stumbling upon good luck, and sticking it in the pocket of his Wrangler jeans, hanging on to it till he needed to spend some.

He owned a fairly large piece of property and managed to have gotten into the high-cost game of breeding horses. She, and everyone else, assumed he must have financed all of that with earnings from his stint in the rodeo. Though she couldn't imagine he made all that much money doing the occasional bull riding competition circuit.

And Jack never shared. He just kind of smiled and winked. And everyone let it go, and women fell at his feet, and he moved on. An enigma wrapped in a mystery, wrapped in flannel.

But whatever his flaws he was a good friend, and he had proven it over and over, not just today, but when dealing with Connor over the past few years. She'd gone into caregiver mode. Jack had made it his mission to make Connor smile. And he'd done a damn good job. But then, Jack made everyone smile.

"Are you nervous?" Connor asked Eli, who was pacing the length of the barn.

"Nerves are for people who don't have an early lead in the polls." And yet it was clear that nerves were also for Eli, in spite of the lead.

"I heard that polls can be superinaccurate," Kate said, perched on one of the long tables that would later hold pie and drinks. "Because data can be skewed."

"Who have you been talking to?" Connor asked.

"Some of the old guys who come into the Farm and Garden," Kate said, blinking slowly.

"You need some friends who aren't paranoid old men," Connor said.

"I have friends. The other girls who barrel race. I hang out with Sierra West during competition." Kate crossed her arms. "See? Friends. Friends who are women. And my age."

"Yeah, Katie. Your social life is hopping."

"People who live in glass houses that are actually

Jack Daniel's bottles should not throw stones, Connor," Kate said, her tone dry.

"For your information," he said, "I'm sober. I have been."

Kate's eyes widened, and Eli turned to look at him. "You are?" she asked.

Liss's throat tightened, and she fought the urge to excuse herself. Because she felt conspicuous, standing there during this moment, which was clearly a big one. Connor's drinking wasn't something that the family could ignore. It wasn't something anyone could ignore. And yet as far she knew, none of them had ever talked about it.

"Yes. I haven't gotten drunk in weeks."

"I didn't know you were trying to stop," Eli said.

Connor looked at her. "Yeah, well, I stopped around the time Liss moved in. I figured she didn't need to deal with me being hungover."

"You never minded me dealing with you hungover," Eli said.

"I minded," Connor said.

"Well, I feel like I already won the election," Eli said, smiling. "Now it doesn't matter what happens."

Connor frowned. "Really?"

Eli slapped him on the shoulder. "Hell, no. I'm happy for you, but I need to win this election."

Connor laughed. "Good. That was way too much sincerity."

"Seriously, though, that's amazing." Eli shook his head. "I'm proud of you."

"It's really nice that you're able to be proud of me for no longer being an asshole. I'll try to set the bar higher in the future."

"Men," Kate said, sliding off the table and crossing the barn, throwing her arms around Connor and hugging him tight. "I'm really proud of you." She kissed him on the cheek and took a step back.

"What was that for?" Connor asked, his voice rough.

"Because you scare the hell out of me," Kate said. "I don't want you to leave me, or die, like everyone else."

Liss swallowed hard, blinking rapidly to keep from weeping all over a moment she had no right to invade.

Jack chose that moment to walk into the barn. "Why are we all looking somber?" he asked.

"Connor is sober," Eli said.

"Well, fuck. Going to the bar is going to be a lot less fun now," Jack said. "Nice for your mental health and stuff, though."

"Thanks, Jack," Connor said. "That sentiment is more my speed. Anyway, tonight is about Eli. This family has been down a few times in the course of our history, but we're not out. Eli, you've proven that big-time."

"You've done more than you think," Eli said.

"Both of you are the best. Now, I propose we have some beer… No, soda," Jack said. "A toast for all the excellent shit that's happening."

"Good thing we have soda," Sadie said, finally coming over to their end of the barn, crossing the space and giving Connor a side hug.

Liss wished that she could hug and kiss him. But she couldn't, not here. She realized she was the only one who hadn't said anything when Connor had made his announcement. Because, of course, she already knew. It would expose some of the intimacy that was growing between them. But then, they had always had a certain level of intimacy. And she did live with him. She wasn't sure what she was supposed to do now.

Was commenting acting casual? Or was not commenting more casual?

This sucked. She didn't normally have to think through her interactions with these people quite this hard. She didn't normally have to think about them at all. In fact, these friends, this family, this group, were the only people she didn't overthink things with.

Because it wasn't all checks and balances, and making sure she was worthy. And she hated that she was feeling all nervous and insecure now.

Because she and Connor were… What even were they right now? They had established the friends and lovers thing. With the intent that they would sleep separately, have sex, but not be in a relationship.

But something had changed last night. Something major.

She wasn't sure what to do with it.

Especially not right now. So she just sort of stood there awkwardly, not certain of what to do with her hands.

"It was nice of you to get soda, Sadie," Jack said, digging around in one of the ice chests that was shoved against the back wall of the barn, waiting to be transferred to a more decorative metal bucket closer to starting time. "For the kids. Like Katie."

"Fuck you up, down and sideways, Monaghan," Kate said, extending her hand and accepting a can of Coke from him, even while she insulted him.

"It's so cute when you try to use grown-up words."

"I could punch him for you if you want," Connor said.

"I can't," Eli said, "because I can't risk a violation

of the law at this point. But I'm with you in spirit. I'm punching him in the face in my head."

"Go on," Kate said, looking at Connor. "Hit him."

"Sorry, Kate," Connor said. "Jack would have to do something pretty bad for me to punch him. Seeing as I didn't punch him the time he talked us into skinny-dipping and we got caught by those older girls…"

"You talk about that like it's my fault. It was embarrassing for me, too," Jack said.

"You were not embarrassed," Eli said. "You hit on them. You were a scrawny, naked thirteen-year-old hitting on seventeen-year-olds. You had no shame then, and you have no shame now."

"That is what my headstone will say."

Kate shook her head. "You won't even punch him for your own sister."

"He isn't allowed to," Sadie said. "Because Jack might bleed on the floor. And everything is perfect. I do not have time to go scrubbing bloodstains out of wooden planks."

"There you go," Connor said. "The most compelling reason of all not to punch Jack. Sadie would get mad at me, and I am afraid of Sadie."

"Rightfully so," Sadie said, making a severe expression that wasn't all that severe. "Okay, enough standing around. Jack, you're supposed to be supervising the meat."

A lopsided grin crossed Jack's face. "Okay, Sadie. I guess I will go supervise the meat." He raised his can of soda in salute and walked back out of the barn.

"Eli," Sadie said, "you probably need to put on something you haven't been working in. And I probably do, too."

"Right," Eli said.

Kate moved toward the barn door. "I might go and see if they need more help with the food," she said, stepping out.

"I guess we'll just stay here and wait for people to start arriving," Connor said.

"Okay, we'll be back in about an hour," Sadie said, grabbing Eli's hand and leading him from the barn.

As soon as the door closed behind them, Liss turned to Connor. "They are just escaping to have sex, aren't they?"

"Oh, absolutely," Connor said.

Liss cleared her throat, unhappy to discover that the awkwardness had not escaped the room along with the others. "Everything looks…nice," she said.

"Are you okay? You've been very quiet. In fact, I don't think you've said anything for the past twenty minutes."

"Sure I have. I asked if you thought Eli and Sadie were going to…you know."

"What's up, Liss?"

She sighed. "Well, I knew already that you weren't drinking. And it's hard for me to know what to do in front of everyone else. And now that I think about it, I was probably looking a lot more conspicuous than if I had just tried to fake surprise and join in. But I kind of forgot how to act naturally." She made an exasperated noise. "No, you know, the thing is I didn't forget how to act naturally. It's just that what feels natural now isn't something I can do in public."

Connor's eyes darkened. "Oh, yeah? What feels natural to you?"

"This," she said, closing the distance between them and kissing him.

"Feels good to me, too," he said, a smile curving his lips.

"We'll figure it out." She had to believe that. The alternative didn't bear consideration.

CHAPTER NINETEEN

THE ENTIRE TOWN of Copper Ridge appeared to have turned up at Eli's party. At least as far as the town was concerned, Eli had the vote. But they would have to wait and see what the county decided.

Dinner had been eaten, dancing had been going on for quite some time and most of the pie that had been spread out on the long tables inside the barn had been eaten, too.

And the countdown to the announcement was winding down.

Eli was ahead in the count with most precincts reporting, but Connor knew his brother wouldn't start celebrating until it was more of a certainty.

Still, Connor figured they would be calling it soon. Even if the counting didn't finish for another few hours, Eli was ahead by enough of a margin that there would be no way for his opponent to close the gap.

A local camera crew had assembled to film the results, TVs mounted to the walls playing continuous footage of ever-growing percentages. Measures that were passing and failing, city council positions and, of course, the race between Eli Garrett and David Wright for the position of Logan County sheriff.

Eli had a lead of over ten points, but even with that level of certainty, Connor felt nervous. Because there was a lot at stake here for his brother, and he found he cared a whole hell of a lot more than he'd anticipated he might.

It was kind of refreshing. To care about something more than making it through the day.

To feel all right about the prospect of going to bed, and what dreams might find him there.

The screen on the television changed back to the news anchors' faces, with percentages on the side.

Sadie stood up and started to clank her fork on the side of a Mason jar, trying to get some quiet in the barn. But the noise continued, everyone oblivious to what was going on around them. She tried again, this time clinking more insistently.

Suddenly, a high-pitched whistle cut through the din. Connor turned toward the sound and saw Kate climbing up onto her chair, planting her boots firmly where she had just been sitting. "Hey!" she shouted. "Be quiet now, my brother is about to win an election."

She tugged down on the brim of her hat, nodded her head and sat.

Connor turned to Liss, who was sitting next to him. "Damn, I could use her to herd cows."

Sadie turned the volume up on the TV and stood next to Eli, her arms wrapped around his waist as everyone turned their attention to the announcements.

Measure 62 passed and so did measure 64. Connor felt slightly guilty at the realization that he had no clue what in hell those were. Measure 47 failed. Most of the city council positions remained the same. And when the results for sheriff flashed up on the screen, it was with a kind of anticlimactic speed. There was no pause or drumroll, just a clear and quick announcement that Eli Garrett was the new sheriff of Logan County.

A cheer rose up through the barn, hats flying through the air, and the sound of thunderous applause echoing off the walls. Eli grabbed Sadie and kissed her, dipping her low, which only caused everyone around to cheer louder.

He looked over at Liss, and he found he wanted to kiss her, too. But he didn't.

Instead, he stood and joined in the clapping and boot stomping.

Liss was beaming, and he could've sworn he'd never seen a more beautiful sight. "He did it!" she shouted over everyone else.

He couldn't kiss her, but hugging her, putting his arm around her, would be normal enough. She was right; it was hard to know what to do.

He moved closer to her and wrapped his arm around her shoulders, squeezing her tight. She leaned in, putting her hand on his chest, and he felt a rush of desire flood through him.

He pulled away from her and she looked at him, hurt and confusion visible in her eyes.

He leaned in and whispered in her ear. "It's too much for me to handle."

"Then maybe we should go somewhere more private."

He should say no. He should absolutely not sneak out of the barn during his brother's moment of triumph. Not for something as base as sex. Saving a kitten from a tree, or a puppy from a sinkhole, sure. But sex? No.

"Let's go," he said.

Of course he was going to do it. Whether he should

or not. He couldn't say no to this. Couldn't say no to her. And he didn't want to.

She gave him a look that lit him on fire from his chest down to his toes.

And then she turned and walked out of the barn, weeding through the crowd of people. And he followed. Because he could do nothing else.

He tipped his hat and smiled, and tried to look as if he was paying attention as people greeted him, all the while keeping an eye on Liss. The back of her. From the glossy waves of copper hair to her perfectly rounded ass.

He didn't want to lose sight of her.

She managed to slip through the thickest part of the crowd, and he stopped making eye contact with people. No, now he was just busting through. Every man for himself.

And to hell with them if they thought he was rude. He didn't care. Not right now. All that mattered was Liss. All that mattered was this.

She flicked a glance at him over her shoulder, the Mason jar lights from overhead casting a golden glow onto her hair, making it shimmer like it was on fire. He hoped she was on fire. Because God knew he was. He was burning. Burning like his barn, and he didn't know if there was any chance of him ever being rebuilt. But if not, if in the end all that was left was a big pile of ash, it would be worth it. For this. For her.

He was moving forward, one foot after the other. Him after her. After a feeling that he'd thought was long dead. She made him want. Made him need. Made him crave when for a whole lot of years he'd been trying to sink into the cushions of his couch and dissolve completely.

She made him want to feel when he'd spent years bathed in an alcohol haze. He didn't want a haze when he was with Liss. He wanted her, all of her, burning hot and bright and sharp. Pleasurable, painful, anything and everything.

And that scared him. Scared him to death.

But there was still nothing he could do but follow her.

They escaped the lights in the crowd, the noise and music fading behind them. And when he was confident no one was around, he closed the distance between them and took her hand in his. She looked up at him, her smile stoking the fire inside him. He loved that he could make her smile like that. He could even smile back, and it wasn't hard.

They walked down the dirt road that led to the old barn. He didn't use it for anything anymore, and the red paint was faded, worn and revealing the natural wood planks beneath. There were a couple of holes in the roof, which he'd been meaning to fix, because he didn't want the place to fall into total disrepair.

This was the barn that had been the center of his father's ranching operation. The one that had become Connor's responsibility at a very early age. Part of the reason why the Garrett Ranch lived inside him. Why the dirt on his hands had settled down beneath his skin, gotten into his blood. Yes, he'd poured too much into it and not enough into his marriage, but the fact remained he would always pour into this place.

Because it was home. Because it lived all around him and in him.

And coming here with Liss now felt right. Possibly

because they were going to have sex, and nothing at all felt wrong about that right now. Seeing as he had spent so much time feeling as if everything was wrong, he would take this whatever the significance was.

He pushed open the side door and pulled her inside and up against his body.

"Finally," she said, the word almost a purr.

It slid down his spine, settling in the pit of his stomach and down lower, his cock getting hard just thinking about kissing her, touching her, having her. "My thoughts exactly," he said, holding on to her hips tight, walking them both backward against the rough wood siding. This was what he wanted. To screw her up against a wall. To show her just how desperate he felt. Just how much he needed her. Another thing he'd never done before.

Because he was always lost, halfway somewhere else, his brain on the cows, the weather, the land. But he was in it right now, in it with her, and he couldn't spare a single thought for anything that wasn't Liss.

"I have a feeling this is going to be quick," he whispered, kissing the side of her neck and reveling in the sound she made.

"That's fine. I'm feeling pretty quick myself," she said.

He pushed her top up, exposing her lace-covered breasts. He tugged the bra down, exposing her skin, her perfect, rosy nipples. Damn, he loved breasts. He couldn't believe he had gone this long without seeing them.

More specifically, he loved Liss's breasts. So damn much that looking at her hurt. So damn much that he doubted he would ever be able to look at her again without thinking about her like this. Without picturing this.

He pushed that thought out of his mind, because it was irrelevant right now. Because right now she was getting naked for him. Right now he could look at her if he wanted to. He could taste her. And he did. Lowering his head and sliding the flat of his tongue over her nipple. She arched against him, a hoarse cry escaping her lips, and he sucked the tightened bud in deep, grazing his teeth over it lightly, relishing the moment she dug her fingernails into his shoulders.

He unbuckled her belt, undid the snap on her jeans and pushed them down her hips. "Those are gonna have to come off all the way, honey."

She made quick work of undressing while he shoved his pants halfway down his hips, taking his wallet out of his back pocket and fishing out a condom and rolling it on.

He cupped her ass and slid his hand down to her thigh, hooking her leg up over his hip, opening her to him as he thrust deep inside. He pressed his lips to her neck, holding her tight as he withdrew and thrust harder. "I've never done this with anyone before," he whispered. "I've never wanted someone so badly I had to sneak out of a party, fuck them up against a wall."

He didn't talk to women like this. He didn't do shit like this. But someone had broken free inside him, a beast that was on the loose now, prowling around, chasing after him while he tried desperately to stay ahead of the jaws threatening to close tight around his throat.

She shuddered beneath him, rolling her hips in time with his movements. That, combined with the tight, hot clasp of her body, sending him straight to the edge. He held on tight for as long as he could before he couldn't hold back any longer.

"Connor." She shuddered, her internal muscles tightening around his cock as she came hard.

Her name on his lips, the force of her release, cut his control loose. His blood was roaring in his ears, his release coming on with all the force of a freight train. And all he could do was hang on tight while he was consumed.

When it was over, he was shaking, unable to catch his breath. But so was she.

He kissed her lips, moving away from her and disposing of the condom in a bin in the corner.

"Aren't you worried about foxes?"

He turned to face her. "Who the hell can think about foxes with you standing there looking like that?" he asked.

"Well, a couple weeks ago you could." She moved away from the wall, wincing. "Now you really will be picking splinters out of my ass. And my shoulders."

"Shit," he said. "I'm sorry."

"Don't be," she said, bending down and collecting her jeans, putting them on quickly as she righted her top. "I've never done anything like that, either. With Marshall it was all comfortable. And…I should not be talking about this right now."

"Why not?" he asked. "I always talk about my stuff. Talk about your stuff."

"There is not much stuff. I mean, I stayed in a relationship for far longer than I should have, because… because I didn't know what other relationship I would ever have. There wasn't one I wanted to be in more. At least, not one I could have. And he…he likes to be taken care of. He needed it. And that made me feel needed. And when I feel needed I feel secure. At least, I did. Because if someone needs me they can't get rid of me. And dammit, I should have wanted to get rid of him. Instead, he left me. And he took my truck and ruined my credit. Because I am a pushover who put up with a whiny baby of a boyfriend who was really bad in bed."

"I'm better in bed than he is, right?"

"On riverbank, against barn wall. And I really shouldn't prop up your ego like this." She pointed her finger at him, and he reached out and grabbed it, tugging her close and nipping the tip. Her eyes widened. "You bit me."

"And you liked it," he said, smiling.

He liked this. The intensity, followed by talking, and then something fun, funny. It was all the pieces of his relationship with Liss coming together and making something that he hadn't even known could exist.

"Fine," she said, leaning forward and kissing him. "I liked it."

"Yeah, you did," he said, kissing her back. "Never settle. I mean it."

"I won't."

He cupped her chin and angled his head, kissing her deeper, longer. He could drown in this, in her, and be happy with that.

The sound of the door opening caused him and Liss to break apart, jumping back as though they'd had cold water thrown on them. Jack was standing there, a woman Connor couldn't name standing with him, both their eyes wide.

"Hi," Jack said, looking between Connor and Liss.

"What the hell are you doing here?" Connor asked,

the question coming out a little bit harsher than he'd intended. But seriously, what the hell was he doing here?

"I…" He indicated the woman standing next to him. "I think we had the same idea."

"Jack," the woman said, "I'm going to go."

"No, don't go," Jack said, with very little conviction to the words.

"I didn't realize we would have an audience." And with that she turned on her heel and walked back down the path.

"Jack," Liss said, her voice small. "Don't you need to go after your…"

"No. She'll be fine. I don't even know her name. So this is where I say what the hell?" He turned his focus entirely onto the two of them.

"There is no hell to what the," Connor said, clenching his teeth. "You didn't see anything."

"Fine," Jack said. "I'm only one of your best friends, and I would've thought we could talk like adults."

"There is nothing to talk about," Connor said, his throat closing down tight. No one was supposed to know about this. Because once people knew about it, they would have to call it something. Because as Jack was proving, they would have questions. And he didn't know what to call it. He didn't know what to do with it. He wasn't ready for this.

LISS FELT AS THOUGH the entire scene before her was playing out in slow motion. She was still dazed from the orgasm Connor had given her, still feeling a buzz from the words he'd spoken to her. From the feeling of closeness that was warming her heart even now. And now this. Jack had seen them. And Connor was flipping out. The warmth in her heart was fading now.

"And if you say anything to anyone, especially to Eli or Kate…"

"Are you threatening me?" Jack asked, his tone incredulous. Frankly, *Liss* felt a little bit incredulous.

"Just don't say anything," Connor said.

"Would it be that bad?" Liss asked, her voice shaking. She knew she shouldn't be doing this here, knew she shouldn't be doing this now, in front of Jack, but it seemed like they were. "Would it be the worst thing in the world if everybody knew?"

"Knew what?" Connor asked. "That you and I had sex? How is that his business?" He gestured to Jack. "How is that anyone's business?"

"It's more than that," she said, her throat tightening. He shook his head. "It's not."

"Somehow, I think this isn't a conversation that needs to involve me," Jack said, turning. Then he stopped and faced Connor again. "Connor, I'm really glad you stopped drinking. Maybe also try to stop being such an asshole to people who care about you. And I don't mean me. But if you could make an attempt to not fuck up the best you have? Yeah, that would be good. That's your next step." And then Jack turned and walked out of the barn.

Leaving Liss with Connor. Leaving Liss with her heart racing, her head spinning and her throat aching. A pain that was spreading, expanding down to her chest. This was it. And she knew it. She didn't want it to be the end.

"So that's it? It's not anything more than us having sex?"

"It's complicated."

"No, it's not. Not for me." She knew she would regret this. She regretted it already. But she had to say it, anyway. "As far as I'm concerned there isn't anything complicated about this. I love you, Connor."

"Don't," he said. "Please, don't do this, Liss."

"I will do it. Because I've spent years not doing it. Connor, I…I've wanted you forever. And I've been too afraid to have you. And I'm tired of being afraid. You just told me not to settle, well, I'm not settling. I'm not settling for friendship when what I want is everything."

"I gave everything once. I can't give it again. Not to you. Not anyone," he said, the fear that was lacing his voice real, visceral.

And she cared. Cared about what he'd been through, how it had affected him. But she also knew that he couldn't live in it forever. That couldn't be the beginning and end of him. Just like this couldn't be the beginning and end of them.

"I understand. I understand what you've been through. And I understand that it's hard. But, Connor, you can't…"

"Do not tell me that you understand. Because you don't. Nobody does."

"Connor…"

"No. Who did you love that you lost?"

"You, dumb ass. When you fell for someone else. When you married someone else. Somebody that I also loved. And so I put it aside. Because that's what friends do. Because I would never ever have done anything to come between you and Jessie. I let it go when I had to. I sat on our swing—it was our swing to me—and I cried like I would never see you again. Then I lost you again, when she died and you fell into a bottle. I have lost you over and over again. I know what it means." She took a shuddering breath, trying to hold back her tears. "But I don't have to let it go now. I wasn't ready for you then, anyway. All I was ready for was half-ass declarations and a comfortable relationship. I loved the idea of you, but I never had the courage to do anything about it. But I do now. You know, they say timing is a bitch. And yeah, it kind of has been in the situation. The one time I thought I was ready to change our relationship, you proposed to someone else. And then I moved on. And then life... I don't want you to misunderstand and think that somehow your marriage ending like it did was something I was waiting for or something that I wanted. I respected the fact that you married her. I moved on. I never wished anything..."

"I know," he said, the words tight.

"I needed you to know that, though. Just like I need you to know that I've had feelings for you for a long time. And that I love you now."

"I can't do this. Please don't make me do this."

She wasn't sure what he meant. If he meant love, or if he meant ending what they had.

She didn't want to end it. But she'd realized in a blinding flash when he'd said all that to Jack, that she was doing the same thing she always did. Taking care of him, seeing to his needs and crushing what she wanted underneath that. So that she could have a piece of him, when what she wanted was all of him.

She hated this. Hated watching it crumble around her. But what the hell else could she do? Live the rest of her life loving him like this, knowing what it was like to be with him, but never being able to have him in the way that she wanted? Because sex wasn't enough. Sex and friendship wasn't enough. She loved him. A real, all-consuming kind of love that didn't want fences or division.

Yes, she was his friend. But she could never be his friend in the way she had been before. Come to that, she didn't want to be.

"I'm not making you do anything," she said, feeling weary down to her bones. "This is just what's happening."

"No," he said, the word intense, shaking. "I am tired of things just happening. I have choices, dammit. I am not choosing this. I want things to stay the same."

"They can't," she said, her throat getting so tight she could hardly speak. "Because they aren't."

"Damn you, Liss." He shook his head and took a step back from her. "I've lost too much. Please don't make me lose you, too."

"You have to make a choice. If you lose me, it's because you are choosing to lose me. Because you're too afraid to—"

He cut her off. "I'm not choosing to lose you. You are changing the rules. You're supposed to be my friend."

"I am your friend," she said. "But I can't ignore the rest of what I feel. Not even for you."

He closed the space between them and wrapped his arm around her waist, pulling her against him, his expression intense. "What is it you want?"

She blinked back tears, her heart beating so hard she was afraid the fragile thing would crack against her breastbone. "I want…"

Connor swore and reached into his pocket, pulling

out his cell phone. "I have a text," he growled. "Eli proposed."

"They need us to come back?"

"Yeah," he said, putting his phone back into his pocket.

"Great." She tried to smile, but she was pretty sure she lost the ability to force the corners of her mouth to curve up.

She followed him out of the barn, keeping a heavy distance, her heart pounding dully in her ears as they approached the lights and the revelry that they had left behind only forty-five minutes ago. How had they gone from that wonderful, intense moment, when he had taken her up against the barn, shaking, to this? How had it all fallen down so quickly?

Nothing had caught on fire tonight, but something had been destroyed nonetheless.

She worked as hard as she could to force a smile as they walked through a knot of people and into the barn, where Sadie was grinning from ear to ear, holding her hand out, showing her ring off to everyone around them.

Kate's face was flushed, joy radiating from her. Even Jack looked happy. And Eli... Well, the man had become sheriff and gotten engaged to be married in the same evening. He was reserved, always had been, but right now he was grinning so hard she thought his face might break.

She needed to say congratulations. She needed to be happy for them. But she wasn't. Because she wanted that. She wanted to be engaged to Connor. She wanted to marry Connor. She couldn't spend the rest of her life in a halfway point between being friends and lovers.

She couldn't spend the rest of her life being an employee to her relationships. Working hard, waiting for her reward to be given to her, waiting for a good progress report. Hoping she had done well enough to keep the job. Connor was right. She had to want more. And it had to start with him, because it was the hardest place to start.

Of all of the people in her life, she needed him most, and losing him scared her more than anything. But what she wanted mattered. She couldn't give the rest of her life in the service of buying him groceries, having sex with him when he needed sex, being a friend when he needed a friend. Not when she needed more.

"Isn't it beautiful?" Kate asked, gesturing to Sadie's ring.

Kate looked all dreamy and wistful all of a sudden, which was unusual for her.

"Yes," Liss said, knowing her answer sounded as forced as it felt.

Sadie moved closer to Liss and Kate. "He had a whole little private alcove all set up with more Mason jars and candles and Christmas lights. It was all golden and glowing, and private and perfect. And then everyone was here so we got to announce it right away." She was beaming, for happiness brighter than any of the lights strung up in the trees. "And I really want both of you to be in the wedding," Sadie said.

Liss's face burned. She sincerely doubted she would be invited to the wedding after all of this finished between Connor and herself. Just the thought made her chest seize up, made it impossible to breathe. And at the same time, seeing this, knowing there would be a wedding, it solidified in her what she had to do. It solidified what she wanted. And she knew that no matter how much it would suck, her decision had been made.

"I've never been in a wedding," Kate said, looking as if she'd been given a particularly good Christmas gift.

"You'll have to wear a dress," Sadie said.

Kate's smile dimmed a little bit. "You sure I can't be a groomsman?"

"I promise to keep ruffles to a minimum."

"You're going to have to keep ruffles at a zero count. I do not do ruffles."

"We have a while for you to worry about it. I have a feeling the wedding is going to be a monster. The whole town was here for the engagement, so we can't very well exclude them from the wedding."

Connor was talking to Eli, wearing a smile that was as forced as her own. And her expression and her heart sank straight down into her stomach, and slid farther down into her toes. She couldn't do this. Not now.

"Congratulations," she said to Sadie. "We'll talk more tomorrow, okay? I know there are a lot of people here who want your attention. And I'm just…really tired."

Sadie looked concerned but didn't say anything. Liss forced one more feeble attempt at looking happy before turning and walking out of the barn.

She let out a hard breath, one that verged on a sob. She didn't know how she was going to get through this. She didn't know how she was going to survive when she was sure that her heart was going to be crushed in Connor's hand, squished into a useless, lifeless nothing. And she would be left walking around with a vacant spot in her chest where it was supposed to be.

She walked up the steps and into the house, slamming the door closed behind her. She should pack. Because she had no doubt this would end in her leaving. It would have to. But instead, she flung open one of the cabinets and pulled out her favorite mug. She went over to the tap and filled it with water then put it in the microwave, pulling it out when it was hot and putting in a tea bag. A totally plebeian way to fix a cup of tea, but as a diversionary tactic, it worked.

She heard the front door open and slam shut, followed by footsteps.

"What are you doing?" Connor asked from his position in the kitchen door.

"What are *you* doing?" She tied the string on her tea bag, dipping it in and out of the water. "Shouldn't you be off celebrating with your brother?"

"Unsurprisingly, Liss, I am not in a celebratory mood."

"Unsurprising because you never are?"

"Unsurprising because my best friend has suddenly decided she wants to destroy eighteen years' worth of a relationship."

"No," she said, slamming her mug down on the counter and sloshing hot liquid over the side. "Your best friend wants you to pull your head out of your ass and offer her something better than occasional sex and being your grocery monkey."

"Now who's being an asshole?" he asked, his expression thunderous. "You know you're more to me than that. Don't pretend you haven't noticed. To pretend I haven't shown you. But that does not mean I'm ready for…"

"What? What exactly did I ask you for? I just told you I loved you. I didn't go making demands."

"You want a relationship."

"Yeah, imagine that, I want a relationship with a man I'm sharing my body and soul with. What a monster. How dare I."

"Stop. You're the one reducing it so you can try to strengthen your point."

"Am I? Because you're the one who freaked out because Jack caught us kissing. You're the one who threatened your friend. Because people finding out about us was somehow the worst thing in the world to you."

"I'm not ready to share it."

"Why?"

"Because then we have to call it something. And I don't know what to call it."

She put a hand over her eyes and scrubbed it down her face. "And we're back to this. Because I do know what to call it."

"I don't want to have to say this," he said, looking away, a muscle in his jaw twitching. "You're making me say it."

All of her energy, all of her anger, drained out of her, leaving her feeling deflated. Exhausted. "Say it. Just say it, Connor. If there's one perk to the fact that we're friends, it's that we can be honest with each other."

"I don't love you. I can't. Not like you mean. Not like you want."

There was a small part of her that had been prepared to hear these words from Connor Garrett for the past eighteen years. A small part of her that had always imagined her declaration of love, should she ever have enough courage to make it, would end this way. But there had been a larger part of her, a part of herself she hadn't realized was quite so strong, that believed firmly that he would pull her into his arms and tell her he loved her, too.

But that wasn't happening. He wasn't saying it.

She'd slept with him. Shared his bed. Shared his

body. Listened to his secrets, his pain. She had held him while he cried. And still he wasn't in love with her.

And right then and there she knew he never would be.

"Oh," she said, feeling light-headed.

"I can't." He ran a hand through his hair. "I just... I'm a shitty husband, anyway."

She closed her eyes and shook her head, trying to swallow the lump that had lodged itself in the center of her throat. "Don't."

"What?"

"Don't try to make me feel better with stupid crap like that. I know you, Connor Garrett. You are never going to convince me that I could love a better man. Hell, if it were that easy for me to love someone else, I would have done it by now. But I didn't love Marshall. It's always been you."

"Stop. Just stop. You should want it all, and I'm not that. I am a drunken—" a tear rolled down her cheek "—broken jackass who doesn't do anything but worry about himself and his own pain. I've loved and lost and decided it's not worth it." Another tear chased that one, following the same trail the first one had forged. "You're going to find someone who isn't a terrible person like Marshall. And someone who isn't screwed up like me. Dammit, Liss. No tears for me."

She scrubbed her hand over her cheek, not able to wipe the tears away fast enough. "I'll cry for you if I damn well please. I've been crying for you for years. On your wedding day... Oh, Connor, I cried like I would break."

"Liss..."

"This isn't new. And it isn't going to fade."

"I'm not the man you should be feeling this for. I don't deserve it, baby. Just...don't."

Liss crossed her arms beneath her breasts. "Oh, thank you, Connor. Could you make all of my life decisions for me?"

"That's what friends are for," he said, his voice rough.

"That's another thing. I can't do this. Not like this. You have to understand that things are not going back to the way they were before we were sleeping together just because you have made a blanket statement about how you won't fall in love with me."

"That's bullshit. That is not what we agreed on."

She laughed, the sound completely out of place in the conversation and setting. "Well, that's too damn bad."

"I can't believe you. I can't believe this all-or-nothing crap you're throwing at me."

"You don't understand, Connor." She was shouting now, and she didn't care. "I'm not choosing to do this to you. But my feelings have changed, and what you mean to me has changed. I spent a long time pushing those feelings down. I even let them go for a while. Because I had to. And then this happened. And I really thought that I could do this, and I wouldn't fall in love with you, and that I wouldn't need more. I really did believe it would be enough. But it isn't. I'm not demanding a change. The change happened. It happened in me, and if I went back...Connor, my heart would break every day."

"Liss, if you leave me..."

"You don't love me. How bad could it hurt?"

She picked up her mug and turned away from him. Another tear slid down her cheek.

"You're important to me," he said.

"It's not enough."

She started to walk out of the room. "Are you fucking kidding me?" he asked. "You're going to leave me? After everything? After everything I've lost? You promised you wouldn't leave me. You promised me," he said, shouting now.

She turned back to face him. "I'm not a Band-Aid. You can't slap me over what hurts so I can heal you while I get nothing back. Dammit, Connor, I want to do that for you. Don't you understand? But I can't." She let out a long breath. "I have a feeling we can go around all night. But if you aren't ready to change, there won't be any point. My mind is made up. I know what I want, and if you can't give it to me, then you have to let me go. Because you're going to have to let me heal."

She walked out of the kitchen and this time, he didn't follow her. She opened the front door and went outside, running down the steps and through the driveway, down past the old barn. She was at the river before she realized where she was going.

The place she'd shared all those summer days with him. The place she'd wept her heart out for him as she'd tried to purge herself of her love for him.

"One more try, I guess," she said.

She walked down toward the bank, and suddenly it hit her what had happened. What she had done. What she had lost. Her knees gave out, her stomach cramping hard. She bent over, sank to the ground, a rock biting into her knee, a sob racking her body. She had lost him. Really lost him. In every version of this scenario in her mind, it had never been this bad. She had imagined him telling her he didn't love her. She had imagined him taking her into his arms. But she had never imagined walking away.

Away, not just from the idea of loving him, but away from their friendship.

She pushed up from the ground and walked to the edge of the river, to the swing. She reached out and grabbed hold of the rope, pulling it over to the bank. Then she grabbed on tight with both hands and jumped, landing on the round, wooden seat. The momentum carried her out over the water, cool, sweet air moving over her face, through her hair.

You were scared, but I told you it would be fun.

Connor's voice, the first night they were together, rumbled through her like a storm.

And you said you had never done it before, but I said you just had to take a chance. And you did, and you screamed and screamed. But in the end, you told me you loved it.

"I took a chance," she said. "I took a chance. But in the end you didn't love me."

You screamed and screamed.

She closed her eyes and tilted her face into the wind, then she took a deep breath and screamed. Because she hurt all over. Because this was the end.

Because she was on their swing.

The scream ended on a sob, her whole body shaking hard. This was her last time on the swing. Her last time on the ranch.

She had to be done. God help her, it had to end.

She couldn't go on seeing him every day. Couldn't pour her whole life into him and expect things would stop revolving around him.

She'd made him everything. And until she changed that, he would remain everything.

She held on to the swing so tight the rope burned her palms, but she didn't care. It didn't come close to the pain in her heart. And nothing ever would.

She sat out there until she was dried out inside. Until there was a drought inside her. She stayed until she was chilled to her bones, shaking and unable to stop.

Then she got off the swing and walked back to the house. Thankfully, when she cracked open the door, Connor wasn't anywhere to be seen.

She walked up the stairs, trying not to make noise, and stole into her bedroom. She moved to the bed, sliding beneath the blankets. She felt too brittle to cry now. A sob would crack her, leave her in tiny little pieces that she would never be able to sweep up and put back together.

So she just lay there staring at the ceiling, her eyes burning.

And along with the burning in her eyes came the pressing sensation that nothing would ever be okay again.

She sat up. No, on second thought she wasn't staying here. Not tonight.

Not for another second. She couldn't handle it.

She took her phone off her nightstand and dialed the number she usually avoided. Her mother.

"Hello?"

"Hi, Mom."

"Hello, Felicity. I was just about to go out. Can you call tomorrow?"

"No. Mom. I can't call tomorrow. I need to… I need to come over."

"I have a date, Felicity."

Liss blinked back tears. "No. Listen to me. I need to come over. I need a place to stay. Please, Mom. I need you. You can still go out. I just… I need somewhere to stay."

Her mother hesitated for a moment. "Okay. Why don't you come on over?"

"Thank you," Liss said.

She hung up the phone and went to get her duffel bag out of the closet. She would come back for the rest of her things later. Or maybe she would ask Jack if he could help. He wasn't related to Connor, or marrying into his family, so she stood the most chance of getting his help when all this was said and done. Plus, he already knew some of what was happening, since he had borne witness.

She stuffed quite a few clothes into the bag then looked and saw the prom dress hanging in her closet. It hurt just to see it. But she was taking it with her. Because it was hers, dammit. It wasn't his. She wrenched it off the hanger and stuffed it into the bag.

She looked around the room, trying not to melt into a puddle of tears. Then she opened the door and walked out into the hall and down the stairs. She didn't see Connor. And that was for the best.

She paused at the door and flicked on the porch light before walking outside into the night, leaving Connor, and her heart, behind.

CHAPTER TWENTY

CONNOR WOKE UP, the same dream he'd had the other night playing on repeat in his mind. His bed was empty. His sheets were cold, and he was sweating and shaking. Because in the dream, Liss was standing there, bathed in the porch light, looking at him, wanting something from him, and he couldn't give it.

He swung his legs over the side of the mattress and stood up.

He made his way over to the window and saw the porch light was on. He had turned it off earlier, he knew it.

He turned away from the window and walked across his room, opening the door and stalking down the hall. The house felt wrong. It felt empty.

You're an idiot. What the hell does that mean?

Except he knew exactly what it meant. He had lived in an empty house for three years.

But Liss had gone to her room. He'd heard her come back inside before he'd gone to sleep. She was still here.

No, she isn't.

He knew it then, as surely as he knew anything else. His heart clenched tight, and he walked down the hall and opened her door without bothering to knock. The bed was empty. The room was empty. He turned and strode back out, taking the stairs two at a time and going to the front door.

He stood there, caught in a moment of déjà vu. How many times had he done this in the middle of the night? Dreaming Eli would be on the other side.

Don't open the door.

He never opened the door. Because there was no point. Eli was never there.

An image of Liss as she'd been in the dream flashed through his mind. Looking at him, begging him.

I love you.

He flung the door open without another thought, and when he saw nothing but empty space the shock hit him with the force of gunfire. He'd really expected her to be there. Looking at him. Waiting for him.

He walked outside, barefoot and in his underwear, down the porch stairs onto the driveway. Her car was gone. He knew it would be. But he had to make sure.

Liss was gone. She wasn't there.

And he was alone again.

She was right. He had made a choice to let her go.

But he didn't have it in him to do anything different.

"Are you drunk?"

"I'm asleep," Connor said, shifting his position, not entirely certain where he was or who was talking to him.

"Are you hungover?"

Connor opened his eyes and immediately shut them again. The sun was shining in his face. And he was very obviously not in his bed. In fact, he was freezing his balls off. He shifted again, becoming aware of how uncomfortable he was. Of just how stiff and sore he felt.

"I don't think so," he said, rubbing his eyes with the palm of his hand before he opened them again. He was outside. On his porch. Sitting in the uncushioned wooden chair that was right by the door. And Eli was standing there, arms crossed, looking disapproving. "No, not hungover."

Because last night came back to him far too readily. Way too clearly. And his chest hurt more than his head.

"Then what the hell are you doing?"

Was there any point in lying about it? He didn't think so.

"Liss left."

"Did she find another place to stay?"

"Not as far as I know."

Eli frowned. "Then why did she leave?"

"Because I ruin things," Connor said, sitting up straighter, pain shooting through his neck and back. "I ruin everything. Yeah, that about sums it up."

"Sure, but she knows that. And you've been friends for long enough, and it's never seemed to bother her."

"Big surprise, I ruined that, too," Connor said, the bitterness that had lodged itself in his chest flooding out with his words.

"What did you do?"

"I slept with her."

He watched his brother's face run through about four different emotions. None of them positive. "You what?"

"Please tell me I don't have to repeat that."

"No. Sorry. That was reflexive. Because I can't believe it. You slept with Liss?"

"Yes."

"What the… Connor. If you are ready to get back out there, there were a lot better ways to go about that."

"It was not that simple. It's complicated. It was and continues to be complicated."

It's not complicated...

He could hear Liss's words echoing in his brain. Broken, soft, sad. He had made her sad.

He'd spent a fair amount of time hating himself over the years, but he hated himself more now than he could ever remember.

Eli was right. He should not have dragged her into this.

Yes, she had jumped in with both feet, but he had kissed her first. Knowing that he couldn't give more than a physical relationship. Knowing that he was unwilling. And he'd told himself all kinds of lies to make it all seem okay. Because it had felt good. Because he had felt good for the first time in so long. At her expense.

"So what happened?"

"I need coffee," Connor said. "I don't think I'm ever going to be able to straighten my neck again." He reached back and ran his hand over his sore muscles.

"Then we'll talk inside."

Eli was being stubborn, and Connor knew from experience that when Eli was stubborn there was no getting around him.

Connor stood, staring his younger brother down. "Fine."

Eli walked past him and pushed the door open, holding it for him. "I'm the new sheriff, and I would appreciate a little bit of respect."

"You're looking in the wrong place," Connor muttered as he walked past him and into the kitchen.

Connor set about putting coffee on, ignoring Eli's presence as best he could. Heart-to-heart conversations were not his favorite thing in the world, and he had a feeling he was headed for one. He also knew that short of chasing him out with a shotgun, he wasn't getting rid of Eli until they had it.

He switched on the coffeemaker, and the sounds of imminent caffeine filled the room.

"Just stop," Eli said. "Stop making a concerted effort to stay miserable."

Connor turned to face his brother. "What are you talking about?"

"Connor, you make a serious effort to be unhappy."

"It doesn't take that much effort to be unhappy when you lose everything," Connor said, bristling against Eli's words.

"It's more than that. It's more than just being sad because you miss her. You push everyone away. You do your very best not to share anything with anyone. You are committed to staying unhappy. And I've never seen someone take that commitment more seriously than you."

"Go ahead and tell me how you would have acted differently, Eli. Go right ahead. But you can't guarantee that. You can't know that."

Eli rocked back on his heels. "I don't have to know it. I just have to convince you to knock it off."

"For what reason?" Connor slammed his hands down on the countertop. "I'm serious. Give me a reason, Eli."

"So you don't die alone. How about that, asshole?"

"That's the way I'm headed, anyway, isn't it? No matter what? I mean, show me an indicator that I'm not. Dad is dead. Mom left. Jessie died. And Liss is… She's gone. I can't… I can't keep people with me. It's like trying to grab on to a handful of sand. It just all drains out in the end, and you're left with a fistful of nothing. What's the point?"

Eli put his hands on his hips and looked down. He took a deep breath, raised his head and met Connor's eyes. "The point is that when you can let go of all that, of the fear, and the anger, there's something better on the other side. Trust me."

"I'm a lot further gone than you ever were."

Eli leveled his gaze on him, his dark eyes grave. "Do you love her, Connor?"

The question made Connor's heart freeze, a cold sweat breaking out over his skin. "I don't see what that has to do with anything," he said, unsure of why he couldn't just say no. He had told Liss he didn't love her, so saying it again shouldn't be hard. And yet the words wouldn't come.

"It's the only thing. If you love somebody, then you work the rest out."

"I have something pretty cynical I could say about that."

"There are no guarantees. You aren't going to get one. But if you aren't going to take any chances you might as well start digging your grave now. Because what's the point?"

Connor gritted his teeth. "The point, Eli, is that I cannot go through something like that again. Or I really will die. Or drink myself into the ground, just like Dad."

"But you didn't. You went through more than he did, and you didn't."

"I can't," he ground out.

Eli broke his hands over his face then turned away from Connor, taking a deep breath. "Connor, is she dead?"

"What the hell, Eli?"

Eli turned around again. "Is she dead? That's what you asked me when I told you why I couldn't make it work with Sadie. You told me that if she wasn't dead there was still hope. Take your own damn advice."

Connor didn't plan his next movements, he simply acted. Next thing he knew he had his hands wrapped around the collar of Eli's shirt, and he had his younger brother's back pressed hard against the kitchen wall. "Don't you dare talk to me about that. Jessie *is* dead."

Eli stared him down. "Liss isn't," he said, his words hard. "You aren't. So stop existing like you are."

"That simple?"

"No. Not that simple," Eli said, pulling out of Connor's hold and tugging his shirt back down into place. "After years of grieving, drinking, quitting drinking, finding someone new. You've been through hell, I know that. But now you've reached the other side, and you can walk out. So do it."

"You have no fucking clue," Connor said.

"I have more of one than you think. You know… I saw the medical report." He took a deep breath. "I know. I know about the baby. But I never said anything in case…"

"In case I didn't know," Connor said, feeling the heat drain from his blood.

"Right. And I'm sorry, Connor. I'm so sorry. I can't imagine everything you've lost. And I've never pretended I could. But I can tell you that you have to let go."

Connor looked out the kitchen window at the trees, the wind blowing through the branches, so calm and peaceful. Because the storm was too busy raging in his chest. "You haven't said anything about the baby for three years, so why say something now?"

"Because I… Well, with the way things have gone, how you've responded, I figured you knew. But if you didn't want to tell me, I wasn't going to force it. But now…now I have to force some things. Even if you didn't know…it's something you have to get through. It's time. Dammit, Connor, you're my older brother and I admire the hell out of you. You were brave, getting married after what our lives were like, after we watched what our parents went through…"

"No," Connor said, cutting him off, "I was never all that brave. I never have been. I got married, and I held my wife at arm's length until…until it was too late. And I can't… I can't do this with Liss. She's… There is no holding her at arm's length. Because she's been under my skin for years. She's my best friend and if…if she becomes anything more she'll become everything, and I can't handle that."

"You know, at some point, it might be good to learn from your mistakes instead of just repeating them."

"You think you can Monday-morning quarterback my grief?"

"I think someone has to take the time to point out that grieving is a process, and you're not getting through it. I sure as hell expect that you'll love the woman you married for the rest of your life, that you'll remember her birthday and that when the anniversary of her death rolls around every year you'll go to visit her grave. And I damn sure expect you'll think of that baby. How old he would have been, when his birthday might have been. Yeah, I expect that will stay with you forever. But I also expect that at some point you need to start arranging that pain around your life, rather than arranging your life around your pain."

Pain sliced through Connor's chest like a razor. "Get out of my house," he said.

"Connor, I'm reaching my hand out, and I want to save you. Liss wants to save you. For God's sake take someone's hand."

An image of being at the bottom of a dark pit filled Connor's mind. A hand reaching out in the darkness. But the darkness felt so safe. Such a great place to hide.

"Get out, Sheriff." He gestured toward the door.

Eli stared him down for a moment, as though he were waiting. For something else. For a different answer. For Connor to break down in tears and pull him into a hug.

He was shit out of luck there.

"Suit yourself. See you around." Eli turned and walked out, slamming the front door behind him.

And just like that, his house was empty again.

Liss HAD BEEN completely stunned last night when her mother had opted to cancel her plans and stay home and listen to what was going on with Liss's life.

It hadn't been the most in-depth conversation, but it was more than she usually got out of her mom.

Still, she knew that she couldn't stay there long-term. So she was sitting in The Grind, trying not to cry crocodile tears into her coffee while she looked at apartment listings online, knowing full well that the chance of getting one was slim. Thanks to Marshall. Because, even though she was turning over a new leaf, she was still paying for that period in her life when she'd been a little pushover.

A hand lowered right in front of her, and another

mug of coffee was placed beside her nearly empty one. She looked up and saw Cassie, the owner of The Grind, and one of Liss's clients, looking down at her, her brow wrinkled. "Are you okay, Liss?"

"Yes. No. Not at all."

"Oh, dear." Cassie sat down across from her. "What's up?"

"It's a saga."

"It so happens that I'm on a break. And my break is about saga length. Go for it."

"Well, I got evicted. About a month and a half ago. But the biggest problem with that is that my credit is bad because of my stupid ex-boyfriend. So instead of letting me get thrown out on the streets, Connor Garrett had me move in with him. He's my friend. He was my friend. Anyway, some things happened…and now I'm looking for a place to live again."

Cassie frowned. "Things happened, huh?"

"Yes."

"What kinds of things?"

"The kinds of things that happen when men and women are in close quarters," Liss said.

"Oh."

"Yes, *oh*. So basically it's all bad. If I look like I lost my best friend, it's because I have lost my best friend. And I'm homeless."

"Well, I can't help you with the best-friend thing, but I might be able to help you with the homeless thing."

Liss wrapped her hands around her coffee cup. "You can?"

"Jake just finished renovating the old family farmhouse, so we're going to move out to the property. In fact, we started moving yesterday. Anyway, the upstairs apartment, which is huge, since we combined the two into one, will be empty."

"Oh, that's so nice of you… It's just that…the credit thing…"

"I don't care about that. I know you. And I'll know where you live. I know you're stable. I use you to do my books, so you better be." Cassie told her the rent rate, which was more than fair. "See? I'm not giving out charity. But I do want to help you."

"Oh, that's fine. I can afford it. I just haven't been able to find anyone to rent to me."

"Well, I will. What's the point of living in a small town? If people won't cut corners and do things for you based on knowing you, rather than what a federal bureau says about you?"

Liss tried to force a smile. "That's a good question. Cassie, thank you so much for this. Of all the things I have to worry about right now, it's nice to cross one off the list."

"Sorry I couldn't do more for you."

Liss sighed. "I suspect it's one of those things that only time will take care of."

And time would take care of it. It had to. That was the entire point of cutting Connor out of her life altogether. Just the thought sent a sharp pain slicing through her chest. Yes, that had to get better. Otherwise it would just be a matter of learning to live with the ache. Maybe that was what grief was. Because this was certainly grief for her. For their lost friendship, for the loss of a dream.

Which meant that both she and Connor would spend the rest of their lives wandering Copper Ridge with pain in their chests. That seemed appropriate in some ways. Though she didn't wish that on him. Even now, she didn't wish it on him.

She didn't wish it on herself, either, but it seemed inevitable.

This seemed like the moment to call a friend, maybe Jeanette, get a gallon of ice cream and a spoon and watch chick flicks. It was what people always did in movies to get over broken hearts. But Liss didn't want to do that. She wanted to put on an oversize sweater and crawl under a blanket and never resurface. She could live forever in a cocoon of knitted yarn, never talking to anyone about what happened, never facing reality. She could resurface for hot beverages and cake, and nothing else. That sounded much better than sharing her pain and being social over a movie starring Hugh Grant.

Anyway, inevitably, Hugh Grant would start talking about his feelings and sharing with his leading lady, and then Liss would just want to punch him in the teeth for daring to be so much more sensitive than the asshole she had fallen in love with.

She sighed heavily and stood, breathing in deep, the sharp pain in her chest a companion to the breath, not as notable as it had been only a moment ago. This was, she had a feeling, her new normal. Pain and breathing.

"Is there a good time for me to come and look at the apartment?" Liss asked Cassie.

"I can give you a key and you can go up now if you want."

Liss hesitated for a moment, because it was a step toward making all of this reality. Leaving Connor for real. Which was exactly why she was going to say yes. "That would be great. Thank you."

"Just a second. I can't leave the shop but you're welcome to poke around. Most of our stuff is gone. Just a few pieces of furniture left."

Cassie hustled behind the counter and bent down, pulling a key off a little hook that was screwed into the wood cabinet. She popped back up and reached over the counter, handing the key to Liss. "You can go through the store here, and use the inside stairs. Go on up," she said, smiling.

Liss managed a smile back, and she felt somewhat triumphant.

She followed Cassie's instructions and walked up the narrow staircase that led to the apartment over the coffee shop. She put the key in the door and jiggled it, pushing the door open. It was a beautiful space. Exposed brick, wood floors, high ceilings and a large open floor plan. Way too big for one person.

She wandered over to the window that faced the main street of Copper Ridge. She could see the row of little businesses that comprised the old town, the American and Oregon flags blowing in the wind, and a slice of brown sand and gray sea beyond.

It was beautiful. Better than the house she lived in before.

But not better than living with Connor.

She had a feeling she would always long for that house. Set back in the trees, in the mountains, a testament to the hard work of the man she loved.

The man who didn't love her.

She turned away from the window and walked over to the couch that was positioned at the center of the room. She sank onto it slowly, resting her forearms on her thighs, leaning forward and staring straight ahead.

She wasn't even sure what she was looking at. Just the empty space, maybe.

Really, no matter how beautiful the apartment was, no matter how nice the view was, it didn't really matter. Not right now.

"But it will. It will matter." She said those words out loud, because she needed to hear them.

Yes, this hurt. But she wasn't going to die. And she didn't need to sink in despair and self-loathing. Her worst fear had been realized. She'd done something wrong, and it had resulted in the end of a relationship she prized. It was the thing she had worked her entire life to avoid. And yet, now that she was staring it down, she realized two things.

One, it hurt a lot more than she could have imagined. And two, it wasn't about her.

It was Connor's baggage. Connor's pain. And maybe, even without all of that, he still wouldn't have loved her. But it didn't mean there was something wrong with her. It didn't mean she should have worked harder. And failing didn't mean she was worth less.

A small burst of hope settled in her heart, right next to the ache. Yes, it was terrible. And yes, she still thought the large sweater and cozy blanket seemed like viable options for her future. But she hadn't lost all her faith. She hadn't lost her faith in herself.

She would get through this. Because the alternative was becoming… Well, the alternative was becoming like Connor. The alternative was holding on to hurt as if it was a lifeline, as though it was the only thing keeping you rooted to the earth.

It was so tempting to hold on to the past. But if her

hands were full of all that, she could never grab on to anything new.

She would live. Because she deserved to. Because she deserved to be happy. No matter how the relationship with her mother, the relationship with Connor, worked out, she deserved happiness. She deserved something she didn't have to work quite so hard for.

She stood up, her legs shaking, and walked back out the door and down the stairs, back into the warmth and noise of the coffee shop. There was something comforting about the sounds down there, something that she hadn't recognized only a few moments earlier. The clanking dishes, the chatter, the smiles on everyone's faces, reminded her now that life went on.

And thank God for that.

She made her way back to the counter, back to Cassie. "It's perfect. I'll take it."

CHAPTER TWENTY-ONE

IT WAS SO EARLY the sun was just now creeping over the edge of the mountains, a golden band highlighting the peaks and ridges, the edges of the fir trees glowing while the valley before him remained dark.

Connor maneuvered his horse through the landscape, the only sound the pounding of hooves on grass. The air was so cold it numbed his face, made his eyes burn. Which made it more difficult for him to confront the emotions that were rioting through him. Which was just how he liked it.

He didn't want to feel. Didn't want to feel the emptiness in his home, and most especially not the emptiness in his chest. He didn't want to miss a woman whom he could have if he would just break free.

That was the worst part. Right now he was in a hell of his own making.

Because he was a fucking coward.

He pulled back on his horse's reins and slowed her, before stopping her completely. In some ways a death was easier than this. Not less painful, but the actions were easier. Because there was no choice to make. It was a blow dealt by life that you couldn't argue against. But this…

For God's sake take someone's hand.

He heard his brother's voice again, and he squeezed

his eyes shut, fighting against the wave of emotion that crashed through him.

The simple truth was that at a certain point his grief had become safe. It wasn't comfortable. But it was safe. Because as long as he stayed down deep in the darkest part of his pain, no new pain could touch him. He'd used his barn as evidence that caring was dangerous. Had used it as another piece for his case.

But the barn had been rebuilt. And the ranching operation had gone on. And Connor was still standing in the ashes of his life, refusing to budge.

He dismounted, sliding off the back of the horse, his feet planting on the soft ground without making a sound.

He walked forward a few steps before stumbling, falling down onto his knee. The cold and the wet soaked through his jeans, and he didn't care. What was a little more discomfort?

When Jessie had died, there had been no decisions to make. No one had asked his opinion. There had been nothing but pain and alcohol. There had been no one standing around waiting for him to decide whether or not he wanted to live without her. He was living without her. And there was nothing else that could be done.

But now…now there was a decision to be made. A terrifying decision. Now he was choosing to walk through the darkness. He couldn't deny that. He'd already had the revelation that he couldn't stand still anymore. But he'd applied that only to the easy things. To sex, to the ranch. He'd managed to keep little pieces of himself back there in the past, managed to grab hold of a bit of the present, and at the same time hoarding his grief.

He could keep a hold of his grief and still be in the present, but there was no way he could have a future unless he released his hold on everything that was behind him. And that was really the threshold he was on right now. Did he want to exist, taking only little pieces of what felt good now? Or did he want dreams again? Hope for the future, for bigger and better things, no matter how much it might hurt if he lost them?

He knew the cost of loss. Knew it better than most. Knew what it was like to lose not just the people he loved the most, but his future, his identity.

Knowing that, knowing that pain, how could he possibly open himself up to that again?

A picture of Liss's face swam before his eyes, and his heart clenched tight.

Dammit. He loved her. He loved her already, whether he wanted to or not. And he was a fool. She had been there for him, for every moment, always. As a friend, whether or not he had been a friend in return, she had been there. And as a lover. She had been everything he'd ever asked her to be, and more. Everything he wasn't worthy of. Everything he had no right to ask for.

He thought back to the past three years. To every demonstration, no matter how small, of her love for him. Because it had been there. From the beginning. No matter what manner of love, she had loved him. Romantic, friendship, it was all love. And it had been in every meal she'd shared with him while he sat there in silence, hungover and grumpy, the worst possible company. It had been there every time she had brought groceries to fill his cabinets, every time she had yelled at him for drinking too much. Every time she had smiled at him, for him, when he hadn't had the strength.

She loved him. He had done nothing to deserve it, nothing to earn it, and she loved him. It was a gift that no man deserved, least of all him. And he had it. And he could still have it, if he hadn't fucked it up beyond repair.

If only he wasn't afraid.

If only he wasn't holding on.

You have to let go.

More words from Eli.

And it was the absolute hard truth.

And so he let himself remember. His engagement, that moment he'd slipped the ring on her finger. His wedding and all the vows he'd made, and meant from the bottom of his heart. His marriage, the good, the bad, the ugly. Finding out he was going to be a father. So terrifying and beautiful. The way that Jessie smiled, the way her blue eyes crinkled up tight. And the way she frowned when she was about to tell him off.

And then he remembered the day she died. And he let himself *feel* it. It was like a storm inside him, and all he could do was lower his head and let it wash over him until it passed.

"I have to let you go," he said, even though he knew she couldn't hear him. Just in case. He had to say it just in case. "I'm not going to forget it. But I can't hold on anymore. Because there are people here that I have to hold on to."

He stood slowly, rising along with the sun. It flooded the valley with light, the warm rays touching his skin. He closed his eyes and faced the light, taking a deep breath, letting it wash over him.

And for the very first time in three years, the light

of a new day touched his soul. For the very first time
in three years, he felt the sun rise.

LISS LOCKED HER NEW apartment door and walked down
the stairs, taking the door that led outside, behind The
Grind. She had been moved in for a couple of days,
and it was going well. In that achy, desolate kind of
empty way.

She sighed, her breath visible in the cold air. It was
inching closer to Thanksgiving, which sounded like
absolutely no fun to her. Seeing as she usually spent
Thanksgiving with the Garrett clan, and she imagined
that this year her invitation would be revoked.

Oh, well. She could go eat in the diner by herself.

Or perhaps, if she had progressed to chick flick and
ice cream stage by then, she could do that.

She shoved her hands into her pockets and walked
around to the front of the building, heading down the
street where she had parked yesterday. That was the
only real problem with the apartment. Besides the emptiness and the desolation. The parking.

The wind whipped across her face, pulling part of
her hair from its bun, the loose strand sticking to her
lips. She ran her fingers down the side of her face and
tugged it free, shaking her head reflexively.

Another gust whipped down the street and pushed
more hair into her eyes. She slid her hand up her forehead and pushed it back, raising her gaze as she did.
And then her heart stopped.

Connor was standing there. Wearing a cowboy hat, a
tight black T-shirt and faded jeans. And his beard was
gone. He was clean-shaven for the first time in years.
And she had to wonder if she was hallucinating him.

Because he was more like the Connor she remembered. And also, she wanted to see him so badly that it wasn't too far-fetched to think that he might be nothing more than a very sexy figment of her imagination.

But then he started to walk toward her, and even though everything in her screamed for her to turn and go the other way, she started to walk toward him, too. And she didn't vaporize, or turn into mist, so she knew for a fact it had to be him.

"CONNOR," SHE SAID, because she could say nothing else.

He started to walk faster, closing the distance between them, and pulling her into his arms, hugging her tight. She melted into him for a few seconds then pushed back. "No," she said. "It isn't fair. You aren't supposed to come and find me. You aren't supposed to stand there looking all sexy when I can't have you. You sure as hell cannot just walk down the street and hug me." A tear slid down her cheek, and she wiped it away. "You lost that right, Connor. Don't hurt me anymore. Please, don't do this to me."

He took hold of her arms, gripping her tight. "I don't want to hurt you. I'm done with that. And I'm done hurting me, too."

She shook her head. "I don't believe you."

"I got up this morning completely sober. And I hurt like hell, but I wasn't hungover. And then I went for a ride. And...I let go. There's a difference between forgetting and releasing your hold on the past. I'm not going to forget. But the funny thing is, I wasn't even really letting myself remember. I was lost in the after bit. I was lost in that moment when Eli came to the door and told me that she was gone. And that moment had become my entire life. I thought by holding on to that, I was holding on to her memory. But that was the furthest thing from the truth. I let myself forget. I let myself forget the good parts. And when I let go…I got my past back." He looked down for a moment then back up at her. "Then along with that came some hope for the future."

She sucked in a shaking breath, her hands trembling. She wanted to yell at him and send him away, but how could she do that now? "Oh, Connor," she said, "I'm… I'm glad to hear that."

"I'm not finished," he said. "I wasn't only clinging to my grief to try to preserve her memory. Nothing quite that selfless. I was protecting myself. Because I knew that as long as I wrapped myself up in that old pain, there would be no way any new pain could get inside. When you're living in your darkest day, then you know things can't get worse. If you don't want anything better, you can't be disappointed again. And I was a coward. Because I had you, and I let you get away. Because I was too afraid to make the choice. I told you I was tired of life just handing down sentences to me, but the simple truth is I found that a whole lot easier than getting off my ass and making a decision. But I'm tired of it. I'm done with it. I'm making a choice," he said, his voice rough, dark eyes intent on hers. "I love you, Liss. And no matter what the future holds, I want that. No matter what problems we might face, I want to love you through them."

Connor's words were echoing in her head, and it took her a moment to unravel them. To let the meaning fully sink in. Right now she was the one who was afraid. Because this was far and beyond anything she had ever dared fantasize. Anything she had ever dared dream of. "You...you love me?"

"So much. And that terrified me. I couldn't even let myself think it, Liss. Love is different this time around. You were my friend first, and you mean the world to me because of that. And then...then you became my lover. And I crave you. Your body, your heart, your soul. And I know the risk. I know the cost of love, and I want it anyway, and that makes this feel more exhilarating, more terrifying, more precious, than anything else I've ever experienced. I'm not the man I was a decade ago. And because of that what I want, what I expect, what I need, has changed. And what I need now, now and forever, is you."

Liss threw her arms around him, kissing him deep on the lips. "I need you," she said, tears falling down her cheeks. "You have no idea how much."

"I do. Because it's the same thing I feel, too."

"I love you, Connor. I love everything you are. I know who you were back when we were young, back before all of the sadness. And I have seen your strength, and your weaknesses, too. And I love all of that. I can't guarantee that everything will be smooth from here on out, but if there are going to be storms, we'll walk through them together."

"I know that. I believe it. I thought back on everything you've done for me in the past few years. And I am an idiot. I should never have been shocked by hearing you say that you loved me. Because you showed me. Every day you showed me. But I was too caught up in myself to get it. I was too afraid to see it. But I'm not now. And I'm not afraid to give it back."

"Is this really happening?" she asked, kissing him

again to make sure he was here, to make absolutely certain she wasn't hallucinating. "When you've wanted something for so long, and you finally get it, sometimes it's hard to believe."

"I know what you mean. It feels surreal to me, too. I've been in the dark for so long, I'm just kind of blinking against the light right now. But it feels really good."

"It feels weird to kiss you without a beard."

"Yeah, well, I thought it was time to let that go, too. But if you miss that, I can always grow it back. I'd rather grow it for you, then just have it because I was too lazy to take care of myself anymore."

"I get that. We can discuss the beard later."

"And...I have to say something about the tattoo."

"Connor, I will never ask you to not love Jessie. I love her. I always will. She's in my heart, and I expect her to be in yours. I respect the fact that you loved her enough to marry her. I respect that marriage, the fact that she was your wife."

"I appreciate that. But I wasn't going to talk about that. Because I already knew how you felt. I think it helps that we both love her. But...of course, it's not the same now. You're the woman I love. And I will always have Jessie in my heart, but she's not my wife now. She's not here now. I'm not in love with her now. That's you. Only you. I need you to understand that. I have never, and I will never, wish that you were someone else. Like I said, I've changed. What I need has changed. And you're the woman I need now. You are the woman I love now." He leaned forward, pressing a kiss to her forehead. "I think we had to break our friendship down. Like melting metal. It has to lose its shape so you can make it into something new. But it's all the same materials. Just like us. We're still made from the same stuff, it's just in a new shape."

Another tear escaped, and this time she didn't bother to wipe it away. "That is the most perfect thing you could've said."

"Which brings us back to the tattoo. They are Jessie's flowers. But the meaning of them has changed for me over the past few days. Actually, it kind of connects back to the barn."

"I'm listening," she said.

"Flowers die. People die. Barns burn. But as long as there is life, there is hope. We rebuilt the barn. I want to plant roses again. And I'm in love again, when I never thought I could be." He reached out, brushed his thumb over her cheek and wiped her tear away himself. "No matter how dark things get, life is still there. Love still grows."

She tightened her hold on him, kissed his cheek. "I know my love for you has grown. And it will only keep growing."

"I want to marry you," he said. "And I'm making an ass out of myself, because I don't have a ring with me. And I didn't get down on one knee. But I want to marry you."

Liss blinked. "We don't have to get married right away. I'm not going to rush you into anything."

"I'm not rushing. It took me eighteen years to get here with you. And I won't waste another minute. So do you want to marry me or not?"

"Of course I want to marry you."

"I might not be the best husband."

"I never said I wanted the best husband. I just want my best friend."

"Then you're in luck. Because you have me. I won't be perfect, but I will love you. Now and forever."

She reached up and took his hat off his head, putting it on her own. "That's the best promise I could ever ask for, cowboy."

CONNOR GARRETT WAS a grown-ass man. And he knew that there was nothing to be nervous about when it came to giving good news to his family. Even so, given that he had asked Liss the question, and put a ring on her finger, only a few hours ago, he was nervous.

Eli walked in, holding Sadie's hand. Sadie was holding her orange-and-black Beavers bowl in her other hand. In behind them came Kate, followed by Jack, who was holding pizzas from a local restaurant, since dinner had been his responsibility for tonight's game.

Everyone stopped and stared at him and Liss when they came into the dining room. Because either directly or indirectly they all knew now what had passed between them. But nobody knew what had happened today.

"Liss," Sadie said, "you're here."

Beside him, Liss nodded.

Jack looked between them. "You guys are…okay?"

Connor cleared his throat. "Actually, we're more than okay." He reached down and took Liss's left hand in his, raising it slightly so that they could see the diamond on her fourth finger. "I asked Liss to marry me."

"What?" This incredulous question came from Kate, and Connor realized that the only person who might have been in the dark about recent happenings was his younger sister.

"We were together, then we broke up, and then he proposed," Liss said, offering a quick recap.

"No one ever tells me anything," Kate said.

"I would have told you eventually," Eli said. "But I was too pissed off at him to tell the story without a lot of swear words."

"Like that's ever stopped you before," Kate said. "The saltier parts of my vocabulary are courtesy of you and Connor, after all."

"True," Eli said. "But back to this… You're really getting married?"

"Yes," Connor said, and this time he didn't have to force his smile. This time he couldn't hold it back.

Eli closed the distance between them and pulled Connor into a hug, clapping him on his back twice before letting him go. "Welcome back," he said, a slight mist covering his dark eyes.

Connor felt a little mist in his own. "Good to be back," he said, looking at Liss. "Yeah, it's really good to be back."

"So who wants to play some poker?" Jack asked.

"Me," Kate said, scrabbling for a place at the table.

"Me, too," Eli said.

They all took their usual seats, but he kept hold of Liss's hand.

He thought back to the game they'd had a little over a month ago, when he'd observed the look that had passed between Eli and Sadie, the one that made him envious down to his bones. He turned his head and looked at Liss, and she smiled at him. And that smile was like the sun breaking over the mountains all over again.

He felt for a long time as if he'd lost his star, as though he'd lost his compass. As if he'd lost his way.

Oh, he might not be certain of his exact destination. But he knew for a fact he would be walking there with Liss. And that was all he needed to know.

* * * * *

Don't miss Eli and Sadie's story,
PART TIME COWBOY,
available now!

And read on for a sneak peek
of Kate and Jack's story,
BAD NEWS COWBOY,
coming soon from Maisey Yates
and HQN Books!

KATE HEARD THE DOOR open again, and then Eli's and Sadie's voices. Now the gang was all here. And she could focus on playing cards, which was really what she wanted.

Sadie led the charge into the dining room, holding her now traditional orange-and-black candy bowl in front of her, a wide grin on her face. Eli was a step behind her looking slightly abashed. Probably because his fiancée was breaking sacred football laws by bringing the colors of an opposing team onto hallowed ground.

But she did it every week. And every week, Connor made a show of not eating the candy in the bowl. Eli didn't eat it, either, but didn't make a big deal of it. While Jack ate half of it without giving a crap what anyone thought. Which summed them all up, really.

Kate always ate the candy, too. If only because she didn't see the point in politicizing sugar.

"Fish-and-chips!" Sadie exclaimed. "That makes a nice change from pizza. And pie!"

"The feast is indeed bountiful tonight," Liss said, eyeing the pie. "We have Kate to thank for that."

"Excuse me," Jack said, "I brought the pie. I will have you all know that Katie has a lemon meringue pie hidden back in her cabin. And she did not bring it to share with you."

Kate lifted her hand to smack Jack on the shoulder, and he caught her wrist. Her heart hit the back of her breastbone so hard she was afraid it might have exploded on contact. His hand was so big his fingers wrapped all the way around her wrist, holding her tight, a rash of heat breaking out from that point of contact outward.

Her eyes clashed with his, and the sharp remark she'd been about to spit out evaporated on her lips.

She tugged her wrist out of his hold, fighting the urge to rub away the impression of his touch with her other hand. "I didn't bring it because I don't want to share my pie with you," she said, looking at Jack.

"Selfish pie hoarder," he said, grinning at her in that easy manner of his.

And her annoyance tripled. Because him grabbing her wrist was a whole event for her body. And he was completely unaffected. That touch had been like grabbing hold of an electric fence. On her end. Obviously it hadn't been the same for him.

Why would it be? It shouldn't be that way for her.

"I am not." And she cursed her hot cheeks and her lack of snappy remark.

"I might have to side with Jack on this one," Liss said, her tone apologetic. "Or maybe I'm just on the side of pie."

"Traitor," Kate mumbled. "Are we going to play cards?"

"So impatient to lose all of your money," Jack said.

This was a little more normal. A more typical level of Jack harassing her.

"To me," Sadie said, her grin turning feral. Sadie, it turned out, was a very good poker player for all her wide blue-eyed protestations to the contrary when she first joined their weekly games.

Kate opted to stay silent, continuing on that way while the cards were dealt. And she was dealt a very good hand. She bit the inside of her cheek to keep her expression steady. Sadie was cocky. Jack was cockier. And she was going to take their money.

By the end of the night Kate had earned several profane nicknames and the contents of everyone's wallets. She leaned back in her chair, pulling the coins toward her. "Listen to that. I'm going back home, dumping all this on the floor and swimming in it like Scrooge McDuck." She added a fake cackle for a little bit of dramatics.

"Then I will keep all the pie," Liss said.

"That's my pie," Jack said.

"You have to stay in fighting form, Monaghan. Your bar hookups won't be so easy if you lose your six pack," Liss said cheerfully.

"I do enough work on the ranch every day to live on pies and still keep my six pack, thank you very much."

"You aren't getting any younger," Sadie said.

The conversation was going into uncomfortable territory as far as Kate was concerned. Really, on all fronts it was getting to an awkward place. Jack and sex. Jack's abs. Yikes.

"I would return volley," Jack said, "but I'm too much of a gentleman to comment on a lady's age."

"Gentleman, huh?" Eli asked. "Of all the things you've been accused of being, I doubt that's one of them."

Jack squinted and held up his hand, pretending to

count on his fingers. "Yeah, no. There have been a lot of things, but not that one."

"Anyway," Kate chimed in, unable to help herself, "you comment on my age all the time."

"I said I never commented on a lady's age, Katie."

She snorted. "I am a lady, asswipe."

"I don't know how I missed it," he said, leaning back in his chair, his grin turning wicked.

For some reason that comment was the last straw. "Okay, hate to cut this short, but I have an early morning tomorrow." That was not strictly true. It was an optional early morning, since she intended to get up and spend some time with Roo. "And I will be stopping by The Grind to buy a very expensive coffee with the money I won from you."

Jack stood, putting his hands behind his head and stretching. "I'll walk you out. I have an early morning, too, so I better get going."

Dammit. He didn't seem to understand that she was beating a hasty retreat in part to get away from him. Because the Weird Jack Stuff was a little more elevated today than normal. It had something to do with overexposure to him. She needed to go home, be by herself, scrub him off her skin in a hot shower so she could hit the reset button on her interactions with him.

She felt like she had to do that more often lately than she had ever had in the past.

The thing was, she liked Jack. In that way you could like a guy who was basically an extra obnoxious older brother who didn't share genetic material with you. She liked it when he came to poker night. She liked it when he came into the store. But at the end of it she was always left feeling...agitated.

And it had created this very strange cycle. Hoping she would see Jack, seeing Jack, being pissed that she had seen Jack. And on and on it went.

"Bye," she said.

She picked up her newly filled change bag and started to edge out of the room. She heard heavy footsteps behind her, and without looking she knew it was Jack. Well, she knew it was Jack partly because he had said he would walk her out.

And partly because the hair on the back of her neck was standing on end. That was another weird Jack thing.

She opened the front door and shut it behind her, not waiting for Jack. Which was petty, and weird. She heard the door open behind her, and shut again.

"Did I do something?"

She turned around, trying to erase the scowl from her face. Trying to think of one thing he had actually done that was out of line, or out of the ordinary at least. "No," she said begrudgingly.

"Then why are you acting like I dipped your pigtails in ink?" he asked, taking the stairs two at a time, making uncomfortable eye contact with her in the low evening light.

She looked down. "I'm not."

"I seem to piss you off all the time lately," he said, closing the distance between them while her throat closed itself up tight.

"You don't. It's just…teasing stuff. Don't worry about it."

Jack kept looking at her, pausing for a moment. She felt awkward, standing there, but also unable to break away. "Okay. Hey, I was thinking…"

"Uh-oh. That never ends well," she said, trying to force a smile.

"What does that mean?"

"I've heard the stories Connor and Eli tell. Anytime you think of something, it ends in…well, sometimes broken bones."

"True," he said, chuckling and leaning against the side of his truck. "But not this time. Well, maybe this time, since it centers around the rodeo."

"You don't ride anymore," she said, feeling stupid for pointing out something he already knew.

"Well, I might. I was sort of thinking of working with the Association to add an extra day onto the rodeo when they pass through. A charity day. Half-price tickets. Maybe some amateur events. And all the proceeds going to…well, to a fund for women who are starting over. A certain amount should go to Alison's bakery. She's helping people get jobs. Get hope. I wish there had been something like that for us when I was a kid."

Kate didn't know anything about Jack's dad. As long as she'd known him, he hadn't had one. And he never talked about it.

But she got the sense that whatever the situation, it hadn't been a happy one.

And now, mixed in with all the annoyance and her desire to avoid him was a strange tightening in her chest.

"Life can be a bitch," she said, hating the strident tone that laced its way through her voice.

"I've never much liked that characterization. In my estimation, life is a lot more like a pissed-off bull. You hang on as long as you can, even though the ride is uncomfortable. No matter how bad it is on, you sure as hell don't want to get bucked off."

"Yeah, that sounds about like you."

"Profound?"

"Like a guy who's been kicked in the head a few times."

"Fair enough. Anyway, what do you think about the charity?"

Warmth bloomed in her stomach. "Honestly? I think it's a great idea." She couldn't even give him a hard time about this, because it was just so damn nice. "We only have a couple of months until the rodeo, though. Do you think we can pull it off?"

"We?"

Her stomach twisted uncomfortably. "Well, yeah. I think it's a good idea. And I would like to contribute in any way I can. Even if it just means helping the pros tack up, or something."

"When are you going to turn pro, Katie?"

She gritted her teeth, and it had nothing to do with his unwanted nickname for her. "When I'm ready. I'm not going to waste a whole bunch of money traveling all over the country, entering all kinds of events and paying for Association cards when I don't have a hope in hell of winning."

"Who says you don't?" he asked, frowning. "I've seen you ride. You're good."

The compliment flowed through her like cool water on parched earth. She cleared her throat, not sure where to look, or what to say. "Roo is young. She has another year or so before she's mature. I probably do, too."

He reached out and wrapped his hand around her braid, tugging gently. "You're closer than you think."

Something about his look, about that touch that should irritate her if it did anything, sent her stomach tumbling down to her toes.

Then he turned away from her and walked around to the other side of his pickup truck, opening the driver's-side door before getting inside and slamming it shut. He started the truck engine and she released her breath in a rush, a wave of dizziness washing over her.

You'd think she'd been staring down a predator, and not one of her family's oldest and dearest friends.

Freaking Jack and all the weirdness that followed him around like a thunderclap.

She walked over to her pickup and climbed in, starting the engine and throwing it into reverse without bothering to buckle. She was just driving down the narrow dirt road that led from Connor's house to her little cabin.

The road narrowed as the trees thickened, pine branches whipping against the doors to her old truck as she approached her house. She'd moved into the cabin on her eighteenth birthday, gaining a little bit of distance and independence from her brothers without being too far away. Of course, it wasn't like she'd really done much with the independence.

She worked, played cards with her brothers and rode horses. That was about the extent of her life. But those activities filled her life, every little corner of it. And she wasn't unhappy with that.

She walked up the front steps, throwing open the front door that she never bothered to lock and stepping inside. She flipped on the light switch, bathing the space in a yellow glow.

The house was small, but it fit her life just fine. In fact, she was happy with a small house, because it reminded her to get outside where things were endless and vast, rather than spending too much time hiding away from the world.

Kate would always rather be out in it.

She kicked her boots off and swept them to the side, letting out a sigh as she dropped her big leather shoulder bag onto the floor. The little lace curtains—curtains that predated Kate's tenure in the house—were shut tight so she tugged her top up over her head and stripped off the rest of her clothes as she made her way to the shower.

She turned the handles and braced herself for the long wait for hot water. Everything, including the hot water heater, in her little house was old-fashioned. Sort of like her, she supposed.

She snorted into the empty room, the sound echoing in the small space. Jack certainly thought she was old-fashioned. All that hyper concern over her not owning a computer.

Steam started to rise up and fill the air and she stepped beneath the hot spray, her thoughts lingering on her interaction with Jack at the Farm and Garden. And how obnoxious he was. And how his lips curved up into that wicked smile when he teased her, blue eyes glittering with all the smart-ass things he'd left unsaid.

She picked up the bar of Ivory soap from the little ledge of the tub and twirled it in her palms as she held it beneath the water, working up a lather. She took a breath, trying to ease some of the tension that was rioting through her.

She turned, pressing the soap against her chest, sliding it over her collarbone.

Yeah, Jack was a pain.

Still, she was picturing that look he got on his face.

Just before he said something mouthy. She slid the bar of soap over her breasts just as she remembered her thwarted retaliation for his teasing tonight. The way his fingers had wrapped around her wrist, his grasp firm...

She gasped and released her hold on the bar of soap. It hit the floor and slid down between her feet, stopping against the wall.

She growled and bent down, picking it back up, ignoring the pounding of her heart and the shaking in her fingers.

The shower was supposed to wash Jack off her skin. He was not supposed to follow her in.

Another jolt zipped through her at the thought, because right along with it came the image of Jack and his overbearing presence sharing this small space with her. Bare skin, wet skin...hands on skin.

She turned and rinsed the soap off her chest, then shut the water off, stepping out and scrubbing her skin dry with her towel, much more ferociously than was warranted.

She needed to sleep. Obviously she was delirious.

If she didn't know better, she would think she was a breath away from having a fantasy about Jack Freaking Monaghan.

"Ha!" She all but shouted. "Ha, ha, ha." She wrapped her towel around her body and walked to her room before dropping it and digging through her dresser for her pajamas.

She found a pair of sensible, white cotton underwear and her flannel pajama pants that had cowboy hats, lassos and running horses printed onto the fabric.

There could be no sexual fantasies when one had cotton panties and flannel pants.

With pony pajamas came clarity.

She pulled a loose-fitting blue T-shirt over her head and flopped down onto her bed. Her twin bed. That would fit only one person.

She was sexual-fantasy proof. Also, sex proof, if the entire long history of her life was anything to go by.

"Bah." She rolled over onto her stomach and buried her face in her pillow. Who needed sex? She had arena dirt, pounding hooves, the salty coastal wind in her face, mixed with pine and earth. A scent unique to Copper Ridge and as much a part of her as the blood in her veins.

She had ambitions. Even if she was a bit cautious in them.

She didn't need men.

Most of all, she didn't need Jack Monaghan.

Come to a small town in Oregon with
USA TODAY bestselling author

MAISEY YATES

for her sexy, heartfelt new
Copper Ridge series!

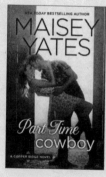 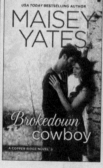 

Available now!   Available now!   Coming July 28, 2015!

Can these cowboys find the love they
didn't know they needed?

Pick up your copies today!

www.HQNBooks.com

PHMYCRS15

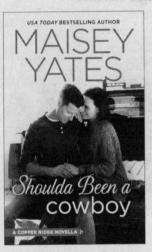

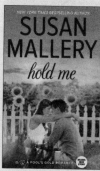

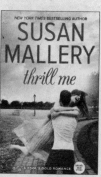

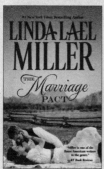
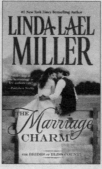
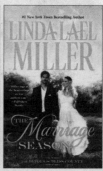

Get 2 Free Books,
Plus 2 Free Gifts -

just for trying the Reader Service!

ROM15CT